OUTLAWS

OUTLAWS

TIM GREEN

Turner Publishing, Inc.

ATLANTA

Library of Congress Cataloging-in-Publication Data
Green, Tim, 1963–
Outlaws / by Tim Green. — 1st ed.
p. cm.
ISBN 1-57036-198-3 (alk. paper)
I. Title.
PS3557.R37562098   1995
813'.54—dc20   95-18342
CIP

Published by Turner Publishing, Inc.
A Subsidiary of Turner Broadcasting System, Inc.
1050 Techwood Drive, N.W.
Atlanta, Georgia 30318

Distributed by Andrews and McMeel
A Universal Press Syndicate Company
4900 Main Street
Kansas City, Missouri 64112

First Edition
10 9 8 7 6 5 4 3 2 1

Printed in the U.S.A.

For my parents, Judy and Dick Green, and my grandparents,
Betty and Raymond Edinger, who put books into my life and created
a world that enabled me to grow up and write them.

And for Illyssa, always Illyssa.

OUTLAWS

PROLOGUE

HIS FACE WAS GAUNT, CLEAN-SHAVEN, AND TAN, and his thick black hair was cut stylishly short. He wore small round sunglasses, and his tall, lean frame, full of angles, gave him the appearance of a menacing insect. He was known as Striker. Sitting in his dusty Pontiac on a rise overlooking a dreary strip mall, Striker's keen eye scanned the parking lot, the bustling Wal-Mart entrance and roof, and surrounding buildings. Heat rose in continuous, shimmering waves from the pavement. Pickup trucks and big Americans cars crawling aimlessly around the lot glimmered like a mirage in the dense heat. It was Striker's habit to check everything. He was thorough, that was one thing Striker prided himself on, and the thought curled the edges of his mouth into a thin smile.

A white Jeep with woodlike door panels pulled off the road and circled the lot twice before pulling up next to a blue Taurus. Striker's eyes narrowed behind his dark lenses as he watched a man get out of the Jeep. He scanned the area again for anything that looked amiss. It wouldn't be anything obvious but something small, like someone talking for too long on a pay phone or a car creeping through the lot without parking. Details like this could mean the difference between success and failure, life and death.

The man who left the Jeep was now at the window of the Taurus, and Striker saw him talking. He wore khaki slacks and a white polo shirt, and the highly polished shoes that Striker could see from such a distance contrasted with his informal attire. The man suddenly started to gesticulate wildly. He looked up, searching the parking lot, obviously angry. Something was not right.

"I'm here," Striker whispered to himself. "I'm right here."

As if he heard him, the man became calm and then turned and reached through the open passenger-side window of his car and pulled out a gray metallic carrying case. He took one last look around and walked around the back of the Taurus to its passenger side. Striker pursed his lips and started his own engine as the man got in the car and it began to pull out.

Striker reached the road that met the mall exit just as the Taurus pulled onto it. He began following it from a discreet distance. He hadn't seen anything unusual so far. Eventually the car pulled onto the highway and headed north on Route 87, up the panhandle. Striker tailed the car for a long time, almost to the Canadian River, searching the horizon periodically for aircraft.

After about an hour, the car slowed and pulled off the highway, heading west on a dirt road. The sun was lower and glaring just above the rim of the mesas, casting long dark shadows amid the barren rocks but blinding the drivers as they drove into its light. Between the glare of the sun and the cloud of dust that rose in the wake of the car ahead, Striker wondered what the hell Peter was doing driving for so many miles on this dirt road. He muttered and cursed Peter until the car stopped in the shadow of a towering rock formation. Despite Striker's impatience, he had always felt Peter was competent and reliable, as anyone could have been in his position. Peter was a bag man, Striker's drone, an errand boy; he wasn't a player, and no one would notice him if he kept on working for Striker indefinitely or just disappeared altogether.

When the dust finally settled, Striker unfolded his long limbs and got out of his car. His faded jeans matched the vest that he wore over a plain white T-shirt, and his black, alligator cowboy boots added two more inches to his six-foot-two frame. He climbed nimbly onto the roof of his car and surveyed the landscape with a pair of military-issue high-power binoculars. Peter and the man stepped from their car and approached Striker as he jumped down and reached into his front seat to retrieve a leather briefcase. They stopped before they got too close to Striker.

"What the hell is this shit about?" The man's light blue eyes burned with anger. They were the eyes of a man who demanded respect and got it. A leader. His gray hair was cropped, and his face was too tan. "Who is *this* guy?"

Striker shot an ironic smile at Peter. He was almost a full foot shorter than the general, but Striker knew that Peter could tear the bigger man's testicles off and pull the eyeballs out of his head in a sneeze. Peter looked to the ground and rolled a pebble with the tip of his boot.

"This is Peter, and he was helping me make sure that this was what it was supposed to be. It's not that I don't trust you, but I'm *very* cautious. You know that," Striker said pleasantly, but with a blank, cool stare that bored into the general's eyes. "Well, now that we all know each other, I'd like to see the pit."

The general looked at the case in Striker's hand. "Is that the money?"

"Of course," Striker said flatly, and he set the case on the hood and opened it. Packs of hundred-dollar bills were stacked neatly inside. The general nodded and hoisted his own case up beside it. He spun the tumblers several times and carefully popped the latches before slowly opening the case. In the center of a gray foam mold sat a perfect silver sphere about the size of an orange. The pit: weapons-grade plutonium, extracted from a disassembled American thermonuclear warhead. It looked as useless as an oversized ball bearing. Peter stepped closer for a look.

Striker took half a step back and with his left hand removed a sleek long-barreled .22 caliber semiautomatic from the shoulder holster inside his vest. He pressed the gun into the general's nose. Striker looked into the general's cold eyes. There was no fear in them; there was nothing. Striker smiled.

"I love you, Peter," he said, and in one stroke he swung his arm in an open, magnanimous gesture, brought the gun to Peter's ear and pulled the trigger three times. The short pops of the small-caliber gun echoed off the nearby rock.

"You're a sick fucker," the general said coolly as he turned, closed the leather case, and grabbed the handle.

"Yes, well, you could say I'm a bit emotional at times. And I do regret this." Striker had a smirk on his face as he nodded toward the lifeless body at their feet.

"Now," Striker continued, "I have a reminder for you, Mr. General. This is the first of three exchanges. I don't want you to make the mistake of taking this money and trying to disappear. I can't have that. This is a package deal, and if you breach our agreement . . . Well, let's just say that while you play hide-and-seek, I'll always be one step ahead of you. As you can see," nodding again toward the corpse, "I take no chances."

"Don't threaten me, Striker. You get what you want as long as you bring the money."

CHAPTER ONE

V

THE OFFICES OF GEM STAR TECHNOLOGY were on the third floor of a mid-sized office building just off Congress Avenue on Eighth Street in downtown Austin. The rest of the floor served as the library of the Ridley & Shaw office and was accessible only from the firm's office on the fourth floor. It was rare for anyone other than William Moss or Clara Jones to get off the elevator on the third floor. In fact, very few people knew there even was an office on that floor. That was the way Bill Moss liked it. He didn't want people around, didn't want them to see him come or see him go. Clara knew that went for her as well.

Clara had been working at Gem Star Technology for seven years. She worked regular hours, was paid and treated well by her boss, and really didn't have very much to do. In fact, she often wondered how the firm stayed open at all. Bill Moss seemed to do very little business. He rarely had her type a letter, and he received very few calls. Mr. Moss, when he was in at all, would most often sit in his high-backed leather chair behind an ornate mahogany desk, listening to classical music and staring off into space. What she did know of his business seemed to explain his strange comings and goings, and how one man could maintain such nice offices and her salary on so few transactions.

Clara knew that Bill Moss sold weapons. There were many manufacturing plants in Texas that produced weapons. She had a cousin who worked at the American Arms Co. just north of Austin, and she knew there were lots of others like it. Texans, she knew, liked their weapons. Clara herself wasn't against weapons, only handguns on the streets. What Mr. Moss did was different. Clara had typed letters to people in strange places, arranging for shipments of things like automatic rifles, grenade launchers, camouflage clothing, even tanks, armored personnel carriers, and missiles. These letters were copied to officials in Washington, D.C., who held positions in places like the Treasury Department, the Pentagon, and the F.B.I., so she knew that what was happening was legitimate. She wouldn't have said anything if it wasn't. She was the kind of person who just lived her life and hoped no one bothered her. But things were not going so well at the present time.

Clara chewed her lower lip and wondered if her boss would ever arrive. He had been out of the country for two weeks. She knew he was due back this morning, and usually after a long trip he would appear like the ghost he was, silently entering his office. Occasionally though, even after she knew he was due back, he wouldn't appear in the office for weeks.

Part of her wished that would be the case now. She dreaded asking her boss for anything, but this was an occasion where she felt she had no other choice. Mr. Moss was quiet and strong, and that made her nervous. Although she had worked for him for seven years, she could count all the conversations they'd had on one hand. The most talking he had ever done was during her interview for the job. He had given her the idea that he would be an amiable and pleasant person to work with. He wasn't unpleasant, but certainly no one would describe Bill Moss as amiable either.

She hated to ask him for anything, especially a favor, but this was certainly one time she could make an exception. The constant terror in which she and her son were living was making life unbearable. Something had to change, or else she would have to leave Austin. The only place she could really go would be to her sister's in Chicago. Clara's home, small and simple as it was, was not even close to being worth what she had paid for it. She'd have to walk away on the bank to get out of her neighborhood, and if she did that, she'd ruin her credit. She'd do it, though, and move, if something didn't change soon.

She knew, though, if there was one thing Mr. Moss didn't want, it was to be involved in her private life. She knew that from the beginning. He had told her so, and it had never bothered her. But now she had no one to turn to. She needed help. The police refused to take action; the school said there was little they could do. All she had lived and worked for over the last sixteen years and the health of her son were in danger. He'd never been entirely well, and the pressure he was under was becoming too much for him.

At first it was simply name-calling. She had expected that. Reggie had a clubfoot, and he stuttered. When he was very young, Reggie didn't go to a normal school. That was fine with her. She loved him. She wanted to take care of him. Then someone who didn't know any better decided that kids like Reggie should be in the regular schools. Things got bad.

When the boys in the neighborhood became teenagers, things got worse. Reggie began returning home from school with feces and urine smeared into his clothes and hair. Clara kept him inside after school, but they still got him between the bus stop and the front door. They were a sick bunch of kids. She knew that. They were part of a gang—a bad one. There were three of them, and they had taken it upon themselves to torment and terrorize Reggie as part of their daily routine.

Next came the beatings. She called the school. None of the abuse took place on school grounds, so school officials told her to call the police. Reggie was hysterically afraid of the police. He screamed uncontrollably if she mentioned calling them. She knew his tormentors had told him the police would take him away forever because he was a retard and a loony. He believed them. When she came home from work one day to find him under her bed with cigarette burns on the back of his hands, it was too much. She called the police. Reggie wouldn't tell them anything. The police were sorry. There was nothing they could do. They had people being killed every day. A few burns on the hands of a frightened teenager did not rank high on their list of things to fix.

Clara had no one. She needed help. The only person she could consider turning to for help was Mr. Moss. It was almost unthinkable, but she had to do something or face throwing herself at her sister's feet and living on charity until she got herself back together. She looked up at the clock. It was after noon. She pulled a brown bag from her bottom drawer and had begun to unfold her lunch when her boss walked in through the heavy wood door. Clara uttered a quiet greeting and stood up. Mr. Moss was in his office and already shutting the door before she could even get his attention.

Finally she blurted out, "Mr. Moss."

Striker looked at his secretary as if seeing her for the first time. It was unusual for her to speak to him. She knew he didn't like to speak. And he knew that didn't bother her, which was one of the reasons he'd hired her and paid her good money to do relatively little work. He knew everything about Clara Jones before he hired her. She was a large, homely woman who'd moved to Austin from Chicago when she learned she was pregnant. She had never been married, and he guessed she never would be.

Striker knew she was ashamed, and that was just as well. She had no friends or family close by, and she didn't want any; she had her son. He was fine, too. Striker even knew the son was not retarded. His IQ was slightly below normal, but his stutter and his physical deformity had tracked him in special education classes at an early age. He was a good drain on Clara's time. Striker didn't want Clara to have time or friends or family. He kept her on for as long as he did because she kept to herself, almost completely.

"Can I speak with you about something, please, Mr. Moss?" she said.

"Come in, Clara," he said in a way that was not unfriendly.

Clara nearly tripped over the chair trying to get her bulky figure out from behind her desk. By the time she got into Striker's office, he was already seated in his chair, his feet propped casually up on his desk.

"Sit down, Clara," Striker said.

"No, that's all right, Mr. Moss," she said, keeping her eyes trained on the floor in front of her.

"So, what is it?"

"I—I—I don't know how to start," Clara said, wringing her chubby hands as she looked up meekly. Striker could see that she had tears in her eyes.

"Clara," he said in a gentle voice she had never heard before, "take your time. Tell me what's wrong."

Clara took a deep breath and began. "It's my son, Mr. Moss. Me and my son. I have a problem. I don't have anyone, I'm sorry. I have to ask you for help. I know if you were to call, then the police might help. They won't listen to me—"

"Wait a minute, Clara," Striker said, holding up his hand abruptly. She thought he was going to rebuff her.

"Tell me what you're talking about," he said.

Standing there, wringing her hands as if she could wash the whole thing away, Clara breathed a sigh of relief and told her boss the entire story of the boys who were tormenting her son.

"If something doesn't change, Mr. Moss," she finally said, "I'm gonna have to leave."

"What do you mean, 'leave'?" Striker said. The last thing he wanted right now was to lose her. He didn't have the time it would take to hire someone else. He needed a secretary now that he could trust and rely on. The timing was horrible.

"I mean," she said hesitantly, staring at her shifting feet, "that I would have to go north, Mr. Moss. I'd have to leave here and go live with my sister."

Striker didn't have to ask why. He knew her financial situation. It was the way he wanted it, to keep her on a tether, not paying her too much, not paying her too little. Simply buying out her mortgage to the bank wouldn't do either. That would draw attention.

Striker sat pensively for a few moments with his chin resting on his steepled fingertips. He then asked her a few questions about the thugs. Clara couldn't help becoming excited. This was what she had hoped for.

"Well, Clara," Striker said finally, "I think the best thing is for you to call the police again. This is something that they should take care of for you. Maybe things will work out."

Striker took his feet off the desk and began going through some papers that were on the desk. Clara stood for a few embarrassed minutes before she realized that he was through with her. She said nothing. Her fingers trembled as she reached for the door handle and pulled it closed behind her. The phone on her desk rang mercifully. She pulled it from the receiver and answered it as she plopped down into her seat.

"Gem Star Technology," she said in the same flat voice she had used to answer the phone for the past seven years. She was too numbed with disappointment to feel anything. But later she would feel the full weight of his crushing rejection, and the hopelessness of her situation would tear her insides apart.

They came again that same night. The gang tormented her and her son, banging on the windows and doors, laughing and mimicking the terrified screams they heard from within. Finally she pulled Reggie into a closet and held him close, humming to him in an attempt to drown out the noise. After a while the boys grew tired and left. Clara wondered how long it would be before the gang wanted more, before they broke into the house and . . .

Striker watched them as they left. It wasn't hard to follow the three hoods. They left a trail of broken bottles and headlights, and made plenty of noise. There was one among them who was the obvious leader. He walked slightly behind the others who pranced around him like circus dogs, checking to see that everything they did or said met with his approval. He was the skinniest of the three and not the tallest, but Striker knew he was not only the leader but the most dangerous. He kept his hands in the big front pocket of his large, hooded sweatshirt, where Striker suspected he carried a gun. That was smart, keeping his hands on his weapon, but Striker knew the punk wasn't too smart or he wouldn't be wasting time terrorizing a disabled teenager and his mother.

Striker kept back and walked down the sidewalk on the opposite side of the street. He was dressed in dark jeans, a black T-shirt, and a black sweatshirt. Those who saw him suspected he was crazy. Any white man dressed the way he was and walking in that neighborhood after dark was just asking to get killed.

Occasionally a chrome-lit foreign car would creep down the street, sending a heavy bass sound pounding through the windows of the tiny row houses that lined the block. The three punks darted into the shadows when one of these cars passed, like minnows scattering from a big game fish that had wandered into the shallows. Striker faded too when these cars approached. They would be trouble, and he was not there to clean up the streets. He was focused on a single purpose.

Striker watched patiently as his quarry openly sold drugs to other teens at street corners and in garbage-strewn driveways between gutted buildings. Finally one of them cajoled a bum into buying a case of Colt 45 Malt Liquor from a run-down corner store, and the three made off toward an empty garage in an abandoned lot. The garage was the only thing standing in the empty lot that was surrounded by what Striker knew must have been a picket fence. Nothing was left of the old house that had once been there except some scattered pieces of brick and charred lumber covered with twisted rusty nails. Tall weeds poked through the uneven ground covered with garbage and dotted the lot with menacing silhouettes.

After a few minutes, a glowing, orange light shone through the broken windows of the garage. Striker saw smoke billow up through breaks in the roof before it disappeared into the clear night, and he let them get settled inside for a while. The night turned chilly, and he zipped his jacket up to his chin and pulled it up over his mouth to stay warm. Occasionally gunfire would split the night. Striker thought about going in. He could do what he had to with the three of them stone sober and armed to the teeth. But out of habit Striker would give himself the absolute best possible advantage. He would wait until they were intoxicated.

At twelve-thirty Striker limbered up, rotating his arms and legs. He removed his gun from inside his jacket as he crossed the lot and slipped into the abandoned garage through the side door. Two of them were sitting in old beat-up armchairs while the third, the fat one, stood by the fire gesticulating wildly as he told some story. Striker instantly zeroed in on the skinny one, the leader, and leveled his long sleek .22 at the youth's head. The end of the barrel was fitted with a silencer. For everyday use Striker carried a Beretta 9mm, but when he had a special job, he brought Lucy, his .22.

"Stand up," Striker ordered in a calm voice. The skinny kid gave him a smart-ass grin, and Striker put a bullet through his ear just to let him know that he wasn't a cop, and that they didn't have any rights. The blood drained from the kid's face. He grabbed at his torn ear. Blood seeped through his fingers, and he grimaced in pain. The other two remained frozen in disbelief. The quiet spitting of the gun almost made the whole thing seem like some kind of gag.

"Now stand up," Striker said in the same tone. Before he could blink they were all standing, facing him with their hands in the air.

"What the fuck?" the fat one whined.

Striker stepped in and whipped a front kick into the punk's groin. He collapsed in a heap, gasping for breath. Striker never let the gun waver from the skinny one. He knew better. There was no fear in the skinny one's eyes, and Striker knew that he was dangerous. The realization gave Striker a rush. He would have to change his plans. He knew better than to let an animal like this kid see another day. This kid would get him if he didn't get the kid first. It was too late to go back.

Striker stepped forward, but the skinny kid was expecting it, and he ducked under Striker's kick and went for the gun in his sweatshirt pocket. Instead of backing away, Striker shifted his weight while his kicking leg was still in the air and landed solidly right beside the kid. At the same moment that his foot hit the ground, his elbow smashed into the side of the kid's head and knocked him unconscious just as he pulled a Glock from his pocket. The gun clattered on the concrete floor. The other kid, whose face was riddled with acne, froze in his spot.

Striker aimed his gun at the boy's face and slowly advanced the muzzle toward him until it tickled his nose.

"Pick up the gun," Striker said in that same voice.

The kid bent down and picked up the Glock.

"Now, take the money out of your buddy's pockets," Striker said. This kid had seen enough to know that anything but obedience would be trouble. He pulled wads of money from the skinny kid's pants pockets.

"Now," Striker said, "put the gun up to his head, right to his ear. Right there!"

"Oh, man," the kid whined, "oh, man. Oh, no, no man, no. . ."

"Shut the fuck up," Striker snapped. "Now, pull the trigger. . . I said *pull* the trigger, you piece of shit, or I'll blow your fucking brains out!"

The kid began to cry, and Striker put the barrel of his gun to the kid's ear. He pulled back the hammer. The kid was hysterical.

"Do it!" Striker screamed in a rage. The tiny garage exploded with the sound of the big-caliber gun. The kid dropped the gun and collapsed to the ground, sobbing. Brains and blood were all over the place. Striker got a charge out of the mess, the hysterics, and the hot, pungent smell of the gun powder. The fat one started to squeal on the floor in terror, and Striker kicked him hard in the side of the head to shut him up.

"Now pick up the fucking gun again, you piece of shit!" Striker had a crazed look in his eyes. He was riding a crest now, and he let it carry him. This pimple-faced kid would take the rap, no fuss, no muss.

"Pick it up!"

The kid did it.

"Shoot that fat fuck in the head."

"Oh, fucking man, oh, motherfucking man!" cried the kid, pulling the gun behind him as if he could hide it. "Why? Oh man, fucking please, no man. . ."

"Go ahead," Striker growled. "You want to be a big fucking bad guy. You want to scare people! Do it, bad guy!"

Striker grabbed a handful of the kid's nappy hair and twisted it hard, forcing him over toward the fat one. Then he put a vice-grip on the boy's wrist and forced the gun up to the fat one's ear.

Striker punched his thumb into the pressure point between the kid's thumb and his wrist and screamed right into his ear, "DO IT, YOU MOTHER-FUCKING BAD GUY! DO IT! DO IT!"

The Glock exploded, and before the terrified kid knew what had happened, Striker was gone.

CHAPTER TWO

MADISON MCCALL WAS LATE FOR LUNCH. She was always late, though. Marty usually expected her about fifteen to twenty minutes after the assigned time, so he didn't mind. Still, Marty himself could never be anything but punctual. That was a tax lawyer's most common trait. The early spring sun was shining. It was warm enough for the café to open its outdoor seating area, and it was there that Marty sat, sipping a Perrier and waiting. He saw Madison coming from halfway across the little park that sat between the café and the Travis County Courthouse. She negotiated her way through the scattered benches and lunchtime crowd. People and pigeons bustled about, scurrying for places to sit and things to eat. At the opening to the park stood a large statue of a cowboy on horseback and a fountain that splashed noisily. Madison gave the fountain a wide berth to avoid the spray being carried by the breeze as she made her way to the café.

Marty liked to watch Madison walk. In fact, he liked to watch Madison do just about anything. She was pretty. There was something soft about her, but at the same time you knew she was tough. Marty couldn't think of anyone else like her. She was one of a kind. When she saw him, she waved and smiled in an easy way that suggested a successful day. That was Madison. She could tear the district attorney to pieces one minute and then be that sweet and beautiful southern belle the next. Her legs weren't long, but they were shapely, like the legs of a sprinter. She wore a dark blue suit, and her light brown hair was pulled back into a French knot by a comb, showing the fullness of her face.

She was spectacular. Her eyes seemed to fluctuate between slate gray, light blue, or a greenish color, depending on the color of her clothes. Her cheekbones were high, and her nose was thin. She didn't have the face of a model or a movie star, but she was a sophisticated if not unique beauty. She rarely wore makeup or got "dolled up," as she put it. Madison believed that a jury mistrusted a pretty woman made up with lipstick and rouge. She relied on her brains and her sharp tongue as her only weapons of persuasion. Marty thought if he were on a jury, he would give her any verdict she wanted, but that was Marty.

Madison had to go inside the café to get to the outside tables where Marty was seated. He scowled at several men whose eyes followed Madison's figure to his table.

"What are you glaring at, Marty?" she said, sliding easily into a chair across from him.

"Don't they have wives?" Marty said, continuing to glare.

Madison glanced over her shoulder and laughed lightly. She was used to that kind of attention and ignored it.

"Please, Marty," she said, "you don't have to be my big brother."

Marty turned his attention back to her and smiled. "So, how's it going?"

"With what? Brayson?"

Marty nodded. Madison was in the middle of preliminary hearings for the murder trial of an aging and once prominent local physician who had given his wife a lethal injection of morphine. The woman had been suffering from a painful and incurable form of bone cancer. Most people looked at the act as one of mercy, but the nurse on call at the hospital where he'd administered the fatal injection was morally opposed to euthanasia and protested loudly and vehemently. God told her to protest loudly and vehemently. District Attorney Van Rawlins, in a political move to cement the religious right in the upcoming fall elections, had taken on the state's case with the fervor of a Baptist minister.

"Oh," Madison said, absently picking up the menu, "I think I've got the needle suppressed."

Madison wasn't going to wage an ethical battle with Van Rawlins if she could help it. It wasn't that she didn't feel that her client was right, or even that she couldn't win that way; but she preferred simply quashing any conviction by knocking out the real evidence if she could, and in this case she thought she could. The doctor, after giving his wife the injection, put the needle back into his bag. It stayed there until two days later, when the police searched the doctor's home. One of the investigators saw the doctor's medical bag in the next room and confiscated it. The DA was trying to argue the plain-sight exception to the Fourth Amendment's protection against illegal search and seizure. Madison countered that the bag in and of itself gave the officer no probable cause for a search, as it was the needle inside the bag that was incriminating and not the bag itself.

"You think you got it out? That's great!" intoned Marty.

Madison closed the menu and looked around for their waiter. "Yeah," she said absently. "It's good."

"Good?" Marty said. "Hey, what's wrong with you? This is great news. Van must be grinding his gold caps. . . . Are you okay?"

"Yeah, I'm fine, Marty," she said, and finally got their waiter's attention with an exaggerated wave.

They ordered, then Marty cleared his throat several times and pushed his heavy glasses as far up on his nose as they would sit before he said, "Madison, I want to ask you something."

"Okay."

"I want to ask you to dinner."

"What do you mean, 'ask me to dinner'?" she said warily. "We have dinner all the time. Why did you say it like that?"

"I said it like that because I mean it like that," Marty said, his face flushing. His big, flat palms were cold and clammy. He'd gone over this scene a thousand times. He had hoped that she would gaze back into his eyes and say dreamily, "Of course, Marty, I'd love to." Instead he hit the glitch. He was smart enough to know how she would probably react, so he wasn't shocked, but he decided to press forward.

"Madison," he said with a sigh, "I can't pretend any more. You have to say yes. I know you care about me."

"Oh, Marty," she said, her face showing sadness, "of course I care about you. You're my best friend. I—"

"Don't say anything," he pleaded. "Just listen. . . ."

The waiter brought their salads, and Marty waited with a pained expression for him to leave.

"You don't have anyone," he continued in a desperate whisper when they were alone again. "I don't have anyone. We're together all the time. I love you. Don't shake your head, Madison. You don't have to be head over heels for me. Just give me a chance. If you'd just try, I think it could work. You know we have a great time together. We laugh. We cry. We do everything."

"We're exact opposites, Marty," she said, but he could see she was weakening.

"That's exactly right!" he said triumphantly. "That's why we get along so well. Opposites attract! Madison. . . " Marty reached across the table and took her hand.

"Please . . ."

"I have to think, Marty," she said, allowing him to hold her hand. "It's not you. I don't know if I want anyone. I've got Jo-Jo—"

"Don't you want him to have some brothers and sisters?"

"Marty, you're way ahead of yourself," Madison said incredulously. "I'm not thinking about getting married again. . . . Kids? I don't even know if I want a relationship."

"We've already got a relationship," he said.

"Not that," Madison replied with a wave after gently pulling her hand away from his. "And I don't mean to demean our friendship. I don't know what I would have done without you, but I just have to think about it."

Marty slumped down in his chair. The two of them sat with their private thoughts until the rest of the food arrived.

"Really, Madison," Marty said glumly. "I don't mean to dredge up muck, but how did you marry Joe anyway? I tried to tell you back then that he wasn't right for you. I mean, all these years I've known you both, but I never knew why. You never wanted to talk about it so I didn't ask, but I think it might be part of the reason why you can't get on with your life."

"I have gotten on with my life," she protested.

Marty said nothing. He didn't believe she believed it, and he didn't think she really had, either.

Madison looked up at the clock on the face of the courthouse and anticipated its chime on the half hour. After the bell had resonated through the street, she looked at Marty.

"It was Jo-Jo," she confessed.

"Jo-Jo?" Marty said, raising one eyebrow. "But he wasn't born until almost a year after you got married."

"I lied . . . about when we were married."

Madison was a second-year law student when she met Joe Thurwood. Back then he was called "Big Joe," and he still liked to be called that today. He was the starting fullback for the Outlaws at the time, and one of the team's biggest stars. The team was at its pinnacle after having gone to the playoffs three years in a row. Joe was a hunk of a man, with blond hair and blue eyes and a suntanned body that had reminded her of a Rodin bronze. Every sports fan in America knew who Joe Thurwood was, and every woman wanted him. That was the way Joe liked it, too.

She met him at a bar, of all places. Madison wasn't one to hang out at bars;

the bar scene wasn't her idea of evening entertainment, but that one night had been an exception. Her trial team had won the regional moot-court competition, and the celebration had spilled from the courthouse into one of the popular downtown clubs. Madison, who'd made a spectacular closing argument that had put the University of Texas team over the edge, joined her teammates for an evening of celebratory laughs and drinks. Joe Thurwood caught her like a doe in the headlights of a fast-moving car. She was definitely out of her element, socially disoriented, and she never knew what hit her.

It was fate really, at least that's what she had told herself at the time. The group had actually left the bar and was heading home when Madison realized she'd left her wallet behind. When she returned to the bar to look for it, Joe Thurwood swooped down on her like a hawk. All Madison knew was that this handsome stranger was one of the nicest people she had ever met. He accompanied her on her search of the night club, politely jostling other patrons out of the way and calming her with assurances that they would find her wallet. He insisted on borrowing a flashlight from the manager to search under the tables and in every last corner. She was impressed with his chivalry, as were the manager, the bartenders, and the numerous patrons, who noticed this gallant stranger acting like an overgrown Boy Scout.

They never found her wallet. She'd left it at home, but she was so taken with Joe that she accepted an invitation to go to a quiet piano bar and then allowed him to take her home.

Madison realized that the thing that had drawn Joe Thurwood to her as much as her good looks was the fact that she was not only unfamiliar with who he was, but she was indifferent to his athletic accomplishments. To Joe Thurwood, Madison was the ultimate challenge, plus she was beautiful, smart, sophisticated, and one woman who didn't want to jump into bed with him.

To Madison McCall, Joe was such an unlikely suitor, he was tantalizing. And more desirable because he was so foreign and out of reach. Madison's father was never a sports fan; she had no brothers, and her and her sister's extracurricular activities had been limited to the band and the debate team. Madison's father was a highly respected trial attorney in Dallas, and she wanted nothing more in life than to follow in his footsteps. If it didn't have something to do with the law, Madison McCall had no real use for it. Joe Thurwood changed that.

He was a whirlwind of brute charm, and the fact that there was no expense that Thurwood spared or act of kindness he was reluctant to express, endeared him to her even more. For the first few months of their relationship, Madison would do nothing more than kiss him. Because they had met in the springtime, Thurwood had little more to occupy his time than weight training, running, preparing for the best game he could ever play, and making Madison his personal obsession. Those who knew him and saw him with Madison couldn't believe their eyes. Joe, who could be crude, crass, and incredibly egocentric, was sensitive and suave. As smart as she was in the classroom, and as shrewd as she was at her assessment of people, Madison's vision of Joe Thurwood was clouded and she never clearly saw what she was getting into.

It happened that summer. After classes ended in May, Madison had gone north to Dallas to work with her father on a murder trial. Every weekend, Joe traveled from Austin, where he was training with the team, to spend as much time with Madison as he possibly could. When they weren't together, Joe would call her, and they'd talk on the phone well into the night. Madison was being seduced. Everything about Joe Thurwood was right. When she looked back on it years later, she would realize that his apparent perfection should have caused her some concern; nobody's perfect. But Joe seemed to be the exception, and as a student of the law she had learned to always consider the exception. That summer she fell madly in love with him.

In mid-July, Joe asked her to spend a weekend with him in Corpus Christi. Joe would be going to San Angelo State College with the Outlaws for over a month of training camp. With the prospect of a prolonged absence looming, Madison could no longer hold back. For all her cautious ways, Madison McCall was as passionate and sensual as any woman. When Joe asked that they spend an entire weekend together at a beach condo outside the Texas coastal town, she agreed. That weekend, the only beach they saw was from the terrace that overlooked the ocean from their bedroom. As much as Madison now despised Joe Thurwood, she would never regret, or forget, that weekend. Total physical pleasure, ecstasy like she had never known before or since. . . . And nine months later, her beautiful son, Jo-Jo, whom she loved more than anyone or anything in her entire life, was born.

It was mid-August when Madison knew she was pregnant. She had taken precautions, but again, fate intervened. She was scared when she found out, and she felt all alone. She wanted to tell Joe in person. Her first opportunity came after the Outlaws had played an exhibition game against the Cowboys in Dallas. Madison said she needed to talk to him, and Joe had gotten permission from the team to stay overnight in Dallas.

The players didn't have to report back to camp until the next night. It was their first day off since training camp had begun in late July, so Joe was more than happy to spend it with his new lover. It was midnight before he gimped out of the locker room, sore from a bruised thigh he'd acquired earlier in the week during practice and exacerbated in the game. Joe was cranky from exhaustion and pain, and although Madison understood, she was impatient to be alone with him to talk. Joe wanted to be alone too, but not for talking. He'd been cooped up at Angelo State for a month, and although he'd bedded several groupies who had haunted the camp, he was anxious to get his beautiful new trophy on her back without any complications or discussion. When they got to his hotel room, he groped at her the minute they stepped inside the room and actually tore her blouse.

That was Madison's first glimpse of a side of Joe that would soon come to define his entire character. In tears she told him she was pregnant. He told her she'd have to have an abortion. Madison screamed that she would never do it, then she collapsed onto the bed, sobbing. Joe calmed her and gently told her that he loved her, but it was three A.M. when he finally gave up hope of convincing her to abort the baby.

Joe Thurwood knew when he was beaten. One thing he would not do was father a child out of wedlock. Marriage was something he'd planned on one day anyway, and on that night he couldn't imagine a better mother for his children than this beautiful and spirited law student. In a way that he thought was gallant and magnanimous, Joe Thurwood announced that they would get married. Madison, exhausted and confused in a way that she had never been before in her life, surrendered herself, physically and emotionally, into Joe Thurwood's arms. They made love then, over and over, until they finally collapsed as the sun began to rise. Later that day they made hasty arrangements. The next Saturday, the day the Outlaws broke training camp and returned to Austin for the season, Madison and Joe married in civil ceremony in Corpus Christi. Their honeymoon was spent in the same seaside condo in which they had conceived their son. By then, things were already different. The gallantry was gone and, although the difference in his treatment of her was slight, Madison had a sinking and unshakable feeling that she had gone from the role of damsel to bed wench in one short week.

When Madison returned to school the next week, she quietly let it be known that she had married Joe Thurwood in mid-May, right after finals for the spring semester. She hadn't lied for herself as much as for the son she would bear. No one was surprised. Madison had always been the private type who would keep even her own wedding confidential. Everyone already knew that the football star was madly in love with her. All her classmates had seen him waiting for her after classes in his red Porsche Carerra. It had been the talk of the law school last semester. Madison successfully sold the lie to her close friend and classmate Marty Cahn. They had spent all spring slaving for a huge firm in Manhattan, and she hadn't spoken a word of her new relationship or condition until fall. Marty was crushed but determined not to let his disappointment separate him from the girl he secretly loved. If he couldn't be her lover, at least he could be there as her friend. Marty was smart enough to figure that Madison would need him later on. When she did need him, he intended to be there.

And Marty had been right. After six years of Joe's infidelity and the vociferous arguments that characterized their marriage, Madison finally called it quits. She knew that the only thing worse than a single-parent home for Jo-Jo was a dysfunctional family environment. Like every football player, Joe had gotten old and battered during all the years of his playing. He was replaced by younger and healthier men. No longer the toast of the town, Joe became belligerent and vicious toward a wife who was not only the family's bread-winner but a respected member of the community. Madison gritted her teeth and tolerated the drinking and even the cocaine, but when Joe took his first swing at her, she put the legal system she knew so well into motion and quickly stripped Joe Thurwood of what he considered his last remaining possessions: his home, his wife, and his son. That had been only two years ago. After a humiliating series of newspaper articles chronicling the complete demise of the local superstar, Joe Thurwood, angry and privately vowing revenge, had disappeared. Madison heard rumors that he returned to his hometown, a small farming community in Iowa, but for almost two years, she had not seen or heard from her ex-husband.

Marty, as he had intended to so many years ago, stepped into Madison's life and was the kind of stalwart friend she needed in a crisis. He maintained an even keel through it all. He stayed by her side, sleeping on her couch like some lanky, underfed guard dog, through the divorce proceedings and custody hearings. Madison was scared of Joe and what he might do. He had openly threatened her and Marty, whom Joe resented for helping Madison. This only stiffened Marty's resolve to help Madison to secure exclusive custody of Jo-Jo.

Marty not only allowed Madison a more peaceful sleep at night, he made breakfast in the mornings, dinner in the evenings, and got close to Jo-Jo. But that had been almost two years ago. With Big Joe's absence, things settled down. Madison and Jo-Jo adjusted, and Marty felt that things were normal enough in everyone's life now for him to state his intentions to Madison. If pressed for a candid answer, Marty would have admitted that he felt he had earned the right to court the woman he had loved for so long.

Marty's one consolation was that before Madison and Joe separated, she had convinced her husband to allow Marty to negotiate what would be the last contract of his NFL career. Although he studied tax law as a practical matter, it had always been Marty's dream to represent the elite athletes of the NFL. He got Joe a great deal in an age before free agency made big deals the rule rather than the exception; and although Joe did everything he possibly could to squander the money on bad oil and real estate deals, Marty's crafty negotiating had assured that at least there was a lot to spend. That deal, and Marty's subsequent successes at the negotiating table throughout the NFL, had resulted in a small stable of top-rated players. Marty, ever pragmatic, continued to devote most of his efforts to the less glamorous but steady work of tax lawyering. But the agency work was Marty's prize accomplishment. The deals he did for football players were embarrassingly easy, but they gave Marty a direct tie to the macho, physical world of the NFL. Everyone who knew Marty knew that this work and his friendship with Madison were the pride of his life.

Marty pushed his plate away untouched and signaled their waiter for the check. "I'd give everything I have to have never had you marry that animal."

"Don't, Marty." Berating her ex-husband served no purpose. "What is done is done."

"It's true, Madison," he said, holding his hands up in surrender. "It's true."

Madison stared out at the fountain in the park, lost in her thoughts and the white noise of it's steady spray. "He's back," Madison said, as if she was hypnotized.

"What?" Marty said, stiffening as if someone had doused him with a bucket of ice water. "Who?"

Madison's eyes came into focus. She turned and stared intensely at Marty while reaching inside the breast pocket of her suit jacket. She pulled out a folded paper, which she set down on the table between them. It was a summons. Like most lawyers, Marty knew what it was without more than a glance.

"Joe," Madison said flatly.

"What is it, Madison?" Marty said patiently, slipping naturally and easily back into his role as the consummate friend.

"A summons."

"I know. But for what?"

"Joe wants to challenge the divorce settlement and the custody arrangement," Madison said, her eyes losing their focus in the fountain once again. "He wants alimony. . . . He wants Jo-Jo."

"He can't do that, Madison," Marty said as gently as he could, using every ounce of control he had to keep from bursting out with rage. "The order has been settled."

Madison huffed at the irony.

"I know, Marty," she said, looking directly at him with a twisted smile, "but, like *you're* always telling me, the law is in a constant state of flux and *anyone* can sue *anyone* for almost *anything*."

"He said he didn't want Jo-Jo," Marty reminded her.

"Apparently," Madison said quietly, "he's changed his mind."

"Mr. Moss?"

He had just finished an overseas call regarding a deal for some sonar equipment for the Italian navy when Clara stuck her head just inside the door to his office.

"Come in, Clara," he said.

She stepped inside the door and immediately started to wring her hands and shift her weight from one foot to the other.

"I wanted to tell you that everything's okay now," Clara mumbled, looking at her restless feet.

"What are you talking about, Clara?"

"Those bad kids, the ones that'd been scaring me and my son . . ." Clara turned her gaze bravely toward her boss. "They're dead."

"Why are you telling me this?"

Clara looked back to the floor.

"I don't know," she said.

"I don't know, either."

"Would you like your coffee, Mr. Moss?" she said.

"I usually do about this time, Clara," he replied flatly.

"Yes," she said and turned to go.

"Clara . . . "

Striker leaned back in his leather chair, elbows on both arms and placed his steepled fingers under his chin. "Sometimes God works in mysterious ways."

CHAPTER THREE

WHEN MANY PEOPLE THINK OF TEXAS, they think of oil rigs and vast expanses of dry, hot flats dotted with sagebrush and cactus. But set on the edge of rolling foothills in the center of the state is Austin, a lush, green landscape speckled with large blue lakes and gently running streams and rivers. An extremely desirable and welcoming place to call home, it is the capital of the second most populous state in the nation. Austin has a world-class university and has attracted a steady flow of industry and high-tech companies. The fact that the city boasts a competent NFL team, the Texas Outlaws, gives it a cachet shared by its better known rival cities, Dallas and Houston.

In the foothills northwest of the city, a golf and tennis community called Wild Oaks boasts homes beginning at four hundred thousand dollars. All are set back off peaceful, winding streets, and most enjoy either a view of the golf course or an even more spectacular view of the distant city and the river that rushes toward it. The Greys had a home with a view of both. When they first arrived in Austin almost nine years ago, Cody and his young wife, Jenny, lived downtown in a fashionable apartment between the river and Sixth Street, the center of Austin's night life. The neighborhood suited their lifestyle perfectly. Cody not only had the distinction of being an NFL player, he was a handsome man with dark hair and an angular face and physique. Jenny also had dark hair, long and silky, creamy white, unblemished skin, and a face that was almost perfect. She was tall, only a few inches shorter than her husband who was six-foot-two, and she had the kind of body that turned men's heads wherever she went. Her eyes, though, were her most striking feature, ice blue, like the eyes of a Siberian husky.

From the moment they arrived in Austin, Jenny, more than anything, wanted to establish herself and her husband in the high life of Austin society. She wanted to be important and rich, to be invited to all the right parties, and dine at all the right places. Cody was a celebrity, and that meant that they were always welcome, but he had no desire for any of it. He wanted to play football, that was all. Networking, something Jenny perfected during her four years at Princeton, was something completely foreign and distasteful to him. He only knew that Jenny liked to go to every party, every charity luncheon, and spend every free minute at the Wild Oaks Country Club, which he had no desire to attend. He didn't golf all that well because it was something he'd never done: tennis to him was a joke, something for rich people and women. No matter how much money Cody made, he never thought of himself as rich. But Jenny had insisted on all those things that smacked of glamour and displayed wealth.

Cody Grey was one of the most visible and well-known Outlaws players in the city of Austin, and Jenny's taste for celebrity status was fueled by the attention people gave to her husband. At first, Jenny liked it when they went to a restaurant or a club on Sixth Street and people stopped to ask for Cody's autograph. Soon, however, she began to resent the constant attention that was paid to her spouse while she stood idly by, ignored. She had brains, and she had looks. She also believed she had talent. Jenny wanted to be a star too. She was often told she was beautiful enough to be in the movies, and she had always secretly wanted to. She decided to do it. Austin, she already knew, was the fourth biggest place in the country for filmmaking behind L.A., New York, and Chicago, and it was growing by leaps and bounds.

Just months before completing her Ivy League education, the thing she had struggled so long and hard for, Jenny realized she wanted more than the job interviews and the scramble for placement in corporate America. Certainly a Princeton business graduate had a wonderful leg up in the job market, but Jenny wasn't satisfied with the idea of making eighty thousand a year, out of the limelight. She had seen the effects of real wealth up close and all around her during her four years at Princeton, and she wanted that. But she knew that wealth alone wouldn't make her happy. She needed fame as well as fortune, and in the city of Austin on the arm of a well-known NFL player, Jenny believed she could find both. She started thinking about a plan to get her acting career off the ground in Austin.

From the very beginning, Cody Grey was a player who drew a lot of attention from the local media. Even the negative publicity his violent temper occasionally generated could help Jenny with her plan. She understood that the connections important in the world of business were even more crucial in the filmmaking industry. Besides an incredible stroke of luck, to get anywhere you had to know the people making the decisions at the top. The people at the top attended the same social occasions that Cody was invited to. Even though Cody preferred to avoid this scene, he wasn't one to stand in the way of his beautiful wife's ambitions. In fact, he was her biggest fan. Cody wanted Jenny to get what she wanted. He was a decent husband, and he wanted his wife to be happy. But he secretly hoped that if she were to achieve even modest success in her acting that she would settle down, spend more time at home, and maybe even be ready for the children he dreamed of having.

Cody's dreams of family and his professional goals were tied up together, and he hoped he could achieve even some of them. If he drove himself hard enough, maybe he would. On the football field, dreams are directly related to productivity, and productivity for Cody came in the form of tackles and interceptions. The Outlaws was the perfect team for him. Even when he was still in his rookie season, and he played nothing more than special teams, his violent brand of football earned him a cult following. The Outlaws had two exceptional cornerbacks that enabled their defense to play primarily man-to-man coverage. This allowed Cody, as the free safety, to be a run-stopper first and foremost; and that became his forte, because stopping the run was all about hitting. In only his second season, Cody became the starter at the strong safety position. In his third and fourth years, he was considered a solid player. As the seasons stacked up, more and more fans would appear at Texas Stadium in #40 jerseys with GREY printed on the back. The crowds would cheer wildly whenever he made one of his heat-seeking missile hits that inevitably laid the offensive ball carrier out on the grass. It was something the fans in Austin came to expect. Many of them considered his hits alone worth the price of a ticket. When Cody tackled, he went up high, for the head. An occasional unnecessary roughness penalty thrown by some over-cautious official would draw deafening boos in Austin. They wanted their assassin turned loose, and Cody seemed to never disappoint them.

In his fifth year, Cody had eight interceptions to go along with his team-leading one hundred sixty-seven tackles. The team went to the playoffs, and although they lost in the first wild-card game, Cody went to the Pro Bowl. He was by then a household name in Austin and most of Texas.

But unfortunately for Cody, from a financial standpoint the timing was not good. As a third-round draft choice he was happy to get a four-year deal worth just over a half-million dollars. And when he was up for renegotiation after four years, free agency in the NFL was still a dream, and he considered himself lucky to get another four-year deal worth nearly $1.5 million. Locked into the four-year deal, his Pro Bowl appearance, something that would have made him millions in the free agency market of the nineties, did nothing more than earn him a fifty-thousand-dollar incentive bonus. And fifty thousand dollars to Cody Grey wasn't what it once was.

Upon signing his second contract, Jenny insisted they move to Wild Oaks. Cody, warned repeatedly by his agent not to buy the house, couldn't convince Jenny that the million and a half dollar contract wasn't guaranteed, and if he got hurt they could end up sitting on an expensive house with a big mortgage and no way to make the payments. She would hear none of it. Cody never got hurt, she reasoned, and even if he did, by then she would be making it big herself. Besides, they both believed that he was only going to get better, and after this contract there would be another even bigger one. If free agency ever came about, Jenny knew as well as anyone that she and Cody would have all the money they needed.

She told him they had to think big. Wild Oaks was where "everyone" lived. Of course living in Wild Oaks wasn't enough in and of itself. Jenny fell in love with a six-bedroom Spanish stucco with a red tiled roof. The property came complete with a pool, a small pool house, and possibly one of the ten best views in the entire community. The price tag was $735,000. The team agreed to give Cody the first hundred and fifty thousand of that year's salary up front so that he could make the down payment. It was the least they could do for the player who was already the toast of the town and the leader of their defense.

Armed with a place in the hills, four years of arduous acting classes at the University of Texas, and a celebrity husband, Jenny began to get steady work. Cody's trip to the Pro Bowl and Jenny's success in her budding career made everything seem right. The two of them seemed destined for only bigger and better things to come. None of Jenny's work, however, was anything major. She would get a few lines here, a few lines there, and a lot of background scenes as a glorified extra. At first, just that had been enough to thrill her, and she and Cody were happier than ever. As time wore on, though, she was harder and harder to please, and she became increasingly frustrated with the fact that she hadn't gotten her big break. She knew everyone in Austin who was anyone in the industry, but when the time came for the final cut, there was always some casting director or some out-of-town director or producer who would nix her. Once she got a real role, albeit a minor one, in a feature western. She appeared in three scenes and had several lines each time she appeared. She thought this film would be the answer, but it never made it to the theaters.

Frustrated and embittered, Jenny became more and more difficult to get along with, not just for Cody but for everyone. She couldn't keep the same agent for more than six months, and despite her social ties, the big producers stopped taking her calls. The Greys were still welcomed at every event, but that was because of Cody. Jenny became an annoyance, and at times, if she drank too much, she was even an embarrassment. Sometimes, if Cody was surrounded by a throng of admirers, he would finally break free only to find Jenny off in some corner talking and smiling with some unsuspecting man. He and Jenny would fight about it. She protested that he couldn't smother her, that she was doing nothing wrong. Cody could never articulate what bothered him, but his instincts told him he had a right to be angry.

More than once, such an evening would end with punches being thrown. Young bucks, undeterred by Cody's size, were stirred to action by his flirtatious wife and an evening of drinking. Cody soon developed a reputation as a roughneck. He wasn't the kind of man to lose a fight. Sometimes he turned vicious. Noses were broken. Three times lawsuits had ensued and Cody had paid dearly to avoid more bad publicity than he already had. Jenny seemed to enjoy the fiery turn their lives had taken. She believed that any publicity was better than no publicity at all. More and more it seemed Jenny prompted Cody to anger. More and more they fought, openly and bitterly, privately and publicly.

Near the end of the 1993 football season, Cody's worries got worse. The day after a game in Philadelphia, his knee swelled, and his leg was locked in one position. All he could do was hobble into the trainer's room the next day. The team's orthopedic surgeon, Dr. Randy Cort, examined him and ordered an MRI, predicting that they would find some kind of cartilage damage. They did, and the next morning Cody went under the knife for the removal of all that remained of the cushion that kept the two main bones in his leg from rubbing together and grinding each other into dust.

After the surgery, Cody was shown a videotape of the procedure performed on his knee. He sat quietly with Cort in a tiny office that contained nothing more than two chairs, a TV, and a VCR.

"You see that there?" said the surgeon, pointing to a tattered flap of cartilage that had wedged itself between the two bones. "The edges are worn smooth. This is an old tear, real old. It should have been taken out when it first happened. Do you remember when you first hurt it?"

"No," Cody said. "My knee has been fine. It gets a little sore every once in a while, but it never seized up on me like it did."

The doctor nodded. "Well, you may not have even noticed it, but I would think that a tear this big would have given you at least some pain and swelling for a few days."

"You know," Cody said thoughtfully, "in college I had that for a few weeks, but it got better."

The doctor frowned. "Well, there's nothing we can do about it now. That torn piece in there over the years is what ground the rest of the cartilage into hamburger. It's like having a loose bit of metal floating around in a gear box. Before you know it, everything's ruined." The doctor got quiet again, and together they watched the screen as the enlarged image of the microscopic instruments cut and snipped and sucked the tissue out of Cody's knee.

"I had to take it all out," the doctor said solemnly. "Once it seizes up on you like that, you've got to get it out. Otherwise you can't play. But you should be ready to go again in three to four weeks."

The doctor stood, but Cody nodded with an absent look on his face and remained seated. He was used to this sort of thing. He'd accumulated a series of injuries like most NFL players. His body was battered with scars and hampered by joints and muscles, damage that would never allow him to lead a life free from physical discomfort. Nothing to date, however, had actually been removed from his body. Hardware had been added, a plate in a broken arm and some staples in his other knee, but this was the first time he'd lost cartilage forever. "What's it gonna do?" Cody asked slowly.

"Excuse me?" said Cort.

"What's it gonna do?" Cody asked again.

"What do you mean?" the doctor said, nervously adjusting the round rimless glasses on his face.

"I mean, I got no more cartilage. What happens to my knee?" Cody looked intensely at the doctor's face. He wanted to know.

The doctor averted his eyes and said, "You can play—"

"Yeah, but what happens after?" Cody persisted.

"Well, this could give you some problems," the doctor said briskly, jamming his hands into his white lab-coat pockets. "You know, football causes a lot of wear and tear on your body. But, hey, those two bones might just wear into a nice groove that allows you to play with a real tolerable level of pain."

"So what kind of problems? Worst case," Cody added.

"Well, worst case, you get a knee replacement, when you're older of course, and only if it bothers you a lot. If it does . . . well, sometimes it's not that bad."

"Have you ever known of a football player who had this and it didn't turn out bad?" Cody asked.

The doctor thought for a minute. "I really couldn't answer that. When players leave the team, I rarely see them again."

Cody digested that information and nodded slowly. He stood, and the doctor held out a prescription bottle filled with fat, white codeine pills, a sort of peace offering. Cody's knee was screaming now. It was a deep, low, guttural scream of pain. He took the pills.

"Thanks," he said.

"Hey, no problem," the doctor replied. "It's the least I could do."

Cody thought that might not be far from the truth.

He worked the knee as hard as he could, doing everything that was asked of him by the doctors and the training staff. After the third week he was back on the field. He could play through only after having the knee, which seemed to be permanently swollen, drained and then refilled with a mixture of cortisone and Xylocaine. Cody called it high-octane. With his knee relatively numb and the swelling temporarily reduced, he could almost play like his old self. The only problem was that he hadn't practiced with the team the entire week, and Cody knew he wasn't at the top of his game. But the coaches didn't want to disturb the chemistry of the team that late in the season, so they kept Cody in the starting lineup despite his lack of practice and hobbled performance. The Outlaws were playoff bound again. They would eventually lose in the second round, but Cody was one of the mainstays.

One thing that was obvious though, to Cody and his coaches, was that since his operation he wasn't making as many plays as he normally did. He wasn't certain whether or not this was because the deadened knee was slowing him down or because of the practices he constantly missed. Either way, when the team watched game film together on Mondays, Cody heard his name called out less and less as an example of how things should be done.

Then, for the first time in his career, a sportswriter used the word "old" in the same sentence as Cody Grey. It hit him hard. It was like a crack in the dike, and once the water started to come through there was no way to stop it.

Cody started to notice things in the mirror. When he pulled his hair back, he could see patches of white hair covertly taking over his scalp. The aches and pains seemed to bother him a little more, or maybe it's just that he noticed them more. Either way, by the time his eighth NFL season with the Outlaws was over, Cody Grey was considered old and beat-up, and at thirty years of age, he was.

CHAPTER FOUR

∨

STRIKER LOOKED OUT OF THE GLASS DOORS that led to the terrace of his penthouse apartment. The clear night sky was filled with brilliant stars. The moon was not yet up. The skyline of the city stood around him like tombstones in some titanic graveyard. Striker stretched his naked frame and yawned loudly before taking a mouthful of red wine from the crystal goblet. He slid open the glass door and the wind rushed in. The steady breeze on Striker's face made him feel alive. He finished the wine in his glass and turned his attention back toward the bed.

She was up from her midnight nap. In the light of the city and stars, he could see her dark hair blowing gently in the cool stream of air. Her skin was milky white, and in the shadows she looked more like an apparition than a woman. She was on her knees, this thin white figure, facing him. One of her hands moved gently to the dark patch between her legs while she reached out across the open space for him with the other. Striker felt the blood rush to his loins, and he moved closer to the bed.

She fixed her free hand on his shaft and began to jerk him roughly. As he grew she reached out with her other hand and grasped him before plunging him into her mouth. She held him firmly with both hands and continued to jerk as she spun her tongue wildly. Striker arched his back and ran his hands through her long silky hair while she worked. His abdominal muscles were stretched like banded steel. When he was almost there, his hands instinctively tightened, gripping her hair. The muscles in his stomach began to convulse. She stopped, pulling away from him with a wicked smile. She lay back on the bed completely naked and spread her legs invitingly.

"Now fuck me," she said. It wasn't a suggestion. It was a command. Striker felt the adrenaline rush from his heart and fill his body. He kneeled over her, smiling at her wicked face and her wicked words. He positioned himself, then plunged inside of her for the second time that night. Striker arched his back, driving deep and rising up on his hands to watch the beautiful pale form beneath him writhe like an impaled serpent.

Around one-thirty, Striker lay back on the sweaty sheets and shut his eyes. A small smile pulled at the corner of his lips. He heard her rustling at the bedside, and he opened his eyes without lifting his head. She was dressing in a hurried, distracted manner. Striker spoke without moving any part of his body except his mouth.

"Going somewhere?" he said.

"Uh-huh," she said casually.

Striker was amused at the way she dressed herself, like a man would do after sleeping with a cheap whore. She pulled a sheer white evening dress over her head and wiggled into it as she tugged at the hem. She took one more swipe between her legs with a tissue before she pulled her panties on and wedged her long foot into a shoe at the same time.

"Home?" Striker asked, tilting his head now so he could see her better. It was a small thing, the way she was leaving him, but Striker had a keen eye for detail, and he had never seen anything quite like her.

She looked at him straight in the eye. "Yes."

Striker rose up on his elbow, wide awake, intrigued. "And where is home?"

"That's really not your concern," she said, lifting a gold-sequined purse from the night table and fishing daintily around until she found her keys. She snapped the purse shut and, keys in hand, turned for the door.

Striker got up off the bed. He had to scramble to beat her to the door and stiff-arm it closed to prevent her escape. He laughed in an uncomfortable way.

"Wait," he said. "I want to see you again." Striker felt the complete fool. He couldn't remember the last time he had acted this way. It must have been while he was still in high school, more than thirty years ago.

"What's your number?" she said impatiently.

"What?" Striker asked.

"What's your phone number?" she said.

"556-5690," he said. "How about yours?"

"Maybe I'll call you," she said, then pushed his arm down and slipped out the door.

Striker watched her walk down the hall and wait for the elevator. "Don't you want to write it down?" he called to her.

The beautiful woman said nothing. She didn't even look back at him. She got into the elevator without another word and without even a sideways glance. Striker huffed and smiled to himself, shaking his head as he shut the door. He walked over to the living-room window and pushed the curtains aside, waiting to catch a glimpse of her car. A few minutes later her candy-apple red Porsche 928 raced down the street under the white lights and disappeared like a puff of smoke around the corner of another building. Striker let the curtain drop. He chewed lightly on his lip as he poured himself a straight scotch. He put on a CD of Carl Orff's opera, *Carmina Burana*, and slumped down on the couch with his drink as the urgent pleas to Fortune's power reached a crescendo and filled his head.

He pictured their sex as the music washed over him. The music grew in intensity, and in his mind's eye he saw her as vividly as he first had, sitting in a chair with her long legs crossed, her mouth turned down in a distracted pout that added to her beauty. She was surrounded by doting men but in a world of her own. Then she saw him looking, and there was something small, a flicker of recognition in her eyes, although he had never seen her before. Striker shifted in his seat as the voices on the disk rose in a tempest of music. He saw her now, rising and falling in the heat of his bedroom. He tasted blood in his mouth and realized he had bitten the inside of his lip. He knew that he had to see her again.

Cody woke up. He was alone in his living room. The bags of ice packed around his knee had turned to water. One of them was leaking. It had soaked the towel and half the couch. He'd run on his knee too hard, and he would pay the price for the next four days. It happened every week. Cody would push the knee to its limits, anticipating that one day soon it would be well. He knew that sooner or later the day would arrive when he wouldn't have to suffer for running hard. It was nothing more than the basic training regimen necessary to prepare for another NFL season. He had to do it.

His skin was soggy from the leaky bag and his bottom itched uncomfortably. The TV snowed and hissed. Cody looked at the glowing digital clock on the VCR above the set. It was 2:23 A.M. He heard the door shut, and he sat upright, swinging his bare legs out of the wet mess and rising to his feet. He stood there, his hair mussed and his face creased with sleep, wearing a wet, baggy pair of flannel boxer shorts and a T-shirt cut off at the waist. His legs looked bony and pale, and he felt silly standing there. Then he got angry.

Jenny walked in with composed majesty and set her purse on a side table.

She looked him right in the eye as she began to pull off her earrings and slip out of her pumps.

"Hello, Cody," she said calmly, as if she had every right to walk into the house at this hour. "Are you feeling okay?"

Cody flushed. "Where the *fuck* have you been!" he demanded. "Do you see the time?"

Cody could see the fire in his wife's narrowed eyes.

"You're not my father, Cody," she hissed. "Don't talk to me like you are. I'm tired of it!"

"You're tired? You're fucking tired?" Cody ground his teeth. He didn't normally curse like this, but he was enraged. "I don't care what I sound like. Where the fuck were you?"

"I don't have to listen to this," she said and turned back out toward the hallway and went up the stairs.

Cody hobbled behind her as quickly as his stiff knee would allow.

Jenny was at her sink when he caught up to her. She was wiping makeup angrily off of her face. The white balls of cotton she rubbed over her eyes came away smudged with coal-black mascara. She threw them at the brass waste basket. Some missed. She didn't bother to pick them up.

Cody gulped the bile in his throat down into his churning stomach. He knew better than to let this scene disintegrate into a shouting match. She would fight him toe to toe. It never did any good. They never got anywhere.

"Jenny," he began, then took a deep breath, trying his best to mask the rage of a jealous husband, "we've got to talk—"

"About what, Cody?" she snapped, continuing her work at the mirror. "About how you couldn't come with me tonight because you had more important things to do? About how you treat me like a little girl that you can punish or like some football player that you can threaten? I'm not a little girl, Cody. I'm not a football player. And I'm tired of your lack of trust. It's like you want me to be unfaithful. You're always accusing me. I have to hear it constantly, about where was I, who was I talking to, why wasn't I following you around like a damned whipped puppy. So what do you want to talk about tonight?"

Jenny let her hands drop to her sides, and she stared at him in the mirror without turning around.

"I had to do that dinner, Jenny," Cody said, angry at himself for sounding defensive. "I've been telling Greer since last season that I'd do that dinner, and

I couldn't say no, you know that. It was for the Leukemia Society, for God's sake! His kid's sick with it—"

"Here's what I know," she barked, unzipping the back of her dress and wriggling out of it. "That party tonight was important to me. Clarence Wyzanski was supposed to be there. He doesn't have a leading lady yet. That movie could be the break I need, Cody. I had to go, and you should have gone with me. Is Greer going to pay the bills when you can't play anymore?"

"Supposed to be? You mean he wasn't even there?" Cody said incredulously.

"That's not the point," she huffed.

"What do you mean when I can't play?" Cody said with a scowl when he suddenly realized what she had just said. "Who said anything about not playing? That's got nothing to do with this. I'll be playing for a long time. I'm not thinking about *not* playing."

Jenny shook her head and the dress dropped to the floor. She kicked it into the corner where the marble floor met the teak-framed Jacuzzi tub. Cody felt the sexual desire for her boil up inside himself. She stood there in a black thong with a strapless bra made of black lace. Her body was still hard, and her smooth, white skin was unblemished. He wanted to cross the space between them and touch her. He wanted to take her where she was, angry and impudent, bend her over the vanity and take her right there in the bathroom. The thought excited and angered him even more. Here he was, her husband, but somehow she was off-limits. That was the way sex was with him and Jenny. If she was in the mood, they did it. If she wasn't in the mood, he waited until she was. He couldn't remember how it got that way, but there it was. He hated the feeling. It was complete helplessness.

Jenny took her toothbrush out of its gold wire holder and gobbed on the toothpaste she had taken from the drawer.

"It's like everything else, Cody," she said before sticking the brush into her mouth, "you don't want to look at the way things are. You're hurt. How much more do you think that knee can take? How much more time have you got? They won't keep you if you can't run. Get smart. You can speak at a dinner for Greer every night from now until the season starts, but if you can't cut it, you're gone."

It was the way she said it. Cody sensed she was almost glad, like she was laughing at him.

"You're supposed to be my fucking wife, Jenny. What the hell are you talking like this for?" he snarled.

She spit in the sink and looked at him. She looked almost sad. It made Cody take half a step back.

"Cody," she said with a calmness that he didn't like. A thin line of white foam circled her lips. "You don't see it, do you? You don't see the big picture?"

"What the hell are you talking about?" he said.

"Either I make it big fast," she said, "or we're in trouble, Cody."

"What do you mean, 'we're in trouble'?" he said. "Why'd you say it like that? What the hell does that mean?"

"I mean we're in trouble," she said simply. "Everything's in trouble, for you, for me, for us. We need things to go our way. I like the way we live. I don't want to change it. I don't plan on it."

"What the hell does that mean?" He was prepared for an argument but not this. This kind of talk was bewildering. It created a nauseous feeling that closely resembled fear, although Cody would never call it that. For all his tough exterior, Cody couldn't tolerate the thought that his wife, his life partner, would ever not be there. For all his suspicion and resentment, Cody's dependence on Jenny was almost addictive.

"See?" she huffed. "That's how you are, something's got to mean something negative. What do you think I'm saying? I'm just saying that I've got to get things going, Cody, for when the time comes when you can't play anymore; not now, but sometime, later. Don't you want *me* to succeed?"

"Of course I want you to succeed," he said, twisting his mouth.

"Well maybe that's what this is all about," she replied with a thoughtful look into the mirror.

"This is bullshit!" he said suddenly. "I was talking about why the hell you waltzed in here at two-thirty, and you've turned it around to me not wanting you to succeed! This is so fucking typical of you."

"You want to talk about me coming in like you're my damn father?" she screamed. "I thought we were past that! I was giving you the benefit of the doubt, Cody. I was going to let your possessive crap go by, but you want to talk about it? I'll talk . . ."

Cody nodded with a scowl, "Yeah, where the fuck were you?"

"I'll tell you, and then I'll tell you why it is so fucked up that you're treating me like some child!" she said, turning on him in a fit of rage.

"I went to the party. I went alone. Wyzanski didn't show up. It's the same old thing! I'm in the same old rut, Cody! I want a life! I want something to happen! Don't you understand that?"

Cody continued to glare.

"I went out for a drink with Peg," she said, throwing her hands up in the air. "We had a glass of wine; we had two. We kept drinking, Cody. I had to talk to someone, and you weren't there, not that you'd have talked if you were."

"I don't believe you," he said flatly.

"It's true, Cody," she said, looking him straight in the eye. "If you don't believe me, then I'm sorry for you. There's nothing more I can do, there's nothing more I can say. It's true."

Cody searched her face for the truth. He thought he found what he wanted. He digested it patiently before crossing the space to kiss her. She responded, but then pulled away.

"I want you," he whispered, pulling her close, his hands slipping inside her panties and palming her muscular buttocks.

She turned her head and pushed away gently. "Not now."

"I want you, Jenny," he said urgently.

"I know," she said quietly, with her saddest eyes, "but I'm tired. I'm depressed. I don't want to. I want to go to sleep. Think about what I want, Cody. Think about me for a change. Please?"

Cody nodded resolutely and removed his hands from her behind.

"Okay," he said, "let's go to bed."

She hugged him to her and kissed him lightly on the cheek, but to Cody she was a million miles away.

CHAPTER FIVE

ⅴ

ON THE OTHER SIDE OF THE COLORADO RIVER, Marty and Madison were dining at the Four Seasons. The restaurant sat on the water's edge. From their table they could see the nearby hills to the west. The lights from the bridges shimmered on the river's surface. It was a peaceful and elegant evening. At first the conversation between them was strained. Both of them were uncomfortable. Neither knew quite what to say or how to say it. Madison didn't want to be too familiar and thus suggest that this was something more than it was, but on the other hand she didn't want to be too distant and hurt the feelings of a good friend. What it was, though, was a date. In the excitement of the not-guilty verdict she had won for one of the firm's biggest clients, in a vehicular manslaughter case, Madison had rashly agreed to Marty's proposal. She regretted that now, and it wouldn't surprise her, from the way Marty was squirming uncomfortably in his chair, if he wasn't having second thoughts of his own.

It was the wine that saved them. Marty chose an excellent German Riesling. Even before their meals were served, they ordered another bottle. Things started to loosen up. Talk turned from their law firm to a more intimate subject. Marty finally confessed in a forthright but inoffensive way his obsession with Madison dating back to their days in law school. Madison was flattered with his description of how much she meant to him. She was sad for him when he described the pain he'd experienced when she had taken up with Joe. The story was poignant, but the wine, and Marty's easy smile, didn't make Madison uncomfortable.

She looked across the table at Marty and found herself actually wondering if she could love him. He was tall and lean, with a hard jawline and bright blue eyes; not unattractive at all. There was something about him, though, that just didn't get her excited. She wondered if she shouldn't put the notion of animal attraction behind her. Joe had attracted her. From the moment she met Joe she was hungry for him. Now she knew firsthand the value of such an attraction. But Madison was a dreamer, her father had always told her that. When she lay awake, alone in the bed that was once Joe's as well as her own, she would think about finding someone, out there somewhere, a man whom she could adore the way she adored Marty, but whom she desired the way she had desired Joe. But maybe that was nothing more than a dream. Maybe she was a fool who hadn't seen the answer to her happiness when all along it was right before her eyes. She said none of this to Marty because she wasn't sure. Wine or not, she was smart enough to know not to hurt him that way. She was determined not to give Marty false hope.

The meal was as good as the wine, and afterward they walked out the back of the hotel and down to the river walk. A full moon drew a brilliant, dancing beam across the surface of the river, and the bridges loomed above them like sleeping giants adorned with sparkling jewels. Madison pushed her breeze-blown hair behind her ears and crossed her arms. Marty noticed immediately and removed his jacket to wrap around her. The cool night air seemed to break the spell of dinner.

"How's it going with Brayland?" Marty asked, referring to her case with the doctor who allegedly killed his wife.

Madison shrugged and said, "Could be better. The trial is just around the corner, and I can't convince him not to take the stand."

"Why don't you want him on the stand?"

"Because he'll tell the jury he did it," Madison said. "I talked with a psychologist about it. She told me that he needs to say it to the jury to reassure himself that what he did was right. If he kept silent, it would be paramount to admitting that he really did murder her, which he doesn't believe he did. He spared her suffering."

"There's a difference between moral murder and legal murder. Doesn't he understand that?" Marty said, kicking a stone off of the asphalt path and into the grass.

"No," Madison said. "He doesn't want to understand."

"So," Marty said, "you've got a client that's going to get on the stand and basically tell the jury he did it. That's a tough one."

"Yeah, and combine that with the fact that the judge on the case, Walter Connack, keeps asking me to take on a pro bono murder case to defend some kid who shot his two friends in the head for some drug money, a case I have no intention of taking."

Marty stopped walking and took Madison by the shoulders, turning her toward him. He looked down into her eyes. They were illuminated by the moonlight. Marty didn't think he'd ever seen her look so beautiful. His voice shook when he spoke.

"Madison, can I kiss you?"

Madison gave him a small, gentle smile. She knew how hard it was for Marty to ask. It was so unthinkable that they should kiss, really kiss. They had been together alone countless times. They had kissed each other on the cheek countless times. Because of all that history, a passionate kiss was unimaginable to her. She knew that he knew how she felt, and she admired his bravery.

"Yes, Marty," she said, closing her eyes and resting her hands on the insides of his arms, "you can kiss me."

Marty leaned over awkwardly and touched his lips to hers.

"Hey!"

Marty pulled away and looked over Madison's shoulder. The shout had come from above, on the grassy bank. A large figure was moving down the slope toward them. The voice and the body were a man's. He had long hair, Marty could see that, and he appeared to be wearing some kind of windbreaker that flapped around him as he jogged their way. Marty couldn't see the man's face in the darkness. Adrenaline pumped through his body, and he had to stifle the urge to run. Instead he pulled Madison behind him and stood protectively between the advancing man and the woman he loved.

"Hey!" the man barked again.

Marty's heart raced. The river was not known to be a dangerous place, even at night, but the man who was loudly advancing toward them didn't look or sound familiar. Marty wished that he had a gun, or that he knew how to fight. He gritted his teeth and clenched his fists. He'd do what he could, or whatever he had to. If it meant Madison's safety, Marty wouldn't go down easy.

The man got right up to Marty, and he pulled up short, only about three feet from Marty's face. Marty could only vaguely make the man's features out beneath the shadow of his long hair. He had a thick beard and mustache, and his hair hung limply down to his shoulders. The man was even bigger than he had looked running, and even though he was no taller than Marty, he probably had a hundred pounds on the tax lawyer. Marty was afraid. Madison stayed safely behind her date. Marty held his fisted hands slightly in front of his body at about his belt line. His stomach sank.

"I hate to interrupt you two young lovers," the man said with a rude chuckle. His voice was gruff. He had a big gut, but he was powerfully built.

Marty could smell whiskey on the man's breath.

"But," he continued, stabbing a finger into Marty's chest, "I had to check to make sure my old buddy wasn't getting in a little over his head here, a little hot water here. . . . Hello, Maddy."

"Joe!" Madison said in a shocked voice, and stepped ever so slightly closer to Marty.

Marty's stomach sank even deeper.

The sun, not quite up, was rising beyond the buildings of downtown Austin. The emerald green water of the Colorado River rolled by. Striker sat sideways on the end of a bench with one leg crossed over his knee, wearing an expensive, dark green running suit. The sweat from his run in the predawn dark was almost completely dry. He alternated his gaze between the river and the open lawn that separated the running path from the towering old trees of Butler Park. Striker liked to run. The trail around the area of the river that was called Town Lake was just over ten miles and included short hops over two bridges. Striker ran it often. Austin was full of beautiful places, but to him there was nothing like the park when the sun was just about to glow above the buildings to the east and swarms of bats made their final flight back to their homes underneath the bridges.

Striker had been in Texas for years. At first he didn't have a choice. The agency wanted an operation in Texas because of the number of arms manufacturers located in the state, as well its proximity to Central America. Later, when Striker was established and had the leeway to go where he pleased, he decided to stay on and make Austin his home. It had what he wanted: warm weather, beautiful golf courses, good restaurants, music, an airport that could take him anywhere, and beautiful women. Basically, it had all the good things that you could ask for in a big city without a lot of the bad things that seemed to be inherent in New York, L.A., Atlanta, or Chicago. Gem Star could really be run out of a closet anywhere in the world. He was Gem Star, not the other way around.

Gem Star had served him and the agency well. Most properties owned by the agency were functional businesses. Very few, however, made a profit. All agency companies were funded by the U.S. government through a series of straw corporations that enabled employees like himself to be paid and to maintain the facade of legitimacy while conducting specialized intelligence work. Striker was a trouble-shooter of sorts. His cover as an arms dealer allowed him to move freely about the globe without drawing unnecessary attention to himself. If the agency had a problem, Striker was the man who could fix it. If someone had to disappear, then they did. Striker always cleaned up quickly and quietly. Part of being an intelligence agent entailed making sure one never got caught. It was essential that Striker never have any connection to the U.S. government. Exposure as an agent would result in his termination—total extermination.

Striker knew that in peacetime, the only sanctioned killing was contracted to criminals with no official ties to the government. Striker's job was to find the appropriate criminal to make the kill. Striker never made it clear to those he retained who exactly he worked for. If one of his people were to be caught, the authorities would be unable to make any connection at all to the agency. The real problem for a janitor like Striker was finding competent criminals. But Striker always seemed to find the right people. He had been so successful, the agency had allowed Striker to indulge himself. No expense was too great for Striker's comfort. The agency could rationalize almost any expenditure because Striker was also making money with Gem Star. That, and his image as a high-rolling arms dealer, only helped his international mobility.

It was Striker's sensitive operations that necessitated his being paid and contacted through his notional, which is what front operations like Gem Star Technology were called within the intelligence community. Likewise, he himself had no name. He was simply Striker, and he took pride in the fact that only a handful of people had ever known his real name. The nature of his work also meant that Striker was not an official employee of the agency. He had no social security number or pension plan. He had no official rank. He was a contract employee, a free agent of sorts, an NFL superstar in the world of intelligence.

Striker had lived well and been paid well. Lately, though, things had begun to change. Striker felt a tightening. His assignments were less and less frequent. He knew this was partly a result of the end of the Cold War. The organization no longer had its fingertips on the pulse of the entire world. In fact, these days Striker could learn almost as much from the media as he could from the agency's intelligence reports. More and more, the agency and its activities were being openly discussed in newspapers and magazines. More and more, Congress was meddling with the protocols and traditions that had set the agency apart from the other sluggish, ineffective agencies of the bloated U.S. government.

Controls and checks and audits and reporting committees had no real place in effective intelligence. The ability to make decisions and strike quickly was imperative. But when the Berlin Wall came down, Striker got nervous. He knew this could be an opportunity internationally for liberal elements to rein in the kind of the military and special forces intelligence work he needed to do. When the armed forces began shipping their nuclear weapons back to Pantex, where many of them had been made in the first place, Striker knew that he had to do something to preserve himself and his ways. Watching the nation that he and others had worked so assiduously to help become the preeminent world power voluntarily remove its own teeth was unacceptable. This was a certain harbinger of the end awaiting intelligence specialists like himself, and Striker was not about to be left out in the cold.

As he sat by the river thinking about his future, he noticed some movement among the trees. A short man in a drab gray suit walked out onto the lawn. Few people besides Striker would have even noticed the two figures that remained behind in the shadows of the trees. Striker recognized Dick Simmons by his gait even before he could make out his face. Simmons looked like a mildly successful businessman on his way to the office early, not too happy, not too sad, the suit not too sharp but not embarrassing; he was a man whom no one would remember. Striker knew that was the way he liked it. Striker also knew it was a rare occasion for Simmons to leave the confines of Langley, and this cloak-and-dagger stuff wasn't really necessary. His days as a spy had been over for a long time. Still, even though it no longer mattered who did or didn't notice Dick Simmons, old habits died hard. Striker supposed that under the same circumstances, he would be the same way.

Simmons sat down beside Striker without saying anything, and Striker turned to face the river, leaning his back against the bench and stretching his long legs comfortably out onto the path. He knew there was at least one automatic weapon trained at the back of his head, but that didn't faze Striker.

"How are you, Striker?" Simmons asked quietly without moving his eyes from the water.

"I like to think I'm excellent," Striker said.

Simmons glanced over at Striker and gave him a quick once-over. "You look well. The good life always agreed with you, though."

"When you've tasted the bitterness of the bad," Striker mused, "you can appreciate the sweetness of the good. But you know me, I adjust."

Simmons nodded. Striker, he knew, had lived everywhere from squalid mud hovels in the Middle East to insect-infested bamboo huts in Southeast Asia, and never looked much worse for the wear. He was one of those rare individuals who could thrive almost anywhere, even under the harshest conditions. Striker was like a weed.

"And you," Striker said, "I can always tell how important you're getting by the shadows you cast. First it was just me, but I wasn't really a shadow, was I? Wouldn't you say we were more like partners? Then, hmm, you had a driver who was also a bodyguard. Then it was a driver and a bodyguard, and of course there are two of them now lurking out there, probably aiming MP–5s at the back of my head as we speak; but we haven't actually seen each other face-to-face in quite a while, Dick, and I know you never trusted me. Still, it must be . . . constricting. I mean, two or three spooks hovering around you all the time. I like to wipe my ass in total privacy, but that's me."

Simmons shook his head and sighed. The comment on trust didn't even merit a response. No one trusted Striker. He was too effective to be trusted. And, Simmons had to admit to himself, it was Striker's effectiveness over the years that was partly responsible for his own advancements. He had been Striker's contact with Langley, a place Striker had rarely seen. They had started together years ago in Southeast Asia and had worked well together. Simmons was a language expert with an IQ of 180. Striker had the same IQ and a willingness to do dirty work. There was no assignment they hadn't completed and left without a string of dead bodies in their wake.

Together they went from special forces to Military Intelligence. After the war Simmons made the move to the CIA, and it wasn't long before he had asked Striker to sign on as well. Striker had no ambition to rise within the agency. He only wanted the flexibility and the challenge, and, he would later find, to live well. Except for the living well part of it, Simmons wanted the exact opposite. Together, with Simmons pulling the strings from within the agency, providing assets and personnel, and Striker in the field, utilizing people and money, they had rarely failed at an undertaking. As the years went by, however, Simmons climbed higher and higher within the agency and found himself less and less in direct contact with Striker. Still, he had ensured Striker's comfort and thrown an occasional challenge his way to keep him placated like a big dog chained out back. And, as always, Striker had proved quite useful.

Dick Simmons had recently been appointed to Deputy Director of Operations. He was the number-one man in charge of all CIA clandestine services. He reported directly to the CIA executive director. His recent boss, the former DDO, had been asked to step down shortly after the Aldrich Ames scandal. Ames had been the head of the counterintelligence division and had systematically sold out agents and double agents around the globe to the Soviet Union and later to Russia. Ames had grown rich, but many of the agents he had betrayed had been executed once exposed. The catastrophe had resulted in the intense scrutiny of the DDO. It was well that Simmons at the time was only the assistant DDO rather than the DDO himself. As assistant, he was high enough to be able to step in and run the operations directorate, but not too high to have had to take blame for the scandal.

As a result, covert operations, its influence waning, had fallen drastically out of vogue. Heads were going to continue to roll. Dick Simmons had been in the right place at the right time, and he intended to keep it that way. Simmons wanted to keep climbing, but he knew that covert operations, once the jewel of the agency, would soon be nothing more than heavy baggage. The future in the agency was all about technology, not people. Satellites and other means of electronic surveillance were becoming so advanced that the number of field agents the agency needed would only continue to shrink.

"I'm leaving operations, Striker," Simmons said, looking intently at his old acquaintance for some kind of reaction. There was none. Striker merely looked up at the sky as if trying to figure the weather for the day.

"I've been offered Deputy Director of Intelligence," Simmons said. It was a lateral move for Simmons, but a smart move.

"That's great, Dick," Striker said. "I'll come with you."

This threw Simmons off balance. There was no place for a contract agent like Striker in the intelligence directorate. Intelligence was for scientists, mathematicians, and linguists.

Simmons stammered and said, "I—I . . . you know that's not possible, Striker."

Striker showed his old partner an evil smile. Simmons realized Striker was having fun with him, but he didn't share the laugh.

"You're an important man, Dick," Striker said in a bored tone of voice. "I always told you you'd be running the whole company one day."

Simmons shifted uncomfortably on the bench. He was a man who was used to making others squirm, but Striker unsettled him.

"It's a far cry from running the company, but I wanted to tell you, and I wanted to warn you," Simmons said.

Striker waited patiently.

"Garbosky is going to be the DDO."

Striker snorted a contemptuous laugh. Garbosky was a young agent who had quickly moved from station manager in Tel Aviv to the CIA top man in the Near East. He had a reputation for doing everything by the book, a perfect man for the "new and improved" CIA. It was bad news for Striker, but he certainly wasn't going to let on how bad.

"Well, this should be fun," Striker said.

"He's going to be watching you," Simmons said flatly.

"Oh," Striker said casually. This was no surprise to Striker. He had been in Tel Aviv several years ago, brokering the sale of some land-to-air missiles, when he'd run into Mrs. Garbosky. It was no big deal to Striker, but the young lady, obviously frustrated with her husband and her life, had made much more of their brief affair than Striker had ever suspected she would.

Simmons pursed his lips and nodded. "He's going to reassess the status and the integrity of everyone in covert operations. I'm not even supposed to know about it."

"What does Russell have to say about this," Striker asked. Walt Russell was Dick's boss, the CIA executive director, the link between the director of central intelligence and the four working directorates of the agency: operations, intelligence, science and technology, and administration.

Simmons sighed, "You know, Russell is old. He wants to please the new boss. He's on thin ice after the Ames thing. He barely kept his head above water. The new boss loves Garbosky, or he loves that Garbosky's uncle is on the hill. Either way, Garbosky it is, and I wanted you to know that he's going to be sniffing around."

"Worried that he might find something that stinks, Dick?" Striker said casually.

"No, Striker, I know you don't leave a mess behind in anything. I just don't want you to do something that might reflect badly on all of us."

"Who exactly is 'us'?"

"'Us,' Striker, is us," Simmons said, "you, me, and every other guy that's worked our whole lives for this country. Things are changing, but it won't stay this way forever, so lay low and ride it out."

"You're wrong about that, Dick," Striker said, gazing at the moving water.

"Things are going to stay changed. It's never going back."

Simmons shrugged. "Still, you'll have to expect that things will be different."

"Things are already different," Striker said. "I haven't been able to operate freely for the past three years."

"I don't know about that."

"I do," Striker said. "What about Turkey?"

"Striker," Simmons said incredulously, "you wanted to sell a plane-load of cluster bombs."

"In the old days," Striker countered, "that wouldn't have raised an eyebrow, Dick. I've made a lot of money for this agency."

"You've made some for yourself too."

Striker laughed in a short burst. "I haven't kept more than what amounted to sales commissions on those deals. I could have been stashing millions if I'd been even a little corrupt. I played the role for years, funded projects all over the world for the agency, then when things get rough, I get cut off. I get squeezed, Dick. I don't like getting squeezed. Now I'm expected to work for Garbosky, and he's got a hard-on for me that goes beyond my lifestyle. How do you think that makes me feel? What am I supposed to say about all this?"

"I think you were the one with the hard-on," Simmons said with a terse smile, unable to help himself.

"You know what I mean," Striker chimed in.

Simmons sat quietly nodding.

"I know," he finally said. "I know all this, Striker, and I know what you've done for me. I can't change the way things are. Like I said, I think they'll change back again. I do. In the meantime, that's why I'm here, because of all you've done. I just don't want you to have any surprises. The way you live is no problem with me; I know you've earned it and more. I'm just telling you that Garbosky's not going to like it. He's heard about your condo and your cars and your vacations, like most people have. He doesn't like the James Bond image. He wants accountants and lawyers. He wants numbers crunchers and sycophants. He's going to be coming after you, Striker. I wanted you to know."

"I may have to call it quits then," Striker announced.

"I wouldn't do that," Simmons replied. "I would wait, Striker. Let his goons follow you around for a little while, sniff in your garbage, listen to you flush the toilet, and then after things settle in and you've come up with a clean bill, then walk and go into business for yourself. Let him clear you first, Striker. He's going on a witch hunt. He wants to prove something. If you leave right away, he'll close in on you like a bug in a web. He'll make business bad, or impossible. I know him. Just wait. Wait and call me before you do anything. I'll let you know when it's clear."

Simmons stood up and held his hand out to his longtime associate. Striker took the hand and held it firmly. Striker's grip was that of a man who could kill with his hands. Simmons's hand felt like he'd have trouble hammering a nail. Striker looked up at Simmons. Even though Simmons was five years younger than Striker, he looked ten years Striker's senior. Striker liked it that way. It was confirmation that the path he'd chosen was the right one. He'd never run the agency. He'd never have a directorate. But Striker lived better, felt better, screwed better, and looked a hell of a lot better than the man many people would say was the more successful between the two of them. And soon he'd be rich, cashing in the way he should have long ago.

"Good luck, Striker," Simmons said.

"Thank you, Dick," Striker said. "I'll miss you."

Simmons shifted uneasily on his feet. He had never grown used to Striker's sudden emotional outbursts. The man was like blue steel, devoid of emotion, and then, without warning, he'd tell you he loved you or something weird like that. Simmons gave an awkward smile and half a wave before he turned and headed back toward the trees.

Striker cranked his head around to watch Simmons go. He watched and he thought. Garbosky was a problem. If what Simmons said was true, and Striker knew it was, then completing his transactions between the general and his foreign plutonium investors could prove to be quite difficult. He would need some help, without a doubt. But it would have to be from someone outside the community. It had to be someone who couldn't turn on him even if they wanted to. It had to be someone alone, someone isolated, and someone very smart. Intelligence was essential to Striker when he considered working with someone.

He knew of agents over the years who preferred imbeciles because they were often easier to direct. They never got it into their heads that a fool was the most dangerous type of person. Sure, they knew you were smarter, and they accepted your authority, but imbeciles made mistakes, and mistakes got you killed. Smart people were more likely to succeed. They could figure things out on the first run. Intelligence made up for a lack of experience; and a smart person could be managed, so long as they weren't smarter than you. That was one problem that Striker had never really had to worry about.

The idea of the girl came into his head like a bolt. It was perfect. He thought of the danger they could share. That would be good. The girl would like that. Danger would be like a drug to a girl like her. She was proud, and she was smart, but she was also greedy, not just for money but for excitement. Striker could see that in her by the way she performed in bed. She was a woman who needed excitement, who would be at her best when things were on the edge.

The more he thought about it, the more Striker liked the idea. He could recruit her the way he'd recruited dozens of women before her, women who had slavishly done his bidding in dangerous places with dangerous people. Sometimes they made it, sometimes they didn't. Sometimes, like with the case at hand, Striker would have to eliminate them himself even if they succeeded, the same way he had with Peter.

He thought about her, about her long, lean limbs, her soft skin, her icy blue eyes, her dark hair that flowed like silk. He thought about her proud, almost obnoxious way. She needed a lesson in the ways of the world. She needed to know that money and power only came from going where others would not go. She needed to see the abyss and walk on the edge. Then how arrogant would she be? Then she'd see him for what he really was. Not a suave sophisticated businessman who was blown away by her beauty and infatuated with her every word, but a reaper of souls. The Grim Reaper. Striker turned his head back toward the river and smiled broadly. He needed someone, and it was time for her to learn. He would teach her.

CHAPTER SIX

AUSTIN, LIKE MOST MAJOR CITIES, and certainly every state capitol, has a federal office building, home to hundreds of United States government employees and civil servants. Not the least important of these minions are the men and women of the Internal Revenue Service, who work diligently to extract the taxes that are, according to the government, each person's fair contribution to the workings of this great country.

It's not surprising, though, that U.S. taxpayers are resentful. Over-spending and misappropriation, waste, chicanery, the savings and loan debacle, government corruption run amock, it was all so discouraging. But each year, the IRS employs new and more effective collection methods and a new breed of tax collector to implement them. The IRS makes its own rules and is accountable to who knows what other part of government; and its interpretation of these rules is its own, and, not surprisingly, very difficult to challenge. Most IRS agents are simple, hardworking accountants, doing their best to meet quotas. Anonymous zealots working for the benefit of this country, who are rarely recognized for their service. And because of the unusual power that they command, occasionally an IRS auditor becomes intoxicated by this power. There is always some group that, if squeezed just the right way, can actually yield some extra fat for the larder. Some years physicians are more carefully audited, other years it may be actors or people who own their own businesses or architects or car dealers or restaurant owners, and some years, the targets are professional athletes. This year, fourteen-year veteran IRS agent Jeff Board was going to put the squeeze on someone.

In his late thirties, overweight, an accounting major whose grades and LSAT scores weren't good enough for law school, Jeff Board was a bitter man. His caustic personality, awful habits, and sloppy attire had made it hard for him to land a job with any of Austin's accounting firms. But with the help of an aunt who was high up in the civil service union, Jeff Board sought and found a job in government. He was underpaid for an accountant, but he believed that if one could only hang on in the paid service of the government, things got easier. The money got better, and soon he planned to name his own hours and vacation days without worrying about the higher-ups. Government advancement had almost nothing to do with productivity or merit, but rather length of service. So Board was in for the long haul and, not unexpectedly, desperate for recognition.

Jeff Board knew that in the past the agency had singled out professional athletes, but he had never audited one himself. If there was one type of person that Jeff Board singularly despised, it was jocks. He knew how they ate. He knew how they smelled. He knew how they thought. When he was in college, they had tormented him. They lived like animals, squandered their education, and treated people around them with complete disrespect. But all the girls loved them. In Jeff Board's mind, athletes were spoiled and rude, and probably very corrupt—the worst tax offenders. When word came down that he would be reviewing the tax returns of every active member of the Texas Outlaws, Board laughed out loud.

"Double trouble for you guys," he said to himself as he tore into the box of Outlaw returns that had just been delivered to his office.

He started at the beginning with Ace Atkins, the first on the Outlaws roster. He pored over the tax returns for days, earmarking little abnormalities that he would later go back and check against employers' records and bank accounts. Usually there was something, at least a minor thing, on almost half of the returns an agent examined. Board would make a file of these glitches. He would go back to them later. He would send notices and ask for documentation that substantiated certain deductions and write-offs. If there was no documentation in any specific case, he would levy taxes and penalties with the very real threat of jail. The prospect was titillating.

With the IRS, unlike any other arm of the government, a citizen was guilty until he could prove himself innocent. The letters alone would be enough to jolt most of the players out of their reveries of wealth and leisure. The smart ones would call tax attorneys who would slow him down and make him work more carefully. But the lawyers would cost the players money, and in any event, he would make sure that these people dealt with him face-to-face, whether they had a lawyer or not. Board had big plans for this project. He would watch them squirm like bugs under a magnifying glass in the hot sun.

"What's the matter, Cody?" were the first words out of Marty Cahn's mouth as he slid into the booth.

Cody made an exaggerated motion to get a clear view of his watch.

"I don't know, Marty," he said. "When you were recruiting me to sign with you for my last contract, you used to wait outside the facility for me in your convertible Mercedes and chauffeur me to the Texan for lunch. Now I'm sitting here waiting for you for forty-five minutes at Taco Man, and I've got the feeling you forgot your wallet, so I'll have to pick up the tab."

Marty's cheeks flushed slightly. As long as he'd known Cody Grey, he'd never been able to quite figure him out. It was usually somewhere between the content and the delivery of his words that Marty could figure out what Cody meant. As with every enigmatic person, sometimes Cody meant exactly what he said, and sometimes he didn't mean it at all. Marty never got the feel for when Cody meant to be funny in a dry way or was just being confrontational. He looked for a smile on his client's face and thought he saw one.

"Sorry," Marty said, picking one of two menus off of the table and concentrating on the selection. He glanced up. Cody was smiling, having fun with him. That made him relax.

Cody signaled to a waitress. "Now I'm in a rush, Marty. I've got to do a talk for some kids," he explained.

The waitress was a young, plump Mexican girl with dark hair, dark skin, and a pearly smile. Cody ordered a Double Supreme Burrito Platter, enough food for a mid-size family. Marty wanted the fajita salad, strips of grilled, fatless chicken on a mound of dark, leafy lettuce.

"When I retire, I'm going to eat like you," Cody said.

"I can't imagine you ever eating like me," Marty replied.

"I can't imagine ever retiring."

Marty looked down at his red, plastic water glass. He picked it up and swirled the contents as if he were fascinated with this particular mixture of slush and water.

" So, can you?" Cody asked.

"Huh?" Marty said, looking up.

Cody rolled his eyes. Marty was so wimpy sometimes. When Cody first met Marty, he thought that with a little weight work and some conditioning, the lawyer could have been one hell of a tight end. He had the body type and big hands that could suck in a football like a Hoover Deluxe. It didn't take long to see that Marty just didn't have the heart for contact sports. Besides catching the ball, a tight end had to live in the land of the defensive backs, mostly safeties like Cody, who longed to hit them so hard the flesh between their ribs would tear.

"So," Cody said, staring intently at his agent, "what did they say?"

"They don't know," Marty said. His fingertips tingled with nervous energy as he tapped them on the table. For all Cody's granite facade, even Marty could sense the knot in the football player's gut.

"They don't know if they're going to pay me a million dollars, or they don't know if they're going to offer me a contract?" Cody's voice had a desperate edge that Marty had never heard before.

"They don't know either right now," Marty said, bravely looking Cody in the eye.

"God, Marty, it's June and they don't know?" Cody asked dejectedly.

Marty shrugged. "It won't be a lot of money, I don't think. They said we should pursue other opportunities, that they appreciated all you've done for the team."

"What the hell," Cody barked. "I bust my ass for this team for eight damn years and they tell me to pursue other opportunities? I don't have other opportunities, do I?"

"No," Marty said, squeezing his lips as though on a lemon. "Not with your knee. I've spoken with every team. Maybe, if someone gets hurt in training camp, they'll need someone."

"So now I just sit around hoping that the Outlaws will find it in their hearts to sign me to some half-ass contract for the minimum salary?"

Cody stared at some distant point in the clear blue sky outside the window. The noises of the restaurant filled the silence. Mothers hushed screaming kids. Conversation hummed. Plates were scraped with silverware. The heavy smell of fried chips pervaded the air. Their waitress returned with two plates of food and cheerily asked if she could get them anything else. She had spilled hot sauce down the front of her bright yellow apron, the colors of a fiesta. Marty answered politely for them both and poked tentatively at a strip of grilled chicken.

"Hey," Marty said, "look, we've got time. You'll get well. They'll see it, and they'll want you back. I think you'll be there by the time the season starts. It may not be what we want, but it won't be minimum. They won't do that to you. They won't. It won't be what you're used to getting, though."

Free agency was the worst thing that could have happened to most NFL players. The older ones, nearing the ends of their career, were the hardest hit. To compliment a severance package that was cut in half, and a meaningless pension increase, the football Players Union had gotten free agency with a salary cap in their negotiations with the NFL owners. The owners could barely contain their delight. For the players the cap meant that a select few marquee guys would get the vast majority of the money available for the teams to pay out in salaries under the cap limit. The rest of the players, most of the young players, older veterans whose skills were declining, and anyone who was recovering from an injury, could only look forward to a crammed-down salary. For Cody, free agency had come four years too late.

Cody continued to stare out the window.

"I thought you'd want to know the truth," Marty said. "It's not that bad. It could be worse. I think they'll end up signing you. Your knee will be better. How is your knee?"

Cody looked at him. "It's better. It's good. It's not completely better, but I don't think it ever will be. I can play with it like this. They know I can play like this. What about mini-camp?"

"What about it?"

"Am I going?"

"I think with or without a contract you should. The coaches want you there. We're not really in a position to play hard to get."

They sat quietly for a moment before speaking again.

"I don't think you should take this personally," Marty said, invoking his best lawyerly frown.

Cody set his jaw and looked back out the window.

"Eat, you'll feel better," Marty said after he had a mouthful of his own food.

Cody looked at his watch, then attacked his food, saying very little to Marty while he ate. Then he rose abruptly.

"I gotta run," he said. "Can you take care of this?"

Marty waved his hand to say of course. "Where are you speaking?"

Cody was already starting for the door, but he stopped.

"I told you. I gotta speak to some kids. At a school. You know me . . ."

"Just keep working out. Do what you're doing and don't worry," Marty reassured him. "It'll all work out, Cody. I really think it will."

Cody thanked his lawyer from halfway across the restaurant with what might have been a smile and walked out into the hot afternoon sun. He reached for his sunglasses like an old man reaching for his heart pills. His vision was cooled the instant he got the glasses on his face. For a moment he forgot where he parked. He scanned the lot until he saw his blue pickup. Jenny hadn't wanted him to drive a truck. She said it was crass. But there were some things even Jenny said that he just didn't care about.

Cody left the door open to drain the heat while he fired up the engine and the AC. When it got hot and humid in south Texas, which was May through September, you usually didn't get your truck cooled down until right before you got to where you were going.

Sweat had pooled under his arms during the drive, so after he parked at the school, Cody blasted the cold until he felt presentable. The John Houston Elementary School was on the north end of town in a lower-middle-class suburb that was similar to the one he grew up in. The Outlaws had a community relations director who lined up players to speak at special functions and appear at different charity events throughout the community. Cody was her most requested and, because of his willingness to help, her favorite player. Injured or not, old or not, the kids in Austin all wanted to meet Cody Grey.

"This and a bad knee will get you half your severance," Cody mumbled to himself as he limped toward the single-story brick building.

Usually the players in the most demand were the least likely to accept invitations to speak at nonpaying events like an elementary school's Drug Awareness Day. Cody was different. He had done more than his share in the way of civic duty in the city of Austin since the day he arrived eight years ago. If it had something to do with kids, Cody had a hard time saying no. Jenny bristled at his willingness. It seemed to her, and he admitted that it was sometimes true, that it was harder for her to get him to go to a social event with her than to some sports awards dinner for a bunch of nine-year-olds.

Today was the first time Cody found himself in full agreement with his wife's disgusted sentiments. He had done this routine for eight years, talked with the kids, signed their autographs, answered their questions, helped raise money for good causes. He hadn't done it because he thought he'd get something out of it. He did it because he thought it was right. Despite his reputation as a violent bad-guy, he liked being around the kids. It was fun for him to show the public, and himself, that he could tear heads off during a game but be the kind of guy to visit kids in his spare time. But even though his motivation hadn't been to get something in return, that hadn't kept him from expecting that in the end he would get something anyway. He couldn't imagine having given so much of himself not only to the Outlaws but to the community in general and then getting the message that he should seek other opportunities. Maybe Jenny was right about a lot of things. Maybe he was a fool with his head buried in the Texas sand.

Cody talked to the kids and smiled at the teachers. Then he got up on the cafeteria stage to do his thing. There was a crowd of adults by the doorway. Among them was one young woman whom Cody could not keep his eyes from wandering back to. She had blond hair and bright blue eyes that were set like sapphires in the face of a golden idol. She looked like a younger version of the movie star Sharon Stone, only without the attitude. In fact this woman, one of the teachers, he guessed, seemed shy and quiet. She wore a plain white blouse and dark slacks. Her hair was pulled back into a girlish ponytail, but even that couldn't contain its golden brilliance. When their eyes met, she would drop her gaze, but he sensed that she couldn't help looking at him any more than he could at her.

While he delivered his speech from memory, Cody thought of nothing but the pretty blonde schoolteacher. He was a married man. He knew that, but whenever he saw someone as attractive and unadorned as this girl was, he couldn't help himself from wondering what it would be like to know her. He would imagine himself and some shy flower like this blonde, living happily in a simple suburban home, taking care of their kids, baking cookies. It was a crazy thought; it was a dream that overtook him at times and gnawed at his heart from within. He wanted to talk to her, to single her out right there from his platform and ask her to have dinner with him. All the while he was conscious of the fact that he was married and loved his wife. It was that crazy.

The kids were stone silent. He looked at the rest of the teachers as he finished his message. Even they were in awe of him. The ferocious Cody Grey could actually speak. His message was simple: work hard in school and don't do drugs. It was a boring message that these kids heard all the time, but he was assured by everyone that it was never heard more clearly than when it came from him. He wasn't so sure of that, but he did as he was asked.

When he finished, he sat at a table down in front of the stage and the kids swarmed around him for his autograph. He lost sight of the pretty teacher in the mayhem and didn't see her again. He never would. It was one of those fantasies that transports a person into an entirely new universe, a different life. He could have fallen in love with that teacher, gotten a divorce from Jenny, gotten over his love for Jenny, and moved on, possibly to better things. Cody had experienced these fleeting fantasies before in the past four years. He wondered if the day would ever come when he would break through the walls around him and see something new. He doubted it. Like most people, whether it was wise or not, it was Cody's nature to stay on the path he had chosen and make the most of it.

The kids were going crazy for his signature. They just didn't know any better. They didn't know that his value on the open market of professional football right now was bottoming out. The kids were the last to forget. To them, he was larger than life. The smile he wore for them was twisted with his private pain. They didn't understand yet that when an athlete outlives his usefulness, he is quickly replaced and just as quickly forgotten.

CHAPTER SEVEN

∨

CODY'S PRESENTATION TO THE SCHOOL CHILDREN was a success, and at the bell announcing the end of the day, the kids were slow to leave. Cody said a few nice words to the lingering teachers and searched fleetingly for the blonde, too embarrassed and not motivated enough to ask anyone who she was. Then he walked out through the throng of kids making their way to the waiting school buses and headed home. Jenny was out at the pool. The water heater was broken, and despite the hot days, the nights had been cool and the water was still on the chilly side. Jenny was never a big swimmer anyway. For her the pool was more for looking than swimming. Cody stood by the poolside and assessed his wife across the water. She lounged on a comfortable chaise under an umbrella. She wore a straw sun hat, sunglasses, and a white frilly bathing suit that he guessed cost about five hundred dollars. On her wrist was a gold Rolex and a diamond tennis bracelet. Her long dark hair spilled out of the hat and draped onto her bronzed shoulders. Her lips and her nails were painted a brilliant red. They were like an invitation and a warning at the same time. She could sexually satisfy you or gut you, or both.

Jenny was talking on the cordless phone, a perfect image of wealth and beauty. She looked almost nothing like the high-school girl he knew in Pittsburgh, Pennsylvania, as Jenny Gretzsky, at least she didn't remind him of that Jenny. She had come a long way. Because he couldn't see her eyes, Cody wasn't sure whether she'd seen him. Jenny was like that sometimes. She could sit and talk on the phone or read a book or watch TV and not see or hear anything around her. There were other times, though, when she simply ignored you.

Cody said nothing. He just took a step toward her and plunged straight down into the pool. He came up and broke the surface with a yell in a spray of spit and cold water. Jenny was up on her feet now, and he saw that the phone was no longer in her hand.

"Are you crazy?" she shrieked. "You scared me to death!"

"Help," Cody gurgled and flapped his hands desperately at her. His jeans and suede boots filled with water and dragged him down. He kicked against the weight. It hurt his knee, and he wondered just how foolish he'd been to jump in. He was a few feet from the other side now, and Jenny, still disconcerted, bent down to give him a hand. He pulled her in.

She broke the surface screaming and clawing for the edge of the pool like a wet cat. Cody climbed out alongside her and pulled her toward him. She fought him, sputtering and enraged. Cody could feel the sun already warming him. His laugh shook his whole frame, and she almost got away. Jenny's hair was matted down on her head and clung to her shoulders like black Saran Wrap. He looked into her eyes and realized that this was a moment in his life that would make a difference. There were so many things that were wrong between them, and he guessed that was why he'd pulled her in, to shock her, to remind her who she was and who he was and why they were even there together in the first place. She was still struggling when he pulled her even closer and kissed her. She was stiff and cold, and if he'd stopped it would have been over right then and there. Nothing would have been left but the formality of drawing up the papers and splitting what little was left from their eight years of living so well. But Cody didn't stop, he'd gone too far, and he knew that all the chips were on the table. Jenny was a horse you couldn't just lead to water. You had to make her drink. He would hold her and kiss her until she either tore out his eyes with her nails and got away or relented and kissed him back.

It was like a long slow dance while they wrestled there, soaking wet in the early summer heat. But as her body warmed and recovered, she struggled less and less. Then she let him kiss her. Then she kissed him back. Then she began to devour him. He slipped the straps from her shoulders and pulled the top of her bathing suit down to expose two perfect breasts. He groped at her like he did the first time they were together. She put her arms around his neck and wrapped her legs around his waist, pulling his face to her breasts. He carried her like that into the small pool house. The sliding glass door was open. Cody dumped her onto the soft double bed. She squirmed desperately out of her suit, and Cody tore every button on his shirt getting it off. They made love until the sun began to turn the sky red-orange in the west, and the long shadows of the hills crept toward the city below them, plunging it into darkness. Then they slept.

Cody awoke first. There was a half-moon shining in through the heavy glass doors of the pool house that lit Jenny's face. She was nestled in the crook of his arm, and she wore the innocent smile of a child.

It was cooler now. Cody shifted to pull the bedspread on top of them. Jenny groaned. Her arm briefly tightened like a soft cord around his waist. Cody's mind wandered back in time to when they were only kids, in high school, in love, with nothing in the world between them. It used to feel just like this.

It was a half hour before she awoke. Her smile made him happy, and he gently rubbed his palm along the side of her cheek, smiling back at her.

"You're beautiful," he said.

"You always say that," she replied with languid pleasure.

"Because you are."

She nuzzled her nose into his skin and sniffed deeply, as if he were a bottle of subtle cologne.

"What do you want to do?" he said in a dreamy, husky voice, careful not to upset the moment.

"Put on a dress and some shoes," she began with another smile at his indulgence, "eat dinner and drink champagne at the Four Seasons, then go to Sixth Street to dance."

"That sounds great," Cody said with as much enthusiasm as he could muster.

Besides a fancy party in the hills, Sixth Street was Jenny's favorite spot in Austin. There, between the government buildings and the river, was a vast collection of bars and clubs that generated some of the best music in the world.

"Really?" Jenny said, perking up at his pliancy. "Oh, good!"

They returned to the house to change and get ready to go out. When Jenny stepped from her closet in a blood-red silk dress and matching heels, Cody tried to take her again. Jenny kissed him deeply, but then pushed him away with a school-girl giggle and the promise of more later, if he behaved. The way she said it wasn't unpleasant at all. Unlike one of her normal sexual rebuffs, this was more like a seductive promise that left Cody with none of the bad feelings he had grown accustomed to.

It was nearly midnight by the time they found their way into a small bar called Los Bravos. Jenny recognized the name of a band within on a chalkboard sign on the door. The band was nothing more than four college kids dressed in torn, faded jeans and T-shirts; three boys and a girl with two guitars, a bass, and some drums, but their music spilled over the crowd inside like a tonic. People swayed and tapped to the fast-paced but somehow mellow sound and the rich voice of the lead guitarist. There was a small area in front of the band where the stools and tables were pushed back so a tight crowd could dance together on the floor.

They were half-drunk from champagne already, but Cody muscled his way to the bar and ordered a beer for himself and a vodka tonic for Jenny. He needed a drink. Crowded places were not his thing. Jenny pulled at his arm before the drinks even arrived, and she said what he knew she would say. It was what he wanted to hear less than anything he could think of at that moment in that place.

"Let's dance."

Her eyes were expectant and bright. She loved to dance. He hated to dance. He asked her in the pool house what she wanted to do, suggesting the night was hers, and this is what she wanted to do. For her, this was the perfect end to a perfect evening. His was their bedroom.

"Let me get a drink first," he said. He needed time to think about it still. He needed at least another beer. Dancing to him was ludicrous and stupid. He felt awkward and self-conscious doing it. He rarely did dance, and on the few occasions he gave in, he regretted it the minute he got on the floor.

"Are you sure you'll be okay?" Jenny asked him. She knew better than anyone that once Cody was drunk, he was a different and dangerous person.

"Yeah," he said with an assuring smile.

"Okay," she said cheerily, graciously doing her own part to keep the magic of the evening alive. If he needed to get totally lit, that was fine. As long as she got to move to the music out there, she'd be happy.

Cody staked out a little space at the bar so he and Jenny could watch the band and drink their drinks. He even found himself tapping his foot to the infectious beat and wondered what a sound like this was doing in a little dive on Sixth Street, then he remembered that this was where a lot of the big artists, like Stevie Ray Vaughn, had actually started. After his fourth drink in quick succession, Cody felt good and numb.

It happened the way it always seemed to happen to him. The more drunk he got, the meaner he got. Instead of getting more amicable, he got resentful. Why the hell should he make an ass out of himself out there? Why should they be here in this crowded, smoky dive in the first place?

Jenny patiently danced in place, waiting for him to be ready, waiting for things to be different, waiting for the night to end the way she wanted it to, and not in some fit of anger the way so many nights in the past had ended.

"You go ahead," he said to her through the noise.

Jenny looked like she'd been slapped. "Excuse me?" she said, as if she'd heard him wrong.

"Go. You dance. I'm not. I'll watch you."

Jenny's eyes narrowed in a scowl. "Don't do this, Cody," she said. "Just relax and go out there with me. Don't do this."

"Go ahead," he said nonchalantly in a dull, drunken voice. "I'll watch."

"I will then," she said, her chin held high.

Cody watched her make her way to the floor. The crush of people parted for her. Jenny melted into the shaking group of dancers, but her red dress and beautiful, flowing black hair made her clearly discernible from the rest of the crowd. Her gyrating body matched the rhythmic swaying of the music as though her movements had been choreographed before the music had even been written. Jenny could dance.

Cody signaled for another beer, and by the time he got it and turned back around, there was a big corn-fed Texan stomping his pointed boots and shaking his ass right alongside his wife. The Texan wore faded jeans and a matching jean shirt. They were the kind of clothes that had seen some hard work. He stood at least six-foot-seven with the boots, and long, yellow hair hung to his shoulders. A drooping mustache and sky blue eyes adorned his rugged, tan face. Cody stared malignantly. After a few minutes, Jenny looked over at him and gave him a flat, emotionless stare that lasted thirty full seconds before she turned her gaze upward to the big Texan and smiled.

Cody felt a wave of violence rise up underneath his feet, and he smiled the smile of the heroin addict who no longer feels that great high but who still welcomes the comfortable release brought on by the presence of an old friend. Nausea turned to thrill as he stepped forward, pushing his way through the throng. He grabbed Jenny firmly, but not so as to hurt her, and started to pull her toward the door. She shook free and yelled above the music.

"You told me to dance!"

"Now I'm telling you to stop," Cody commanded, grabbing for her again.

The Texan reached over and put his hand on the back of Cody's arm, up high near his shoulder. Cody grinned with pleasure as he felt the big man's long thick fingers dig into the flesh under his arm like the tines on a back hoe.

The assault stripped away any guilt that Cody felt for his own violent outbursts. The Texan freed his mind. Cody zipped into the tunnel of his own private wave and became engulfed in its roaring power. He leaned away from the Texan and lowered his hand almost like he was reaching down to pull a piece of gum off the heel of his shoe. When the punch came, it came from the floor. When his fist hit, it hit the Texan on the point of his cleft chin. The impact rolled his eyes back in his head, and he teetered before dropping backward like a grand redwood in a forest of firs. He took three other people with him to the floor, he was so big. Then Cody was on top of him. He jackhammered three quick jabs into the Texan's face, breaking his nose with the first punch and scattering the pieces through his nasal cavity with the other two.

Cody saw or sensed a flash of light in his brain. He knew it meant that something was wrong, and he turned to his back. In the faces of the pushing, screaming mob, he couldn't decide what had happened, or who had done it if anyone had. His left arm felt warm and wet. Three bouncers tangled him up in a web of arms and dragged him to the door. He let them do it. He had no beef with anyone but the son-of-a-bitching Texan. He wondered while they made their way through the crowd if there was a connection between the tight grab the Texan had had on his arm and the wet warmth he now felt. It was only a coincidence.

The bouncers threw him out into the street as passersby stopped for just one more Sixth Street spectacle. Cody brushed off his shirt and pants in the most dignified manner that he could muster and then stared around, spinning in a three-hundred-sixty-degree circle to make sure there were no visible snickers from the onlookers. Cody felt the backside of his arm while he spun, and when he had assured himself that the coast was clear, he checked out the sore spot more thoroughly. His free hand came away dark and shiny with blood. When the shock subsided, Cody felt the pain and knew that in fact the blood on him was his own.

He looked around for Jenny. She was nowhere. He went back toward the door to the bar. The bouncers were there and would not let him in.

"My wife," he said.

They told him if he didn't leave, they would call the police. Cody began to argue, but when one of them pulled out a cellular phone and began to dial, he retreated to the street. He staggered around on the sidewalk like a sick alley cat, expecting Jenny to walk out any second. After ten minutes, Cody got into a cab and told the driver to take him to the emergency room. He stared fiercely at the cabbie in the rearview mirror so he wouldn't notice that Cody was bleeding all over his backseat. It worked.

Cody needed twenty stitches in his posterior deltoid muscle and another thirty to sew up the gash in his skin. The doctor was a young resident from the university who recognized him and understood why Cody didn't want to get involved with any kind of a police report. He told Cody that if the wound had been six inches closer to his spine, he'd be on a slab in the basement. For his part, Cody knew that if you were still breathing and you had no idea who had stabbed you in a fight that you started, you weren't likely to get a lot of sympathy or action from the police. With his volatile reputation, the cops would figure he got what he deserved.

Cody was almost out the door before the doctor warned him not to use his shoulder for at least six weeks. Cody stopped short. In his pain and anxiety, he hadn't even considered what this injury would do to his training.

"I can't not use my shoulder for that long," Cody said, turning to face the young doctor.

"You don't really have a choice," the doctor said. "If you use that muscle for anything strenuous and tear those stitches, you'll have to start all over again. This isn't something you can just tough through. If you don't get this thing healed right, you won't even be able to pass a physical, let alone play a game of football."

Cody murmured thanks, to be polite, and walked out of the hospital into the early moments of dawn. He didn't feel thankful.

In a few minutes he found a cab and slumped into the backseat, giving his address in the hills. Cody was as close to tears as he could remember having been in a long time. He had come so far in life, only to find that at the top of his mountain were sharp, craggy stones jutting out from the precipice. He couldn't even enjoy his view from the top of the world. Maybe because his fall had been too imminent. Now, with no contract forthcoming and no other teams in the wings, he had squandered his most prized asset, his physical readiness to play a five-month season of bone-crunching football. He would be nowhere near as ready as he should be by the time training camp rolled around with a six-week recuperation imposed.

Cody eased back into the seat of his cab. The doctor had given him some Percoset. He'd already dropped three of them. He was comfortable with prescription drugs. Like most football players, he had been using them to reduce swelling and manage pain since his college days. As much as his shoulder hurt him, though, he was more tormented by the certainty that what he'd done would be impossible to undo. His mind twisted like a dying man on the end of his rope as he ran through the painful possibilities of what might have become of Jenny.

Mercifully, the narcotic began to soften the edges of his screaming wounds and the tormenting images in his mind. As the cab thumped across the bridge over the Colorado River, Cody gazed into the half-light of the retreating night. But he was still racing into the darkness, and he couldn't imagine how things could be any worse for him or for anyone. It was almost just as well that he had no idea how bad things were going to get.

CHAPTER EIGHT

THE BIG TEXAN STAGGERED TO HIS FEET. Jenny caught him under one arm, and another man caught him under his other arm. Together the two of them got him off the dance floor and over to a chair next to a round cocktail table whose surface was covered with a cluster of empty Bud Light bottles. The blood that ran down the big Texan's face was already beginning to darken and dry. His bloody face looked like the sloppy brown muzzle of a St. Bernard.

"You okay, missy?" the big man mumbled.

Jenny almost smiled. The big guy had just gotten pummeled and he wanted to know if she was okay.

"I'm fine," she said.

"I'm Peter Royce," he said. "This is my brother Jamie."

Jamie looked at her with a stern face and nodded without a word. His eyes roamed frantically about the bar like a caged ferret, or like the eyes of a man who had just stabbed another in a crowded bar.

"Hello," she said.

"Jamie don't say too much," Peter explained. He reached out with his big, beefy hand and rested it gently on Jenny's bare back. She could feel the rough calluses against her skin. His hand was warm.

"I didn't catch your name, missy," Peter said.

"I didn't pitch it," she replied.

"Who was that guy?" Peter asked, taking a different tact. He worked his jaw around to test the damage as he spoke.

"My husband," Jenny replied without emotion.

"Can I buy you a drink?" he said.

He was very handsome and suave despite his bludgeoned face. In her mind she played out a little scene between her and the big man that wasn't too far from Cody's worst nightmare. A little smile danced on and then off of her face. Jenny enjoyed the power she had over men.

"No," she said, rising from the table and pulling their eyes like two kites on the same string, "I just wanted to make sure you were all right."

The two men rose from the table in deference to her. She tried to remember the last time anyone had shown her that kind of respect. She liked people who showed respect, but she'd already made up her mind where she would go. She needed to go somewhere, of that there was no doubt. But she also felt the need to feel safe and comfortable and not go through the tangled motions that would lead to her to fucking some guy she'd just met in some bar and who she'd never see again. At the same time, she had no intention of going home. Cody had pushed her too far. She would teach him a lesson in a way that would never allow him to forget.

Striker was awake. He sat in a large leather chair in front of the unlit fireplace under a reading lamp. He folded the newspaper he was reading and set it down on a side table next to a half-empty glass of scotch and ice before he rose to answer the door. He knew before he was halfway there that it was her. Striker had a sixth sense about things. He stopped before unlatching the heavy wooden door, tucking his reading glasses into the front pocket of his shirt.

For all the death and beauty Striker had seen in his forty-plus years, he couldn't remember a sight stopping his heart with quite the abruptness as the sight of Jenny standing there alone in her red dress on the thick green carpet in the hallway.

"I needed someplace to go," she said in a quieter and less sure tone than he had yet heard her use. He stepped aside and she came in. She didn't continue into the living room but stood there, looking away from him.

Striker took her hair in his hands and pulled it aside, exposing her long white neck. He kissed her there lightly several times. She turned to him.

"I need you," she said.

Striker picked her up like a new bride and carried her into his bedroom without another word.

"I'm heading home, sir," the young lieutenant said, peeking his head in through the door. "Anything else I can do for you?"

The gray-haired general looked up from a pile of papers. "Go get yourself some pussy, son," he said with a twisted smile.

This suggestion would have been far more humorous to the lieutenant had he not been married.

Smoke from the ashtray spiraled through the glow of the desk lamp and curled about the general's face, accentuating his already hellish appearance. In contrast to his flushed and craggy features, the general's clear blue eyes were cold, completely devoid of compassion or pity. At home, the lieutenant referred to his superior as "General Scratch," but only to his wife, and then only when he was sure they were alone.

The general made his way through some paperwork for another forty-five minutes before he checked his watch and rose from the desk. He picked up the metallic case that seemed to always be with him. It was too small for a suitcase and really too fat for a briefcase. Since he began carrying it almost a year ago, no one had ever commented on the general's unorthodox case. Normally at the end of the day there were papers to be extracted from the bulky case and more still to be stuffed inside. Today, however, nothing went in or came out.

The general left the office with his usual brisk stride, but instead of heading for the administrative parking lot, he set off down one of the concrete paths that ran through the complex maze of buildings. Almost everything above ground was administrative in nature. There were a few labs, but most of the real work with the heavy metals was done underground. The theory was that an underground facility, if bombed, wouldn't leave a pothole the size of Texas and a dust cloud blocking out the sun from the rest of the earth for ten thousand years, the way an aboveground facility certainly would.

The United States Department of Energy had created one hundred three metric tons of plutonium during the course of the cold war. Ninety of those tons were weapons-grade material, developed for thermonuclear devices. Much of the plutonium and weaponry had been made at Pantex, and much of it was steadily finding its way back there now. Even the plutonium that had been produced at one of the country's other two nuclear weapons facilities, Rocky Flats in Colorado and Savannah River in Georgia, was wending its way to Pantex. From subs and silos and airfields across the globe, bombs and missiles were being turned in like the badges of a disassembled posse. Rocky Flats and Savannah River were no longer producing weapons-grade plutonium. So it was Pantex or bust for the man-made element Pu 239. Of the thousands of warheads that had been so painstakingly constructed over the years, six thousand had already been retired. Fourteen thousand more were scheduled for retirement, and at least six thousand of those would also be stored at Pantex. The government was still undecided about where to place the remaining eight thousand.

When a weapon was retired, it was essentially disassembled. At the end of the process there remained the heart of every thermonuclear device—the pit of pure plutonium. There was no real way to dispose of the pit. To convert it to usable fuel would cost more than the electric energy it could produce. Instead the pits were buried about a quarter mile beneath the earth's surface in a series of vaults at Pantex. Security was extraordinary. The general not only oversaw the continuing security for the entire Pantex facility, he oversaw the design and construction of the storage system for the now useless pits of plutonium. From the series of three barbed-wire fences, the dogs, the sound and sight sensors, to the camera systems, the codes, the clearance checkpoints, the SWAT team, the security forces, and the sophisticated sensors in the plutonium vaults, the general was ultimately responsible for it all.

Sometimes, he would lie awake in the middle of the night, digging at his hemorrhoids through striped cotton pajamas, wondering at the simplicity of the whole thing. For all the systems and the training and the checks and balances, it was he, an underpaid, overworked, and frustrated military commander, who was the ultimate chink in the armor that protected the material that made the United States the most powerful nation on the face of the earth. He would gnaw on this thought, searching over and over in his mind for his oversight. Somehow there had to be a check for him. But there wasn't. That was so very clear now. Already he had delivered one of the precious pits to the man he knew as Striker, a ruthless pirate. Nothing had happened. The money was in a locker at the Amarillo bus terminal, and there was a lot of it. Half a million dollars. There was much more to come. Striker would see to that.

As he walked down the concrete path, the general gazed up at the pocked, cheese-white moon and thought about Striker. At first he was certain that Striker was a trap, a test to see if he could be bought. That would make sense. The only safeguard against him was a yearly evaluation by Military Intelligence. With so much at stake, he had been certain Striker was not for real. He had known of Striker for years. During his time with MI he had come in contact with Striker from time to time. No one he ever knew could say what the man's real name actually was. The general did know, however, that Striker's past service had included time with the army's Special Forces. Striker had served in Vietnam and was a trained killer who had actually practiced his craft.

Like the general himself, Striker had served in intelligence. Whatever work Striker had done for MI, something the general didn't know of, it necessitated the creation of a new identity. The general did know that Striker eventually left the service and became an active contract agent for the CIA, and that he ran a front corporation dealing in international arms. Rumor had it that Striker was not only a janitor for the CIA, cleaning up their various messes around the globe, but that he turned a healthy profit for the agency and himself in the arms market. Striker had a reputation in the intelligence community as being a fast-moving, freewheeling operator who was out for number one, but who also always got the job done. That was something people in the community never took lightly.

That Striker, a CIA agent, would be personally involved in a sting directed against a military officer of the United States Army seemed unlikely, but the general was naturally suspicious. Finally, Striker had convinced the general that it was worth the risk, explaining that this would be the general's last opportunity to take care of himself. The military had capitulated to politicians. The strength was being sucked out of the country. The plutonium that made the country strong was being packed away. The demise of the Soviet Union and the disassembling of the nuclear arsenal meant that it would only be a matter of time before the very same material being so cautiously guarded at Pantex became freely available on the international arms market. The time to get the big payoff was now, before the commodity became readily available and far less expensive. Already there were rumors of people securing plutonium from the Ukraine. Striker was offering him a once-in-a-lifetime opportunity.

More importantly, Striker pointed out that the general's life work had been meaningless. The general was a proud man but also realistic, and he knew this to be true. Like a fireman who was trained to put out a fire but never got the chance to do it, the general was a soldier who had never really soldiered. Caught between the Korean War and the war in Vietnam, the general had never served a tour of combat. It had stifled his career in the army, even in MI. Combat veterans were a special fraternity whose members always seemed to get ahead faster.

Nevertheless, throughout his career the general had put his shoulder to the wheel and pushed ahead, certain that his chance to do something of real importance would come. When he finally got the star he had slaved for and got the post as head of security at the country's most coveted military asset, it was payback time for all his years of loyal service. Then, even before the last pieces of furniture had arrived for his new office, a man he considered to be nothing more than a whining deserter became the commander in chief of the United States Armed Forces. The humiliation of the military began. The forces were cut, and more horrifying yet, the arsenal that separated the United States from the rest of humanity was marked for destruction. Plutonium production lurched to a halt. Nuclear weapons were retired, the Pantex facility became a glorified junk yard, and the general became nothing more than a glorified Fred Sanford with a uniform.

For his lifetime of service, the general had a house in the suburbs, an overweight wife who drank too much, and a military command that quite suddenly amounted to nothing more than cleanup and storage. So, Striker had reasoned, what difference did it really make? The general could take the money and run, literally. The general had the knowledge and the means to rig the system so that no one would know the pits were missing until some time in the future when someone decided that it was a good idea to reassemble all the weapons they were now so expensively disassembling. By the time the production cycle ever came around to the point where the pits were going to actually be used again, the general felt certain he would be dead. He would certainly be long gone from Texas.

His plan was to finish the business with Striker, put in for immediate retirement, move to Miami with his wife, and then disappear on his fishing boat one day when the weather got heavy. His wife would be left with his pension, and he would enjoy the rest of his life traveling from place to place, living off of what all told would be three million tax-free dollars. The interest the sum could earn in a Swiss bank would do him very nicely. It was a good plan, and as Striker had so accurately put it, it was his payoff. With half a million already in the bus locker, and one pit already delivered, the general knew that if Striker was setting a trap, it would have sprung. The thing that bothered the general now more than getting caught taking the pits was Striker. The general didn't trust him.

The general approached a relatively small building on the edge of the complex. It looked like nothing more than a large guard post. This was the entry point for the underground facility. Everyone working below the earth's surface passed through this central location. Parking lots were outside the ring of barracks. Materials, raw and finished, were transported via truck, tractor, and aircraft directly to storage points in the desert. Each underground facility had what amounted to its own aboveground shipping and receiving depot, but the people who designed Pantex thought it would be wise to direct all the workers through one checkpoint. It was easier to monitor the influx of people this way, and with the underground distribution, none of the people who worked at Pantex would ever be sure where the materials were stored. With a sharp salute, the general passed through a checkpoint of armed soldiers and proceeded to the building.

Once inside, the general shivered slightly and breathed into his hands to warm them. There was a breeze kicking up from the west, and even though it was June and the days were warm, the temperature still dipped into the low forties at night. The dark desert night was strangely silent. This was his doing. Once a week the entire one-hundred-thousand-acre facility was dusted with an insecticide that eradicated the cricket population. This was to ensure the accuracy of the sound sensor equipment that was an integral part of security. Crickets created white noise, a nuisance to any sound surveillance device. The general could think of a dozen environmental groups that would raise holy hell if they ever knew about the spraying. Of course they never would know. That was one beautiful thing about Pantex. There were no rules that couldn't be overcome in the name of national security.

In the center of the small structure, a bank of elevators plunged down into the earth. There were ten different levels below ground. On each of the different levels, a web of tram-cluttered tunnels stretched out beneath the desert floor to numerous production sites. But only one level could access the tunnel that wound its way to all the plutonium vaults. That level was unmarked and accessed only with a special key.

When the general stepped out of the elevator, he was met by two security guards armed with MAC-10s, short machine pistols designed for cutting down a dozen people in a small space with one burst of fire. The general's pass was checked, and his palm was scanned. He complimented his men on the fine job they were doing. He made this safety inspection once every four months. It was supposed to be a surprise, but because he did it every four months like clockwork, everyone knew it was coming. They didn't know the exact day, but they knew that about midmonth of every June, October, and February, they'd better be on their toes.

After the appropriate stone-faced salutes, the guards opened a door that led into a tunnel containing a single open tram car. The general sat down in the car. He pushed a green button on the dash in front of him, and the tram began to wind through a tunnel that would twist and turn its way to the plutonium vault. The vault was buried deep within the earth, but a nuclear explosion whose vortex was directly above the vault could theoretically set off a reaction within the vault itself and create an apocalyptic explosion. The whole thing—the security system, the facility, the operations—sounded wonderfully complex and secretive, which was exactly what the lawmakers on the hill seemed to like. The expense had never seemed to matter.

Of course the general was one of the few men who knew the exact coordinates of the vault. After the initial construction of the underground steel and concrete framework by workers who themselves never knew exactly what they were constructing, one tunnel was modified by special facilities workers and became the only access to the vault. There was one long, winding tunnel, and at the end was a chamber where the tram came to a stop. Only a single officer sat outside the chamber, at a raised control panel that included video monitors of the chamber and various other camera views of the tunnel track. There were various buttons and levers, one of which could seal the chamber off from the tram, as well as a computer that was hooked up into the pit room.

"Good evening, sir," were the only words the officer had for the general as he passed the console and punched the keypad that let him into the vault.

The pit room door opened and the general stepped inside, closing the vault behind him. He knew the officer at the console could hear and see everything he did. The room looked very much like a large safe-deposit box vault. Each pit was stored in its own lead-lined box that had a separate digitally coded combination. There was one small shelf jutting out of a wall of safes, and the general set his case down there. He extracted from it a laptop computer and plugged it into an interface jack in the wall just above the shelf. The general flicked on his computer and began to stab at the keys.

He punched in a series of commands and looked up at the camera that was in the corner of the vault.

"Can you see me?" the general asked, knowing full well he had disengaged the video camera above him.

"No, sir," came the officer's slightly nervous voice over an intercom speaker.

"Good, now pay close attention," commanded the general.

The general accessed the coding for box #3379, a random selection. There was a low beeping tone and the door to the small safe for the #3379 pit slid smoothly open. The lead-lined drawer was eye level with the general and only two feet to his left. He reached up and extracted the pit from its resting place, setting it gently down into his open case. The low tone was replaced by a piercing high-pitched beep-beep-beep. The general punched some numbers into his computer and the beeping stopped. Before reengaging the video camera, he placed the shiny metallic pit in a small concealed compartment in the case.

The general would have loved to have taken the three pits he needed at one time, but that wasn't in the manual. It said that each check would be conducted on one random vault during every inspection. It was probably better for other reasons as well. The shiny metal exterior was nothing more than a protective alloy shell, and because of that shell, the pit itself gave off no harmful radiation whatsoever. But the general knew enough about plutonium. Eventually the bombardment of alpha particles inside the shell would deteriorate the alloy lining and the radiation would seep out. Although a little external exposure to Pu 239 wouldn't harm a flea, unlike the deadlier Pu 240 version, the general was still a little nervous. Three kilograms of the Pu 240 plutonium emitted enough radiation to kill a person almost immediately. Even though a single pit of Pu 239 wasn't deadly, or even dangerous, two or more pits close together risked a nuclear reaction. Two plutonium pits leaking radiation in close proximity wouldn't explode like a bomb, but the meltdown would kill everything in the immediate area. So the risk, along with the need to conduct his inspections according to the manual, led the general to wisely insist to Striker that he deliver the pits one at a time.

"Tell me what just happened, soldier," the general barked out to the dead air that surrounded him.

"Sir, in accordance with the Nuclear Weapons Safety Manual Rule 6.27-B, you just extracted pit #3379 and then replaced it, sir," came the voice through the intercom.

A small smiled teased the corners of the general's mouth. He reached up and shut the opened vault door. Until the unforseeable day came when someone was ordered to extract pit #3379, no one would know that it wasn't right there were it should be.

Madison watched the green LED numbers on the clock turn from six-twenty-nine to six-thirty. She'd been watching since five-seventeen, and before that she'd watched it until around three. Dinner last night with Marty had gone well enough. He seemed to handle pretty well her insistence that they no longer pursue anything more than a friendship. The hardest part about the whole thing had been convincing Marty that her decision not to get involved had nothing to do with the sudden appearance of her ex-husband. But the strain she'd put on her friendship with Marty wasn't why she couldn't sleep. When she'd arrived home last night, Jo-Jo was still awake. He was excited. Any young boy would have been. He'd gotten an unexpected visit from his father.

Lucia, Madison's housekeeper, had been a nervous wreck, but not Jo-Jo. His eyes shone with pure delight. It was the first time he had seen his father in almost two years. Instead of growing to resent his absence, Jo-Jo still worshipped him. Understandable. The name Joe Thurwood was known to all Jo-Jo's classmates. He was the former NFL superstar fullback. It was a source of pride for Jo-Jo that his father was Big Joe, but also a hidden source of shame that he never saw his famous father. Madison knew that Jo-Jo somehow blamed himself for his father's absence and didn't know what to do about it.

When Madison finally got Jo-Jo settled down and in bed, she tore into Lucia like a lawnmower for letting her ex-husband into the house. By court order, he was denied access not only to her home but to their son, unless he first obtained her consent. She told Lucia before the divorce even went through to never let Joe in the house, and she had warned her repeatedly since the day she first heard Joe was back in Austin. She was afraid of something like this, afraid of the effect it would have on her son, and if pushed, she would admit that she was afraid of what Joe might do to her. Through her tears Lucia insisted that she hadn't let Joe in, and when Madison told her she must have left the lock undone, Lucia assured her again that she had checked as she was supposed to do, and that every access into the house had been locked.

So except for a few fitful hours, Madison had lain awake thinking. She felt certain that what Joe had done was planned more to distress her than to reestablish his relationship with his son. Tomorrow they were having a summary judgment hearing, and the judge had expressed her desire to see both parties with their attorneys in order to determine whether or not to dismiss Joe's suit as a matter of law without even bothering to adjudicate the facts. Joe knew Madison well enough to know how this would effect her, and after consideration, she became more and more certain he'd done it on purpose, tempting her to explode in front of the judge tomorrow. Joe wanted the judge to see firsthand what a temperamental bitch she could be. But Madison would not be beaten. She would maintain her calm and get through this so she could get back to her normal life.

Madison knew two things about her ex-husband. First, he was crafty, and he only had to learn something once, then he never forgot it. Joe had learned the hard way how the legal system worked. Going through the divorce and custody proceedings the first time, she had run circles around him. He'd skimped on an attorney, and she'd gotten the best her firm had to offer. Joe would not make the same mistakes again; he would try to use the strategies she'd used against him to his own advantage. Second, Madison knew that Joe was a ferocious competitor who possessed an inordinate amount of pride. Joe had been programmed—or born—to win. He wanted more than anything to take Madison back to court on her own ground and beat her at her own game.

It was obvious from her recent encounter with Joe that he had studied carefully, or consulted with someone who knew, just how far he could go without infringing on anyone's legal rights. When he followed her and Marty by the river, it was creepy and embarrassing, but there was nothing illegal about it. She was certain that Joe had learned where to draw the line. He had been careful to humiliate Marty without doing anything that resembled a threat. He hadn't raised a fist or even his voice, but his words had been worse than a fist to Marty's face.

"I don't think it's very nice, Marty," Joe had said. "You were supposed to be my friend, that's what you said when Maddy introduced me to you, didn't you? Didn't you say that when the time came, when things went bad for me, all the other agents would look away, but you'd still be there? Didn't you say that was the advantage of having an agent who was more of a friend? I think you did. Now I find you together with my wife, kissing her."

Madison saw Marty shaking with fear. The Joe Thurwood they both knew was capable of ripping him open with his bare hands.

"I'm not your wife, Joe," she had interjected venomously.

Joe looked at her longingly for a moment, and then in the moonlight. She watched the longing transform into barely controlled hatred, a loathing from the pit of his soul. Madison was afraid, and she knew that Joe knew she was afraid, because he smiled in a way that seemed to suggest he was enjoying her fear, and that this was somehow only the beginning.

Madison shuddered, then got up to use the bathroom. She dressed and went downstairs to let Abby, their yellow Lab, out in the backyard before waking Jo-Jo. The house was a large split-level. Only the master bedroom was upstairs, so Madison had to simply walk down the hall past the kitchen to reach her son's room. Jo-Jo woke with a broad smile on his face, remembering how only last night he had seen his father. Madison was sure that it hadn't mattered to Jo-Jo that his father had gotten fat or that his hair and beard were long. He was still Joe Thurwood, the star of the Outlaws. People said there hadn't been a fullback quite so good since his father's retirement, and Jo-Jo doubted there ever would be.

Jo-Jo's room was covered with NFL posters. Most of them had something to do with the Outlaws. His bookshelf was jam-packed with books and game balls awarded to his father during his playing days. In the corner was an elaborate computer system. Jo-Jo was smart, and he could run through the various programs in his computer almost as well as Madison, but he would be a football player too when he grew up. He told everyone that, even if they didn't ask. Madison wanted nothing of the kind. She felt that the vicious world of football did nothing but turn boys too quickly into men and men too quickly into animals. She said nothing, though. She knew better. She loved Jo-Jo too much to squelch his spirit. Instead she used his fervor for sports to prompt him in his schoolwork. For all her indulgence, Madison made it clear that if he didn't do extremely well in school, the sports thing wouldn't happen. She held his body hostage to his mind without the slightest moral reservation. In fact she was proud of it.

"Hurry, Jo-Jo," Madison said with a warm smile. "I've got to drop you off a little early today."

"Mom?" he said, swinging his feet out from under the covers.

"Yes."

"Can I see dad again today?"

Madison was ready for this.

"Yes, Jo-Jo, you can."

"Wow, that's great!" Jo-Jo exclaimed, running over to hug her waist.

"Dad said you'd never say yes, but I told him you would. I told him you're the greatest!"

Madison smiled. "Thank you, Jo-Jo," she said, kissing him on the head. "Now hurry. Breakfast in ten minutes."

It wrenched her to concede so easily to Joe's manipulation. She dug her nails into her palms as she left her son's room. It was so blatant. It was so wrong. She thought of all the things she could do to him, slap a temporary restraining order on him for violating the court-ordered visitation rules, maybe file a complaint with the police for unlawful entry or harassment. There were things she could do with the law. She could manipulate the system and bring it crashing down on Joe Thurwood's head. That was her world, the justice system. He wasn't supposed to be able to just pop into her house. And how did he get in? He broke in, that was breaking and entering. Madison's heart raced as she considered all the things she would have to do to set the machinery in motion against him.

Then she stopped. She would do none of it. Joe would ultimately get out of any bind she could entangle him in. There would be publicity, too. It was easy to shelter a five- or six-year-old from an ugly divorce, even if it involved drug use and physical abuse, even if it was in the papers. With a boy of eight, it was an entirely different matter. More damage would be done to Jo-Jo than anyone. Joe knew that, and again she suspected he knew that she knew it as well.

Madison walked into the kitchen and apologized to Lucia for her ranting the night before. Lucia was outwardly relieved, and that made Madison feel better. She let Abby in, then poured herself a glass of orange juice. Lucia set breakfast out on the table while Madison quietly considered her strategy for the hearing as she waited for Jo-Jo to come to the table. They ate without saying too much, and that was okay. That was how it was most mornings. Most of their conversations took place at night, when the day was over.

Madison dropped Jo-Jo off at school with a kiss and a wave and made her way into the city for the hearing. The judge was a woman named Iris DuBose. Judge DuBose was a late-middle-aged woman with white hair who wore steel-rimmed bifocals. Most people assumed that a female judge in any case would be more sympathetic to a woman plaintiff's viewpoint. But Madison found quite the opposite to be true. In a world that was consistently gender biased, women had been so mentally battered that often when they did finally get into a position where they could turn things the other way, they often used their power to further the status quo. It seemed to Madison that women judges were so afraid of not being fair to male parties that they compensated by being more sympathetic.

In their divorce two years ago, the judge had been Garrison Peele. Judge Peele was an elderly southern gentleman who had no sympathy for a strong young man who was involved in extensive drug use and who had hit his wife.

Madison supposed that if Judge Peele had had his way, Madison would not only have been given exclusive custody of Jo-Jo and a highly favorable financial arrangement, but Big Joe would have been drawn and quartered in front of the courthouse. Of course, sometimes in law a judgment that is too favorable can come back later like a wounded grizzly to bite you. If a ruling of any kind was way out of line with the norms of the time, it was an easy target for someone to challenge later on down the road. That was the case today.

Despite what Joe had done in the past and despite the original ruling, he had rights as the father of Jo-Jo. As bizarre as it seemed, he also had rights as Madison's ex-husband. With the passing of the days when men worked and women baked cakes and had babies went the days of women cashing in on divorce settlements. Today, women were subject to the same financial perils as their counterparts.

A woman like Madison, who made well over two hundred fifty thousand dollars a year and had completed her law degree and established a practice during the years of her marriage, would have to fight for an equitable property division upon divorce. Forget that Big Joe had earned almost a million dollars a year and that he had managed to squander not only that, but much of what Madison made as well. All those things happened while they were married, and so any losses and any gains were losses and gains to them both. No one partner in a marriage ever took the sole credit or blame for financial earnings or indiscretions.

So Joe's reappearance and his demand for a whole new settlement annoyed Madison, but at the same time it let her know that he was getting some good advice, much better than he'd gotten the first time around. Of course, then Joe was a crazed lunatic strung out on heroin. One day in the courtroom, old Peele actually had to have him physically restrained.

The judge's chambers for family court were in the basement of the courthouse. High on the wall were small rectangular windows through which Madison could see the ankles of passersby outside. The hearing took place at what looked like an old cafeteria table. It was a far cry from the offices upstairs where Madison tried criminal cases against the state of Texas. There the judge's chambers were paneled with richly stained wood. The trim around the bookshelves, doors, and windows was ornate and spoke of a time when criminals were hung by the neck for stealing horses. Today the courts spent more time regulating how many hours a delinquent father could spend with his child and how Christmas vacation would be divided rather than deciding between life or death for a thief and murderer. Madison supposed it was appropriate that such business was carried on in the basement.

Despite the shabby setting, Madison, like every attorney, knew that a judge was a judge whether the floor of their chambers was covered with marble or linoleum, and that all judges demanded respect. After all, if there was no respect, then how could people be expected to adhere to the authority of the decisions meted out? Respect required everyone to dress as though they were just stopping by on their way to church and that all the formal nuances of lawyering be observed. The most correctly enunciated Latin legal terms and the most extravagant mix of conjunctions, adjectives, and verbs could always be found in the shabbiest judge's chambers. Judges tended to be egotistical as a rule, and so they were particularly sensitive to weak symbols of their power, and almost always determined to make up for it with formality.

Glen Westman, the best divorce lawyer in Madison's enormous firm, was already sitting at the table, as was Joe's lawyer, Paul Gleason, a highly competent attorney who had his own small but successful practice. Madison knew a battle between these two lawyers could be like a fight between two champion rottweilers. Judge DuBose sat at the head of the table, looking through a file on the case. Madison said hello to everyone and sat down quietly. She and Glen had mapped out their strategy extensively the day before, and there was nothing more to discuss between them until Joe and his attorney put at least some of their cards on the table.

When Joe walked into the room, Madison had to do a double take. He was clean-shaven and his hair, although long, was pulled back into a tight, neat ponytail. He wore an expensive suit that had been tailored to make his large gut look like the prosperous girth of a tycoon rather that the sloppy bulk of a derelict. Despite his size, Joe looked good. He not only gave off an aura of power, but his demeanor and facial expressions denoted composure and even a slight hint of condescension. Madison tried to swallow, but her mouth was too dry. Joe was going to create real problems for her. She had been counting all along on his ragged appearance and his volatile personality to help her maintain the bulk of what she'd won two years ago.

"Your honor," Joe said, taking a moment to shake Judge DuBose's hand before sitting down.

"Well," Judge DuBose began without wasting any time, "now that we're all here, I'd like to remind you, Mr. Gleason, and you, Mr. Thurwood, that this matter has already been litigated fully and formally, so I am highly averse to changing what for two years has proven to be an effective arrangement in regards to the best interests of the child. Of course my feelings are the same regarding the distribution of the marital property. This court, like any other, is loathe to adjudicate things twice. Ms. McCall's movement for summary judgment is quite in order . . . "

The judge let her words hang in the air. Madison had to bite the inside of her mouth to keep the smile from creeping out onto her face. These words were the proper ones. They reflected her position on this matter almost verbatim. Her sentiments would surely result in the summary judgment, throwing the matter out of the court with only the slim chance of renewal based on some constitutional appeal. Regardless of what most people thought, once a decision was reached at the trial-court level by the judge hearing the facts, it was rare that any decision would be overturned at the appellate level.

"However . . . "

With that single word, Madison's stomach fell. "However" was one word that every lawyer dreaded. It meant there was more to come, all of it bad.

" . . . in light of the fluctuating nature of this particular body of the law in the state of Texas, and in light of the assertions filed in the complaint, I am inclined to reevaluate the situation on its merits."

Even Joe, the only nonlawyer in the room, knew what the judge's words meant. A slow, evil grin spread from his lips to his cheeks, and he gazed malevolently at Madison. Then it was gone, and Madison wondered if it had only been her imagination. Joe cleared his throat, and suddenly Madison saw nothing more harmful than a two-hundred-ninety-pound choirboy. But this was an act she had seen before. It was the Joe Thurwood she fell in love with nine years ago, when she was a naive law student.

"Your Honor," he began in his quiet but booming voice, "I know that it is not my place to speak right here and right now, but I am the only person here who lacks a formal education in the law, so I hope you will forgive me."

The surprise created by this impromptu speech allowed Joe to pause and continue uninterrupted, even by the judge.

"It's just that I have to say how much I appreciate what you're saying. I want you to know, I guess I want everyone to know," here he gave Madison the long, pitiful look of a convicted murderer who had found Jesus, "that I'm sorry for the way I was. I was sick, but now I'm well. I can't undo what I was, or what I did, but I can try to make it up to our son. I can be the father I know he needs."

84

"As far as any money, Your Honor—and everyone . . . " Joe glanced around at them all, "I don't want to ask for money. I'm not proud that I am. I'm ashamed of it. I am. I'm not proud that it took every resource I had to get well again. I wish it hadn't happened. But it did.

"So I want you to know, Your Honor, that I'm fully prepared to be badmouthed and trampled on." Joe stared woefully at Glen Westman and then back to the judge. "That's part of the game. But I wanted you to know that I'm well enough now to feel ashamed of the whole thing. If I could have my way, I'd undo all of it. I would. And Maddy and Jo-Jo and I would all be together as one family, as I know we should have been, and would have been, if I hadn't gone off the deep end. I'm sorry." Joe looked ashamedly down at his thick paws that were clamped together in front of him on the cheap Formica tabletop.

Madison looked over at Judge Iris DuBose. There weren't tears in her eyes, but Madison knew the older woman was battling them fiercely. Madison could read a judge. She could read a jury. That was what made her so good as a trial lawyer. She knew what people wanted and what they needed. Iris DuBose needed to be assured that in the great state of Texas, men were still big and tough, and that even when the modern world broke them down they could still come back, even better than they were before. Iris had a need to feel that there was an order that ultimately ruled even the most tempestuous forces in this life. Joe Thurwood had just given her a big slice of that reassurance, like a fat wedge of apple pie. Joe Thurwood had just assured her that the big hometown football hero who had once brought everyone so much glory was back. He'd been down, yes, but it wasn't for good. He was back and everything would be as it should be, if they all could only give him the chance he needed.

The judge cleared her throat, "Well, you're right, Mr. Thurwood, your words are slightly out of order, but this is not a formal court proceeding, and I find your candor refreshing. Still, we have a great conflict here that must be adjudicated according to the laws of Texas. So, Mr. Gleason, I'd like to hear your side of this, then, Mr. Westman, yours. My hope in all this, more than anything, is that we can reach some sort of equitable agreement that will allow both parties to coexist in a way that will serve not only justice but the child in question here."

After pausing a moment to give weight to what she'd just said, Judge DuBose continued. "Mr. Gleason, please begin."

"Thank you, your honor," Gleason said with a nod. "Your honor, let me begin by saying that we are fully aware that this divorce settlement and custody arrangement has been fully litigated and that the law does not take into account the quality of the council for any party who has previously been heard by the court, with the exception of gross malfeasance on the part of his former council. Although there is nothing for which formal charges may be brought against Mr. Thurwood's former council, I must say that without a doubt his interests were not zealously advocated to the court. Again, your honor, I know this is of no legal relevance, but I did wish to include it in what I'm saying so that the court, and Mr. Westman and his client, can fully appreciate our sentiments regarding this entire matter."

The judge nodded. She was very satisfied with the way in which Big Joe's attorney had said in legal jargon that he'd been screwed over the first time around.

"Also," Gleason continued, "we would like the court to know that Mr. Thurwood voluntarily entered and successfully completed a drug and alcohol rehabilitation program in his home state of Iowa, and that he has returned to Austin to be closer to his son and to use his own experience and status as a local celebrity to help the youth of this community to avoid the same pitfalls of which he himself has been a victim."

Madison bowed her head. She could barely contain a sarcastic laugh. Joe Thurwood was now a victim. She'd heard it all.

"Mr. Thurwood," Gleason continued, "despite having many lucrative opportunities in various areas within the world of business, sports, and entertainment, has forgone everything to take a job here locally as a youth counselor at the YMCA."

Madison looked up at her ex-husband with this news. It was hard to believe. Joe returned her stare with a peaceful, repentant countenance. Only deep within his eyes could she see his unbridled hatred of her. She looked back down to the table in front of her. Gleason droned on about how wonderful Big Joe Thurwood really was.

Despite the importance of her mental focus on what was being said and how the proceeding progressed, Madison faded out. Judge DuBose's earlier words clung tenaciously to her thoughts like the heavy gray Spanish moss that choked the old oak trees of the coastal Gulf towns. Both parties coexisting sounded like a nightmare to Madison. It sounded like Joe stopping by after work to take Jo-Jo to a ball game. It sounded like him bringing Jo-Jo home later than expected, or calling and saying maybe Jo-Jo would just spend the night with him. It sounded like Joe living off of her growing practice since she was now the substantial wage earner of the two. It sounded like hell.

She knew where this whole thing was headed, and it had only just begun. The outcome, though, seemed as predictable to Madison as if it were already written. Only one ray of hope lit her misery. It was the hope that Joe Thurwood was in this only for the money, which was entirely possible. She would gladly buy him off. His fine demeanor and his humble words had no effect on her. He was bad and a threat, and she knew it.

CHAPTER NINE

∨

CODY GREY LAY AWAKE ON HIS DOUBLE BED. The air conditioning blew all it had directly on him. It was just enough to keep him cool. On top of the other bed a fourth-year free agent by the name of Derell Biggs lay naked and spread-eagled. It wasn't bad enough that Biggs was brought in to replace Cody; the Outlaws had seen fit to have the two of them room together so Cody could help teach him the intricacies of the defense. Cody was expected to hammer the nails into the framework of his own gallows. Beyond the obvious annoyance with Biggs's mere presence, Cody was certain the younger player's septum had been removed, mangled with the aid of some type of out-dated farm machinery, and then reinserted into his nose with rawhide stitching. He'd never heard anyone snore so loud. But even that wasn't what was keeping him awake.

He flopped off of his stomach and sat up against the headboard. He dialed his home number and got the machine again. It could be that Jenny had simply gotten in late, forgotten to check the messages, turned off the ringer, and gone to sleep without calling him. She told him he had to give her some space. Maybe this was part of what she meant. Cody was sick of hearing about her space. That was the main topic of almost every conversation they'd had all summer. To Cody, it meant simply putting up with a lot of bullshit. But he put up with it ever since the night he was stabbed. She told him she'd spent the night in a hotel and that he had to trust her. He had been in no position to argue. What he'd done in the bar when she was dancing with the big Texan was stupid any way you looked at it.

As recently as a year ago, Cody would have gone home and checked to make sure she was there. Two things kept him in the hotel down the road from the Outlaws facility where they were holding a midsummer mini-camp. First, he wasn't in the position to screw around with the curfew. He didn't even have a contract yet. He was here on good faith, hoping that the Outlaws would find room for him on their roster before the real training camp began. Second, there was something deep within him that didn't want to go home. He didn't want to find something that would only make things worse. This was a cowardly approach to his decaying marriage, but he didn't allow himself to think of it that way.

As soon as his mind went too far down that path, he would think about something else. It wasn't too hard considering all the other things that were swirling around in his mind: his career, his body, his bank account. As bad as his marriage was, right now it looked like it had more buoyancy than any of his other choices. So he wasn't thrilled with the idea of going out of his way to sabotage what security still remained. For all their problems, Jenny had always been there, or so he told himself.

Cody lay back down and waited for sleep to come. He ran through the events of the day. The team had tested each potential player's strength, speed, and endurance in the morning. Between the limitations of his surgically-cut knee and his fight-cut shoulder, Cody tested worse than he ever had as an NFL player. The afternoon had been devoted to meetings and a basic practice session where most of the new guys and rookies took the bulk of the repetitions. For Cody, the day had been the beginning of his painful assimilation to the role of backup player, and even that role was tenuous. The inner torment was almost enough to make him walk off the field.

For eight years he had been one of the team's stars. Before that, in college, even before he'd made a name for himself, everything good was in front of him. Now everything good was behind him. He had always been respected by his coaches and at times almost revered by his teammates. Whether it was true or not, in Cody's mind those would now be things of the past. He had to catch himself several times that afternoon from running out onto the field when the first team defense was called to action. It was as though everyone was watching him stand there on the sideline, out of the action, a man marked for pity. It was sickening.

Cody threw back the sheet and jumped up out of the bed. He limped to the sink and took out of his shaving kit a couple of cold tablets that caused drowsiness. He washed them down with a glass of warm, cloudy water from the sink. Biggs snored on. Cody was halfway back to his bed when the pounding in his knee sent him back to his shaving kit for a double hit of Motrin. He needed to contain the swelling in his knee as best he could. Physically, he could do everything now, maybe not as quickly as he did before, and there was definitely pain involved. After only the first day of a mini-camp, when the players weren't even dressed out in their full gear, a knee had no business feeling as bad as his did.

He would say nothing to anyone, though. He would treat himself with leftover prescription drugs from previous injuries, the way any smart player who was hurt but not yet signed to a contract would. Only after the dotted line was signed could he go to the team physician and get some really heavy-duty drugs to reduce the swelling in his knee. Once he was signed, he was their risk for the season, and they would do everything they could to keep him on the field, even if his contribution to the team was nothing more than playing on one of the kicking units. They'd rely on nothing short of acupuncture to get their money's worth out of him or any player. Until then, though, he had to keep his damaged knee under wraps. If the Outlaws sensed he was too far gone, they wouldn't even risk the hundred-and-sixty-two-thousand-dollar minimum they would have to pay him for a veteran's salary.

Cody lay back down and waited for the cold tablets to take effect. Between the air conditioning and the snoring he might as well have been in the vortex of a nuclear blast. Soon the cold tablets made him drowsy, and the noise became not only tolerable but somehow comforting. In this state, before he dropped off to sleep, Cody did something he hadn't done in a long time. Maybe it was the drugs, but he started to pray to God. He hadn't bothered with God when he was a rising star. It was shameful, he knew. He'd always felt that his climb to success was his own doing. Now he needed something, someone, and it seemed to him that an appeal to the Almighty could fix a mess as big as what his life had become.

The general cursed out loud, then kicked the air -conditioning unit. It blew only tepid air into the sweltering room. He was in a cheap roadside motel on the outskirts of Big Spring. The temperature outside was one hundred four, and the general was certain it was even hotter inside. The general surveyed his room. A sagging bed lay in the middle of the gray threadbare carpet. On top of the bed were his overnight bag and his metallic briefcase. The general couldn't even change rooms. Room 117 was where Striker had told him to go and wait. He wondered if Striker hadn't done this on purpose.

The general took an inflatable doughnut from his overnight bag and blew into it until he was slightly dizzy. He put the doughnut down on the edge of the bed and then sat carefully on top of it.

He thought about Paris. He'd go there in the spring, before the tourists came in droves. There were a lot of places the general would go and a lot of things he would do. He was almost there. He could taste it. Only a thin tether of risk and time separated him from a new life. The risk was well worth it, even if it meant prison. He felt like he was in a prison already.

The phone rang. He got up slowly and went to it.

"Hello," he said.

There was nothing.

"Hello," he said again.

There was a low electronic humming at the other end of the line and several clicking sounds before he was disconnected. The general put down the phone and went over to the window. He pulled back the musty, translucent curtain and looked outside. His Jeep sat alone in the midst of the U-shaped, dilapidated motel, baking in the hot, dusty parking lot. A noisy tractor trailer belching black diesel exhaust sped by on the highway, leaving a hazy cloud of dust and pollution in its wake. Across the road lay a desert of brown scrub brush that extended to the horizon. There was nothing else. The general didn't like the situation, but he sat back down anyway. He'd come too far to turn back.

Striker put the small digitized tape recorder back into his briefcase and hung up the phone. One of the goons was watching him from the other side of the baggage claim. Striker was careful not to give any indication that he knew he was being watched. He left the terminal the way he'd come, only now he was moving against the heavy flow of people. At 3:25 there was a flight to Dallas. It was always packed with businesspeople trying to make it back by the end of the day. The heavy traffic guaranteed that one person coming or going wouldn't be noticed.

When he pulled into the airport, Striker had slowed down just before the terminal and parked illegally, forcing the blue Crown Vic that was following him to go well past him before it stopped too. From where the other car was parked, Striker knew the driver would not be able to see any activity around his car. As expected, only one of the men had followed him into the airport. Airports were useful workplaces for anyone operating with a tail on their back because they were crowded and had plenty of pay phones. Striker needed both on this particular day. The package could arrive at his car unnoticed, and his phone call could be made without a trace.

It hadn't been long after the visit from Dick Simmons that Striker first noticed his two shadows, a pair of blond-headed farm boys in suits. There were four of them actually, but he only saw two at a time. He knew they were taking twelve-hour shifts. They weren't half bad at what they were doing, and Striker figured it would have taken him even longer to notice them if he hadn't known they were coming. That was the way it always was. Once you knew they were there it seemed obvious. It was like one of those optical illusions.

When Striker got back to his car, he got in without a glance in either direction. As he sat down he saw that his package had arrived. It was under a blanket in the backseat. Striker took the recorder out of his briefcase as well as a notebook computer. He connected a cable between the two before turning them on and starting up a program that would allow him to read the voice he'd recorded on the phone. The program allowed him to match that voice to the one he knew belonged to the general. This exchange was almost as dangerous as the first. If someone inside one of the agencies was wise to his operation, they could have certainly allowed the first pit to be delivered without much concern. They might have done so to track its final destination. Three kilograms of plutonium was an expensive paperweight. Two pits, six kilograms, was an entirely different story. Two pits was enough material for a bomb. His clients wanted three pits. He tried to explain that two were sufficient, but the contract called for ten kilograms of weapons-grade plutonium for twelve million dollars. For that kind of money, Striker wasn't arguing.

Even if the general wasn't double-crossing him, someone could certainly be following him without his knowing it. The voice ID assured Striker that it was in fact the general who was waiting at the hotel. Technology allowed him to be certain of this without saying a single word over the phone. That would be foolish on his part. Anyone who had worked for or within the intelligence community knew that talking on the telephone was tantamount to skywriting. People were watching and listening all the time. He started the car and worked his way to Route 35, heading south to the city.

When he got to within sight of downtown, Striker sped up to eighty miles an hour. He had to weave through the afternoon highway traffic to maintain that speed.

"My God! What are you doing?"

The muffled voice came from the floor of the backseat.

"Relax," Striker said. It was a bad sign that she'd said a word. He wanted to see how well she could follow instructions. They'd have to have a talk about it later.

The windows of his silver BMW 740i were tinted, but there was no sense in taking more chances than were necessary. Even the slight shadow of another form would tip off a careful observer. The people behind him were extremely careful; they were professionals and might notice something as simple as the movement of his lips as he spoke to her. That's why he'd instructed Jenny to stay down and keep quiet. In the rearview mirror, Striker could see the Crown Vic sedan doing its best to keep up. This would be the last time Striker could be certain he was losing them until he checked out of the country for a final time. After this stunt, they would take the whole thing much more seriously. Garbosky would have kittens if he found out they'd lost him. Mr. Moss would return by tomorrow and carry on with his routine as though nothing untoward had happened. If he did, and if he didn't pull something like this again, those men would wonder to themselves if he'd lost them on purpose or if it had just been a coincidence. Striker couldn't shake them again without setting off all kinds of alarms, which would include border and airport alerts. The next time he shook them out on the open road like this, he'd make sure it was when he wouldn't have to worry about coming back.

Just past a bend in the road he decelerated quickly and skipped across two lanes to an exit in a mayhem of horns and screeching tires. At the bottom of the ramp, Striker took a sharp left and darted back underneath the highway, quickly losing himself in the city streets and then working his way back north and east until he hit Route 183. This would take them to the heart of Texas, where they would then head north to Big Spring.

Striker had originally planned to let Jenny get out from under her blanket as soon as he'd cleared the city limits. After her failure to obey his directive, he decided he'd let her sit until they hit Brownwood, halfway to Big Spring. But by the time they reached Lampasas, he missed her too much to keep her back there any longer, so he reached back and uncovered her. He made a mental note of the fact that he was being soft. He'd have to make sure that this was the exception rather than the rule, or he'd get one or both of them killed.

"Come on up," he said.

"I know why you kept me back there," she said. Her long black hair was pulled tightly back in a clip, and she wore a simple white blouse with a pair of jeans and sneakers. She took the big outdated sunglasses that he'd insisted she wear from her face and looked over at him seriously.

Striker said nothing. He just looked straight ahead and continued to drive. There was a heavy bank of clouds moving in from the west, and as the sun set between them it looked as if they were headed into the mouth of a red-hot furnace. Beauty of this kind was never lost on Striker.

"I know what I did," she said. "I talked. You told me not to. I don't have to learn things twice. I'm sorry."

Striker was surprised, not at her being sorry or even at her saying it. He was surprised that she'd stayed back there so quietly even after she'd figured the whole thing out. It was a good sign. Striker wouldn't have to say another thing. It was important that she learn quickly, and she had. Striker didn't have time to train her the way he would have liked. They could only talk. Everything was theory. But she was a brilliant student. Once Striker had made the decision to include her, and once she'd accepted, she had eagerly sucked the knowledge from him like it was the last bit of milkshake in a straw.

Striker recruited her much in the same way he'd recruited so many other agents for the agency through the years. Jenny was a textbook case of a frustrated woman with high intelligence and low achievement. She was fascinated and titillated with the whole idea of espionage. At first he told her nothing more than that he was an arms dealer. She liked that. She liked the way he threw money around. She liked his taste for fine things. She liked his looks, his body, even his age. Most of all, though, he sensed she liked the mystique of what it was he did for a living. He fed her desire for intrigue over the early months of the summer, dropping hints and making innuendoes that he had some connection to the CIA. Another part of his plan was to subtly encourage her to continue to live with her husband.

Staying home served two purposes. First, he needed her to establish the pattern of a mistress. It had to be regular, nothing spectacular. He knew the goons in the Crown Vic would be watching, and he didn't need them thinking she was anything more than just another wife he'd decided to tag. The second reason was to keep Jenny off balance as far as what she could expect from him in the future. He knew she was a careful woman who wouldn't jump one ship until another better and more secure opportunity presented itself. He wanted her at home until he was ready to leave the country, whether it was with her or without her. Although his initial plan had been to dispose of her, Striker had grown quite attached to Jenny. He was almost certain that he would bring her with him when he disappeared for good, but it wouldn't do anyone any good to let her know that now, not yet. It was too early in the game.

Striker carefully built a world of excitement and intrigue for Jenny Grey. In a way it was the movie set she'd always dreamed of, and she was the star. The only difference was that this was real, and the stakes were higher. Striker originally had no intention whatsoever of involving another soul in the enterprise that would pave his way to a life of total freedom and luxury. After what he had to give the general, there were nine million tax-free dollars for him in this deal. He hadn't wanted to share it with anyone. More importantly, he hadn't wanted to leave any trace of himself for anyone to follow him and ultimately indict him. That was why he'd killed Peter months ago in the wilderness outside Amarillo. But necessity now demanded that he use someone else. With Garbosky's men on top of him, he needed a partner. None could be better than an intelligent, beautiful, and highly motivated woman with no connections to the intelligence community, who at the same time wanted to keep things as quiet as she could to preserve her marriage in case of an emergency. And she had simply walked into his life. She was perfect, and he could solve the problem of leaving a trail by taking her with him. If she wouldn't go for some reason or he changed his mind, well, of course that would be a shame.

Jenny leaned over without a word and kissed him long and hard on the mouth. Striker allowed himself a smile.

"Hungry?" he said with a wicked grin.

"Always," she answered.

Joe Thurwood was working late in downtown Austin. He walked down one of the side streets just off the university campus toward an old run-down apartment house. He wore a pair of old Wrangler jeans, tennis shoes, a shabby, gray hooded sweatshirt, and a St. Louis Cardinals baseball cap. He looked like an overweight garbage collector. He felt naked without his pistol; Joe had carried a gun since he first came to the great state of Texas to join the Outlaws. Gleason, however, had insisted that he leave his piece at home or in his car until the proceedings were over.

"That's the last thing we need," Gleason had told him, "for you to be picked up somewhere with a gun on you. I'm telling you, Joe, don't even cross the street without making sure the light is green until this thing is over. I know this is Texas, but it won't fit your new image if one of the kids at the Y sees a gun sticking out of your pants and tells someone."

There was no one else on the street. Joe had taken a job as the heavy for a small-time drug dealer near the university. It was nothing glamorous, but nothing dangerous either. He basically had to scare the shit out of wise-ass college students who thought they were smart enough to be able to fuck around with their supplier. His boss dealt almost exclusively in marijuana. The big time stuff, cocaine and heroin, were handled by the really bad people who drove around in big cars and wore dark suits.

Even though Joe's boss was a twenty-six-year-old long-haired freak, he was a pretty competent motherfucker. At least that was how Joe described him, and he paid his employees in cash. Joe needed that. He wanted to look poor. He planned on sucking enough cash out of his bitch ex-wife's bank accounts so that she'd never forget he was right there breathing down her neck.

That was his goal now, to remind her, to punish her. She had fucked him over worse than he could ever have dreamed anyone would. He had provided for her since the moment they met, and her fashion of repayment was to humiliate him publicly and rob him of the equity he rightly deserved, a piece of her legal practice. But that was then. This was now. She caught him the first time around in a state of weakness, when he was so fucked up on drugs and booze that he didn't know if he was coming or going, let alone who should represent him against his wife.

Joe thought about how his attorney had fucked him over. It was two years ago. He wondered who had fucked him worse, his ex-wife, his ex-attorney, or his ex-team who had cut him to save money in the final years of his career. Now he knew better about the attorney end of it, though. He knew that when you hired an attorney, it wasn't something that you fucked around with. You got the best and went from there. It was like a doctor. You didn't just go out and get any swinging dick with an M.D. to remove your gall bladder; you got an expert who took those little bastards out three times a week and never got sued for doing it wrong. Same thing with lawyers. Joe knew that now. Just like a bad doctor could fuck up your life, a bad lawyer could fuck it up too, only twice as bad. If a bad doctor fucked you up, chances are that you'd die. If a bad lawyer fucked you up, chances are you'd have to live with the shitty consequences for years to come. That was exactly what had happened to him.

Fortunately, the way the legal system was these days, nothing meant anything anymore. Criminals got parole. Death-row scum bags lived for ten years off the fat of the land. People sued people for sneezing in the wrong direction. Every decision ever made was appealed and re-appealed and then sometimes repealed altogether. Laws got bent so bad, no one knew what the damn things really meant anymore. Winners could be the losers and losers half the time were the winners. It was the perfect system for a guy like Big Joe, who was willing to lie and cheat, all the while feigning choirboy sincerity. It was a system that would bind him to Madison McCall for the rest of her bitchy life.

Joe got to his destination and walked in through the front door. The light was low and yellow. The traffic patterns in the hallway had worn the wood floor to a dirty gray. When he got to the last door on the right, he knocked. It got quiet inside where he'd just heard noise from a TV and some talking. He knocked again, pretty loud this time, and put his thumb over the peephole in the door. The light leaking from the crack under the door went out. There was some scuffling around on the other side of the door, and Joe thought he heard a window bang open. He spun around and headed for the front door.

By the time he got around to the alleyway, the two kids from inside already had their feet on the ground. Joe yelled at them to stop. They took one look at him and ran. It was the wrong decision. Joe could run, even though it hurt him. And a football player hurting would only get madder and be more determined to hurt back. Joe grimaced at the pain in his joints and back as he shot down the street after the kids. Even worn-down and overweight, he still had enough speed to make most people's mouths drop. The college kids not only made the mistake of running, they made the mistake of running down some dark alley that led between a couple of old abandoned houses.

When Joe got within about six feet, he launched his bulk toward the backs of the two kids' legs, twisting their ankles and knocking them over. They went down like pins. Joe popped up with the quick feet of a wrestler. As the two students started to rise, Joe grabbed each by a handful of hair and smashed their heads together like coconuts. He then proceeded to kick the stuffing out of them, stopping only to grind his feet on their ankles and knees while they screamed in pain like little pigs caught in a gate. He wanted to make sure they felt even worse than he would tomorrow morning. That was a rule he'd learned in sports long ago. Win, lose, or draw, you always made sure you did more physical damage to your opponent than he did to you.

When they started to bleed, Joe slowed down. When they lay still, he hiked his pants back up onto his gut and ambled away. When he got to the street, he checked both ways and wiped his brow with his hat while he ran his other hand through his long locks of hair, pushing them out of his face. When he got himself under a street light, he glanced at his watch. It was 2:17 A.M.

He cursed. He had to be at the Y for the little brats by ten. The day this thing with Madison was over, he planned on telling them all exactly what he thought of them, a bunch of screaming little low-life bastards who'd never amount to a pile of shit. On his way up the street, Joe spotted a pay phone he'd seen on his way to the little grass-brains' apartment. He stopped and fished around in his pocket for a quarter.

The phone rang seven times before someone picked it up.

"Hello," came a sleepy and bewildered voice. "Hello? Hello?"

Joe stuffed the back of his enormous hand into his mouth to squelch a giddy laugh. He listened while she got worked up into a real panic, then he hung up the phone and allowed the mirthful sound of a fat man laughing to bubble out of his chest. One thing that had always annoyed him about his wife was how upset she got over a little late-night crank phone call. He never imagined he'd be able to get such a charge out of it.

CHAPTER TEN

THE GENERAL DIDN'T SLEEP WELL AT ALL. Even the darkness did nothing to assuage the heat. By 3:00 A.M. he gave up all hope of any meaningful rest. He showered, shaved, and dressed for the day, then flipped on the light next to the bed and sat on his doughnut to read Tom Clancy's *Patriot Games*. He liked spy novels lately. He fancied himself something of a spy, even though he was more of a thief. After a couple of chapters, the general stood up and walked over to the window to gaze out from behind the curtain at the rising sun. There was nothing remarkable about it at all. The sun just came up with a blinding white light. There were no beautiful colors, no fanfare. The general stood there, alone in his little rattrap, ramrod straight, chin held high. He knew life was nothing like a novel. Novels took the skirmishes and the battles and the love scenes out of life, and lumped them together for the reader to enjoy. Real life was filled much more with little insignificant moments like this, where it seemed like you had to wait forever for what you wanted, and the sunrise was nothing more than someone turning on the lights. Much of life was so boring and so bewildering to the general that he wondered if people wouldn't all be better off if they lived in caves the way they had thousands of years ago, when their time was spent worrying about things as simple as how they were going to eat or stay warm through the winter.

People in caves was an interesting notion. Maybe what he was doing would somehow lead to that. It was possible. He had no idea exactly who was going to end up with the plutonium he was stealing. He imagined it would end up in the hands of some third-world lunatic, or more likely with some fundamentalist madmen who would unleash it on millions of people in the name of God. One thing was certain, both the United States and the former Soviet Union had too much of this stuff floating around to keep it out of other people's hands for long. He was simply ahead of the curve, and because he was, he had to cash in.

The plutonium was the hard part. Unless you could get it raw like what he was selling, you had to go through a lot of trouble to make it, and people would know. There were satellites everywhere. But the real stuff, weapons-grade PU 239, could be hidden in a suitcase and sent anywhere, undetected. Missiles could now be purchased from China by almost anyone. It was certainly conceivable that once the plutonium started to leak out of Russia, a number of radical organizations around the globe would be fully armed with nuclear weapons. People liked to nay-say this. Of course they did. No one had wanted to believe that Imperial Japan would attack the United States in the 1940s. No one had wanted to believe that Hitler would take Poland. The world, especially Americans, were always burying their heads in the sand until confronted with disaster face to face.

Striker's thoughts on disaster were interrupted by a silver BMW pulling into sight on the road. The car slowed down and turned off of the highway into the motel parking lot, pulling up next to the general's Jeep. Striker got out with a woman. Both were wearing small, round black sunglasses and were dressed in jeans and cowboy boots. The general ran his hand through the stubble of hair on top of his head and straightened his shirt. He let the curtain drop but continued to watch through a crack as they approached the door. The woman was radiantly beautiful. Striker didn't knock, he simply stood at the door waiting, as if he knew the general was watching. The general tucked the inflatable cushion into his duffel bag on the floor, then opened the door and let them in.

"General," Striker said amiably, as though they were meeting for drinks at some neighborhood bar. He held a briefcase in his left hand.

The general nodded and fought to keep his eyes from crawling all over the woman.

"This is my associate," Striker said. "You can call her Lucy."

The general snorted at this. "I hope you're not planning on leaving her in the same state as your last friend."

Striker pulled the glasses from his face with one swift motion and gave the general a furtive wink. "Not yet. I wanted you to meet Lucy because she will be making the final exchange for me."

The general considered this information for a moment. Any deviation from the original plan was fundamentally against his nature. He liked things to be done by the book, as planned. Of course it meant something that Striker was changing things. The general stared coldly at his partner. Was Striker in some kind of trouble, or was he simply planning to use the girl as bait, waiting in the wings for a chance to kill him and make off with the last pit without paying him the final two million? Anything was possible. He would have to be cautious the next time.

"You said you didn't like surprises, Striker," the general said. "Neither do I."

"This is my operation, general," Striker said coldly. "I'm paying the bills. I make the rules."

"I'm sure you're not paying this bill on your own, Striker. I'm sure you're getting a lot of money for this deal, a hell of a lot more than I am."

"General," Striker said flatly, "I took a great risk coming here now because I knew you'd be put out by the littlest bump in the road. You never were one for adjusting. That's why I came this time. I won't be here the next, but my commitment to our contract being fully carried out remains the same."

"I think changing the format must be worth something," the general continued. "I think I'd like to see another million in that little briefcase of yours next time, Striker. I figure your take on this must be somewhere around ten million. I think you can afford more than what you're giving me—"

"I'm not going to change the terms of the deal," Striker said in disgust. "You know that."

Striker put his case on the bed and popped it open as if nothing had happened. The sight of all that money was enough to draw the general's complaints to a close. He was glad Striker hadn't bargained with him. It would have meant Striker was planning to double-cross him. He knew Striker didn't renegotiate anything.

The general went to the other side of the bed and pulled his metallic case from the floor. He kept its replacement in the back of his Jeep. He put the case on the bed next to money, and carefully turned the tumblers until it clicked open. Striker lifted the pit from its resting place and held it up for the girl to see. She took off her glasses, and the general sucked some of the stuffy air in through his teeth. Her eyes were like blue ice.

"Very good," Striker said, replacing the pit and shutting the case. "As always, I will await your call to my office. Next time you will say your name is Ken Frost. My secretary will take a message. Leave your number but add one to the first six digits and subtract one from the last four. When I get your call, I will call that number—a pay phone, remember—exactly twenty-four hours from when you made it. I will then give you the place and time. You will meet Lucy and make the final delivery. She will give you two millions dollars in cash.

"I am going through these little details, general," Striker explained, "because this is not your line of work, despite your years in the army. I'm reminding you because it is always when an operation is within minutes of completion that even the best and smartest people seem to lapse into a false sense of security. There can be no mistakes, general. We both know the consequences."

The general didn't like receiving instructions. He was too used to giving them. He took the case of money off the bed and picked his duffel bag up off the floor as if he hadn't been paying all that much attention.

"Striker," he said, "you're a legend in your own mind."

Striker smiled.

"Thank you," he said.

Jenny and Striker sat in their car and watched the general pull out onto the highway.

Unable to contain herself any longer, Jenny said, "That guy's a creep," then looked over at Striker for his response.

Striker looked at her in a sad, fatherly sort of way, the way he sometimes did when he took on the role as her instructor.

"I'm glad you feel that way," he said.

"Why are you glad?"

"Because it will help you feel more comfortable with the idea that we're going to kill him."

Jenny laughed. Striker would say things sometimes just to get her to react.

"Okay, fine," she said.

Striker started the car and pulled out onto the highway, heading in the opposite direction. They sat for a while in silence. Jenny could handle silence. It seemed the men in her life had always been silent. She wondered if that was her choosing, or just fate. The big difference between Striker and Cody was that from time to time a torrent of emotion would burst like a dam from Striker, while Cody would let it out in nothing more than a trickle, only enough run-off to keep the pressure from bursting through.

Jenny didn't want to think about Cody and Striker though. She didn't like uncertainty, and her love life was nothing but uncertain. She liked the way Striker lived. She liked him. And he was rich. She could see that.

The problem with Striker was that for all his gallantry, for all his tender caresses, he had yet to talk about a future together. When it did come up, Striker made vague suggestions about what they would do and the things they would see, but as to any concrete plans, he was evasive. Jenny felt Striker couldn't be trusted. She couldn't put her finger on it exactly, but something told her Striker was never completely candid. She suspected that was so because of the kind of business he was involved in. Not that it mattered; she was ready to leave Cody. But Striker made it clear that even though she was growing to despise the very sight of her husband, it was important for this operation that she stay with him. When the plan was complete, whatever happened with Striker, Jenny made it clear that she was leaving. Striker had promised her a lot of money if everything went smoothly and she did her part. With a half million dollars, she could start over again almost anywhere. She'd go with Striker if he asked her, but she hadn't said as much to him. She knew better than to put all her cards out on the table for him to see. For all their intimacy, she and Striker were like two knife fighters, circling each other carefully, testing each other's strengths, weaknesses, and tendencies; mixing dodges and feints with real thrusts and parries. If she ended up with Striker, it would be because he asked her, not because she had manipulated him into taking her.

"I'm serious about the general," Striker said from out of nowhere, and she knew he was. "You have to understand that a man like the general will come back to bite you."

Jenny thought about this for a moment and wondered if it would bother Striker to kill her.

"What was the general saying to you about your last friend?" she asked.

"I killed him, for the same reason I have to kill the general," Striker said with the casual manner of a Federal Express man talking about the packages he delivered. "It would be foolish to go through all this only to leave a trail for people to follow. They would find us, and we would be killed or jailed. That's not acceptable."

"You said 'us,'" Jenny pointed out.

"Yes, I did, didn't I?" he said with a pleasant smile. But this was a discussion he wanted to have at a later time. That was a hook he was saving.

"Would you please reach into the back and take... There's a manila envelope in the side pocket of my bag," Striker said, motioning behind him and changing the subject completely.

Jenny did as she was told. The envelope was made of a heavy-grade paper, and it was fat with something. She held it out to him.

"Open it," he said, "it's yours."

Jenny straightened the tabs that held the envelope shut and reached in to find five thick packets of hundred dollar bills.

"It's your cut for this part of the operation," Striker said. "It's a hundred thousand dollars. You'll get more as you do more. It's simple market economics: the higher the risk, the greater the profit. We're partners."

This was a perfect example of what Jenny had just been thinking about. Just when the conversation took a turn toward their future, Striker muddied the waters. But a hundred thousand dollars in cash was one hell of a way to do it. The inky feel and smell of the freshly printed bills was intoxicating. Jenny liked the idea of money that was hers, money that no one could take from her or make her feel she hadn't earned. Cody never talked like that to her, but she knew he thought it. She knew he resented the way she spent their money. She knew he felt like he earned it and she did nothing but spend it. Now she was earning it.

"Don't spend it all in one place," Striker said. "I mean, you can go shopping for some clothes or something like that, but don't go out and buy a new car or anything enormous. This is the kind of money you can only spend a little at a time. You don't want to draw attention to yourself. Just put it somewhere safe where no one will find it."

"Jenny," he said, taking her hand and bringing it to his lips in a reassuring way, "I'm going to teach you how to survive. I will never hurt you."

Jenny tucked the envelope under her knees and rested her head against the leather seat. Striker opened the sunroof and all the windows. He punched up music from the Cars, and the heavy beat pounded through the hair-whipping breeze. Outside, the flat Texas landscape raced by in a hundred-mile-an-hour blur. Jenny smiled. She didn't know exactly what was going to happen, but that was okay. She knew the whole thing was just like a movie.

Cody watched in a daze as the first team defense jogged out onto the field. They broke the huddle and Derell Biggs took his position in the middle of the field, exactly where he was supposed to be. Cody cursed under his breath. The guy wasn't stupid, either. He hated to wish someone else ill, but he couldn't help it. He wanted to be on this team. He wasn't ready to end it now. He wasn't ready financially or emotionally. He knew he could still play in this league.

The offense lined up, and Cody watched in silence as the defense adjusted to an unbalanced, three-receiver formation. Biggs rolled over the top of the heavy-receiver side, exactly where he was supposed to be again. The quarterback called out the cadence, then dropped back to pass. The receivers streaked down the field and then split apart like Blue Angel stunt planes, each going in his own direction. Biggs locked on to the deepest man and opened up his stride into a full sprint. The quarterback lofted a long ball out in front of Biggs and the receiver he was covering. The two strained forward, one to catch the ball, the other to ensure that no one caught it. It was only practice, but in the NFL, players know that careers can be made or lost on any given day in any given practice.

Biggs suddenly crumpled into a heap and tumbled along in the grass until his inertia was spent. The younger player clutched at the back of his leg, and Cody knew in an instant that Biggs had blown out his hamstring. Cody tried not to get too excited, but it was hard. A hamstring could be four weeks, or it could be eight. It could be twelve, or it could even end a career. They were tricky things that sometimes never healed correctly or at all. It was like super gluing something back together; you always know the crack is there, and sooner or later it's going to break in the same place again. The trainers ran out onto the field with the urgency of a 911 call. When a high-paid free agent went down, even the trainers knew they better get there fast. If a rookie free agent were to drop, or a minimum-salary veteran, they would probably take their time.

Cody looked nervously from Dryer, the head coach, to a second-year kid named Jon Wesley. Wesley was Cody's backup last season. He was a young free safety out of Baylor. The kid had some ability. He liked to hit, and his speed wasn't half bad. The problem with Wesley was that he tended to screw things up. About one out of every five plays, Wesley would do the wrong thing. On the defensive line, a screwup meant the other team got a five-yard run instead of a two-yard run, and it usually gave the other team a touchdown. There was a big difference. Cody knew that there was great significance in whomever they called out to replace the downed Biggs. If they called Wesley, it would mean they felt the kid could be ready to fill in this season behind Biggs. If they didn't feel confident that they could put the kid out there in a game under fire, they would opt for Cody. Even though they feared he would be physically limited because of his knee, they could count on him to be in the right place at the right time. With Biggs's bad hamstring, even though most people wouldn't even realize it, it was a critical decision for the team.

"Cody!" the coach yelled suddenly. "Take it."

Cody didn't waste a second; he didn't want anyone to change their mind. All he knew was that he was home again. He could barely contain his enthusiasm. When the huddle broke and he was walking toward his position, he fantasized to himself that the whole thing had merely been a ploy to help rejuvenate him, like when you bought a young puppy to pep up the old dog. That was wishful thinking. The fact was that he had been marked as expendable. He was going to be replaced. But now, if Biggs's injury was worth anything at all, the last laugh would be his. That was football, it was a tough way to make a living.

Adam Garbosky sat in his corner office overlooking the wooded hills surrounding Langley. Garbosky was a short man with a nasty streak, the perfect governmental bureaucrat. He had waited for years and given everything he had to give to be sitting in just such an office in the headquarters of the CIA. It was his lifelong dream, and now he had it. He had his own directorate. The second youngest deputy director the agency had ever known. The first was a computer genius named Stuart Lisson. But Lisson was involved in the technological side of things. Garbosky operated people. He was the spy master.

Part of being the master, though, was cleaning the cluttered house left behind by his predecessors. He didn't need the scum and the riffraff that had accumulated in the agency since the early sixties. He envisioned an exclusive club, not unlike the Ivy League fraternities from his college days at Yale. Garbosky envisioned an agency of gentlemen, people who were not only competent, but who had integrity. It would be his legacy to the CIA. If the current president could hold on for a second term, his sweeping changes in one of the biggest black eyes of the American government could earn him a chance to become director of the entire agency. Anything was possible with work. Garbosky believed that. Luck was a ridiculous notion. He knew for a fact that he had worked very hard and that he deserved every good thing he had. There were no coincidences in his life.

He looked at his gold Rolex and buzzed his secretary.

"Send Teitelbaum in," he said.

Bruce Teitelbaum was one of the most seasoned veterans that the agency had. Teitelbaum was in his early fifties. He had salt-and-pepper hair that was cut close. He wore the typical gray two-piece suit. Garbosky knew Teitelbaum wasn't happy with his present assignment, but that didn't matter. In fact it was a testament to the man's professionalism. He was covering the man people called Striker like white on rice.

Teitelbaum walked in and sat down without bothering to shake hands. Garbosky didn't mind. In fact, if Teitelbaum had made some perfunctory gesture, Garbosky would have been disappointed.

"So," Garbosky began, "how is my friend Bill Moss, aka Striker?"

Teitelbaum gave him the disgusted look of a man who was being forced to waste his time.

"I've got four good men on him," Teitelbaum said. "They lost him once, but it was for less than twenty-four hours, so we know he didn't leave the country, unless you count driving across the border to buy some hash in Mexico, but you know what I mean.

"Anyway, it seems to have been nothing more than a slight error by my men. Since you've made it hard for him to do deals, he's not traveling. He has a predictable pattern. He goes to work every day from nine to five. On weekends, he exercises and does other recreational sports around the immediate area. That includes his favorite pastime, which of course is sport fucking. In fact the only thing worthy of mention in his otherwise very routine life is that he's poking the wife of one of the Outlaws players, Jenny Grey. Her husband is Cody Grey, a defensive back for the team. She shows up every so often and cleans his pipes. She's very attractive by the way. Is that what you were looking for?"

Teitelbaum stopped here. Garbosky turned red. He didn't know whether to be angry or embarrassed. He didn't know if Teitelbaum was blatantly referring to his own wife's affair with Striker or just making some innocuous locker-room joke. Teitelbaum's face was no help, it was emotionless. Garbosky said nothing.

"I've had my best man look into his books," Teitelbaum continued with a sigh. "There's nothing there. Striker has been living on an income of about three hundred thousand dollars a year, but he hasn't hidden that fact, either. Dick Simmons approved every cent of it, and I can't say as I really blame him. Striker has made millions for the agency over the past seven years, highly unusual as you know. Most front corporations lose money in at least their first few years, and most stay that way forever."

"Bruce, the man is an arms dealer," Garbosky reminded him. "He has all our contacts, internationally and within the Pentagon. It's really no secret as to why he's been successful."

"I'm not saying there is. I'm just saying that he has been successful, and that he apparently hasn't dipped into the till. I'll be honest with you, I don't like having to use four good men full-time to keep tabs on him and another to analyze all his phone calls. It's getting expensive."

"You said, 'apparently,'" Garbosky said, ignoring what Teitelbaum said. "That suggests that there could be some improprieties?"

"Sir," Teitelbaum said, "with all due respect, this is a huge fishing expedition, isn't it?"

Garbosky put his hands flat down on the surface of his desk and leaned forward.

"Yes, Bruce. It is a fishing expedition. But Striker is a bad man. He's bad, and when you're bad, you always make a mistake somewhere. It's always been that way. We're fishing, yes, but in a pond that has been stocked for years, and no one else has ever bothered to throw in their line."

Teitelbaum nodded with resignation, then said, "Well, I'll keep those men on it. If anything unusual happens, you'll be the first to know."

Jeff Board battled his way through five screens of Mercs before getting squashed by an armored tank that disgorged enemy soldiers at an overwhelming rate. He took a big slurp of Diet Coke from the dripping thirty-two-ounce cup he'd balanced on top of the video machine and began to dig for another quarter. He found one but noticed his watch. It was just past two-thirty in the afternoon. He should be getting back to the office. The thought made him purse his lips and frown.

"Shit," he mumbled to himself.

He was tired of doing what he was doing. He'd been at his list of athletes for months. The trouble was that almost every one of them relied completely on some accountant or tax lawyer to do their returns. The damn things were spotless. After the initial fervor for targeting sports stars, Board was beginning to lose interest. Like most things Board started in life, the idea was a hell of a lot more exciting than the actual work. He'd sent out his notices and talked tough to a few accountants, but the bottom line was that his job entailed thousands of thankless hours poring over documents, trying to find errors in the math. So far, the only errors he'd found were his own.

By the time he got back to his desk it was just after three. He looked at the pile of papers cluttering the surface in front of him and let out a heavy sigh. He picked up the Cody Grey file and sat back in his chair to go through it for a second time. He hated Cody Grey. Grey was everything he reviled in athletes. He was vicious on and off the field, and he was continuously using his celebrity status to get out of the jams his hotheaded temper got him into. His self-satisfied mug was always on the local television doing commercials for everything from pizza joints to car dealerships.

Board had even seen Grey and his wife in person from time to time, strutting around Sixth Street like they owned the place. Grey was a drunk, he knew that. Every time he'd seen the player, he was staggering around, rudely bumping into people and eyeing the world with a suspicious scowl. If Board could put just one professional athlete in his place, Grey would be his first choice. If he could only get something on a guy like Cody Grey, he could make a name for himself within the office, even around town. He liked the idea of taking out the man whom so many people around town feared and revered. Board knew that no one was very tough when the IRS came knocking at the door.

"Hey, Jeff."

It was Loreen, the office director's assistant. Board instinctively ran his fingers through the stringy locks of hair that hung limply to his collar from the back of his head. There wasn't much up front to run through.

"Boss wants to see you in her office."

Board felt all thirty-two ounces of his soft drink start to churn in his stomach. Someone must have ratted on his long lunch.

"Coming," he said, shuffling the papers in the Grey file as though he'd been doing some hard-core analysis.

Board followed Loreen through the maze of cubicles to the director's office. He hitched his pants and tucked in his shirt as he went. There was a mustard stain on the front of his shirt, and he almost went back for his jacket but decided against it. Despite his concern for the summons, he took advantage of his position to enjoy the nice view of Loreen's ass. She was a little old, but Board would jump on her if he had the chance. He thought the possibility wasn't out of the realm of reason. He thought he was a pretty good-looking guy.

"Okay, Loreen, thanks," he said, veering off into Patti's office.

Loreen didn't give him a second look.

"Jeff," Patti said without looking up from her desk, "sit down."

Board licked his lips and sat. His boss's office reeked from cigarette smoke. His mouth was dry, and there seemed to be no way to clear the smell of old

Marlboro Lights that was filling his nasal cavity. He rubbed his nose a bit, cleared his throat with a rasp, and fidgeted nervously with his tie, waiting for the onslaught. Patti finally looked up and took off her glasses.

"Got anything for me, Jeff?" she said as she took a long drag off her cigarette.

"Not yet," he said with great discomfort. "These guys are pretty slick, but I'm hammering away."

Patti blew out more of the foul air and gave him a false smile. She tossed a folded newspaper at him.

"Did you see this?"

"What is it?" Board felt somewhat relieved. If lunch was the issue, it would have been broached by now.

"It's the *Wall Street Journal*," Patti said with another puff. "Look at the article about Darryl Strawberry. Read it."

Board read. As he did, his mouth slowly opened until he was forced to suck some drool from the corner of his mouth to keep it from spilling onto the page.

"Wow," he said. "We could look into this."

Patti looked at him and wondered how it was that with dead-weight like Board she got the kind of results she did out of her office.

"I don't think looking into it is the right term, Jeff," she said, losing patience. "I think you better start digging and digging hard. You begged for this assignment, but you haven't come up with anything so far, and it's been three months. I'm not happy. This is the kind of thing you need to be on top of. You should be the one showing me this article, not the other way around."

"Well, I—I probably would have gotten to it," he said.

"Yeah, well, it's last week's paper," Patti said flatly. "Anyway, do you want me to get someone to give you some help with this? I don't want it blown. When the public sees us putting the squeeze on a high-profile athlete, it's good for business. They know that no one is above the law. They know we're doing our job."

"I was just thinking that, Patti," Board said enthusiastically. "I was just thinking about how these guys think they're above everyone else. You're absolutely right."

Patti twisted her mouth in doubt. She crushed out her cigarette in the mound of gray ash that filled her ashtray.

"I've heard you say that before," she said sarcastically. "Get me something on this. If a guy like Strawberry was getting hundreds of thousands from card companies, and no one was reporting it on either side, you can bet there are plenty of five- or ten-thousand-dollar gigs out there that went unreported, too."

"I'm on top of it," Board said confidently, as though the whole thing had been his idea.

He returned to his desk with a new purpose. He picked up the Cody Grey file and started to work. He'd start with the bank accounts. He'd get those records and really go at it. He'd find something. He had a feeling about this. It was fate.

CHAPTER ELEVEN

"WHAT DO YOU MEAN, IT'S NOT GOING THROUGH?" Striker said angrily into the phone. He was talking with General Lamont Parker at the Pentagon. Parker was putting a hold on the delivery of ten thousand army surplus World War II grenades that Striker had arranged to be delivered to Uganda.

"This kind of thing isn't going to be easy anymore, Bill," Parker said. "The word has come from high up that any weapons transactions that have anything to do with the CIA are to be put back through the agency's general inspector before they can happen."

"You said 'high up.' How high?" Striker asked. "I'll give Dick Simmons a call and have him straighten this out."

"It's way up," the general said. "I don't even know how high. Some people think it goes all the way to the president. You know his fetish for taking the 'covert' out of CIA."

Striker wanted to say he bet it didn't go any higher than Garbosky himself and that the president didn't have a thing to worry about with an asshole like that at the helm of covert operations. CIA agents around the world would soon be wearing scarlet letters so that they couldn't even think of doing anything in secret. Only the most autocratic, anal-retentive, narrow-minded asshole could actually head up covert operations and destroy it at the same time. They had the perfect man. Striker kept quiet about that, though. He did, however, bother to rage on to General Parker a little more. He knew they were listening, and anything but a tirade after learning that his life's blood was being cut off would seem peculiar.

When he was done telling the general what a lackey he was and how the whole country was going to the dogs, Striker hung up the phone and allowed himself a grand smile. Garbosky would probably be giggling to himself somewhere at Langley within the week, thinking he had Striker's nuts in a vise, but Striker was a bit of an actor himself. He wished Jenny could have seen his performance. He'd let Garbosky think he was really making his life miserable. That would put everyone at ease. When he was relaxing on some South Sea island in the near future, having his scotch brought to him on the beach, he'd have to send Garbosky a postcard, and, of course, ask how his wife was doing.

Cody pulled into the garage and shut off his engine. Jenny's car was gone. That pissed him off. She knew he was due back from mini-camp this afternoon. The one time he did finally get in touch with her over the phone, he'd told her he wanted to take her to dinner the night he got home. What did she think that meant?

Cody took his bag from the trunk and went inside the house. The alarm wasn't on, and that made Cody think that maybe Jenny had just gone out for a minute to the store. On the kitchen table was a jumble of mail. None of it was opened. That was typical. The damn girl couldn't even go through the mail. He went to the refrigerator and pulled out a beer. He needed to dull his nerves a little. His knee was sore as all hell. He was tired, and his whole body ached. Getting the call when Biggs went down was good, but it had its price. Well, at least he'd have a contract now. It probably wouldn't be much, but it was a job, at least for another season.

Cody sat down at the table with a sigh and cracked open the bottle. There was a lot of junk in the mail: proxies from some of his remaining stock holdings—he never opened them, credit-card applications, and solicitations for magazines and financial services. Then something caught his eye. It was not a regular letter. It had a government seal on the return corner. It was from the IRS. Cody was mildly disturbed. That could never be good news, a letter from the IRS. He opened it and read. He read it again. It made him more nervous. They wanted things from him. The letter wasn't easy to understand. There were form numbers and terms that he hadn't heard of. He picked up the phone and dialed his tax lawyer and agent, Marty Cahn.

After having Cody carefully read the contents of the letter to him, Marty said, "Well, I don't think it's anything to get concerned with right now. We've been doing things the right way. The only thing that bothers me is that we've sent them a lot of this stuff already. Remember the letter we got from them two months ago?"

"Yeah," Cody said, "that's what I was thinking."

"Well," Marty said, "send me a copy of that letter and I'll get right on it.

Don't worry about it. This is my job. Hey, you've got to be pleased with getting some reps in mini-camp. I read about it in the paper. I was going to call you tomorrow."

"Yeah, I don't like to say I'm glad Biggs blew out his ham, but . . . I'm glad."

"How did your knee hold up?" Marty asked.

"You know, all right," Cody said. "I'm on Motrin. I'm looking forward to getting signed so I can get some Butazolidin, something heavy-duty. I think it will help me move a lot better, but I don't want to ask until the contract is signed."

"That's smart. Any word on how long Biggs will be out?" Marty asked.

"Not for sure," Cody replied, "but I think it's pretty safe to say that they won't be using him much in the beginning of training camp."

"Good. Well, I've already got a call in to the front office, so I imagine we'll get you signed up pretty soon."

"Yeah, I just hope they don't use me for a camp body," Cody said, fishing for reassurance.

"They won't do that," Marty said. "I'll tell them not to bother if that's their plan. We could make a hell of a mess for them in the papers if they did that. There is some value in all the fans you've got around this town. People can stomach an old guy getting cut or not re-signed, but taking a hometown favorite and using him as a camp body is outright rotten. I really don't think they'd ever do that."

"I hope not," Cody said. "Hell, if Biggs can't come back, they'll need me."

"I know that," Marty said, "and I'm sure they do, too. Now listen, don't worry about this IRS thing. Just get me the letter."

"Okay," Cody said. "Thanks."

Jenny looked at the clock and stepped on the accelerator. She wanted to be there when Cody got home. Her trip to San Antonio had taken longer than expected. Opening up a bank account wasn't as easy as one, two, three. She changed her mind several times as she sat there in the downtown office of Home Bank, but she had remained. Striker's words about being careful rang out in her ears even now, but she was smart enough to handle herself. For all his instructions over the past few weeks, Striker's paramount message to her had been to rely on your own intelligence and resources. Espionage was like a complicated game where you had to be thinking five moves into the future. She figured that her money, once in a bank, could then be wired to an overseas account. That was real security. Striker would be impressed. She knew that, and she wanted to impress him.

It wasn't that she thought Striker was more intelligent than she. Maybe he was; maybe he wasn't. But surely her lover had a vastness of experience that she could barely comprehend. She respected that experience and his intellect. She wanted to show him that she was no fool, that she had learned his lessons and taken them one step further. Except for fifteen thousand dollars she'd stuck in her bag for spending money and expenses, Jenny had deposited everything in the bank and made arrangements to have it transferred once she established an overseas account. With the money in an Austrian bank, all traces of it would be lost.

While she was in San Antonio, Jenny also hired a lawyer and opened a safe deposit box. She gave a senior partner in one of the city's oldest law firms a ten-thousand-dollar retainer for the next five years. His only job was to make certain he received a phone call or a certified letter from her on the first of each month. If he wasn't contacted by her, there were instructions and a key in her file on how to proceed. Jenny had documented Striker's plan in its every detail, both in writing and on audiocassette. If Striker thought that his message about trusting no one stopped with himself, he was dead wrong.

She'd written out everything she could think of in her manuscript. She imagined there'd be much more she could add in the weeks to come. Already, she knew that Striker could come and go from his apartment without the CIA knowing about it. Because they watched him, and he had established a pattern of coming and going each day that they had come to expect, he would sometimes go out at night when they thought he was asleep. The building was heated during the winter by steam that came from the university's steam plant. The substation was two blocks away, and there was a tile-lined tunnel that ran between the substation and the basement of the high rise. Striker had a key to the steel door that sealed the tunnel, and he could come and go underground as if it were his own front door.

She didn't know exactly where the plutonium was going, but she knew that she would be meeting a man in St. Martin who was a strict Muslim. Striker had told her that she would be wearing a veil. He was teaching her certain rules of behavior for her exchange of the second pit for two million dollars in cash. The man, he'd told her, would be put out because he had to deal with a woman, so it was important she keep in her place. She knew she would be staying at the Oyster Bay Hotel. She had the code words. She had the times.

She had the places. The money would be temporarily stored in a deposit box at the Kroner Bank on the Dutch side of the island. She knew she probably couldn't destroy Striker. No one could do that. But if he crossed her, she wanted to make certain he would feel her sting.

Jenny pulled up tight to some guy who was blocking the passing lane. She leaned on her horn. The guy still didn't move, so she downshifted and shot past him on the shoulder in a swirl of dust and blaring horns. She wanted to be home for Cody. She didn't need any problems from him right now. She had already tested his patience by being gone while he was in mini-camp. In three weeks he would be going to the team's training camp in San Angelo, and she would have the complete freedom she needed to board a plane for St. Martin, where she would deliver the pit. In the meantime she would make life a lot easier by appeasing her husband and making things look as normal as she possibly could. That was another thing she'd learned from Striker. He was fond of telling her that consistency was the ultimate camouflage.

Even though she was still married to Cody, and even though Striker was elusive about their future together, Jenny was beginning to feel an elation she hadn't felt since she'd landed what she thought was her big role in the Western feature several years ago. Now, like then, she was certain that a new and exciting path had been opened in her life. It was an unexpected relief to finally unchain herself from the vicious sycophantic cycle of chasing producers, directors, and casting agents from party to party. It hadn't worked. That was as simple as it was. Once she was presented with an alternative, Jenny finally saw her situation for what it really was: she was a halfway decent actress whom no one was going to take a chance on. She was already thirty-one, without even a B or C movie credit to her name. Like her husband, she was old in her profession.

Her new dream was to live out this incredible odyssey with Striker and then flee to some foreign country like France or Australia. After years of frustration, and lately, stagnation, Jenny Grey was finally back in control of her life. Striker had come along and presented her with the opportunity of a lifetime. The life she had with Cody was quickly fading away. It was simply meant to be.

When she walked into the house, Jenny's cheerful hello was met with a scowl.

"What the hell?" Cody growled.

He'd gotten up from his seat and stood in a menacing way. There were five empty beer bottles on the table, and she had no way of knowing if that was all of it. Jenny was behind the eight ball. She got contrite.

"Cody," she said warmly, wrapping her arms around his neck and kissing him on the lips, "I am so sorry. I thought you said you weren't getting back until after dinner."

"I said I wanted to *take* you to dinner," Cody said, softening a little already because of her meek attitude and caressing hands.

"I missed you, baby," she said in a husky whisper before kissing him passionately on the mouth.

Cody shifted his weight from his bad knee to his good one. Jenny began to lightly grind her hips up against him until she felt him respond. Cody, although by no means an amateur, was crude and rough compared to Striker. Then again, Jenny could think of no man who wasn't when compared to Striker. She got hot just thinking about him. Cody had no idea what she was thinking. He pulled her clothes off and took her there on the kitchen table. When Jenny gave it to him, he didn't bother asking why, where, or when he just took it.

As she lay flat on her back with her buttocks squeaking back and forth on the polished surface of the kitchen table, Jenny stared at the light fixture above her. She thought about many things, none of which had anything to do with the man on top of her. She mouthed out a few obligatory groans and grunts, but her heart was miles away. One of the reasons she didn't really feel all that bad about planning to leave Cody was that he didn't even have a clue that things had gone so wildly wrong. He thought that if he could elicit a few groans from her while he slammed her on the table, then take her out to dinner, that everything would be fine again, just like in high school. He talked about high school sometimes and the way things were. She really couldn't stand it. She was so far from the girl she had been in high school that she didn't even recognize herself sometimes. She was much more sophisticated now. She'd come a long way. That was the problem with Cody. She knew he would be just as happy driving a Yugo to work as a Mercedes. He'd be just as happy eating at Papa's Ribs as he would at the Four Seasons or drinking sweet tea as he would Moët. He talked about coaching high school players one day. High school. It was inconceivable to her, being married to a high school coach. It would be a complete humiliation. But it wouldn't surprise her if that was really what Cody wanted. He had no ambition.

Cody arched his back and thrust one final time. He grasped for the table's edge, and the empty beer bottles crashed to the floor. Two of them broke. Jenny thought about pancake-breakfast fund-raisers, chaperoning Saturday night dances, hot Friday nights outdoors under the stadium lights, and getting excited when his team beat the other team of kids from the town next door. As he pulled out of her, she shuddered beneath him. He didn't notice. That didn't surprise her. The truth was that Cody Grey would probably be just as happy without her.

CHAPTER TWELVE

∨

IT WAS EASILY MADISON'S FINEST MOMENT as a trial attorney. The closing argument she'd given to the jury resulted in a half-hour deliberation before they came back with not-guilty verdicts on every count. Dr. Brayson, the feeble but distinguished octogenarian, had turned to her with tears in his eyes and hugged her with all his might. He told her that he wished his wife could have met her, that she had always had a great appreciation for women of fine character and intelligence. That was the ultimate compliment Madison knew the doctor could pay, that his wife would have loved to meet her. It was the reverence that the man had for his wife, even now that she was dead, that had given Madison that extra surge of emotion in her closing argument as well as throughout the trial.

It was a crushing blow for District Attorney Van Rawlins. The blustery Republican had put a lot of eggs in this conviction basket. He had told everyone, from his religious-right followers to the press, that the doctor would be serving at least some time in jail; it was simply a matter of how much. At the doctor's age, he'd reminded everyone, almost anything would be a life sentence. Even Madison would admit that under the letter of the law it was unusual that the doctor wasn't at least convicted of involuntary manslaughter, reduced from voluntary because of his mental state at the time.

But Madison had been able to do one of those things that is rare in the life of a trial lawyer. She had convinced a jury to nod and wink and give a verdict that flew in the face of the facts. It wasn't that she asked them to disregard the law. Arguing any case on pure emotion was a mistake for rookies. Although she argued the emotional side of this case with overwhelming fervor, she also gave the jury just a sliver of rational possibility with which to hang their verdict on. First, she argued that there was no murder weapon. She had successfully excluded the needle because the police had procured it without a warrant. More importantly, though, Madison argued that in fact it was entirely possible that Mrs. Brayson had died not as a result of a massive morphine injection but from natural causes, and that the morphine injection her husband had allegedly given her might have only been the fruitless act of love performed on the corpse of his already dead wife.

Madison took great care to explain to the jury that even where there exists the malicious intent to kill someone in cold blood, if that victim is already dead, there can be no murder. It was a remote principle that Madison remembered from a case in law school where a burglary suspect shot a policeman his accomplice had already killed. The second gunman was acquitted based on the same principle: you can't murder a corpse. Madison had paraded expert after expert across the stand, each one admitting that, in theory, the doctor's wife could have already been dead.

Even the god-inspired nurse who had caused the ruckus had begrudgingly admitted on the stand that she could not be entirely certain when the wife died because her monitors weren't being watched when the doctor locked himself in the room with her. No one got back to the monitors until a full thirty minutes later, so no one could say for certain what had caused the wife's death. Madison coupled this with the "beyond a reasonable doubt" standard. This gave the jury all they needed. They freed the doctor to live out the rest of his sad life in relative peace.

Madison held a press conference and answered all the questions with as much humility as she could muster. As she wrapped it up, she wondered if her father would see her in her moment of glory on CNN. She knew he would be proud. She'd have to remember to call her mother and tell them to turn it on. When the last camera light had finally been extinguished, Madison left through the back door and walked down a long marble corridor to the judge's chambers. Walter Connack's chambers were everything Iris DuBose's weren't, right down to the smell of the old leather-bound tomes that filled the towering shelves.

"Congratulations, counselor," the judge said in his booming, baritone voice, holding out a thick, flat hand for her to shake.

The judge was an enormous man with heavy jowls and rolls of skin at the back of his neck like a basset hound. Besides being one of the few people Madison had ever seen who had to stoop to get through a normal doorway, he was the most senior and most respected judge in Travis County. His closely cropped Afro was almost entirely white, but despite his stern voice and his age, he had a remarkably friendly countenance in the privacy of his chambers.

"Thank you, Walter," she said. Madison knew better than to pander to the judge. He had once been an associate with her father and had told her upon their first meeting in chambers that she was to call him nothing but Walter in private and Judge in public.

"It really was one of the most remarkable cases I've ever presided over. It was clever to remind them of the possibility that she was already dead. It wasn't good sense, but it was good law, Madison. And, off the record, I think justice was served," he said solemnly. "Your father will be very proud."

Madison looked at her shoes and tried not to blush. It was the nicest thing he could have said to her.

"Now," the judge began in an entirely new tone of voice, "I've talked with you about taking the Williams case. There's no money in it. There's no glory. But that hasn't kept you from taking cases like this for me before."

Madison laughed nervously. It wasn't an easy thing to say no to the judge, but even for him she could only go so far.

"Walter," she said, "I know we've talked about Yusef Williams, and even with everything else going on in my life right now, I took the time to carefully look at the details of that case. Sure I could do things to slow the process down, maybe delay an execution, but this kid did it, and sooner or later he's gonna get the needle. My taking this case would just waste my time and the court's."

This was met with a blank stare that asked for something more concrete.

"I know, I know," she said, cutting off his lecture before he got a chance to start it. "No one is guilty until so proven. I know that, Walter, but even you have to admit that this is as cut-and-dried as it gets. There is no other rational explanation for what happened. You must know that."

The judge put his hands flat on the leather-bound blotter that protected the gleaming wood surface of his desk. He leaned forward, just enough to give her a little bit of a scare. His brow darkened.

"If this kid, as you call him, was the governor's son, would you take the case? If this kid's dad owned the Outlaws, would you? Would you if he was one of the players at the university? What if his father was the CEO of General Mills? Don't you lose sight of equality under our system, young lady. That is an intolerable quality that I will not allow you to adopt.

"You're too good a friend," he added more quietly, sitting back again and letting her digest his questions.

"Now," he said, holding up his hand this time, "I know this case looks bad. I know that. But you're not looking carefully. You're not giving what you'd give the other people I just mentioned. I've heard the preliminaries of this case, and your counterpart at the public defender's office, Mr. Cherrit, has got this kid on the fast track to death row. I don't know, maybe I'm just a foolish old man . . . but there's something about the whole thing that strikes me wrong. This boy says there was another man there that night."

Madison threw her hands up in the air.

"Please, Walter," she said, exasperated, "a white man in black clothes moving around in the shadows? Who executes two black kids? Why? Williams never said, did he? I looked. It's one of the worst fabrications I've ever heard."

"So you didn't talk to him yourself," the judge said.

"No. I told you, I've been incredibly busy. Though I did read every statement on both sides thoroughly," she added defensively.

"Well, then," the judge said quietly, "you and I will have to talk about this again . . . after you've spoken with the boy."

"Walter—"

"No! You tell me right this minute," he barked out, pointing an accusatory finger at her, "if that was the son of someone important, would you or would you not have at least talked with him yourself?"

Madison bit her lower lip. She thought about what he said for a moment, then nodded her head.

"Thank you," the judge said and then stood, signaling that their meeting was at an end.

"And again," he said, as though the entire conversation had never transpired, "congratulations. I mean it. That's the real reason I wanted to see you, but you know me, no sense in wasting time dancing around. . . . "

Madison gave him a smile as she let herself out. As she walked through the corridors of the courthouse, she begrudgingly admitted to herself that Walter was right. If the boy was someone else, she would have at least talked to him and listened. She could do that much, even if it seemed there was no hope of ever getting anything close to the truth. But then again, maybe . . . Madison thought of something she'd learned when she was still a student. What if it were you, imprisoned wrongfully? The implications of this were what moved her to represent a boy who grew up on the wrong side of the highway in squalor and destitution and what motivated her to be the bane of Van Rawlins and his team of over thirty assistant district attorneys.

Cody spent what he thought were the best few weeks with Jenny since they were young and growing up in Pittsburgh. She had accommodated his every need and desire. She had fussed over him, worried about his going to camp, and even talked about this being his last season so that he wouldn't have to put his body through anymore of the incredible punishment he got as a player in the NFL. It was the first time Cody had ever heard her talk about his retirement in anything close to conciliatory terms. Normally Jenny was prodding him on, challenging his toughness and manhood to continue to battle among the world's finest athletes and bring home one of the world's finest paychecks.

On the morning he left for San Angelo, where he and the rest of the team would stay until the last week in August, Jenny even made him breakfast. It was unprecedented. Instead of making Cody comfortable with the idea that he would have a wonderful life after football with his beautiful and now adoring wife, he was strangely spurred to again excel on the field. He said nothing to Jenny about this. It was his own private romantic notion of modern chivalry. He wanted to be worthy on the field of battle for the lovely lady who would wait for him at home. If Jenny had only known, she could have gotten even more out of her husband in the last eight years than she already had. If she had played the role she played in his final days before that season's training camp, she would have been a much happier wife. But the part of the acquiescent wife was a role completely contrary to her nature, and she could only stomach it for so long.

Jenny's behavior in the days before Cody's training camp was nothing more than acting, but she played the role of her life. She wanted to insure that Cody was tucked away safe and happy in camp so that when he couldn't reach her by phone, he wouldn't be tempted to do something crazy like drive home and raise a ruckus when he didn't find her there. Her visit to the general in Big Spring with Striker was nothing more than a training mission. She had really served no purpose other than to make the general comfortable with her presence for the final exchange.

Now, what she was going to do would be for real. The minute after she'd seen Cody off with a passionate kiss and a wave, she went upstairs and began packing her things. She was scheduled to leave the next day. That evening, she and Striker had dinner at the Texan, a fancy steak house just off of Sixth Street. Afterward they went back to Striker's, where she planned on spending the night. The moment they returned to his apartment from dinner, Jenny took the time to call home and get her messages. Cody had called from a pay phone at training camp as she'd expected he would. She called him back and got through. One of his teammates went down the hall to retrieve him, and for five minutes thereafter she cooed lovingly to him over the telephone. The moment she hung up, she went directly to Striker's bed where she mounted him like a wild mustang and worked herself and him into a passionate sweat. They collapsed only to awaken two more times during the night to make love, once violently, and the second time, at about four-thirty in the morning, with a tenderness that Jenny had never before experienced.

The next morning, Striker was up early. Jenny woke to the smell of fresh coffee. Striker sat waiting for her at his kitchen table. The table was arranged in a glass alcove that overlooked the ornate dome of the state capitol building. Striker had set out croissants and fine china on linen place mats. It looked like the kind of breakfast one would expect at a posh hotel. Jenny ambled in, giving her lover a kiss on the lips before sitting down. Striker poured her coffee and added just the right amount of cream. They ate in silence, enjoying the sunny morning and the wonderful view. Jenny was hungry. When she finally dabbed the corners of her mouth and laid her napkin down on the table, only one croissant remained in a basket of crumbs.

Striker smiled and said, "It's good for you to eat. You'll use a lot of energy over these next few days. Everything will seem like a difficult task, and the anxiety will cause you to burn more calories than you'll realize."

Striker sounded like a coach, giving his final instructions to an athlete about to go into the ring. That was almost what she was doing. Striker had worked with her, taught her many things, and discussed over and over again the many different scenarios that might arise. The best way to survive in this business, Striker told her again and again, was to anticipate the unexpected.

"Now," Striker said, rising from the table and leading her back into the bedroom, "I have something I want you to have. It's a graduation present of sorts. . . ."

Striker moved aside a floor lamp and a heavy upholstered chair. He used a key to open a closet door Jenny had never seen him open before. On the backside were a dozen guns mounted around the edges. In the center of the careful arrangement was a single long black pistol. From one of the places, he took a dull gray handgun that was compact and almost aerodynamic in its design.

"This is the latest weapon of choice for the Israeli Mossad," he said, holding it out for her. "It's a 7mm automatic, not unlike what you've been practicing with. Hold it. It's light. It's ceramic. It cannot be detected by a metal detector. I have a special holster that goes around your waist. The gun rests right here."

He touched the triangular mound of her crotch lovingly.

"The Mossad has as many women agents as men, so this is particularly useful for them."

Madison had been going to a gun range four times a week for the past six weeks. It was exciting to her. Striker had given her an old Colt 7mm to use. He'd familiarized her thoroughly with the weapon at his apartment and then sent her out to use it on her own. She remembered the first time they talked about guns. He asked her if she had ever used one. She told him that Cody kept a .357 in the drawer of the nightstand next to their bed. She went with Cody a couple of times to the gun range several years ago when he first got the gun. She even fired it a couple of times. Striker laughed when she told him this. Since that time with Cody, she admitted to Striker that she had only picked the gun up once on her own, and then only to clean out the drawer. That was her entire exposure to guns. Striker had changed that.

"You can take it right through the airport with you," Striker said. "I have already FedExed three clips to your hotel room at Oyster Bay. Just make sure you get rid of them before you return. I want to make it easy for you. . . .

"You won't need it," Striker said, seeing the worry creep onto her face, "but you should have a gun with you. Really, Jenny," he said, stepping close and kissing her on the lips, "this will be an easy thing for you. But, like I always say, it's better to overprepare. Besides, this all may come in useful for you one day. Who knows?"

"What's that?" Jenny said to him, unable to contain her curiosity and pointing at the long gun in the middle of all the rest. While she was listening to Striker, that one gun had drawn her attention like a deadly black spider in the middle of a web.

Striker looked at the gun, then took it from its place almost lovingly.

"This," he said, "is Lucy."

"I thought I was Lucy," Jenny said, confused but intrigued at the notion that Striker would give her the same name as this dangerous-looking weapon.

"You are," he said. "And this is. This is a Czechoslovakian CZ .22 automatic. I use it only for very important jobs. She's quiet and reliable. This on the end is a silencer. She's incredibly accurate, beautiful, but very deadly. I named it after another Lucy because of the similarities.

"The first Lucy," he explained, "was a French woman I knew in Vietnam. She was about the age you are now, older than me back then. She was lovely. She had seen the world, and in a world of men, she ruled them all. . . . "

"What happened to her?" Jenny asked, not able to keep the jealous note out of her voice.

Striker sensed this and gave her a patronizing smile. "They killed her," he said simply. "She was the queen of Saigon. It was her home. She loved that country, said it was the most civilized place in the world before the war. When the NVA took the city in '73, she refused to leave. She holed up in an apartment building. They say she killed almost a hundred of them before they simply gave up and shelled half the block. Her body was never found. There was really nothing left when they were done. For years after that, the story goes, whenever an NVA soldier or one of the Vietnamese secret police turned up floating face down in the river, people would say that it was Lucy. I don't know, it wouldn't surprise me. . . . Anyway," he said, coming back to the here and now, "you reminded me of her. It's a compliment."

"Were you lovers?" Jenny said in a moment of weakness. She crossed her arms and waited for the answer.

"Yes," Striker said, amused but holding back his smile, "we were."

Then he put his hands around Jenny's neck and kissed her gently on the lips.

"But you, Jenny Blue Eyes," he whispered, separating his lips from hers and gazing into her eyes, "you stand alone."

Jenny disembarked at the Dutch airport on the island of St. Martin. After passing easily through customs, a porter carried her two bags all the way to a waiting rented Land Cruiser. Striker had removed the pit from its metallic case and put it in a box he'd gotten from a novelty store that had contained a crystal ball. In the box, the pit sat on a cheap plastic stand and appeared as innocuous as the plastic ball it had replaced. This, he had explained to her, was overkill. The St. Martin's customs people were notoriously slack. It was a rare thing for them to open someone's luggage, unless one of the dogs that was occasionally walked through baggage claim happened to smell ten kilos of cocaine that some fool hadn't bothered to pack in coffee. Even if the pit's alloy seal was leaking, pure plutonium gave off only alpha rays, an innocuous form of radiation that no modern luggage screening system would even pick up.

Jenny went straight to her hotel. She had studied a map of the island during the flight. Striker told her that one thing that was always imperative, no matter how simple the operation, was to be intimately familiar with your surroundings so that, in the event of an emergency, you would stand at least a sporting chance of eluding someone. Jenny had taken this seriously and memorized the entire road system that wove its way through both the French and Dutch sides of the island. The Oyster Bay Hotel was on the far side of the island from the airport and sat just across the Dutch line on the French side.

Jenny bumped and swerved her way through the battered roads and sprawling native villages filled with colorfully clothed, barefoot people who were as dark as tar. She turned off the main road until she found herself at the top of an enormous hill that looked out over a sapphire-blue Atlantic Ocean. Below was Oyster Bay and the regal Spanish-style hotel that overlooked the expanse of blue, white-capped water. From the moment she pulled up to the immense portico and shut off the engine of her Land Cruiser, Jenny didn't have to lift a finger except to sign the name of Lucy Meara at the register. There was an eager staff ready to assist her with everything. Her five-room suite overlooked the ocean and came complete with her own maid. Jenny accepted this royal treatment as though she'd grown up at Windsor Palace. She even had the presence of mind to notice a tall slender olive-skinned man with a black beard in white robes and a turban who sat reading a paper in the ornate lobby. The man, she noticed, looked furtively from behind his newspaper at her several times while she checked in.

The suite was as impressive as the hotel lobby. The stucco walls stretched twelve feet to the ceiling, and old-world furniture, upholstered in floral prints, adorned each room. Her FedEx package sat on a teak table in the dining room. After the bellman left her bags in the bedroom, she picked up the package and went back into the bedroom where she closed the door. Two of the clips she shoved into the side pocket of her shoulder bag. She untucked her loose white blouse and pulled out the waistband of her long auburn skirt to remove the 7mm from its holster. She jammed the third clip into the gun and snapped a round into the chamber before she put it back in its holster. Jenny felt much better with the loaded gun pressed snugly against her. She took off her large sun hat and glasses and let down her hair. Even though she was planning on being there no more than one night, she unpacked her bags and put everything away before wandering out onto her private deck overlooking the ocean. She sat down in a cushioned lounge chair to soak up the view. Her maid appeared, and Jenny told her to bring a margarita. For the afternoon, she would simply sit and enjoy the luxury that she hoped would soon be an everyday thing.

When the sun set, Jenny put on a long, elegant emerald dress and went downstairs to dinner. She told the maître d' that she was Lucy Meara, and he showed her to a secluded table out on the terrace. Two high-backed cane chairs and a jungle of verdant flowering vines surrounded the table. The man she'd seen earlier in the white suit and turban sat in the chair opposite her. He didn't say anything until the maître d' was gone.

"You must tell Mr. Moss that we are quite unhappy," the man said bluntly. Jenny thought he was rather handsome until he opened his mouth. It was full of large, crooked teeth.

Jenny nodded her head. Striker had warned her that the reception they would give her would be less than hospitable, even though Striker had informed them beforehand that he would be represented by a woman named Lucy Meara for the second of the three transactions.

"I will tell him," she said.

"You cannot see Jamir the way you are," the man said with a look of disgust.

He was of course referring to her elegant dress and her made-up face. Striker had informed her that this would certainly fluster whichever of Jamir's minions he sent to make contact with her. Striker told her it was important to treat anyone less than Jamir himself with disdain. That would ensure that they took her seriously and that they respected her.

"I know this," Jenny said. "I will change into something appropriate when the time comes."

"Are you ready now?" the man said as he rose from the table.

"No," Jenny said, her stomach fluttering. "I will eat first. Then I will join you."

Striker told her to have dinner and then go with the man. That was how he would do it, so that was how she should. Of course the man would not have minded at all sitting through dinner with Striker. He was a man. But for a devout Muslim to be expected to subject himself to the presence of a western whore was too much of an insult to bear.

"I will be waiting for you on the end of the seventh dock," the man said, then turned abruptly and walked away.

Jenny ordered and sat through a five-course dinner. She didn't do much more than pick at her food. She drank only water, despite her urge to gulp down some champagne. Striker had warned her to be stone-sober for her meeting with Jamir.

When the meal was over, Jenny went to her room and changed into a shapeless gray dress and a white veil that covered her head and all of her face except her eyes. As much as she hated to do it, she left the gun and its holster in her closet. Striker had insisted that to do otherwise would be a deadly mistake. She put the pit, still in its box, in her bag and slung it over her shoulder. She was almost out the door when she remembered to go back into the bathroom and wipe the mascara off of her eyes. That done, she went downstairs and outside to the docks. At the end of number seven, the tall turbaned man stood smoking a Camel. When he saw her, he pointedly looked at his watch and began untying the ropes that moored a small Scarab to the end of the dock. Jenny made her way unhurriedly through a row of tall sailboats that were berthed on either side of the main dock. She stepped down into the boat without the aid of the man and sat beside him in a bucket seat tucked up under the windshield.

She didn't know if it was to shake her up or because they were late, but the man raced out of the bay and out into the ocean at an amazing speed. They jounced across the rough, dark water, and Jenny had to hold on with all her strength to keep from flying out of the boat. Soon the dark shape of the island, dotted with hundreds of twinkling lights, disappeared behind them, and they were left to the ocean and the brilliant clear night filled with stars. Jenny made herself think of Striker. She pretended he was sitting right behind her or down in the hold. Waiting there like a deadly cat to pounce out and protect her if she needed him. Of course Striker was hundreds of miles away, and Jenny had the sinking feeling she would never see him again. And she had no doubt that the man beside her would gladly slit her throat and toss her into the ocean with a weight belt around her middle.

The great white form appeared on the dark horizon, and thirty minutes later they slowed down for the first time, easing up alongside the enormous snow-white vessel. Jenny guessed it was about three hundred feet long. The man next to her scrambled out onto the bow of the rocking boat like a trained monkey that had performed the same trick a thousand times before. He hooked a line from one of two separate cranes to the bow of the boat before scrambling back to do the same to the stern. The boat was hoisted smoothly up alongside the larger vessel until Jenny and the man could actually step right out of the Scarab and onto the deck of the yacht. Her bag was taken from her by a sailor. Another man ran a metal detecting wand thoroughly up one side of her and down the other.

Without a word she was led into a spacious cabin that more closely resembled the inside of an English drawing room than the room of a ship. Dark wood panels with ornate trim adorned the walls, and heavy timber beams crisscrossed the ceiling above. Plush oriental carpets sat under three separate seating arrangements. In front of the largest couch in the middle of the room burned a fire. She could see the back of the head of a man who was seated before the fire with his feet up on a coffee table. He was holding a cellular phone to his ear, and he seemed not to even notice her. She stood in front of an overstuffed chair to his right, unsure if she should sit. Jamir finished his conversation in a language she did not recognize, then he shut the phone and turned to her. He leaned forward and stared up at her intently.

"I am Jamir," he said in a heavily accented English. He had dark skin, and his jet-black hair was slicked back with gel. He wore a maroon silk shirt and matching slacks. The shirt was open at the neck and exposed a hairless and muscular chest. He wore only a thin mustache, and unlike the driver of the Scarab, his teeth were brilliantly white and perfect. He wasn't handsome in the least, in fact he had the rather ugly visage of a nineteenth-century pirate but with an aura of power that made him attractive.

Jenny looked down, careful not to stare or even catch a glimpse of his bottomless brown eyes.

"I am Lucy Meara," she said quietly. "Mr. Moss sends his deepest apologies and humbly asks that you accept me as his temporary replacement."

Jamir seemed to relax. He sat back on the coach and gazed at her. She knew he was imagining what she looked like beneath her shapeless clothes. For the first time she felt glad to have them on.

"You have the eyes of a Bengal tigress," Jamir said, studying her carefully.

Instead of looking down, Jenny gazed right back at him. If he was going to come on to her, she wasn't going to put him off.

"Yes," he said, "a tigress. I wonder, is the rest of you just as enticing?"

Jenny said nothing but continued to look boldly into his eyes. She was telling him, without speaking, that she was more than he ever dreamed of.

"I think," he said as he stood, "I would like to find out. . . . "

Jamir walked to the fireplace. Above it, on the mantle, was a small golden chest intricately decorated with sapphires and emeralds. Jamir opened it and took something out.

"Not now, of course," he said. "Not here. I have pressing business, and so do you. But someday."

He handed her what looked like a coin. She took it and turned it over in her hand. It bore the same royal crest on either side.

"One day I would like very much for you to go to a hotel in Paris called Le Muerice," he said. "If you do, there is a man named Gerrod, he is the concierge. Give this to him. He will contact me, and I will send a comfortable jet for you that will take you to a beautiful place. I will meet you there, and . . . well, we will see."

Jenny held the coin tightly in her hand and bowed her head in acquiescence, suggesting that someday, maybe, she would do as he had asked. It was certainly a nice option to have.

Jamir smiled and said, "Very good."

He sat down, and so did she. Their eyes locked, and Jenny continued to calmly hold his gaze. They waited for what Jenny knew was Jamir's chemist to measure the mass of the pit to make certain that it was indeed Pu 239 and not just a worthless ball of lead. It didn't take very long. Another man entered the room after a few minutes and whispered something in Jamir's ear. Jamir's face showed no expression.

"Please tell Mr. Moss," he said to Jenny, "that I look forward to seeing him soon to conclude our business."

The man who had entered the room waited for Jenny to stand. She nodded briefly at Jamir and followed the man out of the room. Jamir was back on the phone before she had gone.

Jenny climbed back into the Scarab alongside the same thick-bearded man that brought her. The boat was lowered alongside the yacht, and they sped off into the clear Caribbean night. When the large white ship was out of sight, Jenny began to strain her eyes for the lights of the island. She was afraid of being alone with the man beside her.

Suddenly the boat slowed down. The driver decelerated until the only motion was the boat's steady rocking on the waves. Jenny looked at the man, who turned to her with a malicious smile. From within the folds of his robe he took out a pistol and pointed it at her face. Jenny stood, but her knees buckled from fear. In that second a million things raced through her mind, but what was happening was instantly obvious. These people didn't care about three pits. They only needed two for a bomb, and that was all they wanted. They gave Striker two million for the first one. Now they had the second, and instead of giving her two million more as had been arranged, they would eliminate her and make off with a bargain.

The thing that bothered her most as she prepared to die was whether or not Striker had known, or guessed, and simply sent her as a guinea pig to test the veracity of these people. She had told herself a million times that Striker was not to be trusted, but here she was, at the end, and she found herself wishing more than anything that he had not betrayed her. The man said something to her, but she wasn't sure what it was.

"I said," he snarled, jabbing the gun closer to her face, "don't move an inch."

Jenny choked back a whimper. Then the man was gone. He disappeared into the hold.

Jenny's hand went absently between her legs to feel if she'd peed in her dress. A burst of noise escaped her throat that sounded like a demented giggle. She thought how strange the sound was and how foolish she had been. The man thumped about below, obviously doing something mechanical, before he reappeared without even a glance in her direction and restarted the boat.

Jenny endured the same rough ride back to the hotel, thinking all the while how wrong she was about Striker. It made her love him in a way she hadn't realized until now. The driver unceremoniously dropped her off and tossed a black leather bag out onto the dock before he raced back out into the night. Jenny picked up the bag and lugged it up the back stairs and into her room. She unzipped it when she was in her bedroom, with the doors shut and locked. Inside were bundles of American dollars. Jenny undressed and showered, then strapped her holster and gun back around her waist before she lay down to try and rest.

She couldn't sleep. Though irrational, she imagined that every noise she heard was the Scarab driver coming back to kill her in her bed and make off with the money. At five-thirty Jenny got up, pulled a light robe around herself, and went out onto the terrace to watch the sun come up. She was glad for the light. She ordered breakfast and coffee and ate outside. Ten o'clock came slowly. When it was time, Jenny was ready with her leather bag and on her way into Phillipsburg, the town on the Dutch side of the island. Kroner Bank sat on the road through town. Jenny walked in with the bag as the doors were first opened and asked to see the manager. She showed him a key, and he led her into the back of the bank and inside a high-ceilinged vault. The manager left her to herself, and she opened a large safety deposit box and put the leather bag inside. Carrying American dollars through customs was as dangerous as transporting raw heroin. As an afterthought, she reopened the vault and tossed her three clips into the leather bag with the money.

When she sat down in her first-class seat on Delta flight 077 for Dallas, Jenny breathed a sigh of relief. She slept nearly the entire flight. By seven-thirty that night, she pulled into her own driveway. She had the terrible urge to see Striker, but that wouldn't happen for three more days. Jenny went to the wine rack and chose a good Pinot. She was giddy with the success of her first mission. She wanted to talk to someone about it, but she couldn't. She wanted to call him, but she couldn't. Instead, she drank two glasses of wine and went to bed, dreaming about the moment she would be back in Striker's arms.

Chapter Thirteen

SAN ANGELO STATE IS A SMALL COLLEGE in the town of San Angelo in central Texas. Any player who had ever been an Outlaw could never think of San Angelo without thinking of heat and pain. It was to San Angelo that they would go in late July and stay for five weeks of training camp. Days began at seven and went until ten at night. Exhaustion was the rule, and no player could prepare himself for the rigors of camp. There was no off-season training program that could ever subject the joints to the constant pounding, day after day, of training camp. It was a dangerous five weeks, and no one but a quarterback could get through camp without being battered, cut, and bruised in a way that would leave most people convalescing for a month.

Cody wasted no time in taking advantage of living better through modern medicine. Once his contract was signed, done a week before at the Outlaws' offices with Marty by his side, he was a season-long investment for the team. Even if he was hurt, they had to pay him for the remainder of that season; and on injured reserve, his salary would count against the salary cap the NFL imposed on every team. Now he could go to the medical staff and get the drugs he needed without worrying about sending up red flags that would keep them from offering him a contract. He already had it.

Cody walked alone down the path that led from the dorm he was staying in to the locker facility just off the practice field where the trainers and doctors did their work on the hurt Outlaws players. The sun was just coming up. His calves and head were sore. Tomorrow his hamstrings and neck would join in the symphony of pain. His head would get worse before it got better. It would continue to swell and he would be forced to grease his helmet with Vaseline just to get it on his head. Soon his entire body would be covered with bruises, welts, and cuts. Today was only the beginning. But all that was normal. The knife wound in his shoulder had healed so that it was no more than an annoyance. It was the gnawing pain in his knee that he had to remedy.

Cody was the first player in the locker room. His teammates were wisely getting as much sleep as they possibly could. They would need it. Cody wanted to get what he needed and get out before the rush of players began. Even after only the first day of practice, there would be plenty of guys who needed medical attention. Before seven-thirty, each of the ten training tables would be covered with players packed in ice or hooked up to electronic high-volt machines to reduce their swollen body parts. The rest would spill out over onto the floors where the trainers would lay down clean white sheets for the injured. It would be a madhouse.

Dr. Burlitz, the general practitioner who the players saw for their everyday ailments, was on his first cup of coffee and still rubbing the sleep from his eyes when Cody walked into the training room.

"Cody Grey," the doctor said in a heavy southern drawl, "how are we today?"

Cody never liked the way the doctor referred to everything as if they were two men alone in a lifeboat, suffering through the same hardships together. No doctor Cody had ever known played an entire NFL game with broken ribs; got their knee drained, got drugged up, and then went running out onto the field. But that was about all Cody didn't like about the doctor. He was a good man with a hard job, a physician whose loyalty was to the patient and the team that paid the bills.

"Knee's not too good," Cody said, entering a separate, closetlike examination room.

"Our bad knee, I assume," said the doctor.

"Yeah," Cody said. "I twisted it yesterday, and this morning it swelled up on me."

He was lying through his teeth. The knee was always swollen, but this was the first time since last season that the team was responsible for the bad joint. Without a contract for the coming season, if Cody had failed the initial physical, the team could have simply discarded him like the cardboard tube from a roll of used up toilet paper. But now, with a contract in his pocket, and the season having officially started, Cody was in the driver's seat. In the past twenty-four hours, Dr. Burlitz had gone from Cody's worst enemy, because he had the power to fail him in the team physical, to his best friend, because he would do everything within medical reason and beyond to keep him on the playing field. At least for now, that's what Cody thought a best friend would do.

140

Marty had finally settled with the Outlaws on a one-year, two-hundred-thousand-dollar contract, one-seventh of what Biggs would be making whether he recovered or not. More important, though, were Cody's incentive clauses. Marty had insisted that the team pay Cody some six-figure incentives if he ended up replacing the injured Biggs for the entire season. He got them, and now Cody needed to do his part by staying healthy enough and playing well enough to make sure that if Biggs couldn't come back, Cody would be the man in the middle of the Outlaws defense.

Burlitz fussed with Cody's knee for a few minutes, twisting and turning it painfully about. Cody wanted to box the old doctor's ears. He was not an orthopedic surgeon, and he really had no business messing around with his knee. But they both knew why Cody was here, so the doctor could pretty much do what he wanted to satisfy whatever ethics he had to wrestle with before he gave Cody the drugs he needed.

"How about some Motrin for a few days and see how this comes along?" Burlitz suggested.

Cody shook his head and said, "You've got to give me some good stuff, doc. I'm not gonna make it through this camp without some Butazolidin."

The doctor raised his eyebrows as if it were the first time he had ever heard the word. Butazolidin was a strong anti-inflammatory drug that worked wonders on race horses and near miracles on human joints. Everyone in the NFL knew about Butte. The only problem was that it also worked wonders on your liver and kidneys. Sometimes you had to pay the price if you wanted to play in the big leagues.

"Well," Burlitz said with perfunctory hesitation, "I guess you know this knee by now. We'll have to monitor our red-blood-cell levels once a week; as long as you don't mind that, I can give you some and we'll see how we respond."

Cody nodded solemnly. Now he was getting somewhere.

"Have the trainers get some ice on that this morning. You'll have to see Dr. Cort this afternoon," Burlitz said, scribbling out the instructions for taking the drug on the face of a small white box.

"Can we practice?" the doctor said, looking up from the pills he was dispensing into the box.

"Yeah," Cody nodded. "This stuff will help."

"Well, I know we've used this before," Burlitz said, "but don't forget to make sure you eat something before you take one of these. I'd hate to see you rip up your stomach with one of these devils."

141

"Yeah," Cody said, "I'm going to get something to eat right after I get some ice on this." "Good," the doctor nodded, all cares and concerns.

"Hey, doc," Cody said as he hopped down off the table and opened the door to get his knee packed in ice.

"Hmm?" said the older man, looking over his bifocals.

"Would you take this stuff?" Cody gave the box a shake.

The question obviously stunned the physician.

"I—uh—I . . . you certainly don't have to. I suggested giving you some Motrin. If you don't want to use this, I don't think you should."

"Nah," Cody said, having had his fun. "I don't care. I just wondered if you'd take it or not. Me? I don't really have a choice."

Before the doctor could start stammering again, Cody left the room. He hoped he'd made Burlitz at least think about how liberally he used the word "we." A couple of rookies limped in with twisted ankles, and Cody realized he needed to get his ice quickly and get down some eggs and toast if he was going to fire up the Butte before practice. The way his knee felt right now, he could use it. Cody climbed up onto the first table in the row and asked Jerry, the head trainer, if he could have some ice for his knee.

"You mean 'our' knee?" Jerry quipped with a wry smile.

Cody lay down on the table and watched without too much interest as the rest of his injured teammates began to file in and go through Burlitz's revolving door before coming out for some ice or some high-volt. It wasn't long before Biggs wandered in, yawning and scratching at his crotch.

"Yo, roomy," Biggs said in his deep voice as he flopped down on the table next to Cody.

Within two minutes Biggs was snoring. He'd let the trainers come to him and massage his leg. He was in no hurry to get well. He knew camp was just a grind. He would wait until it was just about over before he put himself back out on the field. It made Cody wonder why the hell he was doing all this to himself. Butazolidin. Why? He'd pound his way through camp and then hit the bench as soon as Biggs decided he was tired of early morning massages. The answer, of course, was that Cody Grey couldn't imagine a life where he wasn't an Outlaw. Unlike Biggs, he seemed to need the team more than they needed him. Cody didn't resent Biggs for it. Biggs was just smarter and younger than he was.

Soon Cody's knee was numb from the ice pack. Once the pain was finally gone, he lay back comfortably on the table to listen to the radio. Jerry liked to play NPR in the morning, and Cody found himself listening to Bob Edwards talk to some expert about a group of Muslim extremists in the Middle East who claimed that it was their religious duty to destroy as much of the godless western world as they possibly could. Cody wondered why in hell Jerry bothered to listen. What, he asked himself, could that crazy stuff, halfway around the world, have to do with any of them? Didn't they have it hard enough just trying to get themselves through training camp?

Madison was already having a bad day, so the last thing she needed was to have to go to jail. But jail was where she was headed. The boy, as Judge Connack so innocently referred to Yusef Williams, was being held at the county jail until his trial. With the change of counsel the trial wouldn't be for some time, but Madison figured from the kid's file that he was probably just as well off in the county slammer as he was anywhere else. Yusef had no family. He'd been in and out of foster homes since he was taken from his parents at the age of three, after being found with cigarette burns up and down his legs. No one was quite certain where his real parents were anymore or even if they were still alive. Madison doubted that Yusef cared.

Besides the temperature climbing to over one hundred degrees with high humidity, which was enough in itself to make it a bad day, she had received bad news from Glen Westman. Joe and his attorney were refusing to give anything in preliminary negotiations. She had offered one Saturday a month visitation rights for Joe and one additional holiday day at her own discretion with a five-thousand-dollar lump sum to help him get on his feet. This was generous considering that the law had already determined he was due nothing. But Madison had hoped that by sweetening the pot with some cold cash, Joe would jump on the deal and be only a limited pain in her ass.

On Joe's behalf, Gleason hadn't even balked. They were still demanding a lump payment of three hundred thousand dollars, half her yearly income, joint custody, every other weekend visitation rights, and one weekly sleep-over with a rotating split on the holidays. This was the maximum even a model husband could expect where the wife had somehow created some aggravated circumstances, like having sexual intercourse on the living room rug with her lover in front of the child.

"I don't want Jo-Jo to be deposed," she had said.

"I think everyone knows that," Glen Westman responded.

143

"I won't let that happen," Madison said firmly.

"That's what they're obviously banking on."

"Can we get a ruling on this whole ball of fucking wax?" Madison said. "That bitch Judge Iris is way the hell out of line opening this back up."

Glen raised an eyebrow. He'd never heard Madison talk like this.

"Madison," he said calmly. "It's not that far out of line. It's becoming the rule rather than the exception. The pendulum is swinging the other way. It's very vogue to consider the father's rights these days."

Glen didn't have to tell Madison what Joe's demand meant. It meant that Joe and Gleason were ready and willing to take the whole thing to trial. She didn't want that. She could grind him down at trial, everyone had to realize that. But it would be bad on Jo-Jo, everyone had to realize that as well. It was so obvious that Joe didn't care about his son. Only someone who didn't care would push this to the limit. It was such a contradiction. The less he really cared, the more he would get.

It had gotten worse as her conversation with Glen went on. He told her that he had spoken with Judge Iris DuBose and that DuBose was asking that she consider some temporary visiting rights until things were worked out.

"She told me to ask you to think about the best interests of Jo-Jo," Glen had hesitantly told her.

"His best interests!" Madison had exploded. "Why, that dried up old bitch!"

She was close to tears when she leaned across the rich mahogany conference table in the firm's offices and said, "Glen, this can't be happening to me, can it? I mean, I've done everything right. I've tried. He's done everything wrong. We had the law behind us from the start. How—how can she do this now? How can she start talking like this? Is she that blind? Joe Thurwood is a goddamned animal!"

Glen became obviously uncomfortable. Although he was a divorce lawyer and used to spouses becoming distraught, irate, and even murderous, Madison was one of the heavyweights in the firm, and watching her come undone was a difficult thing. Madison recognized this immediately and excused herself. Marty was in a meeting, but he broke it and met her privately in his office. Madison cried and he held her. She had no one else she could turn to, and Marty was more than glad to be there. By lunch time, Madison had composed herself enough to work. It helped, but a dread had fallen over her like a pall.

She pulled up to the guardhouse. It was the only break in the sixteen-foot-high fence topped with concertina wire. She showed her identification and they let her through. Once outside her car, the heat pressed against her like iron. Breathing was difficult in the sweltering humidity. By the time she reached the visitor's door, Madison was sweating hard. Inside wasn't much better. Madison knew there would be some Republican lawmakers who would be delighted to know that everyone in the county jail was receiving no quarter from the heat, especially the defense attorneys.

She was shown to a cubicle where she sat down to wait for her client. She took a blank yellow legal pad from her briefcase and set it out in front of her with a fresh ballpoint pen. Prisoners came and went, up and down the row of cubicles that stretched across the room. Madison didn't have a hard time imagining the heinous crimes many of them had committed. They all seemed to look the part. One was an enormous fat man whose arms hung from his shoulders and spilled like dough out of a grubby white tank top. Tattoos of swastikas and skulls went up and down his exposed flesh. His greasy hair and beard were long and scraggly. Another man had a mouth full of rotten teeth and a demonic set of beady eyes that raped her the instant he caught sight of her. Then came Yusef.

Madison knew now why Walter Connack had continually referred to him as "the boy." He was sixteen, she knew from his record, but he looked closer to fourteen. Because of the gravity of his crime, he would be tried and punished as an adult. His eyes brimmed with fear. His dark, nappy hair was closely cut, and his face was pitifully marred with what looked like a painful case of acne.

Yusef sat down and looked at his folded hands.

"Yusef," Madison said, "I'm Madison McCall, your new attorney. I'm here to try to help you."

Yusef looked up at her words. She had spoken them as though she was a den mother and he nothing more than a scout late for a meeting.

"Can't help me," he said, looking back down. His face scrunched up, and he began to cry. He drove his fists angrily into the corners of his eyes, as if to grind the tears into oblivion.

"Tell me what happened," Madison said without reacting to his unnerved state in any way. She was certain that although he was kept in a special juvenile section of the jail that he had already fully considered and been generously filled in on the joys of dying by lethal injection in the state of Texas. That was what prisoners did for sport, tormented each other.

While Yusef gained control of himself, Madison thought of herself that same morning, dealing with something that she couldn't avoid, something that had already happened and was bearing down on her like the stifling heat outside. It helped her to empathize with the boy, and it prompted her to listen closely, as a good lawyer should.

Yusef recounted the story for her, the way he remembered it, the way he had recounted it several times already. The story about the man dressed in black who followed them into the abandoned garage and forced him to shoot his friends. He was tired of hearing himself say it. No one had believed him from the start. When he finished, Madison sat back and leafed through her notes in silence for a few moments. Then she leaned forward.

"Tell me everything again," she said.

Yusef's face sagged. What little hope she'd pumped into him with her flashy presence and kind demeanor was gone.

"'Cause you think I'm lyin'," he said as a statement of fact rather than a query.

"No," she said, "because I'm a good lawyer and I want to be thorough. Sometimes there are things that even you don't know you remember. They come out sometimes at strange moments. My job isn't to judge whether you're telling me the truth. You're my client. I assume everything you tell me is true, no matter how strange or bizarre it sounds. That's my job, and I'm damn good at it. Didn't your other lawyer tell you this?"

"No," he said quietly in a shameful whisper.

"Tell me what happened again, please," Madison said patiently.

She would do this twice more, forcing the boy to recount the story four times in succession. Details in a client's story would always emerge that either highlighted the glaring lies or suggested important clues that hadn't been thoroughly examined. It was a technique that many defense lawyers didn't bother with. It took a lot of time and clients sometimes saw it as a hostility rather than an aid to their defense.

Madison went back through her notes. Half the tablet was filled now. She went all the way to the beginning and then back again, stopping to clarify inconsistencies and highlight questions that needed to be answered that might help in Yusef's defense. There were two things that bothered her most.

"Here's something," she said, looking up from the pad. "It's a small thing, but the last time you said that before your friend Ramon stood up, the man in black 'capped' him. Why did you say that? The man didn't kill Ramon then? You told me that Ramon was killed with his own gun, and that you shot him."

Yusef stared at her mutely.

"Well," Madison said patiently, "did the man shoot Ramon or shoot at him?"

Yusef seemed to think a minute.

"I guess he shot him," he said.

"Why do you guess that?" Madison asked.

"'Cause . . . " Yusef looked up at her, "'cause I think Ramon's ear was bleedin'. He grabbed at it, and I think I remember blood."

"Why didn't you tell someone this before?" Madison inquired, trying to hide her impatience.

Yusef shrugged and said, "'Cause no one asked?"

Madison nodded and said, "Are you sure about this, Yusef? It's very important. Think hard. Was Ramon's ear bleeding? Was he shot?"

Yusef did think. He scrunched up his face and worked at it before nodding affirmatively.

"Uh-huh," he said. "That man capped him. Now I remember thinkin' that. I was thinkin' then that Ramon was gonna kill that dude sure as shit stinks, if he got a shot at him."

Madison wrote down Capped and underlined it three times.

"There's one other thing that I want to ask you about," Madison said. "Two times you told me, when I asked you what the man screamed at you, that he screamed, 'Do it. Do it. Do it.' Two other times you told me he said, 'Do it, bigshot. Do it. Do it.'"

Madison looked up at Yusef. He was looking at her now, obviously fascinated.

"Yeah," he said, "I don't know why I said that. I don't really remember exactly what he said."

"Well, if he did call you a bigshot," Madison said, "it suggests that you did something to offend him, something that showed him a lack of respect. . . . "

Madison didn't know where this was leading. She had already gone down the road of the man in black being a rival drug dealer or a recent crime victim, but there was absolutely no connection the boy could come up with between the man in black and himself. She let the words just hang out there, hoping that the boy might have an epiphany.

Instead he shook his head and said, "I don't know."

CHAPTER FOURTEEN

"**WHERE ARE YOU GOING?**" Striker asked. He was lying on his back completely naked on top of his bed.

Jenny looked down at his tan body. He stretched. Hard long muscles rippled under the brown skin. He was delicious, that was the word she had for him. Cody had about the same build, maybe a little heavier than Striker. Cody was strong but didn't look incredibly muscular. Unlike Striker, who had a sexy tan, Cody was pale. And Cody didn't have Striker's abdomen either, a washboard of muscle and flesh. Jenny couldn't help comparing the two.

"I'm going to call my husband," she said, running a long, red nail up the length of his thigh as she passed by him. It was ten-thirty at night. They hadn't bothered going out at all that night; instead they'd ordered in Chinese food.

Striker flipped on his stomach to watch her go.

"Why don't you call from in here?" he said. "I'd like to hear what you have to say."

"Leave me alone," she said lightly, continuing into his living room to make the call. Cody liked to speak to her every night. It was annoying, but she understood.

"Soon you won't have to keep him happy," Striker said from the bedroom. "Soon you and I won't have to wait two or three days between the times we see each other."

"You're the one who says I have to keep things cordial with him," Jenny answered from the living room.

"I know." He rolled back over and looked up at the ceiling. "But I don't have to like it, the way you have to call him all the time."

Jenny's face appeared in the doorway to the bedroom.

"Jealous?" she asked.

Striker threw a pillow at her and she ducked.

"Maybe," he said thoughtfully. But he knew he was, very.

Jenny smiled and said, "Good," and then went to make the call.

Since her return from St. Martin, there was no doubt her stock had gone up in Striker's mind. Jenny was elated. She felt more alive than she had in her entire life. Together, she and Striker were outsmarting everyone. Jenny was important now. She'd made the exchange. She was in as deep as he was. Both their lives were at stake now. It was a good feeling.

She dialed the number of Cody's room. He'd gotten his own phone after the first few days at the dorm. He answered on the first ring.

"Jenny!" he said, obviously thrilled about something. "I've been waiting for you to call."

"Hi, love," she said with what sounded like genuine enthusiasm.

"Guess what?" Cody said.

"What?" she asked, pulling aside the curtains to get a clear view of the capitol dome, enveloped by an eerie yellow light across the tree-lined street.

"You know how Biggs came back today?" he said, knowing he'd told her only last night that his replacement was going back in the lineup. "Well, he blew out his ham again! Can you believe it? He's out for at least six weeks, maybe eight to ten! Jenny, I'm back! Hell, I may be the starter for the entire season. Baby, I am the man again!"

Those were a lot of words and a lot of excitement for Cody. Jenny couldn't think of the last time she'd heard him so animated.

"It's wonderful, Cody," she said. She really was glad for him. He sounded so good and so vital that, in a way, it made her miss him.

"I can make my incentives," he continued. "Jenny, I could make almost four hundred thousand dollars if Biggs stays out ten weeks!"

"It's fantastic," she said.

"I know," Cody said, and then there was silence.

Jenny couldn't think of anything to say. She hadn't expected to feel this way, to miss him, to feel even the most remote twinge of guilt that she was deceiving him. She wondered for the first time if she might have made a mistake about Cody. Maybe Cody was going to make a comeback and still had several more years of stardom left. It was too strange. She had just been thinking how wonderfully happy she was with Striker, and she was. Jenny had moments like this often in her life. Just when she was completely sure of one thing, some other, unwanted emotion would pop up and confuse her.

"How's your knee feeling?" she asked. It was the first thing that came to mind.

Cody hesitated, then said, "You know, that's a problem. I mean, it's better with the Butte, but I think they're going to have to start draining it again. But if I can keep this job for another week and finish camp, I'm the man. I can get by if I don't have to run on it too much in practice and I get it drained before the games. I can definitely make it through the season like that. It's been done before."

As quickly as she had become confused about her husband, Jenny went into emotional reverse. Cody was damaged goods. It was nice that he might get the rest of this season under his belt. It would make it easier for him when she finally left him. She didn't know why she had a doubt at all, but that was how Jenny had gone through her life, always worrying that she was missing out on something good. She would get excited about a new lover, or a new house, or a new city, but ultimately, wherever she wasn't is where she would want to be.

Alice Vreland was an assistant medical examiner for the Travis County Coroner's Office. She was damn good at what she did. Madison knew this firsthand. When Alice first arrived on the local scene, fresh from UCLA medical school, Madison had taken a couple of runs at her in some criminal cases she was trying at the time. That was five years ago. Since her first three cases, Madison knew not to bother questioning the credibility of the coroner's office if Alice had been the one to do the autopsy. She was too good to mess with; and the times Madison had attempted to cross-examine her on the stand, it had taken everything she had to recover from the damage, so outstanding was Alice's presence in front of a jury.

Instead Madison had become friends with the chunky redhead. Occasionally they would have dinner together, more often it was lunch when Alice was at the courthouse giving testimony for the D.A.'s office in one grisly murder or another. It always amazed Madison how Alice could give a detailed account of a gunshot wound that removed half a person's skull and then go out minutes later and enjoy a rare hamburger with French fries doused in ketchup. It was at one such lunch that Madison asked for Alice's help with Yusef Williams's case.

Alice looked skyward when she heard the name. Her concentration was so intense that Madison couldn't help also looking up, as if there were some answer in the ceiling above.

"Okay," Alice finally said, breaking her trance. "I know the case you're talking about now. There were two of them, right? Both execution-style gunshot wounds to the head. Real mess from what I hear. A regular blood pudding."

That was how Alice liked to refer to the more grisly killings that came through the coroner's office.

"Let's see," Alice said, looking above quickly for one more tidbit of information, "the Ogre did those jobs. Late night stiffs. He probably messed something up, so anything wouldn't surprise me there."

Alice didn't have to pull any punches when it came to assessing the other people in her office. These were things Madison already knew. The Ogre was an assistant in the office by the name of Ryan Lutz. Lutz was six feet tall and weighed in at about three-twenty, a veritable bear. Hair grew prodigiously from his back, ears, nose, and hands. He was a drunk who clung to his job like a handful of other county workers who made everyone else's job in their office twice as hard.

"Well," Madison said, taking a delicate sip of her iced tea, "I want you to find out if there was a bullet wound in the ear of the victim named Ramon Gustava. I suspect that there may have been another gun involved. And evidence of another gun would help substantiate the kid's story about the man in black."

Alice tilted her head and looked at Madison for the punch line. "And how are you proposing I find out?" Alice said. "With my crystal ball or my tarot cards? Honey, that boy's six feet under."

"What about Lutz?" Madison said. "Can't you just ask him?"

"Madison, dear, are you feeling well?" Alice said with a mock look of concern on her face. "Lutz can't remember what he had for breakfast, let alone the status of a stiff he tore apart at three A.M. several months ago."

"What about the body, then?" Madison asked.

"Honey," Alice said incredulously, "when was the last time you heard of a body being exhumed in Travis County?"

Madison couldn't think of any.

"Exactly," Alice said, taking one big bite to finish off her bleeding burger.

It was Madison's turn to think. She would have to look into the case law. She'd get one of her associates started on it this afternoon. Walter would be the one to give her the ruling, and she had a feeling that if she could give him almost any case law at all to hang his robe on, he would order the exhumation.

"By the way," Alice said, her cherubic cheeks now flushed from the meal, "now you've got to tell me the story behind all this nonsense."

That was no problem to Madison. She thought it was good to rehash a story to someone else, especially someone as smart as Alice. Oftentimes someone else saw things that she didn't. Other times, she realized things by just saying them out loud.

"So why don't you do this?" Alice offered after she'd heard it all. "It sounds like if the kid is telling the truth, there's a bullet somewhere in the wall of that garage behind where Ramon was sitting. Even the Ogre would have found the slug if it was lodged in the kid's head. It would have showed up on the X-rays. Why don't we take a gander at the crime scene? If we find lead, then I bet you'll have a hell of a lot better chance getting a judge to order an exhumation than if you just go in there and tell him the alleged murderer says it's possible the body has another wound and that the Ogre just happened to miss it because he's an incompetent clod."

"Can you do something like that?" Madison asked. "I mean, find a bullet in a wall?"

"Honey," Alice replied, "if I can take a needle-thin bullet fragment out of a brain pudding, I can sure as hell pull a slug out of a wall. I know how to preserve a chain of evidence as good as any cop. You said the building was abandoned, so with any luck at all the chalk marks will still be there, and based on where old Rain-man Gustava was sitting, we can figure out pretty much where to look."

"That sounds great, Alice," Madison said. She was getting excited. If Walter was right, and the boy was innocent, it would be a wonderful achievement to exonerate him. It was the real reason she had become a defense lawyer. The fact was that people were often wrongly accused of crimes and punished based on their lack of fortune rather than their degree of guilt.

"When can we do it?" Madison asked.

Alice looked at her watch. "Damn, not now," she said. "Call me next week, honey. We'll get to it, but right now is bad. Don't look so sad. You're not going to trial on this soon are you?"

"No, and I can get a delay anyway," Madison said. "I'm just anxious to find out."

"Well," Alice said, rising from her seat with a wink, "hold on to your pants until the end of the dance. Contrary to popular belief, us county workers don't have a lot of free time. I'll call you, and we'll do it soon."

Madison smiled and waved good-bye as her friend chugged through the restaurant and out the front door into the hot summer afternoon.

Cody didn't know if it was him or what, but in the three days he'd been back from San Angelo, Jenny had been acting strange. Or he thought she was. He couldn't put his finger on it though. He had been so uptight and worried about camp before he'd left that he hadn't noticed much more about his wife than that she was unusually accommodating. He hadn't bothered to wonder about it back then. He'd just enjoyed it. Now her extra-good behavior was fueling those same old feelings of mistrust and jealousy that he seemed to have had ever since he'd known her.

It wasn't what she was saying or doing that was strange in any way, it was how she was saying and doing it. He was beginning to notice that although she was always willing to have sex with him, her mind seemed to be elsewhere. Also, he would come home from practice and find her sitting at the kitchen table or by the pool simply staring into space. Cody would watch her like this for several minutes before making himself known, then he'd ask if she felt all right. At first Cody hoped that Jenny was going to tell him she was pregnant, but it soon became obvious that that was not the case. Cody brought children up in a conversation they had at breakfast one morning, and Jenny's face visibly dropped. "Cody," she'd said, lying without even a blink, "I'm trying, and I've been trying hard, to make things between us good. Please, don't talk to me about that now. Wait until after this season. We'll see where we are. Then we can talk about that."

Cody thought it was a strange way to answer, but he'd accepted it. From time to time, in the past, Jenny had had her distant and mysterious phases. They weren't uncommon when he brought up subjects that she wasn't particularly fond of, and he simply took this for one of those times.

The next week, on Wednesday, four days before the opening regular season game for the Outlaws, Cody had a message in his locker after practice to call Marty Cahn. Cody hated messages that didn't explain what they were about. They made him nervous. He bothered only to strip off his sweat-soaked jersey and shoulder pads before going to the bank of players' phones just outside the locker room. Sweat continued to run down his back as he waited for the receptionist at the firm to pick up.

"Marty Cahn, please," he said. Cody absently scratched a bleeding scab on his shin with his other foot. A steaming clump of grass fell out of the shoe. Cody knew the equipment man would curse him if he caught him out here with his grass shoes on.

"Hi, Sabrina," Cody said to Marty's secretary, "it's me."

"Oh, Cody, hang on," Sabrina said, almost losing her breath, "he's in a meeting, but I know he wants to talk with you right away."

More desperate mystery. Cody's pulse raced. His stomach tightened. He hated this.

"Cody?"

"Marty, it's me, I can't stand when you leave a message to call immediately without telling me what the hell is going on. What's up?"

"I just didn't want to spread this all around. Now don't get excited, but we've got some problems with the IRS."

Confirmed. Cody knew something was bad. He knew it. "What problems?" Cody nearly shrieked.

"Cody, I have to say that I think we can work something out, but it's not great news. . . . Have you been getting yearly checks for five thousand dollars from America's Trading Cards?"

"Five? Yeah," Cody said, sickening at the sound of his own words. "I have. I really didn't think about it. I guess I have."

"Well, I hate to put it to you like this," Marty said, "but I don't want you to think that I've been remiss in handling your affairs. Now, you know that every year before I send in your taxes that I ask you to go down the line and tell me about any additional income you've had outside of the Outlaws. In fact, Cody, I send you a letter every year. It's in your file. Most of those outside things I've lined up for you myself, so I didn't really give it much second thought. I just want you to know that I haven't screwed you up on this. You really should have told me about this card deal."

"You know, Marty," Cody said, "I remember I signed a career deal with them my rookie year, and I just didn't give it much thought. I think I got a check from them every year, but I didn't really think about it. You know, when Jenny and I get a check, it's usually spent three different ways before it even hits the bank. So, I'll have to pay some back taxes, huh?"

Marty was quiet for a brief moment. It was a long moment to Cody Grey and a moment in which he realized real trouble was brewing.

"I hope we can resolve it that way," Marty said. "That's why I wanted to speak to you right away. I spoke to the agent who's doing the field audit. He wants to see us in person. He was being a real hard-ass on the phone, but the fact that he wanted to see us, you, in person makes me think that maybe we can stroke this guy a little and he'll work with us."

"Why do you sound so concerned, Marty?" Cody said. "If we have to pay, we have to pay. I mean, if I make my incentives, like I will if I can stay healthy, I'll have some extra money to pay it. You make it sound so bad."

"Cody," Marty said, "penalties, back taxes, and interest are one thing, but I have to tell you that this guy is talking about jail time."

Cody thought he might vomit. He was already exhausted and battered from a hard day out on the hot practice field. This news took him close to the edge.

"Not really," Cody said, "the guy didn't really mean that. They can't do that, can they?"

"I don't know," Marty said. "Well, yes. They can. Unfortunately, there's a pattern here. It's not the amount. It's the repeated frau—the repeated error. They did it to Daryl Strawberry already. Let's hope this guy isn't that determined. But we'll know more tomorrow. He wants to see us tomorrow morning in his office at ten o'clock."

"I've got meetings," Cody said.

"I know. I told him that," Marty replied. "He didn't seem all that interested."

Cody thought to himself. He could get the time. He'd have to tell the coach . . . but the game plan went in today. As long as he could make it back for practice . . . He'd have to take some stuff home with him tonight, then they'd let him off. Hell, they didn't have much choice. Cody thanked God the team now needed him. It would make it much easier for the coach to bear. Football coaches didn't like players to miss meetings or practice even for their own funerals.

"You don't really think they'd try to do that," Cody said, "I mean jail, do you?"

"Look, Cody," Marty said, "I don't want to give you any false hope. I think we've got a good chance to avoid something like that. As long as they aren't going to try to make an example of you, I think we can work something out. We're not talking about a tremendous amount of money here. But it's my job to tell you all the possibilities."

Cody was silent. He wanted more. He wanted Marty to assure him. That wasn't happening.

"I think you should come to my office at eight," Marty said. "We can go over everything and go over to the Federal building together."

"Okay," Cody said, "I'll be there."

He hung up and noticed that his shoes had disgorged a three foot circle of grass and dirt all over the carpet. He couldn't have cared less.

Jenny took the news worse than Cody would have expected.

"It's not you alone, Cody," she said. "It's us! We file jointly. We have for eight years. I'm at risk as much as you. I can't believe this! What the hell have we been paying your goddamned agent for? He's a fucking tax lawyer!"

Cody looked up from the table. They were sitting across from each other and he'd had his head in his hands. She seemed to be on the verge of losing control. It fit with her recent strange behavior, but if he hadn't been sure something was up with her before, he was certain now.

"Jenny," he said, as calmly as he could, "it's me they want. You're not part of this. If anything bad happens, it's me it will happen to. They don't want you. They want an NFL player. They want their own local version of Daryl Strawberry."

"Everything they do to you, they can do to me," she snapped at him. "My name is on those returns too. I signed them."

"Jenny," Cody said quietly, looking directly at her, "I won't let anything happen to you. If someone has to pay for this, I will. It's my fault. I'll take care of it. You're my wife, Jenny. I love you."

Jenny couldn't even look at him. Even she was too ashamed.

"Maybe it will be all right," she whispered.

CHAPTER FIFTEEN

WHILE CODY AND MARTY WERE HASHING out their strategy of how to best handle Jeff Board and their bad predicament, Board was shaving in the tiny bathroom of his old, rundown home on 22nd Avenue, in the same university neighborhood where Joe Thurwood did the majority of his work for the young drug dealer. The mirror doubled as the door to a rusted medicine cabinet that had once been white. The glass was pocked with ugly, dark blotches around the edges, and the remnants of an old STP sticker obscured the upper right-hand corner. Board was sweating even though the shower he'd taken was cold. His gut hung over his boxer shorts, stretching the cotton tank top tucked into the waistband.

Board cut himself and cursed. Crimson drops dripped from his chin to the sea of foam and stubble in the sink below. He wanted to look good for today. It was maybe the biggest day in his life. He wanted to look important. Now he was going to have to sport a spot of toilet paper on his face or risk having the nick ooze during the meeting, dripping blood over everything. Either way, he looked at it as a possible opening for humiliation that he was sure a savage like Cody Grey would exploit. Cody could very well laugh right out loud during the meeting. And again behind his back after he left.

"Shit!" he screamed, throwing the razor down on the floor. "Shit! Shit! Shit!"

Board finally got control of himself and picked the razor back up to finish the job. He decided on the toilet paper. He'd use a very small piece. Ten small pieces later, one stuck for what he hoped would be the remainder of the morning. He looked at his watch. He had to hurry. One of his cats was mewing pathetically by the back door that led down a rickety set of stairs to the driveway.

"Damn it, Babs," he whined as he stumbled to the door to let out the cat.

Ten minutes later, Board was racing down Lamar Avenue toward his office. His tie had yet to be tied, but his top button was buttoned. He could get the tie on in the parking lot. He didn't want to be late. He didn't mind keeping Cody Grey waiting, but he didn't want them to see him scurrying into the office at ten after ten. He wanted them to see him busting loose from some important meeting, making time in his busy day to personally take charge of a flagrant criminal affront to the United States Government. Board looked at his watch. Damn. He wanted to have time to get Patti's conference room lined up. He should have done it yesterday. He had to have the conference room. He sure as hell wasn't going to grill Cody Grey and his lawyer in his cubicle.

"Damn, damn," he muttered to himself.

Every traffic light seemed to go against him. Board ended up running through the parking lot to the building so fast that he had a full sweat going by the time he reached the elevators. He knotted his tie on the way up; it wasn't straight, but it was tied. He scuttled out of the elevator and down the hall as fast as he could, trying all the while not to look like he was hurrying. He saw Cody Grey sitting with his lawyer in the row of seats along the wall by the receptionist's desk. They were busy conferring. He was going to make it past them.

"Mr. Board?" the receptionist called.

To Board it sounded like a scream. He froze. Keep going? Stop? Don't look their way? They saw him.

"Shit," he said under his breath.

"Mr. Board," the receptionist said, "these gentlemen have been waiting for you."

Board put on his most dire and concerned countenance and turned to face Cody Grey and Marty Cahn. Cahn was holding out his hand. Grey had no expression on his face whatsoever. Board took the lawyer's hand, giving it his tightest grip to see what kind of a man the sharply dressed lawyer really was. Board believed that a real man shook hands firmly. Marty was caught off-guard and got his fingers crushed.

"Hello, Mr. Board," Marty said. "I'm Marty Cahn, and this is my client, Cody Grey."

"Well," Board said with a scowl, too nervous to enjoy the fact that Cahn had called him mister, "you'd better follow me."

Board thanked God he had the file with him in his briefcase. He hadn't gotten much done at home the night before; he'd spent more time deciding if he should wear his gray suit or his blue suit. But he'd taken the file home, so he had it now.

The player and his agent followed Board silently as he waddled toward the other end of the office where Patti's conference room was located. Board opened the door importantly and took two steps into the room.

The people who were in there stared at him with unabashed hostility. Patti's face turned red. Three people from Washington and office directors from around the state sat around the long table. Patti mashed out a Marlboro Light and exhaled her words.

"Jeff," she said, an exasperated edge to her voice, "I think you're in the wrong place at the wrong time."

Board was humiliated. He backed out with a few gruff apologies and tried his best to act as if some secretary's head was going to roll for the mistake. Frantically he tried to think of a place to go. Then he had it.

Loreen stood up from her desk as he filed past with Cody and Marty.

"Mix-up with the conference room," Board said to her importantly, as if to suggest that she had been the errant fool causing the mix-up. He walked right by without giving Loreen a chance to protest, shutting the door behind them and making out as if the office were his own.

"Sit down, gentlemen," he said pompously, getting himself between them and the front of Patti's desk to turn the name plate on its face before they could read it.

Marty hesitated to sit. The stink of cigarettes was overwhelming, and it looked as if smoke had left a film of grime on all the furniture. He wanted to keep Board as happy as he could, though. He needed to soften him up in any way that was possible.

Board got himself behind the desk, sat down, and peered threateningly at Marty and Cody over the stack of papers that covered his boss's desk. Grey, the son-of-a-bitch, looked right back at him. He was so fucking cocky. Then, for a split second Board got nervous, thinking that Patti could walk in and make him look like a real fool.

"Well," Marty said, realizing that the IRS agent was not going to get things started in the near future, "would you like me to tell you our position, Mr. Board, so we can try to come to some kind of reasonable understanding with all this?"

"You think there's a reasonable understanding?" Board said with a nasty smile as he reached self-consciously to feel if the toilet paper was in place, or if he was bleeding. "I don't think your position can be much of anything but . . . but a bad position."

"Yes," Marty said calmly, "we realize that fully. You are absolutely right. This is a gross oversight—"

"I wonder about that," Board snapped, wanting more than anything for Cody Grey to snap back, to react to something, to lose it. But he didn't see fear. He didn't even see concern. The son-of-a-bitch was sitting there calmly, like this whole thing was some kind of a joke.

"I have to say, Mr. Board," Marty continued as amiably as possible, "that our position for the record is that Mr. Grey did not intentionally misrepresent his income to the government."

Board was sweating under his arms now. He hated the smell of fear. He wasn't supposed to be afraid. He wasn't supposed to be nervous here! It enraged him. Everything was going wrong.

"I'd like to hear what Mr. Grey has to say," Board said, sticking out his chin, just daring Marty to contradict him on this one.

Cody looked at Marty. Marty didn't really have a choice but to tell his client to go ahead. That Board was acting like a pompous ignoramus was just hard luck. Once an IRS agent had your client's file, you dealt with him. If the word ever got back that you'd gone over his head, you'd better pray that the higher-up agreed that the agent had drastically exceeded his authority. But the IRS had so much autonomy, and the agents so much leeway, that ninety-nine times out of a hundred, bucking protocol only made things much worse for your client. Marty looked from Board to Cody, then shrugged and nodded, signaling Cody to go ahead.

Cody looked at the slovenly IRS agent. His gray suit was old and rumpled. The bright red tie hadn't been popular for ten years. The knot was off-center. Board's skin was so pale, it had a green tint to it, and his long, dark hair was so greasy and stringy that Cody could think of nothing but a *Saturday Night Live* skit with the Lupeners.

Then Board absently rubbed his chin, pulling off the tattered piece of toilet paper and exposing a crusty blotch of blood that began to ooze. Board panicked. Cody thought the man's face was too funny. He bit the inside of his mouth to repress a smile. Board caught the glimpse of a smirk, though. The IRS agent turned beet-red.

"I just didn't remember about the card money," Cody said calmly, as though nothing had happened. "I signed a deal with them back when I was a rookie, and I never got any forms or anything."

"You just got a check?" Board said with as much sarcasm as he could muster, pulling what looked like a used tissue from his pocket and dabbing the beads of blood running down his chin. "Did you forget that five thousand dollars a year?"

Cody looked at Marty, then back at Board before saying, "Yes."

"Well, you're a pretty forgetful guy, aren't you?" Board said, as though he were talking to a ten-year-old child.

Cody clenched his fists and held them tightly against his legs. He looked over to Marty for help. Cody didn't take that kind of talk from coaches, men who he knew could rip the balls off of a bull with their teeth. This pile of shit and blubber was way out of line. Marty held up his hand to Cody, trying to keep him calm. He knew by the expression on Cody's face and from his body language that he was starting to lose his composure.

"Just a minute," Marty said, standing up and gesturing with both hands to hold back the storm that was going to break. "Maybe, Mr. Board, you'd like to put down on paper your position so I can review it, then we can go from there. We could talk about it next week."

Board rose suddenly. "I wanted you—him—here today, and I want to hear what he's got to say for himself before I begin what I think will be a very damaging investigation." Board calmed himself before he displayed a malicious smile. "*Very* damaging."

"Mr. Board," Marty said with a judicious tone in his voice, "I've dealt with the IRS before, and I have to say that this is highly irregular. It sounds as though your only purpose in bringing us here was to tell us that you are going to commence a field audit no matter what we have to say in our defense."

"Well, I'm not regular, Mr. Cahn," Board sneered. "I'm not falling all over myself to make you happy because your client is a professional football player. I don't scare so easy, Mr. Cahn." Board's voice cracked, but he gave Cody a challenging look. "I . . . don't . . . scare."

Cody stood abruptly. He looked at Marty and snarled, "I'm out of here."

"You'll sit down!" Board yelled. "This is my office! This is my meeting!"

Cody leaned toward Marty and through gritted teeth said, "You tell this guy to steer clear of me, Marty. You tell him . . . " Cody's voice trailed off as he chose between his fists and the door.

Then he walked past the gawking agent and out of the office.

"We'll see if you walk out when this goes to a trial!" Board bellowed after him, knocking a pile of papers off of his boss's desk as he waved his arm at Cody's back. "I'm prosecuting this to the fullest extent of the law! My next call is to the U.S. attorney's office! You think you're above the law? No one is above the law!"

Marty turned and walked out as well. The man was clearly crazy. He'd have to regroup. The whole thing had fallen apart in a way that was entirely mad. He hurried to catch up to Cody.

When they were gone and his breathing was almost back to normal, Board knelt down and carefully picked up the scattered papers, replacing them as neatly as he could on the desk. Then he walked cautiously out of Patti's office.

"Oh, man," Loreen said, "Patti's not gonna be too happy about that."

"About what?" Board said arrogantly.

"About you just barging into her office and yelling like some kind of nut. Everyone heard you, you know."

Board looked around and caught a dozen faces turn and flit in every direction but his. "I don't care if everyone heard," he said, hitching up his pants and glaring down at Loreen. "And as far as Patti goes, when she gets out of that meeting, you tell her I need to see her. I'm gonna put this office on the front page of every paper from here to New York. You tell her that."

Marty could do nothing to calm Cody down. The man was seething with rage. Cody tried to explain to Marty that his anger wasn't a bad thing, that he had practice that afternoon, and he'd work it out there.

"The truth is," Cody said when Marty stopped on the street where Cody had parked his pickup truck, "I'm the best player I can be when things are going bad. It transfers for me, Marty. Some people, things go bad in their life and they fold. They can't keep focused. They lose their fire. Me? I get twice as mean and I play twice as good. It's always been that way with me."

Cody looked over at his agent to see if he understood. Marty nodded as if he did, but in reality he was thinking about things more important than what happened on the football field. Marty wondered if Cody understood the significance of what had just happened and how dire the circumstances had become.

Cody turned his gaze to the bustling street in front of them. "Maybe that's why I married Jenny," he said, as if speaking to himself.

Marty could say nothing to that. He'd contained his feelings about Cody's wife since the day they first met. He had strong opinions about women who flaunted their looks and bodies, seeking attention from every man within a mile's radius. He'd seen Jenny's sidelong flirtatious smiles at men in restaurants and at his own office. He'd watched as she spent the couple out of any savings they might have had. But he knew better than to ever talk bad about a client's spouse, even if a divorce looked imminent. It was a good way to lose clients. He wasn't going to start now.

Cody didn't bother to look for Marty's reaction. He simply opened the door and climbed out of the car.

"Fuck that guy, Marty," Cody said, leaning in from the street, his mind obviously back on the IRS. "Pull out all the stops. He's going to take this to the limit, so let's kick him in the balls. I've got some connections. People know me. Let's use every favor we've got.

"Look," Cody said with a note of humor that he didn't really feel, "worst comes to worst, I go to the federal hotel for a couple of months and write an autobiography. I'm not going to let this guy fuck with me, Marty. I know the worst he can do, and I'm ready to handle it."

Marty wanted to tell Cody that this wasn't a football game. It wasn't a matter of blitzing every play, and if you lost, well, there was always next week or next year. This was much more serious than that. Marty opened his mouth to speak.

"Let me know," Cody snapped, then he was gone.

Marty pushed his glasses back up his nose and watched Cody climb into his truck before he put his own car into gear. It was going to be a long day. Board was going to make this whole thing a long drawn-out affair, and Marty was going to have to go by the book. He had a client who was used to smashing opponents, and an opponent who held all the cards. It was a bad combination. Cody didn't realize what Marty knew for a fact, that the IRS didn't deal. Favors and chummy promises were best left at the door. The IRS took pride in being impervious to any outside influences.

Because of the Cody Grey situation, Marty worked later than normal, even though he was supposed to have dinner with Madison at eight o'clock. He pulled into her driveway at eight-thirty. Madison wasn't one to get too excited about being late, so he really didn't worry about it. He got out of his car and pulled at his dark suit as he walked up to the door. He was still wearing the same clothes from that morning, and he felt stiff and sticky. If he hadn't been late already, he would have gone back to his apartment and changed. Even though Madison wouldn't be angry about his being late, he knew that after a certain point she would just tell him she'd take a rain check. But he wanted to talk to her. He wanted to get her opinion on Cody Grey's predicament. Madison had good instincts, even regarding areas of the law outside her expertise. If it had to do with people, Madison was a good sounding board.

Marty rang the bell, and after a minute Jo-Jo opened the front door. Jo-Jo looked up at Marty, squinting because of the overhead porch light. Marty could see Lucia's head pop around the corner to see who was there.

"Hey, Jo-Jo," Marty said in his best eight-year-old voice. "How's it going, buddy?"

"Good," said Jo-Jo. He had a red Power Ranger toy in one hand and an authentic looking Glock replica in the other. Marty was surprised that Madison allowed the gun and wondered if it had come from Joe. He knew Madison had conceded to temporary visitations after realizing there was no way to explain to an eight-year-old why he couldn't see his father. Marty stepped into the house and shut the door quickly to keep the mosquitoes from launching a full-scale invasion.

"So," Marty said, eyeing the gun, "how's school?"

"Good."

"Great," Marty said.

"Marty?" Jo-Jo said, looking up at the tall, lanky tax lawyer, "did you ever play football?"

Marty pushed his glasses up and blinked. He kneeled down next to Jo-Jo and tousled his hair.

"Well, buddy," he said, "I played a little, but not too much. It really wasn't for me."

"I mean, you were never an Outlaw, right?" Jo-Jo said.

"No," Marty said with a good-natured chuckle, "I wasn't. I'm an agent for a lot of the Outlaws, but I never played for them."

"Oh," Jo-Jo said, then he turned and walked off into the house.

Marty smiled, but he felt strangely uncomfortable. Why should an eight-year-old's innocent question bother him? Maybe it was because Marty felt other people had wondered the same thing about him, and concluded he wasn't quite man enough. That's what it was about, being a man. Marty suspected that this question had originated with the boy's father. Big Joe had always divided men into two categories, those who were players and those who weren't. Agent or not, Marty had always been somewhat of an outsider in the world of football, especially since he'd never played, not even for fun.

The sight of Madison cut his thoughts short. She looked absolutely beautiful. She'd let her hair down and was wearing just a touch of eyeliner and lipstick. She wore a new black cotton summer dress. It was short enough to show off her shapely legs.

"Why are you down there on the floor like that?" she asked him.

Marty straightened up and took a step toward her.

"God, Madison," he said, "you look—you look gorgeous."

"Thank you, Marty," Madison said, blushing slightly.

"What's the occasion," Marty said, hoping in the back of his mind that she was doing this for his benefit.

"None, really," she sighed. "You know me, Marty. Sometimes I just get tired of being the drab female attorney. I just felt like looking good. That's all."

"Well," he said, looking at his watch, "I know I'm late, but I called and they're holding our table."

"Good," Madison said. "I need a night out. I'm getting tired of criminals and jails and drug addicts and killers. A civilized dinner is just what I need."

Marty opened the door, and Madison called one last good-night to her son and Lucia before stepping out into the darkness.

After they had been seated at their table and ordered a couple of drinks, Marty began to recount for Madison what had happened that morning at the Federal building. When he was finished, they ordered dinner.

"Well, it sounds to me like your client pushed the wrong buttons with this IRS guy," Madison said when the waiter left.

"Haven't you been listening?" Marty said defensively. "Cody didn't do a damn thing! It was unadulterated hatred. Why? I've never seen anything like it. It was as if Cody had done something to this guy personally."

"Maybe he did," Madison suggested.

"He didn't," Marty said. "I asked him. He's never seen the guy or heard of him or known anyone who had anything to do with the IRS."

"Marty, think about it," Madison said. "Cody Grey may have punched this guy's lights out one time and not even remember it."

"Oh, come on," Marty said. "Cody's not like that. You know damn well that people aren't always what they appear to be."

"I know you think all your clients are great guys, Marty," she said, "but they're not."

"Come on, Madison," Marty protested, "don't you think you're reacting to your own experience with Joe? These guys aren't like Joe. Cody is not like him."

"Please, Marty," she said, rolling her eyes. "How can you say that? All you have to do is read the papers to know Cody Grey is a crime waiting to happen. How many times has Rick Capozzo cranked up the civil litigation department to settle with some guy whose nose Cody Grey broke? Ten times?"

"Not ten," Marty said sullenly. "Three."

"Okay, three," Madison said, throwing her hands up in the air. "I'm sorry. Just think, if Van Rawlins wasn't such a good Texan how much trouble you would have had. If they'd prosecuted your guy for all those punches, he could be doing two to four right now."

"Unless you were his lawyer," Marty said with a smirk.

"God forbid," she replied. "Someone like that just gives off bad vibes, Marty. If he didn't punch out the IRS guy or one of his close relatives, or something crazy like that, to cause the guy to have a grudge, he probably shook the guy up by the way he looked at him. Talk to the IRS guy tomorrow. Give him some time to settle down. He'll be easier to deal with without some thug like Cody Grey sitting there staring at him."

"You keep making it sound like Cody is some kind of monster, Madison. I'm telling you, he did nothing wrong."

"Stop giving these people so much credit, Marty," she implored. "They play football. They hit people. They're paid to be nasty. And in a world where nastiness reigns king, Cody Grey is supposed to be one of the worst. You're probably lucky he didn't assault the guy. All the time you spend with him, you're probably lucky he hasn't wiped the floor with you yet."

"Hey," Marty said, "really, you don't know Cody. First of all, he and I are friends. Hell, every time I see him he's running off to talk to this bunch of kids or that bunch of kids."

"Yeah," Madison said skeptically, "but remember, I know how phony that game is. I watched Joe firsthand go out and talk about how much he did for kids. He couldn't stand the kids. It was all a big farce, just like the farce he's pulling right now to try and make my life miserable. But that's what football players do, isn't it? Make people miserable."

Marty held up his hand to signal enough. He rarely cut Madison off, but in this case, he had to. She was wrong. She just didn't know what she was talking about. She was too poisoned because of her own horrible experience with a football player named Joe Thurwood.

"Let's talk about something else," he said.

"Let's."

Dinner was fine, and they began to reminisce about their law school, slipping into that comfortable zone of old stories about old friends and then wondering where they are now. Marty loved to talk about life before Joe Thurwood. When they talked about those good old days, it was easy for Marty to realize why he would always think of Madison as she was back then, idealistic and unspoiled by the harsh realities of the world. No matter what had happened in the interim, to him Madison would always be the closest thing to perfection as a lawyer and as a woman.

They stayed late. The dinner wine had been so good that they each ordered another and drank it slowly before considering dessert. It was eleven-thirty before they had their last cup of coffee, and Marty slipped his gold card underneath the check.

The night had cooled enough for them to put the windows down on the way home. When they got onto the open road, Marty started to close both windows.

"Let's leave them down, Marty," Madison said languorously.

"I'll leave yours down," he said, continuing to close his own. "I don't like the wind."

"Oh, come on, Marty," Madison said with a giggle she only displayed after several glasses of wine. "You don't have to worry about messing up your hair, do you? Why not live a little?"

Marty's face turned to stone. Maybe it was the conversation with Jo-Jo and the talk about how rough and tough all football players are and how Cody Grey could wipe the floor with him. When it came to macho, tough-guy things, like fighting, it was as if he didn't even count. Or maybe it was because though he and Madison spent almost as much time together as a romantically involved couple would, he was still just good old Marty. Whatever it was, Marty was angry. Madison made it worse.

"Oh, Marty," she said teasingly, "you don't get mad, do you? You don't get mad at me."

He wasn't supposed to be tough enough to get mad! Marty pursed his lips and still said nothing.

"Oooooo," Madison crowed, capping it off with another silly giggle.

They sat in silence for the rest of the trip. Madison decided Marty had had a bad day, so she put her head back and enjoyed the cool night air rushing over her face and washing all other noise from her ears. When Marty slowed down to turn into Madison's development, he realized she had fallen asleep. He pulled up into the driveway and shut off his engine as she opened her eyes.

Marty walked Madison up to the door, even though he was still mad. He stepped inside to say good night. She turned to face him with her warm smile and gave him a friendly hug.

"Thank you, Marty," she said. "I really enjoyed dinner. I don't know, tonight was just one of those nights I needed to get out. I didn't mean anything. Don't be mad. . . . "

Marty let out a heavy sigh, and with it, any ill feelings he had. Madison was his friend. He should lighten up.

"I'm not," he said. "Just a long day, I guess. See you tomorrow?"

Madison nodded. Marty gave her a kiss on the cheek and said good-bye before turning out into the night.

Madison stood there for a long while, then she went inside. She suddenly felt completely alone. She wished more than anything that her father was there. Even though she knew her feelings were largely due to all the wine she had drunk, she still wanted him to hold her. He was the only one she could think of who could make her feel better. She wished that wasn't so. It wasn't right that a thirty-five-year-old woman didn't have a man in her life who could hold her besides her father. A single tear rolled down her cheek and onto the front of her beautiful new dress. She sat down on the bottom of the staircase and wrapped her arms around the newel post to sob. Abby came padding in half-asleep from the laundry room and nuzzled Madison until she held the dog tightly.

After a good cry, Madison kissed Abby's head and went upstairs to her room. She heard Abby's nails clicking along the marble floor on her way back to her bed. Madison activated the alarm from her bedroom and got into a hot shower.

As the hot water cascaded over her she thought about why she couldn't be romantic with Marty. It basically came down to sex, or sexual attraction anyway. It just wasn't there. Madison knew she could never be happy with a man who didn't get her excited in a physical way as well as an intellectual and emotional way. She knew from her failed marriage with Joe that the physical element could certainly not carry a relationship. But she also knew for a fact that the other connections without the physical attraction would be just as much of a life sentence. If Madison couldn't have a man she wanted to take to her bed every night, she would have no man at all. Madison climbed out of the shower and went to sleep alone.

Joe Thurwood took one last drag on his joint before stubbing it out and swallowing the roach. A smile crept across his face when he saw Marty's bean-pole figure come ambling away from the house. He didn't want that prick fucking with his wife. It was bad enough that the two of them gallivanted around town like a couple of fools. It made him look bad, real fucking bad. He had plans for Marty, though. That much he had promised himself. He wasn't planning on being around forever. This town was too small for him, and too many people knew him. He had made some contacts in New Orleans. He had a new identity and a job waiting for him in a big-time organization. Eventually he would get his own piece of the action, and that is what he wanted. That is what he deserved. But he wasn't going to show up empty-handed.

First, he was going to put his wife through some serious hell. He was going to make her sorry for what she'd done to him. Second, he was going to squeeze her for every last dollar he could get and then disappear. He'd drive into New Orleans behind the wheel of a Mercedes and set himself up in a nice flat in the French Quarter with the money he got. It would be better to start his new life that way. People would respect him more.

Before he blew town, though, he was going to pay his old agent back for trying to fuck around with his wife. He was going to pay him a visit with a baseball bat and some pliers and leave him with a few mementos of pain that he would never forget. This promise to himself was the only way he had been able not to lose control thus far. It took incredible willpower not to leave Cahn in a bloody heap the first night he saw the two of them kissing at the river.

Joe took a baggy out of his pants and stuck his nose inside, snorting up the last of the blow that was trapped in the corner. The grass made him sluggish, and he needed a little lift. Joe got out of his Blazer and crossed the street. He looked around furtively. Except for the crickets chirring in the balmy night, the neighborhood was quiet. It almost always was. The lots were big enough, and the foliage grew around the homes like a jungle, so he could creep around his house without much concern that someone would call the cops. Of course he always dressed in dark clothes to make it less likely that any meddlers would see him in the first place. If anyone did see him, he had an excuse ready for them. He thought it would make him look good anyway. He would say that he was only trying to get a glimpse of his son. The boy that had been taken from him by the miserable bitch mother, the slick lawyer.

The thought of Maddy gave Joe a charge of adrenaline and then, peering into the windows from the darkness of the shrubbery, he saw her standing in the foyer. She wore a dress that left no doubt she still had the same sensational body she had the first time he fucked her. Joe felt himself beginning to stiffen as his memory and imagination kicked into gear simultaneously. The blood rushed to his groin. With the blow and the adrenaline and the memories, it was all he could do to keep himself from smashing through the glass and fucking her right there on the marble floor. She needed it, he could see. She was crying; he imagined it was because she needed to be fucked so badly.

When Maddy sat down on the stairs and bent over, he could see down the front of her dress. In a trance Joe stared at the luscious curves of her beautiful breasts. He knew exactly what they felt like, and he could feel them now. He undid his pants and let them fall to his knees. In his mind he could actually hear her moans of passion, the ones she used to make in the darkness of their bedroom when he would awake late at night and take her in her sleep, fucking her hard in every imaginable way he could think of. In the safety of the darkness, he stood there, hunched over and stroking himself into a frenzy until he felt the mind-bending release he had felt with her time and time again. He choked himself hard, shuddering until his knees felt weak. He actually staggered before he pulled his pants up and backed away through the bushes with the stealth of a reptile.

Chapter Sixteen

∨

SOME DAYS WERE JUST WORSE THAN OTHERS. That was always the way it had been with football. Some days Cody would wake up and feel pretty good. Other days, he'd feel as though he'd been in a nasty car accident, and every part of his body hurt, including some places he never even knew he had. Sometimes, and these were the worst days of all, one specific injury, be it new or old, would scream bloody murder even before his eyes were open. That was how he felt on the first Sunday of the NFL season. It was cruel that his body would do this to him now, when he needed it the most.

The knee was not only aching as though someone had wedged a rusty nail between the two bones, it was swollen. It happened like that. The night before it had been sore, but no more than usual after a week of practice. Now it was the size of a grapefruit. Not a good sign. It wasn't a matter of him dealing with pain, or numbing the pain, or ignoring the pain. All those things he could do. The question now was whether or not he could use the joint. It was like a frozen wing flap on an airplane; if it didn't go down, you just couldn't fly. Cody took a hot shower, hoping his knee would loosen up. It didn't. He hobbled down to one of the hotel's banquet rooms where the team's pregame meal was being served.

He tried to hide his predicament from his teammates as he stood in line for some eggs and pancakes. No one really noticed. They were used to his bum knee by now, and like most people, football players gradually became desensitized to someone else's chronic pain. Besides, everyone was too jittery to notice. Today was the first game of the season, and most guys hadn't slept well in the hotel, making everyone twice as introverted and grumpy as normal. Every player knew that most of them would have been better off at home with their wives or girlfriends, but that was just the way the Outlaws did it. Like on most NFL teams, anyone who was going to play Sunday had to spend the previous night at some cheesy hotel on the outskirts of town, where the team had been given a reduced rate as a draw for groupies and overzealous fans. It was someone's notion of a battle camp, and like dog crap on the bottom of a shoe, it had stuck.

Cody sat down at an empty table and tried to make himself eat. He would need the energy. The eggs looked like yellow Styrofoam and had about the same taste. The pancakes were heavy and reminiscent of plaster of Paris. He tried to overwhelm the stale flavor with syrup, but it was too sweet and already cold. When he popped open the top of the stainless-steel syrup container with his thumb to see if some prankster had dumped a packet of sugar in it, a fly buzzed out and droned heavily toward the ceiling. After a few more mouthfuls of the eggs, Cody got up and gimped out. The fly and the pain in his knee were making it hard for him to keep the food in his stomach. He was better off trying to hold on to what he had than risk the whole thing ending up in the bowl. Cody got into his truck and headed downtown toward the stadium.

Although it was still three solid hours until the noon kickoff, there was already a healthy contingent of maniacs outside the players' fenced-in parking lot. One old Chevy pickup truck was filled with rednecks sitting on a bed of hay, tossing down Busch beer. They cheered wildly for Cody when he got out of his truck. Cody set his game face and walked past the unruly crew without a word. His reticence made the rednecks hoot and holler even more. There was nothing they loved more than a bad-assed football player.

One scrawny, shirtless man with a grizzly beard and leather Confederate soldier's cap stood up in the back of the truck, hoisting a can and screaming, "Cody Grey, you're so damn mean, you hate your own mamma. An' we love the hell out of ya! Wooooooooo!"

The others cheered with him. Cody shook his head. Everybody loves a good bad-man.

Once inside the stadium, Cody found that only a few veteran players had gotten there before him. They were the really old guys, in their mid-thirties, who had acquired idiosyncrasies over the course of their careers. These older players had a ritualized pregame procedure, so they had to get to the stadium hours before kickoff in order to accomplish their superstitious routine. Normally, the longer a player was in the league, the longer his routine became. Cody's routine included sit-ups and push-ups, the number and sequence depending on how he had played the previous week. If he'd had a good game, or the team won, he'd likely repeat the sequence. He'd also lay out his entire uniform, including all its padding, on the floor. Then, with just a towel around his waist, he'd tape his wrists and forearms and get the trainers to tape his ankles. Then he'd return to his seat and begin to dress from either the top down or the bottom up, depending again on how successful the previous week's order had been. Once Cody had tried to dress from the middle out, but he broke his hand that game. Of course, he never tried that again.

Today, though, Cody didn't have the luxury to perform with his routine. Today he went straight to the training room and looked for Dr. Cort. He needed more than drugs for his knee right now. Cort was having a coffee with Dr. Burlitz and Jerry in Jerry's office. They were saying something about someone's congenital heart defect when he walked in.

"Cody," Cort said in his easy and friendly manner, "how's that knee?"

Cody gave him a weak smile and said, "Not too good."

Cort set his coffee cup down with the same deliberate motion that Cody suspected he used to set aside a bloody scalpel.

"Let's take a look at it," Cort said cheerfully, like they were all going to get to see the newest butterfly he'd added to his collection.

Cody didn't like having the entire medical staff hovering around him, but they were like that. They sensed that something gruesome was about to take place, and they were no different from all those people who stop traffic to gawk at a bloody car accident.

Amid five trainers and the two doctors, Cody watched as Cort punched a needle the size of a cocktail straw into the side of his puffy knee. Cody winced, and everyone but Burlitz looked away as Cort wiggled and pushed the horse needle, placing it just so under the bony cap of Cody's knee. When it was just the way he wanted it, Cort pulled out on the plunger, and the fat syringe began to fill with a yellow fluid that soon swirled with dark red clouds of blood. Cody had to watch it, despite the excruciating pain. It was his blood and fluid that were being drained, and if he wasn't going to keep an eye on things, then who the hell else would?

The plunger was almost all the way out, and it still pulled merry swirls of blood into the syringe.

"Gotta go in again," Cort said matter-of-factly, setting aside the big needle like some bloated mosquito and picking up another empty one for its feeding. Cody noticed a couple of his teammates had entered the training room and were warily eyeing the whole procedure from the far side of the room. They knew better than to get close. That was bad luck.

The second one was as painful as the first, but after the plunger was only halfway home, the knee just had no more fluid to give. Cort fished around a little; then, well satisfied, he removed the second monster needle and picked up a harmless-looking dart-sized syringe that was filled with a clear cortizone-Xylocaine concoction: high-octane. The thin needle was like a pinprick after the big boys; and besides, Cody knew that it spelled relief. There were three in all. Cort shot them into his knee from different angles. By the time the third one went in, the first was already starting to make his knee feel like it was falling asleep. Cort finished and patted Cody's leg.

"Lie there a minute and we'll see how it feels," the doctor said.

Cody lay back as he was told. The crowd dispersed. The fun was over. Cody had time now to smell the sickening aroma of the alcohol they'd bathed his knee in and to see the bloody gauze pads that lay in clumps beside the host of needles lined in a row like spent soldiers.

Cort came back in a few minutes and started flexing Cody's bad knee. He felt a little of the tugging, but the joint itself was not painful. It seemed to flex smoothly, like the perfect knee of a teenage long-distance runner.

"Okay?" Cort asked.

"Okay," Cody said, sitting up and taking hold of the deadened joint in both his hands to flex it as the doctor had done.

Cort smiled, gave his calf a pat, and walked away. Cody was still flexing the incredibly smooth knee when Paul Dryer, the team's forty-year-old head coach, walked into the locker room in his houndstooth jacket, cowboy boots, and tie.

The coach smiled broadly when he caught Cody's eye.

"How's it feeling?" the young coach said in his southern twang.

"Fine," Cody said. He didn't really have much more to say.

"Good, we can't play the game very well without a free safety, can we?" Dryer said, then leaned closer to Cody, putting his arm around the veteran player's shoulder and dropping his voice as if he were confiding in a lifelong friend. Cody could smell pistachio nuts on his breath.

"Now I want you to know," said the coach, "how much we all appreciate what it is you're going through. We all know, and I know, that the pricks upstairs made it hard on you as far as your contract this year."

Cody nodded. He didn't mind looking the coach straight in the eye. What he said was true.

"Well," Dryer said, "I want you to know that what you're doing . . . " and he waved his hand across the air above Cody's drained and injected knee as if he were shooing away a fly, "we won't forget it; the team won't forget it." Then the coach looped one forearm around Cody's neck and pulled him into a hug, suggesting that bigger and better things always came for those who waited.

Cody nodded. He would like to see how well they didn't forget. It seemed to him that they had forgotten him once, this past offseason. He imagined they just might do the same again, so he simply kept his gaze at the coach steady as she goes.

Dryer looked for something more, maybe acknowledgment, maybe even gratitude. Nothing was forthcoming.

"Okay," said the coach, backing away, "let's go out there and kick these guys in the teeth, right?"

Cody nodded slowly. "Yeah," he said, thinking that college was too many years ago, and so were the days that he got psyched up for a game because of some coach's macho bullshit.

"Okay," said the coach enthusiastically, smiling once more and giving Cody a thumbs-up before he turned and walked away.

"Okay, my ass," Cody said under his breath, and then hopped down off the table to test his knee.

It was a strange feeling, but one he'd felt before. It was like everything was normal, except his knee felt like a blob of dough. It worked, though. He could move. The signals from the joint to his brain telling him that something was incredibly wrong were silenced and would be for the next four hours. The only thing bad was the little gremlin sitting patiently in the corner of his mind. He knew it was there, an ugly little demon with a big, crooked, toothy smile. It was just waiting. It knew that sooner or later the drugs would have to wear off, and then it would rule his mind. It would dance and sing and moan and drag chains up and down the corridors of his brain until he knew nothing else but the agony of an injury that had just been exacerbated in the name of winning a game of football. The knee would end up being twice as bad as it was only this morning.

Cody now knew the season would be an unending battle with that gremlin. He would drug his body and it would wait. The drug would wear off. The gremlin would torment him. Then he would spring some new kind of painkiller or anti-inflammatory on the little horror. They would go around and around until one of them finally quit.

Cody dressed himself as quickly as he could. Then he sat. He had some minutes, and he used them to work his thoughts into another mind game. The pain was put aside; now he had to whip himself into a frenzy to play. He took all the poison that was in his life at that moment and emptied it into one enormous mental cauldron. He thought about Jenny. He knew something was wrong. He wasn't quite sure what, and he didn't want to know. For his purposes now, he imagined the worst. She hadn't answered the phone last night. He imagined her naked and fucking some specter like a frantic animal in heat. It was sick, but it worked. That went in the pot.

He thought about Board. The sloppy, greasy bag-of-shit with his octopus skin, bald in front with long greasy hair hanging over the back of his collar. He was the perfect image of a witch's toad. He put that in.

Jail? That was possible, or so augured the toad. He thought about that, the humiliation, the confinement. In.

Then he thought about the Outlaws, about Dryer and his words only moments ago. He thought about how he was nothing more than a disposable part for them, like a razor, and a cheap one at that. He thought about being used for eight years, now nine. He put that in the pot.

Money? He had almost none. In it went.

His body? It was being ruined. That went in too.

"Ten minutes!" came the call from the weight coach, who was counting down the minutes before the team took the field.

Cody stirred the poison. He let it fester together, all the bad thoughts, all the anger, all the resentment, all the fears. It made him mad, and it made him mean. Someone looking in his eyes would look twice and see that in fact their depth had become the bottomless void of a madman's. A strange light emanated from his eyes, and the walls of those infinite tunnels seemed to spin with hatred and rage. Cody never heard the call to the field. Instead he was swept up with the surge of energy when the rest of his teammates sprang from their places and charged for the door. Cody was with them, at the center, and soon they were on the field, and the entire team orbited him like a mass of lesser particles, like the electrons around the nucleus of an atom.

Cody spoke, he ranted and he raged. They listened as they milled about him. He was their leader. He was the one to take them into the game that was so much like a battle. The mass of players suddenly exploded as if Cody had released his energy and burst them apart. Each one of them, each individual electron particle, would now go on to wreak as much chaos as he possibly could.

The Outlaws pounded the Vikings 28–3. Cody was penalized twice for unnecessary roughness and once for a face mask when he brought Warren Moon down by the head. He also had one interception, thirteen tackles, and a quarterback sack on a safety blitz. It was a game commensurate with the internal rage of the player who played it.

Afterward, after the slaps on his back, after cutting the tightly bound tape from his ankles and wrists, after the interviews with TV, radio, and newspaper people, and after a shower, it got quiet. When it was quiet, Cody left the locker room and found Jenny waiting there dutifully for him. He was glad to see her. She was acting strange, but she was there. It was something. He was ashamed of the things he'd thought of her, the things he'd mixed into his poisonous mental brew. But that was how he did it. That was how he got by. That was why he was Cody Grey. He was sorry, but he reasoned that no one got hurt by it, except maybe him, where he'd torn the fiber that held his soul together.

Then a practical question popped into his mind, where the hell was she last night? He wouldn't ask. In a strange way, he knew it didn't matter. His marriage was like his knee. If he numbed it up good, he could get by.

They kissed briefly and walked for the exit. Cody was already starting to limp. They went to dinner. They drank heavily. The needles wore off, but Cody kept the gremlin down with alcohol. Talk came easier with drinking anyway. At home he tried to make love to his wife. She let him. It was nothing special, but it was something. They slept. In the small hours of the morning, when it was no longer night,but not quite dawn, there was a knock at the door. Cody stumbled downstairs and opened it. He was bleary-eyed, and at first he saw nothing. Then he saw him. The gremlin sprang at him with a fury and tore into his knee like a rabid dog with burning teeth and nails.

Cody shot up from the covers with a scream.

"What is it?" Jenny said, frightened.

Cody made the noise an animal might make, fearful, hurt, angry.

"Are you all right?" she said, and in that moment, with those words of concern, Cody didn't think he could love a person any more than he loved her. It was because she was there. She was with him. The gremlin was killing him, eating his flesh from the inside out, but he wasn't alone.

"Get me my black bag and a glass of water," he said between his teeth, groping at his knee with both hands to try and choke off the pain.

Jenny hurried. Cody tore open his black leather shaving kit, tossed two bottles down on the floor but stopped with the third. He twisted the top and shook three Percosets into his palm, gulping them down with the water Jenny held for him in her steady hand. Then he lay back to grit his teeth and wait.

He thought about what the week was going to be like. He wouldn't be able to practice. That was okay. He'd played well enough that they wouldn't think of not starting him, despite his absence from practice. He thought about the pain. It would be bad. He would do the same thing next week, take the same needles, the same drugs. He wished the drug he was using now would hurry up.

It really didn't take long, and once the drug set in, all else was forgotten. The gremlin was tossed into the corner like a battered rag doll, harmless and spent. Cody rolled over toward his wife and fell into the nirvana of an opium derivative.

The yellow tape stamped Police Crime Scene—Do Not Enter was still mostly intact. It was tattered here and there, floating lazily in the hot summer breeze, but that wasn't much considering the investigation had taken place months ago in the spring. It was now the second week of September. The Outlaws had won their first game, and Alice had won her bet with her boss. If the Vikings had won, she would have had to buy him dinner at his favorite restaurant. She even gave him seven points. But the Outlaws beat the spread, and she got a morning off the following week. Madison made time in her own schedule even though she didn't have it.

The ground was strewn with rusted junk and rubble, and Madison did her best in her blue suit and pumps to keep up with Alice, who had worn tennis sneakers and peds to complement her wild floral sundress and hat. She looked around at the surroundings. It wasn't really a wonder that something like this double murder happened here. It looked like a war zone. People scurried like rodents up and down the street to what little shade their decrepit porch roofs provided. Obviously they didn't have jobs. It was Wednesday morning at ten o'clock. Madison wondered what her own son would turn out like if he was forced to grow up in a place like this. It made her glad she had taken this case. She was giving someone a chance who wasn't going to otherwise get one, just because he didn't have the right parents or live in the right neighborhood. She'd have to remember to thank Walter for his insistence.

Inside the abandoned garage, the concrete floor, despite its cracks, made the footing much easier. It was hot and dusty. Four broken windows boarded up with heavy vertical slats of graying wood blocked out what little breeze there was. It was a poor man's sauna.

"Okay, honey," Alice said as she stood between a ratty armchair and the feet of a chalk outline that could still be seen on the concrete floor. "Here's where old Ray-man got his final wake-up call. BANG! So . . . "

Alice consulted the report the way she would the map in a treasure hunt.

"You be the mystery man in black, sweetheart. You came in from that door. Stand like you're on a corner of a triangle connecting these two bodies. It sounds like from everything the kid said that that's about where you'd be. That's it, right there, your second calling."

Alice turned around and with fingers splayed open wide indicated the portion of the wall that was behind her. "This is the spot," she said. "Come on over here and give me a hand. I know better than to think you're just another pretty face."

Madison smiled and took the magnifying glass that her friend had held out to her. Alice began unwinding a thin, sticky string that looked like orange dental floss and marked out a grid on the wall, dividing it up into small rectangular sections. They were wider than they were tall because, as Alice explained, to shoot the boy, who was sitting in the chair, assuming the man was somewhere between five-eight and six-eight, limited how high up the bullet could get lodged in the wall.

"Just a hole is all we're looking for. It might not look like too much depending on the caliber of the gun. When you check a square out real good, mark it with an M," Alice said, handing her a piece of chalk. "That way I'll know if it was you or me who checked the square. If we get done and we've got nothing, I can go back and check yours first. No offense."

"Please," Madison said, "I don't care. You can't offend me. I just want to find out if this kid is lying to me or not."

"That's why we're here," Alice murmured. She was already intently examining a square in the far corner of the grid with her magnifying glass.

Madison began her own meticulous search from the other end of the grid. It was tedious. Twice Madison thought she saw something; both times Alice shook her head solemnly and told her it was nothing. After a half hour, Madison began to feel as though either they were looking in the wrong place or the kid was just plain lying to her. That seemed more and more likely as they worked on in the dry heat.

"Got it!" Alice said suddenly.

Madison stood straight up and focused her attention where Alice had stopped her glass.

"It's doesn't look like anything," Madison said.

Alice was already carefully digging away, forming a larger hole than the one she'd found, so she could extract the bullet without making a mess of it for ballistics.

"It's not a real big one," she said as she dug. Madison could see the tip of her chubby friend's tongue sticking out of the corner of her mouth as she worked away at the wall. Carefully, Alice took a rubber-tipped pair of funny-looking tweezers and removed the lead.

"Well, damn," Alice said, more to herself than to Madison.

"What?" Madison asked, trying to peer over Alice's hands for a clear view of whatever it was that was so spectacular.

Alice held up the spent slug before dropping it into a plastic envelope.

"This is a .22 slug. That's strange," Alice said. Then she gave the entire area a cursory scan.

"Why's that?" Madison asked. "What's a .22 have to do with it?"

Alice looked at her with impatience.

"Madison," she snapped, "honey, when was the last time you heard of one of these kids whacking another with a .22-caliber gun? Never, right? Sure. Honey, in this neighborhood you like a lotta bang when you fire a gun. The noise is almost as important as the bullet. They don't carry around guns like the one this came from, small and quiet. You can't be sure a bullet from a gun like this will do anything. To use a gun with this small a caliber requires an extreme amount of accuracy with your shot, otherwise your victim just might walk away laughing at you or shoot you back. I'm assuming that if your boy is telling the truth, whoever was here that night knew where he was going, knew what was going to go down, and brought a twenty-two anyway. That's no amateur. And I'll bet if you check your autopsy reports, you'll see those boys weren't killed with a twenty-two. Even the rough boys, the mob, and the heroin dealers are using large-caliber guns these days. I've probably only seen three or four slugs this small in my last hundred corpses, maybe more. The last one was a fourteen-year-old kid up on Lake Travis, the one who killed his parents with his squirrel gun."

"Maybe the bullet didn't come from that night at all," Madison wondered out loud.

"Maybe you're right," Alice replied. "But if it did, it's a real humdinger that someone who was obviously bent on doing some killing was walking around this neighborhood with a .22. I'm just saying that if this bullet was fired the night of the murders, then it sure goes a long way toward substantiating your boy's story. It might not be enough to get him off, but it might just raise enough doubt to keep him off of death row."

"But the only way to know if it was fired that night is going to be by exhuming Ramon's body and looking at his ear," Madison said, her mind already whirling with the legal arguments she would use to unearth the corpse.

"That's your department, honey," Alice said. "But if you can dig Ray-man up before he gets too rancid, I can tell you for sure whether or not this bullet went through his ear."

CHAPTER SEVENTEEN

JEFF BOARD HADN'T POURED HIMSELF into something like his investigation of Cody Grey since he'd prepared for his accountant's certification test. He had boasted to many people, from his boss to people in the U.S. Attorney's office. Now he had to deliver. He wanted more on Cody Grey than just a five-thousand-dollar yearly discrepancy. He knew there had to be more. There always was. If you could look hard and long enough, Board knew you could get the goods. The tax code was in a constant state of flux. It was too complex and too irregular to allow perfect compliance. Most agents would be satisfied with what he'd already found. He would normally be satisfied too, if he hadn't done so much talking. But after his meeting with Grey and his assurances to everyone all around, he wasn't taking any chances. So, he dug.

He started eight and a half years back, when Grey first came to Austin. Then he worked his way forward, examining every check that was written, every deposit that was made, and searching for any bank accounts that the player might have had but not claimed. That was always a trick people liked to use. If they deposited less than ten thousand dollars in cash into a bank account, there may not be an electronic trail. Banks were only required to report deposits of over ten thousand dollars. But a careful agent could access different banking systems and run a check by social security number. If more money turned up, the taxpayer would have to explain where it came from. It happened all the time with people who had cash businesses. They got away with it until someone had it in for them. Board was hoping that Cody Grey had some outside endorsements and had taken cash payments, then stashed the money away in a hidden account, never claiming the income.

For a week, Board lived the last eight years of Cody Grey's life. He got copies of every check, deposit slip, and pay stub. He worked twelve hours in the office, and then took more work home with him. On his refrigerator door and the wall of his cubicle, he tacked a publicity photo of his quarry: Grey was frozen in a moment of triumph and exultation on the football field. His arms were raised high over his head and his face was ecstatic. This picture drove Board forward when he would have otherwise quit. Cody Grey's downfall would be his own moment of triumph.

He knew every penny Cody spent and every penny he received, at least everything that was in his name in any lending institution in the United States and most of the world. Board found a few checks here and there that he figured were unclaimed income, but after deductions the discrepancy would probably only amount to a few hundred dollars. After a week, Board began to worry. He wanted more. He needed more, not to make trouble for Cody Grey—he already was in trouble—but to live up to all his promises he'd made about jail and scandal and headlines to his boss, the U.S. Attorney's office, and everyone he'd happened to bump into in the Federal building over the past few weeks.

Board looked at the red digital clock on his desk: seven twenty-seven on Thursday evening. He'd exhausted every avenue. Besides the trading card money, it appeared that Marty Cahn had done a meticulous job of preparing Grey's taxes. Grey had nothing to hide. Board knew it couldn't be true. Tomorrow he would start all over from the beginning. Tonight he would take a few hours, have a few drinks, and regroup. He stood, stretched, hitched up his pants, and headed for Sixth Street. There was a little bar called Rodeo that he liked. It was a fancy place with brass fixtures and polished wood. Despite its name, it garnered an upscale crowd of well-dressed people. Board liked to watch.

He was welcome at Rodeo no matter what he looked like. His drinks came cheaper than everyone else's. Of course he paid. Free drinks would have been illegal, but he had investigated the owner several years back and taken it rather easy on him. Board had a friend for life. He could drink all night, and the bill never amounted to more than ten dollars. Nothing was ever said; it was just the way it was. He took a cushioned stool with a good view of the door. It wasn't even close to the weekend, but the people who frequented Rodeo didn't have to work as hard as everyone else. They could afford a night out on Thursday.

He was on his eighth Amstel Light when a stunning woman walked in. Everyone's head turned. She wore a snug red dress with a low-cut front that exposed the tempting curve of her breasts. The generous slit up the side of the dress gave Board a glimpse of her long leg, and then it was gone. The man behind her was older than she. His eyes were dark and piercing, and when they scanned the room, Board averted his own eyes and pretended to be looking out the window. When the man's eyes had moved on, Board noticed his eighteen-carat gold Cartier Panther and his Bally shoes. He wondered if this man had paid his taxes. The couple moved through the bar to a table in a dark corner in the back. After they passed, Board stared without shame at the woman's ass as it switched beneath her dress. He snickered to himself when the man discreetly ran two fingers down her bare back as they walked, resting briefly on the high curve of her ass.

There was something about the way this little vixen flaunted herself that reminded Board somehow of Cody Grey's wife. He'd seen the two of them around town. Board turned back to the bar and ordered another drink. Then the thought came to him. It hit him like a truck. The wife.

Every account Cody Grey owned was held jointly with his wife. She had written a substantial number of the checks over the past eight years. But Board had neglected to run the wife's social security number through the computer. He had done everything through Grey himself. What if the player had used his wife to hide some money away? It was possible; it just might be the answer. It wouldn't take him more than a day to find out. Jeff Board paid his six-dollar tab and went home. He didn't need any more alcohol. He was flying high with the possibility that he'd just found the answer he had searched so hard for.

On Friday morning, Madison went before Judge Walter Connack in her official capacity as Yusef Williams's attorney. She saw Walter in his chambers before she made the legal motion in his courtroom. Walter was not very happy.

"I can't just have you digging up that boy's body!" he bellowed.

"Yes, you can," Madison retorted, tapping a copy of the brief she'd sent him on the case law of court-ordered exhumations in the state of Texas.

"This?" Walter held the brief almost as high as his eyebrows, which looked as though they might jump off his forehead. "You call this case law?"

"There are some cases in there," Madison replied with an earnest look. "I know there isn't a lot of precedent on something like this, but—"

"Oh, but there *is* precedent!" Walter boomed. "There's precedent against anything of the sort!"

"The argument can be made for it," Madison insisted.

"Did you talk with Rawlins in the D.A.'s office?" Walter asked.

"No," she said, "I talked with Cherrit; he's trying the case. He wouldn't help me, but that's just them. They wouldn't help their own mothers across the street if I asked them."

"What about the family? If you can get their permission, it will make this whole thing a lot easier," Walter said hopefully.

"They said no," Madison replied.

"How against it were they?" he asked.

Madison looked him straight in the eye and said, "I'll be perfectly honest with you, Walter, they were horrified. Very religious. Very superstitious."

Walter nodded.

"Make the call, Walter," Madison insisted. "You can do it."

"I can do it and get turned over on appeal," he said.

"Too late. Alice will dig this weekend. You give me the order. I won't file it with the clerk until just before five this afternoon. The D.A.'s office, the kid's family, and any other friggin do-gooder who wants to protect the rights of a decaying hunk of rotten meat will be too busy getting ready for the weekend to bother. Alice will do the work right away. By the time anyone complains, we'll have the body back in the ground."

"That sounds simple," Walter said, "but I still have to get elected in this county. I can't just make a move like that without repercussions, and you know it. The damn coroner's office is going to have a fit."

"They won't say a word if we're right. They'll be glad to let it just go away. They screwed this up in the first place by not finding the bullet hole in the victim's ear."

"And if you're wrong?"

"Then the kid's lying to me," she said simply. "But I don't think so. These boys were killed with Ramon's gun, a Glock nine-millimeter. This .22 slug puts someone else at the murder scene. In my gut I know that body's going to have a bullet hole in one ear, put there by our mystery man."

Then, like a good lawyer, she turned the whole thing around on him. "You're the one who said you believed him. You're the one with the feeling."

"I just can't believe you're asking me to make a decision that flies in the face of the law!"

"You're the one who asked me to take this case, Walter," she reminded him.

"I didn't ask you to start digging up dead bodies that the family doesn't want uncovered!" he exclaimed.

"I don't advocate without passion, Walter," she said matter-of-factly. "That's what you asked me to do. That's what I'm doing."

The judge pursed his lips. He was thinking. Madison went for the kill.

"I'm doing my part here, Walter," she reminded him. "My firm didn't want me to take the time to try this case. We're backlogged. I'm in demand. Alice? She's taking a risk too. Why? Because she thinks this kid might be innocent and because I asked her. Quite honestly, I didn't think I'd have to spend ten seconds convincing you. I thought you'd do it in a heartbeat. It's thin, but there's enough here in this brief to make a legitimate, if tenuous argument. It's time for you to come out on the limb with us, Walter, and you damn well know it."

Walter Connack gave Madison an angry stare. He wasn't used to being challenged or cajoled. He wasn't used to people talking to him that way. He was doing his part. He could do more good from the bench for a lot more people if he held his seat than if he threw it away on something as foolish as digging up a body. On the other hand, he knew what Madison was saying was right. That's what made him angry.

"All right," he finally said. "Write up the order."

"It's right here," Madison said, purposely not smiling.

Walter lifted the reading glasses that hung around his neck on a silver chain and read the order. He shook his head as he signed his name and handed it back to Madison.

"I hope," he said quietly, "that we're *all* right."

Madison took the order and started for the door. "Thank you, Walter," she said, stopping before she left. "You're a good man."

Walter's chamber boomed with laughter.

"Now I've heard it all!" he said, holding his belly with one hand and wiping a tear from his eye with the other. "Little Madison McCall is telling me I'm a good man! Well thank you, my dear. I'm not laughing at you. It's just the idea of that little girl I used to know giving me her seal of approval. Thank you very much, and I mean that from the bottom of my heart."

Jenny walked in the door from getting her nails done and doing some shopping at the mall. It was Friday at two in the afternoon. Cody would be home about four, and they were supposed to go out for dinner at the Green

189

Mesquite. It was a popular little place down across the river from Sixth Street on the outskirts of Butler Park. It wasn't really her kind of place; it was too plain. Barbecued meat and locally brewed potato beer were things that she could live without, but Cody loved it. She had slipped out last night to see Striker on the thin excuse that she wanted to have a few drinks with one of her girlfriends, so tonight wasn't the time to be putting up much of a fuss. Jenny would be glad when the charade was over, though.

Jenny set her bags down on the kitchen table and went to the desk to play the messages. The first one was from Cody, checking in. Nothing new. The second one was from Cody too. She wondered how in hell he managed to get so many calls out of the Outlaws facility when she knew that the team worked him every minute he was there. Her life for the past nine years would have been a hell of a lot easier if there weren't any phones at all out there.

She didn't recognize the next voice. The first few words she heard sounded official, so she ran it back to hear who it was.

"Mr. Grey, this is Jeff Board calling. You may remember me, I am conducting a field audit for the Internal Revenue Service. I . . . I have tried to contact your attorney, Mr. Cahn, but he is . . . he has not returned my calls today. He is indisposed . . . But I wanted you to know that I have found a very serious problem. I think we will have to have another meeting next week. I want you to know that I have found the temporary bank account you had under your wife's name in the San Antonio office of Home Bank. I know you closed the account, and I know the money has been wired overseas, but while it was there, you did earn interest of . . . yes, sixty-one dollars and seventy-seven cents. That is income, my friend, that you'll have to pay taxes on this year, you know that. But what I'm really interested in talking to you and Mr. Cahn about is where the large sum of money that earned this interest came from. I have the feeling that some very big things are going on in your life, Mr. Grey, and I want to talk with you about them. . . . Have a nice weekend. Oh, and good luck Sunday against the Patriots."

Jenny pulled a chair out from the table without thinking and sat herself down. She was terrified. She had come so far. They were so close. Now it was over. They were caught. She was caught. Her stomach spun downward as if she were going down the big drop on a roller coaster. She clenched her teeth and fists and began to hyperventilate. It couldn't be true! She was too close. She had waited. She had worked so long for her chance. Now it was here. Now it would be gone.

"Oh, my God," she said out loud. "I can't go to jail. I can't go. . . . "

She heard her own words. They sounded frantic. Jenny grabbed her keys off the table and paused to erase the messages from the machine before she hurried to her car. She revved the Porsche's engine and raced directly to Striker's office. She knew she wasn't supposed to go there. He told her that. He told her that only in an emergency should she go there, but this was an emergency.

When Clara told Striker that a Miss Jenny Grey was there to see him, he remained calm. In fact, as was the case in every crisis situation since he'd trained in Special Forces nearly thirty years ago, Striker's awareness was heightened tenfold and not one ounce of energy was wasted on anxiety. He had trained himself not to react on an emotional or physiological level. It had been the difference between life and death for him.

Jenny barged through the door, and he knew before she said a word that his first priority had to be to calm her down.

"Striker!" she exclaimed. "I—"

He silenced her with his look and the long finger he held to his lips.

"I see you're upset, dear," he said without much feeling. "It's your husband, isn't it?"

Striker nodded emphatically for her to agree.

"Yes," she said.

He waved her on, rolling his hand to encourage her to continue talking as he got up from his desk with some kind of electronic device that she didn't recognize.

"He wants to know . . . where I was last night," she said, doing her best to keep up the fake conversation while he swept the room.

Striker hadn't checked his office for listening devices in three days. He didn't normally have the need to. Now he wanted to double-check before either of them went on about something incriminating. The phony dialogue dragged on while he worked. He knew that taking five minutes now might save him later. If he erred, he'd have the rest of his life to think about the five minutes he didn't take while in a jail cell somewhere, and Striker had no intention of doing that. He was too smart and he was too careful. Those were the exact reasons Striker was going to get away with the whole thing. No one on the other side could match him. He knew that for a fact.

When he was satisfied, Striker took a special CD from his desk and inserted it into the sound system. The disk emitted a garbled undercurrent of tones that would frustrate any high-tech directional listening device that might be focused at his office window from the other side of the street. Striker knew there were devices that could decipher the words from within by the minute vibrations voices created on a window pane. The noise that came from Striker's CD was to dialogue what a shredder was to classified documents.

He sat her down on the leather couch in the corner by his books and held her firmly by the shoulders.

"Now," he said quietly, but so she could hear him clearly above the gentle noise that reminded her of rainfall on a tin roof, "slowly and carefully, what is the matter?"

Jenny fought the urge to bury her head in his chest and cry. She didn't want to lose him. She didn't want to lose the money or the life they would soon have. She forced herself, at least on the outside, to act as coolly as Striker himself.

She took a deep breath and began to slowly recount the message from Jeff Board. Striker asked her a few things and thought for a moment.

"I told you, specifically, not to let anyone know you had that money," Striker said sternly, admonishing her not with venom but as though he was studying her, questioning the scientific evidence to expose some underlying secret.

"I didn't leave it there," she said calmly. "I put it in Austria. It can't be found."

"It doesn't have to be found to create problems, as you now see," he hissed. "I don't say things to you that I don't mean. I don't say anything without a reason."

Jenny remained silent. Striker calmed himself and then steepled his fingers below his chin to think.

After a few minutes of concentration, he finally said, "I don't think you should worry. Forget it. Let's just see what happens."

Jenny was astounded. It was so obvious to her that they were in peril. She wondered if Striker wasn't mad, or if he was merely testing her resolve to see how devoted she really was. She was devoted, but she wasn't a fool. That was one thing she knew she'd never be, a fool for any man or anyone for that matter. She wanted Striker to know that. He might be toying with her. He had to be. Nevertheless she wasn't going to take any chances. Now was a good time for him to know that he would have to take her seriously and that she'd learned too much from him to be discarded.

"You say I shouldn't worry," she said calmly, "so I won't. But I want you to know, Striker, if I go to jail, or if something happens to me before I can get there, you're going to be going wherever I go as well."

Jenny let the threat hang out there as long as she could before she backed down a bit and qualified it by saying, "You taught me, Striker, to always be prepared and to trust no one. I have only done what you would do."

"Oh? What is it you did do?"

Jenny boldly told him how she had arranged a safe deposit box and an attorney on retainer who was instructed that if she didn't keep in touch with him, he was to release the contents of the box—an account of the entire operation.

"Which would put an end to you, Striker," she said. "I have to watch my back too."

Striker's face beamed with a smile. He began to quietly applaud.

"Good for you, Jenny Blue Eyes," he said, pulling her head to his breast and hugging her like she was his little girl. Striker was amused. He ran his hand through her hair. She was like a kitten, spitting and clawing at a lion to show the bigger cat that she, too, had claws and teeth, and that she, too, could fight. It was quite wonderful, actually, considering that he had taught her to think like this.

"You have to remember this, though," he said when the amusement had worn off, "I can't be taken out by you or any common lawyer you may have hired. This is my game, love. I make the rules, and you can't beat the man who makes the rules. You just can't. I could be gone without a trace, leaving you, those agents who are following me, and even your secret lawyer all dead. I can do that. I know how to find people, and I know how to kill people. You, my dear, have nothing to fear. But remember, that is only because I choose for things to be that way. I wouldn't let you go to jail, not because I fear you or anyone, but because it would be like caging a wild songbird and covering it with a blanket. I would never do that. I want you with me, Jenny."

"But even now you could be deceiving me," she said warily.

"Bravo, my dear," he said, still amused. "But let's end our little contest of wits now. You're having dinner with your husband tonight, right?"

She nodded.

"Fine, go have your . . . what, your Green Mesquite?" he said with distaste.

"Yes," she said, as unhappy with the idea as he was.

"What time is dinner?" he asked.

"Seven," she said. "But what—" Striker held up his hand for silence.

"Jenny, the truth is, you are overreacting. You did good, though, you came to me right away. You said nothing to anyone. You did good. Now keep doing good and don't worry. When anyone asks, including Cody, you just say that you've been socking some money away here and there through the years for a rainy day. You finally decided that you should do something with it. That's it."

"It's so simple and so stupid," she complained.

"Exactly," he replied. "That's why everyone will believe it. Don't worry. We just need some time. You're not going on trial. You just have to get by for a few more weeks. Nothing may come of it. Things happen. If we need to act, we will. Eight weeks from now, Jenny Grey and Bill Moss will be no more. Relax. A lot can happen in eight weeks. I won't let them come and take you away."

Striker took her face in his hands and kissed her gently and passionately on the lips.

"Feel better?" he said to her.

"Yes," she replied. She wasn't completely happy. It was a stupid story to tell and expect people to believe, but he was right. They didn't have to totally believe her. By the time they found out she was lying, if they ever could, she'd be gone. "I do feel better."

"Good," Striker said, "you go eat ribs, and I'll see you tomorrow night?"

"Yes," Jenny said with hungry eyes. "Cody will be at the hotel all night, so I won't be going home."

"Wonderful," Striker said, grinning wolfishly. "I'll rest up for it."

Chapter Eighteen

⌄

Madison filed Judge Connack's exhumation order with the county clerk at four forty-five. She went back to sign some papers and was still able to leave her office at exactly five-thirty. She always tried to leave by then. Some nights she would work late, but not Fridays. Fridays began her weekends with her son. Because she was so busy, there were times during the week, like this one, when she saw very little of Jo-Jo. This particular week had been extremely busy, and the two of them had had nothing more than perfunctory hellos, how-are-yous, and good-byes over the breakfast table. The weekend, however, was theirs.

Jo-Jo loved Chinese food, and Chiang Juang's, a little place in a shopping center near home, was where their weekend usually began. Madison picked him up at the house without bothering to change her clothes. They ordered what they usually ordered, and Madison indulged in a glass of plum wine while they were waiting. She needed some help unwinding from the week. Try as she might to focus on her son, the thought of Alice and Walter going out on a limb for her with the Yusef Williams case kept popping into her mind. She didn't want to make problems for either of them. She respected them both and cared about not only their friendship but their careers. She hoped she wouldn't end up damaging either with her insistence on the exhumation.

Because she was so distracted, it wasn't until the steaming bowls of chicken, vegetables, and rice were set down in front of them that she realized that something was bothering her son. She knew because usually she had to remind him of his manners when the food came to the table. The way he'd tear into Chinese food always reminded Madison of his father. Big Joe had always eaten with the rushed urgency of a man who was afraid the plate was about to be taken away. The prodigious gut Joe sported, now that he was no longer an athlete, didn't surprise Madison in the least. But now Jo-Jo was simply staring at his plate with his head slightly down.

"Jo-Jo," she said, "the food's here, honey. What's wrong?"

"Nothing, Mom," the boy said, picking up a serving spoon and slowly loading up his plate.

"Don't say nothing, sweetheart if something is wrong," she said. "Tell me, honey. Maybe I can help you."

Jo-Jo just shook his head and repeated, "Nothing, Mom."

Madison knew that something was certainly wrong, but she had to be careful not to cross-examine him like he was on the witness stand. It was so natural for her to pump people for information that they didn't want to give. She had to force herself to slow down and gently work the truth from her son. But Madison worried that Jo-Jo might be getting to the age when he'd rather discuss things with his father, or a father figure. She was aware of the gender barrier, and she hoped that she could somehow circumvent it.

Right now, with everything that had been happening lately, she had the sinking feeling that Jo-Jo's secret had something to do with his father. That made her want to know what bothered him all the more. She forced herself to be calm.

"Jo-Jo," she said patiently, serving herself some rice as she spoke, "you know you don't have to tell me anything you don't want to, and I won't keep asking you because I know that sometimes people have private thoughts that they want to keep to themselves, but I'd be glad to talk with you about anything, son. I love you very much, no matter what."

Jo-Jo nodded to let her know that he knew all this. Madison began eating and attempted to change the subject.

"Did you help your friend Jason with his tree fort after school today?" she asked.

Jo-Jo was silent for a moment, and she knew he was going to talk about what was bothering him.

"Mom?"

"Yes, honey," she said, setting down her fork. She wanted him to know that what he said was important to her.

"If someone tells you to keep a secret," he said, looking up from his plate and searching her face, "and you want to keep it, but you want to tell someone too, what should you do?"

Madison cleared her throat.

"Well," she said, "as a lawyer, I have to keep people's secrets all the time, honey, and it's very important to keep other people's secrets."

196

Jo-Jo nodded emphatically. That's what he thought too.

"But," Madison continued, "sometimes, even as a lawyer, I have to tell other people's secrets. I have to, by law, sometimes."

"By law?" Jo-Jo was amazed. The law was an impressive concept to him.

"Yes," Madison said. "If the secret is something against the law or can cause someone to get hurt, then I have to tell the secret, even though otherwise I could never tell. Does that make sense?"

"Yes."

Madison waited.

"Well," he said, obviously very uncomfortable, "you know how when you and Dad got divorced, Dad couldn't see me, and now he can, only not all the time?"

"Yes," she said, her insides knotting and twisting.

"Well, is Dad seeing me against the law?" he asked.

Madison cleared her throat. She wanted to handle this right, but dammit, she was being pushed into a corner by Joe and had the feeling she was going to have to take a stand soon whether she wanted to or not.

"Yes, Jo-Jo," she said slowly, "your father is only supposed to see you according to the legal parameters—the rules—of our divorce."

"So, I kind of have to tell you, huh?" he said.

Madison couldn't tell him that he had to tell her. She couldn't lie. She had explained the whole thing to him in terms of an attorney-client relationship, but she had distorted those rules somewhat because there was a part of her that absolutely had to know what this was all about. Still, she wasn't going to manipulate him outright. If he wanted to talk, she'd let him. Besides, she knew from what he'd said already that Joe had made contact with him secretly. She wasn't going to pry it out. She remained silent.

"I haven't been taking the bus home from school," he suddenly confessed, looking solemnly at his plate. "Dad picks me up. He takes me for ice cream. He said he couldn't do it unless I kept it a secret. . . . "

"Every day?" Madison heard herself blurt out in shock.

"Mom," Jo-Jo sobbed, looking up at her through tears, "I don't want to keep him away. I don't want to. I don't want secrets. . . . "

Madison had tears in her eyes, tears of love and sadness, and of the desperate fear that she was going to lose her son to a man she knew was a monster. She believed Joe Thurwood was using her son as if he were nothing more than a stage prop.

Madison stayed where she was, and so did Jo-Jo. Even as recently as a year ago, when he was seven, she could have crossed to his side of the table and held him tightly, or he would have crossed to her. Now he was eight, and something was different. In a very primitive way he had begun to assert himself as a man and not a child. It started that young. So, now, she had to simply look at him through her tears and hope that he could feel how much she loved him without her embrace.

She did reach across the table, though, and he took her hand.

"It's all right, Jo-Jo," she said. "It's all right. I know you don't understand. It's very hard. But it will be all right. No one is going to take your father away from you, honey. Don't you worry about that. If you can't see him every day and live with him every day, it will still be all right. It will just make the time you spend with him that much better."

"Mom," he said, still crying, "maybe you guys will be married again? . . . Maybe?"

"Oh, Jo-Jo," she said, squeezing his hand. "Oh, no, honey, we can't. Your father and I can't live together, honey. It hasn't got anything to do with you. You are the light of our lives. It's just he and I . . . we just can't, Jo-Jo. Your father can't, and I can't."

"Mom," Jo-Jo said desperately, "Dad said he could! He said he would come back and live with us if you let him. Mom, why can't he? Why can't we all be together?"

Madison did want a man in her life. If ever she needed a friend, if ever she needed another man in her life, it was now. She felt alone. She felt weakened. Her life was being slowly and steadily pulled apart. She needed a man right now more than anything. She was thriving as a trial lawyer in a man's world, but for all her strength and competence, she still couldn't help the feeling that somehow only a man could hold her life together.

Jenny stopped at her friend Ronda's apartment on her way home from Striker's office. She needed a little something to pick herself up. She was feeling confused and low. A little powder went a long way to help temper those kind of feelings. Cody had never used cocaine. He wouldn't know the difference if she was a little high, but she would be feeling much better for it.

For his own part, Cody stopped for a few cold ones with some teammates to end the week. By the time he arrived home, Jenny was wired up pretty good. She was sitting out by the pool under her umbrella, sunglasses on, with the cordless phone in one hand and a Diet Coke in the other. She had been calling around the country, talking to old friends she hadn't seen or spoken to in a while, letting them in on how spectacular her life was. Cody gimped around the pool with a fresh beer in his hand and sat patiently on the end of her chaise lounge, drinking the beer while she hurried one of her old college friends off the line.

"Hi," she said, hanging up and leaning forward to kiss him. "Hey," he said.

"Knee looks sore," she said.

"It is," he said. "But I'll get it straightened out for Sunday."

Jenny had had enough on that topic, so she jumped up from her seat and, standing over him, said, "Should I get ready? Are you hungry?"

Cody stood slowly, finished off his drink, and shifted his weight to stand on his good leg.

"Yeah," he said. "I want to change my clothes, too. Then we can go."

"Green Mesquite, right?" she said cheerily. "I know you love it there on Fridays during the season. It worked for you last weekend. We gotta do it again."

Cody smiled. He liked her thinking tonight. Sometimes she would do and say things that clearly reminded him why he'd married her.

The Green Mesquite was a simple enough place with green vinyl booths and red-and-white checkered tablecloths. The draft potato beer was served in plastic cups. Special house barbecue sauce sat in plastic ketchup squeeze bottles next to the napkin dispensers at each table. Fancy was one word no one had ever used to describe this place. Jenny seemed oddly content. Normally she would be forced to choke back her disdain just walking into such a place. Cody ordered a pitcher of beer, and Jenny even enjoyed helping him drink it. Cody threw down one glass after another.

"You're quite the drinker tonight," she said.

"Hell," Cody replied, "my damn knee is sore. I spent the whole friggin' week on the trainer's table. But now it's Friday night, and I've got the best-damn-looking girl in Texas for my wife. Why the hell not have a few?"

Jenny couldn't disagree with that. They would go right home after dinner, Cody would want to get a good night's sleep. A short night should ensure that Cody's indulgence didn't end up causing a scene. Instead of badgering him not to drink too much, she just smiled. After the second pitcher was gone, Cody asked the waiter to bring another. He also ordered the meat platter that gave him some of everything from the grill. Jenny waited to order.

"I was going to wait and see how long it would take you, but I can't wait any more. Why don't you take your sunglasses off?" Cody said, then threw down another glass of the dark beer.

"Oh, didn't I tell you?" she said happily, "I'm pretending I'm a spy, and I don't want anyone to recognize me. What do you care?"

Actually, with all the snort up her nose she hadn't even realized she was still wearing them.

"I guess I don't care," he said with a smile. She was right. What did he care if she wanted to be a little goofy? As long as she was being so damned pleasant, he wasn't going to rock the boat. They were having a good time. He was relaxed, and he had big plans for her when they got home.

When Cody's face darkened so suddenly, Jenny thought for certain he'd just figured out that she was wired. She reached up with two fingers and wiped under each nostril as she sniffed, thinking some of the powder had leaked out. Then she realized he was scowling at someone behind her. Her back was to the door, so she turned around to see who it was. There was a man coming toward them that she didn't recognize. He was dressed in a shoddy suit, his tie was too thick, and he looked like he'd just come from a long day at the office. She thought she'd seen him somewhere before. When she heard his voice, she knew who he was and thought she might vomit the Diet Coke she'd had by the pool and all the beer in between.

Jeff Board actually had the audacity to pull up a chair and sit down at the end of their booth.

"Well, what are we having for dinner?" he said, introducing himself to Jenny with a smirk.

Jenny watched as Cody's face turned red. She was certain the first thing that Board was going to do was bring up her bank account. Now, by the look on her husband's face, she didn't know if things were going to get that far at all. She knew Cody, and she knew that look. There was an intensity and a hatred in his eyes that could scare anyone. When he'd been drinking, and he looked that way, she knew things were going to get ugly.

"Get the fuck out of my face," Cody snarled. "I told you, you piece of shit, to start running if you saw me."

Board seemed remarkably confident. Jenny thought the man must be crazy.

"You can't talk to me like that, you think I'm afraid of you? I'm not afraid of you," Board said daringly. He knew he had Cody Grey by the balls, and he wasn't afraid to squeeze. "Yeah, but then maybe you're practicing up for the way they talk in jail. What do you think your wife will be doing when you're gone?"

Cody's hand came out from under the table like a snake. Board couldn't have struck a more sensitive nerve. Cody grabbed him by the tie and yanked him up onto their table like a side of beef on a butcher's block, sending their drinks and the empty pitchers flying everywhere. Then he twisted the long hair at the back of the IRS agent's head in his fist and slammed Board's face down a couple of times on the table, bloodying his nose and noisily rattling the remaining silverware. Jenny let out a screech as the man's blood splattered her eggshell-colored blouse. Cody was on his feet now, and he reversed Board's direction, hauling him off the table by his tie and sending him onto a messy, empty table in the middle of the room. The table, two chairs, and Board all crashed down onto the floor.

"You fucking asshole, Grey," Board shrieked through his cupped hands, trying to stem the flow of blood from his nose. "I'll get you for this! Someone call the police! You'll pay, you son-of-a-bitch! I found your wife's money, you asshole!"

Cody was in a full rage. He took a three-quarters-full pitcher of beer off a nearby table and splashed it in Board's face to shut him up. When he was quiet, Cody spoke with deadly venom.

"You listen to me," he said, stabbing the air in front of the IRS man as he spoke. "You bother either me or my wife again and I'll kill you. Do you understand me? I'll fucking kill you!"

Cody made a lunge for the bloodied, beer-soaked man, who slid across the floor to get out of Cody's way. Cody stopped and pulled two twenties from his wallet, flipped them on the table, and grabbed his wife by the hand before he yanked her from her seat toward the door. The entire restaurant was absolutely still. They were all watching. Jenny was appalled.

"Let *go* of me!" she shrieked, twisting and flailing her arm to get free. Her husband was an animal, a hopeless savage.

"Come on," Cody growled.

"I'm not!" Jenny replied. "I'm not, Cody! You do this all the time, and I'm not taking it anymore! I'm not going anywhere with you!"

"Suit your fucking self," Cody snarled with disgust. "It won't be the first time."

Board was still babbling and moaning about the police and jail. Cody retraced his steps to give him a quick extra kick in the ribs.

Board, cringing with the expectation of another blow, balled himself up into a fetal position. Cody turned, brushed past his wife with a furious limp, and walked out of the restaurant, slamming the door behind him.

Board jumped when he heard the door slam. When he realized it wasn't him that had been smashed again, he opened his eyes. He lay there in a puddle of beer amid a pile of tables and chairs and greasy food. He picked a half-eaten rib off of his pants and slowly got to his feet. Blood was still running freely from his nose. He could feel it and taste it. His shirt front was soaked, and he smelled like beer. Jenny Grey turned and walked out. Every eye went from her to him. He opened his mouth to say something. He was humiliated. He would wait outside for police to get there and issue a full complaint. He'd sue Cody Grey on top of it all. He'd have him arrested. But he wasn't going to endure this gawking for a moment longer. When Board walked out the door, it was as though the final actor had left the stage. The audience began to buzz with excitement.

When Jeff Board woke later that night, he remembered right away what had happened. His nose was still sore as hell, and it had swollen to twice its normal size. He had been enraged that the police wouldn't arrest Cody Grey immediately. They told him the best they could do was to take him in early the next morning. To Board, that was like adding insult to injury. He wanted Cody Grey to have just as miserable a night as he was having.

His room was dark and quiet except for the steady hum of the air conditioner. Something had woken him, though. He thought it was a noise, probably one of his cats, but he couldn't be sure. He rolled on his side with a heavy sigh and whimpered a little bit.

He didn't see or hear anything, but it felt as if someone was standing next to his bed. He shot up from the covers with a burst of adrenaline. His heart was in his throat. Then he saw stars. The first blow came from above. He heard the crunch of bone and flesh, and it knocked him back down on the bed. His left eye had been smashed shut. He tried to rise and throw himself away from his assailant. He got to the other side of the bed when he caught another blow in the back of his neck that knocked him off the edge of the bed. He was whimpering on the floor and scrambling on all fours for the door. It was open, and he could see light from the street spilling into his living room. He thought he could make an escape, but the dark figure cut him off. Whoever it was kneeled down in front of him. Board instinctively covered his head.

The figure grabbed him by the hair and pushed his head facedown against the floor. Board started to cry like a baby. Then he felt the cold barrel of the gun pressed against the side of his head. He cried out with a desperate scream and tried to get away. There was an explosion of white light, and it was over. The figure beside him got up and looked down at the steady trickle of blood flowing from the dead man's brain. It was rapidly soaking into the carpet. The killer scuffed his feet where he stood, then quickly left the room. Only Board's limp body and the smell of hot powder and blood remained.

Detectives Bortz and Zimmer got the call from a squad car that had been sent to investigate a burglary. A neighbor heard screams and saw a man running from Board's house. The uniformed officers knocked on Board's door. There was no answer. Both men noticed a bloody footprint on the back stoop. When the neighbor who'd made the call assured them that Board had definitely come home that night, the officers went in. They found him facedown on his bedroom floor with what Alice Vreland would call blood pudding glopped everywhere. In the middle of the mess were footprints that looked as if they came from sneakers. The prints, which led down the stairs and out the back door, were photographed and sent into the lab for analysis.

The neighbor, an elderly man by the name of Boris Hauffler, had been letting his dog out for a late-night pee when he heard a scream and Board's back door slam. The dog barked frantically. Hauffler flipped on a floodlight and saw a man running from Board's house. Hauffler described the man as about six-foot-two or -three, dressed in dark clothing, with short dark hair.

Bortz had a computer check run on Board and came up with the assault complaint from eight-fifty earlier that evening. The alleged assailant was Cody Grey, the Outlaws defensive standout.

"You believe that?" Bortz said, looking down at Zimmer, who stood a full foot shorter than him.

Zimmer looked up at his lanky partner and shrugged, saying, "This guy's got a bad reputation already. He's been in trouble before."

"Nothing like this," Bortz replied. He knew his chubby partner was prejudiced against professional athletes anyway. He hated sports and the people who played them.

Zimmer shrugged and said, "Let's get a picture of Grey and show it to the old man. We get a positive I.D. along with the motive from the earlier assault, and we can get a warrant by morning."

"You know those funny looking footprints?" Bortz mused. "They looked a hell of a lot like turf shoes to me."

"Turf shoes?" Zimmer said.

"Yeah," Bortz replied. "The kind football players wear."

"This could be a big one," the shorter man replied. "A real big one."

Chapter Nineteen

$\bigvee$

CODY WOKE UP WITH A TERRIBLE HANGOVER. His head pounded, and he cursed himself soundly. His clothes and his boots lay in a heap beside his bed. Next to him the king-size bed was undisturbed. He had slept alone. Downstairs he heard voices. The beginning of last night came back to him with a wave of clarity. How he'd gotten home or much of anything that had happened after the Green Mesquite, he couldn't remember. He did remember losing it, though. He remembered bashing Board around and Jenny deserting him. He remembered heading for a watering hole called Chester's off the main drag downtown. That was about it.

He was suddenly nauseous, and he rolled quickly from the bed, despite the splitting ache in his head. He hurried to the bathroom where he immediately began to puke. It hurt his swollen knee to press against the tiled floor, but the painful knot in his stomach and the pounding in his head almost drowned out the throbbing in his knee. When he'd coughed and spit out the last bit of bile and saliva, he looked up to see Jenny standing there in the doorway. Her face was drawn with shock.

"The police are here," she said in a whisper. "They're here to arrest you."

Cody had half expected it. The police were right behind her. Then there were two detectives standing in his bedroom. They stared at him solemnly. They both wore gray suits. One was tall and thin, the other short and chunky, a regular Mutt-and-Jeff combination.

The taller of the two said, holding out a folded piece of paper, "Cody Grey? We have a warrant for your arrest."

"You guys are a little anxious this morning, aren't you?" Cody said, rising to his feet.

Zimmer, the short one, began reciting Cody's rights. Cody knew the routine. He'd been through it before a couple of times. He'd never been convicted of anything, but he had been arrested. It didn't make him feel any better. He only hoped he could get things over with so he could make the twelve o'clock team meeting. Otherwise he'd have to have Marty call and explain it for him. The team would fine him a thousand dollars for sure.

"You can go ahead and get some clothes on if you want," said the taller one in a courteous way.

Cody went to his closet and pulled on a clean sweat suit with a T-shirt and some turf shoes.

"You wear those shoes last night?" Zimmer asked casually.

"No," Cody said. "Why?"

"Just wondering," Zimmer said mysteriously. "Those the only pair you have?"

"No," Cody said, wanting the questions to stop. His head was pounding. "Do you mind if I take a painkiller . . . for my knee?"

The tall one looked at the short one.

He nodded, and the tall one said, "Okay."

Cody took a Butazolidin from his black bag and washed it down. It might not make his knee feel like new, but it would wipe out even the worst hangover headache in about twenty minutes. Cody forced a smile and then started past the two detectives toward the bedroom door.

The shorter one took out a pair of cuffs and took Cody's wrist in his hand as he passed by. Cody pulled back.

"Hey," he said, "come on. You don't need those. I'm coming. I'm not going to make problems."

"Sorry," the shorter one said, taking his wrist again and slapping the metal band around it with a sharp click, "it's not my choice, Mr. Grey. Rules say homicide suspects have to be cuffed."

Cody went limp as the short detective finished the job with another sharp click. Cody's mouth hung open.

"What do you mean, 'homicide'?" he said with a disbelieving laugh. "I didn't kill anyone! He wasn't dead. I knocked him around a little. He's not dead."

"Someone blew his brains out," the tall one said, leading him out into the upstairs hallway. "We've got two dozen witnesses who say that's exactly what you promised him."

The tall detective led Cody downstairs and walked him outside into the midmorning sun. Eight plainclothes investigators waited outside the door.

"What are you doing?" Cody said as they began to stream past him and into his house.

"We have a search warrant too," the tall one said.

Cody turned back, looking desperately up the stairs. Jenny was standing at the door with a confused and horrified look on her face. The shorter one was talking to her, and two other men were standing beside her now too.

"Mrs. Grey," Cody heard the detective say, "we'd like to get a formal statement from you. Officers Remo and Courtney will drive you down, if that's all right."

"All right," Jenny said. She was in a daze.

"Jenny!" Cody called out to her as the taller one regained his hold and began to tug him toward the police car. "Call Marty. Call him. Tell him I . . . Just tell him!"

"They'll be as neat as they can, Mrs. Grey," was the last thing Cody heard the short detective say to Jenny.

Zimmer jogged down the stairs, took Cody's other arm to help get him into the backseat, then shut the car door.

Marty took an early morning run. When he got back, he showered and poured some orange juice. The phone rang just as he was taking the first bite of his bagel with cream cheese. It was Jenny.

"For what?" he asked incredulously.

"Murder," she said flatly.

"Murder?"

Jenny was quiet for a moment, and Marty's spirits sank.

"I can't really talk. They're right here. He beat Board up at the Green Mesquite. He was drunk, Marty, and that guy just appeared and started goading him on. Cody said he would kill him. Everyone heard it. I took a cab home and went to bed in the guest room. I think I heard him come in about two-thirty—"

"Okay. Don't say anything more. Have they questioned you?"

"Well, a little, but nothing on the record. They asked me to come down and make a formal statement."

"Don't say a thing to them, Jenny. Don't say even one word until I can get there. I don't want you to say one word until I get there, not anything. Do you understand?"

"Yes."

"Because it could be very important and you have a right to have me there."

"Okay, Marty," she said. "I won't say anything."

"Is the officer who's taking you down right there?"

"Yes, I can get him," she said, and he heard her calling out to the officer.

"Hello, this is Officer Remo," came a gruff voice.

"Officer, this is Marty Cahn. I represent both Mr. and Mrs. Grey. I don't want you to try to question either of them until I am at the station, is that clear?"

"Clear," the officer said.

"All right, officer," Marty said in a very businesslike tone, "I am making a note that we had this conversation at 8:27 A.M. I also want you to radio the car that has taken Mr. Grey and tell the arresting officers that I have formally told them that they are not to question him until I am present, is that clear?"

"Fine," Remo replied.

"Thank you, officer," Marty said, "now I'd like to talk with Mrs. Grey again."

"Marty?" Jenny said. Marty had never heard her voice so uncertain.

"Everything's taken care of," he said. "I don't think you have to go down with them, but you might just as well go and get it over with. I'll be there soon. I've told them they're not to ask you a single question."

"I hope I didn't say anything already," Jenny fretted. "I think I might have said something about when Cody came home. They seemed to know everything. I don't know. . . . "

"Don't worry about what you've said," Marty told her. "Just don't say anything more. Are you okay?"

"Yes," she said, "I'm all right. I'll see you there."

"Good," Marty said. "First I've got to see a friend of mine who's the best criminal lawyer in town, then I'll be down there."

"No," Madison said flatly. "I won't represent him."

"Madison, forget that he's an Outlaw," Marty implored. "This is about a client who needs me. I represent him, Madison. I have to get the best. You're the best. I know I can get you to take it, Madison, and I have to. This is this man's life, and he's a friend. He's a client."

"No," she said flatly. She was sitting on her enclosed porch at the back of her house. Jo-Jo was splashing around in the pool with his friends, and Lucia was fussing about, cleaning up after the breakfast she'd served them on the porch. Madison wore a white terry-cloth robe over her bathing suit. Abby was napping at her feet. It was a beautiful Saturday morning. Marty didn't blame her for not wanting to drive down with him to the police station. That was why he had come in person rather than call her. He suspected she would say no, especially considering their recent discussion and her comments about Cody Grey's character. But he knew he stood a much better chance of convincing her to change her mind in person than he did over the phone.

"And I don't want you to take this personally, Marty," she continued. "You know if I was going to do this for anyone in the world it would be you, but I can't."

"Why?"

"Because, Marty, I already have one violent, dangerous football player in my life, and he's ruining it. I don't want another one, not even as a client. I can't represent him without prejudice. I remember Cody Grey from Joe's days with the team. Even Joe used to say he was incredibly violent and had a hot temper, and that was Joe talking. I think he probably did it, Marty. He said he was going to do it, for God's sake!"

"He didn't do it," Marty insisted. "I know him. He's not really like that."

Madison rolled her eyes. She truly felt sorry for Marty. He was so naive sometimes.

"Madison," he said, reaching across the table and taking her hand. He looked into her eyes and pleaded, "I need you. I need your help. Don't do it for him, Madison. Do it for me. Please."

Madison thought for a long while. She looked out at Jo-Jo and the boys screaming and splashing. She didn't want to leave. She didn't want this case.

"I have a capital murder case right now, Marty," she said. "You know I never do two murder cases at once. It's too much."

Marty could see she was weakening.

"Do you want me to get on my knees, Madison, because I'm begging you," he said earnestly.

"No," she said, shaking her head. "I don't want you to beg."

Madison pursed her lips. She thought about how Marty had been there for her through her bad times, when she'd needed him. This would be the second case in two months that was being forced on her. But in the first, she might be able to clear an innocent boy. Maybe in this case she could do some good as well. Even if Cody Grey were convicted, if nothing else, Marty would feel more at peace with himself if he knew that his client had the best representation he could get. Madison let out a long sigh.

"All right," she said, getting up from the table and calling her son onto the porch.

The boy ran up to her and stood dripping on the flagstone. "Jo-Jo, I have to go down to the police station to help one of Marty's friends. I know I said I'd be here all day, honey, but this is an emergency. There's a man who needs my help. Is it all right with you if I go?"

Jo-Jo was thinking. "Can my friends stay?" he asked.

"All right, dear," she said, kissing his forehead, "but tell them that they have to listen to Lucia, and if they don't, they won't be able to go to the movies with us tonight, is that a deal?"

"Okay, Mom," he said with a grin. She tousled his hair before he scampered back out to his friends. They immediately began screaming and hollering again.

"I'll get dressed." She turned to walk away. Marty stood and stopped her by taking her shoulders in his hands.

"Thank you," he said, then kissed her on the cheek.

When Madison came down the stairs wearing slacks and a blazer and carrying her briefcase, Marty knew she was all business from there on out. They got in Marty's car because she wanted to be filled in on all he knew and to think while they drove.

"Marty," Madison asked, "have you talked to the team yet?"

"No," he replied. "I haven't spoken to anyone but you."

"Well," she said, "when we get there, you should probably give someone a call and get them to use their weight to get a judge to arraign Cody today. A call from a judge will get the cops busy, and we can get bail set today. If we don't push it, the cops will drag out their reports, and he'll have to stay overnight in jail. They don't do arraignments on Saturday afternoons. He's got a game tomorrow, doesn't he?"

"Yes," Marty said, "that's a good idea. I'll call. They'll be able to pull some strings. The guy Cody backs up can't even play, so they'll need him out there. They'll do it."

"Good," Madison said, "now tell me what the wife said to you."

Marty recounted his conversation with Jenny.

"Do you think if she told them that he didn't come in until two-thirty that it will hurt us?" Marty asked.

"We don't know when the murder took place," Madison replied. "But we don't have to worry about the wife. The prosecution can't force her to testify against her husband. She has spousal immunity."

"What about what she's already said?"

"Come on, Marty," Madison chided him, "remember evidence? The D.A. won't be able to get her statement in. It's hearsay. Only she can recount what she said if it's being offered as a statement of truth, and they can't force her on the stand because she's his wife."

"That's good," Marty replied.

"Bet your ass," Madison said. "You should have told her to just stay home, though. They couldn't bring her in unless she was under arrest."

"I didn't know," Marty said.

"It's not your fault," she replied, "I don't know how to do tax returns. You did good by telling her not to talk and by telling the cop that no one was to question her. A lot of times a suspect starts blabbing before the lawyer can get there. The Miranda warning is great in theory, but in truth, most people just can't shut up when a cop starts asking them questions. But after you put the police on notice, even if they ask him something and he says something he shouldn't, they could never get it into evidence at the trial."

"I did pretty good then, huh?" Marty said, looking over at her with a smile.

"For a tax lawyer, I'd say you were sensational," she replied, returning his smile. "By the way, I want you to sit second with me on this if it goes to trial."

"Madison," he replied, "you know I can't do that. I don't have any trial experience."

"I know," she said, "but you know Cody Grey, and he trusts you. He's going to be much better at all this if you're right there."

"The firm's not going to be too thrilled with it," he said, pulling into the police station's parking lot.

"Why not?" she said flippantly. "We can bill Grey for your time too. He can pay for it."

"He doesn't have it, really," Marty said.

"After eight years of playing in the NFL, he's broke?" she said.

"Almost," Marty replied.

"Now why doesn't that surprise me," Madison said flatly, as though she was thinking about something else.

Marty followed Madison through the front doors of the police station. She walked in like she owned the place. She demanded to know where Mrs. Grey was and who had already spoken with her. She would see her first. They were met outside Jenny's interrogation room by Detective Zimmer.

"What do you know, Detective?" Madison asked, not bothering with any niceties.

Zimmer gave her a painful smile. He hadn't expected Madison McCall to show up. He knew who she was, and he didn't like her one bit. He didn't have to tell her a damn thing, but she'd find it all out sooner or later, and he was going to relish laying it on her.

"The victim was shot at 1:30 A.M. I already know your guy didn't get in until two-thirty this morning. The wife told me," he said with a broad grin.

"You were told not to question the wife," Madison said curtly. She wouldn't mention that it would never get in as evidence. She wanted him to be cocky.

"She volunteered that information before she spoke with Cahn," Zimmer replied, eyeing the tax attorney. "She also told us, like everyone else, that Grey said he was going to kill Board."

"What else?" Madison asked with a piercing stare.

"Your guy beat the victim up in front of more than two dozen witnesses," Zimmer said, continuing to smile. "He threatened to kill him. We have footprints at the crime scene of a football turf shoe, size twelve. Your guy is size twelve. The victim was killed with a .22. Shot in the head. We haven't found the weapon yet."

"Was my client's home searched already?" she asked.

"We're doing it now," Zimmer said.

"That's all circumstantial, Detective. You don't even have probable cause to arrest my client. You're looking at false arrest. I'm going to get this whole thing thrown out by Monday afternoon."

"Oh? Did I forget something?" Zimmer said sarcastically. "Oh, yes, Ms. McCall, we have an eyewitness who saw your client fleeing the scene immediately after the gunshot. We got a positive ID from a photo . . . And I know something else," he said with a grin. "I know you got your work cut out for you, Ms. McCall."

Madison bit her lower lip. "I'll see Mrs. Grey now."

"Right this way." Zimmer lead her through a swinging the door, opening it for her with a mock-gallant bow.

Madison went in and sat down across the table from Jenny Grey. The two of them had met only briefly years ago, standing outside the locker room while waiting for their husbands to shower after a game.

"I'm Madison McCall," Madison reintroduced herself. "Call me Madison. I'm going to be representing your husband."

"I'm Jenny."

"Jenny, can you tell me what you've told the police already?" Madison asked gently.

Jenny recounted everything she'd said, including the details about Cody's returning home one full hour after Board was killed and what Cody had said in the restaurant. That was about all.

"I hope I didn't do anything wrong?" Jenny said.

"Mrs. Gr—Jenny, don't worry about it at all. They can't ask you another thing; and quite frankly, they can't make you testify against your husband. So anything you may have said will not hurt his case at all."

"Thank you," Jenny replied.

"You're welcome," Madison said. "Now if you want to wait, we can take you home. There's no reason for you to stay. I don't want you to say another word to the police. You won't be able to see your husband, though, until I can get bail set. I can have one of the detectives take you home if you like."

"Will Cody be in jail?" Jenny asked.

"I think we can get him arraigned and out on bail today," Madison said. "Marty is working on that right now."

"Thank you. I'll go with a detective, but can you call me if anything happens at all?" Jenny asked, the very image of a concerned and devoted wife.

"Sure, and you're welcome, Jenny." Madison handed her a card. "I'll call you if anything happens. And if you have any questions for me, my numbers at home and at my office are both on there."

Madison arranged for detectives Remo and Courtney to take Jenny home. Marty showed up and told her he'd spoken with the team owner. Marty felt confident that a call from a heavyweight judge would be forthcoming. Then they had Zimmer lead them to Cody's interrogation room. His mug shot had already been taken, and he'd been fingerprinted and booked. Zimmer had been careful not to let anyone ask the player anything. He had the feeling this case was in the bank with or without any information from Grey, and he didn't want to let him get off the hook on some ridiculous technicalities, which in his opinion set too many killers free.

Cody was sitting by himself in the middle of the white-walled room. He sprang from his seat when he saw them and grabbed Marty around the shoulders in an uncharacteristic display of emotion.

"Marty, damn," he said, "I was never so happy to see someone. You gotta get me outta here. This whole thing is crazy!"

Marty blushed at Cody's crude hug and kind words. He was glad, though, that Madison could see a side of his client that people didn't always get to see.

"Cody," Marty said, turning to Madison. "This is Madison McCall. She is not only my best friend, she is the best criminal defense lawyer in the state of Texas, probably the whole country. I've gotten her to agree to represent you in this."

Cody looked up at the lovely female attorney, noticing her for the first time. She was so attractive that, even under what were extremely trying circumstances, Cody realized it. He also noted that her eyes were alert with intelligence.

"Hello," Cody said, holding out his hand.

"Hello." Madison shook hands with Cody. She hadn't remembered him being such a handsome man. His dark hair and deep green eyes highlighted a face that, except for his sad smile, was almost pretty. Probably, like many athletes, his looks had only increased the likelihood of his downfall. Madison knew firsthand that professional football players got to live by their own set of rules. Good-looking ones received more favors, attention, and leeway when it came to the law.

Cody had an intensity about him that reminded Madison of her ex-husband. That wasn't comforting, but despite the similarity, there was also something decidedly different about Cody Grey. Maybe it was the way his eyes didn't rove up and down her body, sizing her up like some kind of breeder, the way most men's did. Instead, Cody Grey's eyes pierced deep into her own without wavering.

"I didn't do anything wrong," Cody told them. "I beat up on the guy a little last night. I know that was stupid. But believe me, this guy asked for it.

"Marty," Cody said, turning to his agent, "you know what I mean, you've seen this guy. He sat right down at our table and started mouthing off about my wife. I couldn't just . . . well, it *was* stupid, but I sure as hell didn't kill him! That's crazy."

There was something in his voice and in his look that made Madison wonder if he wasn't really telling the truth. She was glad that at least she had some doubt. She would zealously represent her clients no matter what her gut feeling was. That was what was ethically required of her. But the task was much easier when she really did think her client was innocent or at least that innocence was possible. Right now, the thing that bothered her most was the set of circumstances that the police had already compiled against him, especially the eyewitness.

"Well," Madison said, sitting down at the table and taking out a pad from her briefcase, "we're going to try and get you out of here today, but while we're waiting, I'd like to hear what happened last night, from your perspective."

Cody described the entire incident with Board, going back to his and Marty's first meeting in the IRS office.

"After I left the Green Mesquite," Cody explained, "I went to a little place called Chester's, just off the main drag downtown. I got snookered. I figured they were going to get me this morning for assaulting him. He was yelling for someone to call the police. I was pretty depressed about the whole thing. I knew the whole thing was going to be a hassle."

"What time did you leave the bar?" Madison asked.

Cody sat looking at her for a long moment.

"I know you're going to think I'm crazy or lying to you," he said, "but I can't remember when I left. I remember going there and drinking a lot, but that's it."

Madison glanced over at Marty. "Cody, I'm going to have to ask you some questions that you probably don't want to hear. It may sound like I'm prying, but I need to ask them. It's my job."

Madison let that settle in for a minute.

"So," she said calmly, "do you think you may have an alcohol problem?"

Cody was stunned. No one had ever really asked him that question.

"I don't . . . think so," he replied uncomfortably.

"Do you black out often?" Madison asked.

"Only very rarely," Cody replied hesitantly. "When I drink too much, sometimes."

"Have you done anything violent in the past during these periods?" she asked.

"No," he said.

"So, your past violent actions have been when you were sober?" she said sarcastically, unable to help slipping briefly into cross-examination mode.

Cody looked at Marty. "What the hell is this? Is she supposed to be on my side? What the hell is going on here?"

Marty looked at Madison.

"Listen, Cody," Madison explained, "I'm not here to judge or condemn you for anything you've done in the past or the present, but I have to know everything about you. I need to get a feeling right away for what I'm dealing with here, so when I ask for your bail, I know what I'm talking about; and when I talk with the D.A., I also know what I'm dealing with. If I'm coming on a little too hard for you, I'm sorry. You certainly don't have to have me represent you in this if you'd feel more comfortable with someone else."

Cody's jaw hung. He looked at Marty again. Marty shrugged and shook his head.

"I don't think he meant that," Marty said. "I know Cody wants you to represent him, Madison."

"Well," Madison said, looking directly at Cody, "I think he needs to say that."

When Madison heard her own words, she realized she'd said them with a little more disdain than she'd intended.

"What the hell," Cody said, mystified. "I don't know what the hell is going on here. You start pumping me like I'm a criminal, now you're talking about not representing me. Listen, lady, I don't know what your hang-up is, but I can tell you this, you're not acting like any lawyer I ever knew. If you're the best, then yeah, I want you to represent me. But if you've got some kind of problem with me, I think maybe you better think about whether or not you can do the fucking job, because I didn't kill anyone, and I want to get this thing over and behind me as fast as I can."

Cody and Madison locked eyes. Neither blinked.

"All right," Madison said, her voice calm once more. She knew she'd been a little out of line in her tone. "All right. I'll try to be sensitive to your feelings. I don't have a problem with you, and you're right, I am the best there is. But you have to tell me everything straight from the start, and if I ask something you don't like, just remember, you'll be hearing the same question over and over again, because you can bet your life that if this goes to trial and you get on that stand, you'll be asked all these questions. Then you can bet the ranch that the person asking you is not on your side."

All three of them sat for a few moments, digesting everything that had just been said.

Marty got up. "I'm going to go see how the arraignment is coming."

When he was gone, Madison said nicely, "So, tell me about the drinking and tell me about the other problems, fights, scuffles, whatever you want to call them."

"From how long ago?" Cody asked.

"Let's stick to everything since you came to Austin," Madison said, keeping her voice under control, "what—eight, nine years ago?"

"Nine," Cody said. Then he began to tell her about his past fights and how much he'd been drinking and why he'd gotten into them and how it was that he'd never gotten a criminal record despite all his run-ins. He'd never even had the need for a criminal lawyer before, a civil lawyer, yes, but the district attorney had never prosecuted him for any of his fights in the past. Madison already knew that Texas was a friendly place to be if you were a football player, so none of what he told her was shocking.

Next, Madison asked him to tell her about his past alcoholic blackouts. She wondered if the man in front of her might not have killed Board and not remember it. She had seen it before but knew it was best not to talk about. Either way, she was committed to getting him acquitted. He was her client now.

She continued to question him. She asked him all about Board and what his relationship with him had been. Then she wanted to know about any turf shoes he might have. Yes, he had them, several pairs. In fact they were lying around his house everywhere; but last night he'd been wearing his cowboy boots. Madison was writing everything down.

"What else were you wearing?" she asked.

Cody thought a moment, then said, "Black jeans and a black polo shirt."

That wasn't good, she thought.

"Do you own a gun?" Madison said.

"Yes, a .357," Cody replied.

"Board was killed with a twenty-two," she told him, all the while trying to read his face for veracity. "The police already know you own a three-fifty-seven. Is there another gun?"

"No, just that one," he said.

"You're sure, right?" she said. "If this goes to trial, I don't want to have to find out about a .22 you picked up somewhere that slipped your mind."

Cody shook his head and said, "No, I don't have another gun. I never did.

"You said 'if this goes to trial.' Do you think that the whole thing might not get that far?" Cody asked hopefully.

Madison thought for a moment. She didn't want to get his hopes up. On the other hand, he had a right to know what her strategy was going to be.

"The police got a warrant for your arrest based on what you said at the Green Mesquite, a size-twelve turf shoe footprint at the scene of the crime, and a witness that they say identified you leaving the scene—"

"Who the hell is that?" Cody said abruptly. "I don't even know where the guy lives!"

Cody realized that he had interrupted her.

"Sorry," he said.

"That's all right," Madison said with a wan smile. "I'm not saying there's a high probability that this won't go to trial, but if we can show that the sneaker wasn't yours and you never owned a .22-caliber gun, then the D.A.'s not going to feel that strong about this case. Then the key will be whether or not I can suppress the eyewitness's testimony. I'll get a hearing on that and try to totally discredit him in front of the judge. If it was a bad ID, he's blind, or the police coerced him into identifying you as the man who left the scene, and I can get his testimony suppressed, then the whole arrest is unconstitutional. Without the ID, everything else is circumstantial and there was no probable cause to have you arrested. The police will be humiliated, and barring some other incredibly persuasive evidence, the whole thing will go away."

"You think that will happen?" Cody said.

"Cody, I have no way of knowing," Madison said. "The witness is old, so that's good. But it may mean nothing. If I had to bet right now, I'd say you'd better be prepared for a trial. It's better to be prepared and then unexpectedly surprised."

"How long will it take?" he asked.

She shrugged.

"You have the right by law to a trial within six months. They can screw around with motions and so forth only so long. Usually it's the defense that delays things, to build the case and make the prosecution fight for every piece of evidence along the way."

"I don't want to wait," Cody said with certainty. "I want this thing over with."

"That will all depend on what turns up," she said. "If the case against you isn't that strong, if they have no weapon, then I can try to make it happen in six months."

"Not sooner?" Cody asked.

"Not unless the D.A. wants it in less, and I can't see why. He'll want to make his case as airtight as he can."

"By the way," Madison said, "I had the police take your wife home. She seemed very concerned."

Cody snorted and shook his head.

"Is there something wrong between the two of you?" Madison asked.

Cody considered his lawyer and said, "Is that question for you or for my case?"

Madison turned pink, and then almost red.

"I can assure you," she said curtly, "that anything I ask you will not have the slightest connection to anything personal with me. Anything I have to say to you will be as your lawyer. Please remember that."

Cody apologized, "I didn't mean anything. The truth is, there is something wrong between me and my wife. What it is I'm not totally sure of, but things are wrong. I guess they kind of always have been."

Madison remained silent. Despite Jenny's apparent concern this morning, she had guessed there were problems afoot from the stories about Cody's past fights. He had never indicated that his wife prompted them, but Madison was smart enough to see that Jenny was always at the center of things whenever he'd had a problem in the past.

"What about playing?" Cody asked. "Can I keep playing?"

"I don't see why not," Madison said. "As long as I can get bail set, which shouldn't be a problem. I may have a hard time with your traveling to away games. We may have to have a federal marshal accompany you, and the bail might get very high for that. From what Marty tells me, the team needs you, so they should be a help in all this."

"Could they suspend me?" Cody asked. "I mean the Outlaws, if they wanted to?"

Madison said, "They can do anything they want, but I can assure you that if they did try to do something like that, we'd serve them with papers by the end of the day and sue their pants off. You are an innocent man. You should remember that through all this. If you're not convicted of this crime, they have no right to suspend you." Cody was beginning to like the way Madison thought. He was damn glad she was going to be working for him, rather than against him.

Marty opened the door. "We got it! Judge Royster told Zimmer to have Cody in his court before they shut down at noon. The bastard was trying to drag his feet."

"Cody, I called the team," Marty continued. "Dryer knows everything. It's no problem being late today. We'll get you right over to your meetings as soon as we get through with the arraignment. I told them, obviously, that you are completely innocent and that we'll get this whole thing worked out. Dryer said he's behind you all the way, and that he wasn't going to forget what you mean to the team. He told me you'd know what that meant."

Cody nodded but said nothing. He knew he was important to the Outlaws as long as Biggs couldn't run full speed and maybe even after he could, if they were fearful that the injury might be a recurring problem.

Judge Royster set bail at five hundred thousand dollars. That meant Cody had to come up with fifty thousand for a bail bondsman. If Cody was going to leave the state, the bond would be two million and a federal marshal would have to travel with him. Marty took care of the local bond and assured Cody that he would get the team to help with the federal bond and the marshal. Within the hour, walking between Marty and Madison, Cody Grey was set free. The only thing he hadn't anticipated was the storm of media waiting right outside the door.

Chapter Twenty

MARTY DROPPED MADISON OFF AT HOME after they dropped Cody at the Outlaw facility. She spent the afternoon with Jo-Jo and his friends, making sweet tea and helping them find lizards underneath rocks by the pool. As she sat by the pool watching the boys swim, her mind kept returning to Cody Grey. She couldn't keep from turning the case over and over in her mind. She realized that it wasn't the case so much as the client who had captured her interest.

"Damn," she said out loud, setting her glass of tea down on the cocktail table beside her chair.

"What, Mom?" Jo-Jo popped his head out of the pool right beside her.

"Nothing, honey," she said with a smile.

She was mad at herself, though. What was wrong with her? This man was married and probably had just murdered someone. He was a football player. He was another version of Joe Thurwood, a brawler, a spendthrift, and a drinker. Cody was a man she didn't want to like. But when she first laid eyes on him earlier today, she felt attracted by something she couldn't quite put her finger on.

It enraged her, and she wondered if there was something psychologically wrong with her. She knew women went back to the same type of man over and over again. She'd defended women who'd been repeatedly abused. Eventually those women either got killed or got so fed up they wound up killing their tormentors. This wasn't quite the same, was it? Could she be that way? She couldn't be. She wouldn't allow herself to be. She was strong enough and smart enough that it would not happen to her again, no matter what twisted wires in her mind brought on a physical attraction to a man who was so obviously wrong for her. He was married. He was a client. He might even end up in jail for the rest of his life, or on death row. She rose from her chair feeling somewhat unsettled. Madison lit the grill and asked Lucia to prepare some burgers. She was going to cook them for the boys and then take them to a movie. She wished Judge Iris DuBose could see her now: the perfect parent. With a mother like her, Jo-Jo really didn't need anyone else. While she stood there looking into the flames, the portable phone rang and she picked it up.

"Hello," she said.

"Honey," came Alice's voice, "I won't tell you what a body buried in the spring and dug up in the summer smells like, but I'll say it isn't sweet."

"What did you find?" Madison said without bothering to acknowledge Alice's frivolity.

"Twenty-two-caliber bullet hole," Alice said cheerily, "right through the ear. Hell of a mess though, I almost can't blame the Ogre for overlooking it. There's no doubt there was another gun used in that old garage that night. Your boy may be right about someone else being there."

"It's all documented, right?" Madison asked.

"Honey," Alice responded, "do you really think I'd go through all this shit for you and screw it up by not dotting my i's?"

"Sorry," Madison said, realizing she had insulted her friend. "Alice, thanks, really. You may have saved that boy's life."

"Glad I could help, honey," Alice said, "especially when you put it like that. Call me for lunch. You owe me."

Madison hung up and shook her fist in silent celebration. If she won this case, it would be one of the hallmarks of her career, a seemingly hopeless pro-bono murder case where an innocent kid was headed for death row.

Suddenly she was struck with an idea. This was the second homicide she was dealing with in the same day where a .22 had been used. Hadn't Alice said that it was unusual for such a weapon to be used in a killing? But how could there be a connection between the two dead boys and an IRS agent who had been investigating Cody Grey? It was far-fetched, but she noted the coincidence. Lucia interrupted her thoughts with a plate of raw seasoned burgers. "Thank you, Lucia," she said, absently dropping the meat onto the hissing grill.

As the housekeeper walked away, Madison found herself wondering about Cody Grey and Yusef Williams.

"Van!"

Van Rawlins could hear his wife's scream from upstairs in the master bathroom. He was noticing the crow's feet in the corners of his eyes as he tied a knot in his tie. His wife was in the kitchen having a glass of bourbon and a cigarette.

"Van!" she shrieked again.

"Damn, that woman's got a mouth," he said to himself, going to the top of the stairs.

"What, dammit! I'm trying to get ready!"

"Well, you got a damn phone call!" his wife screamed at the top of her lungs.

"Why didn't you say so, you old bitch," Rawlins muttered to himself as he made his way back into the bedroom to pick up the phone by the bed.

"I heard that, you bastard!" his wife shrieked before he slammed the door shut .

"Hello," Rawlins said into the phone without any pleasantry whatsoever.

"Van? It's me, Kooch."

Dale Kooch was Van Rawlins's campaign manager. They were currently getting their asses handed to them by Susan Becker, a local attorney whose son had been killed in a gang-related drive-by shooting. The gang driver had been released from the county jail only the week before; the assault charges against him were dismissed on a technicality. His office had botched the case, and Becker was out for blood, his blood. The polls showed that she was eleven points ahead with only eight weeks to go before the election.

"I'm on my way, dammit," Rawlins said. He was late for a pig-roast fund-raiser that was being held at the Elks lodge in West Hills. He needed the money too. Kooch figured Rawlins had to double his television advertising if he was going to stand a prayer of winning. Van could go into private practice and do pretty well, he knew that. But it wasn't the money that motivated him. It was the power of the office and the thought of losing it.

"Did you see the news?" Kooch asked.

"I told you, I'm tryin' to get to your damned pig roast!" Rawlins said with disgust.

"Well, put on seven, right now," Kooch said, unflustered.

Rawlins picked up the remote and flipped the TV on to channel seven. Van's chin hit his shirtfront as he watched Cody Grey emerging from the police station amid a throng of cameras and reporters. He listened intently as the details of the murder were reported. He let out a low whistle. He knew instantly what Grey's conviction could mean for his campaign.

"You find out who's handling the case and get them to that pig roast tonight," he told Kooch. "I need to know how sound this case is. This could be exactly what we've been waiting for, Kooch."

"I know," Kooch said. "That's exactly what I was thinking."

"The only problem is going to be getting this thing to trial by the election," Kooch said.

"There are ways," Rawlins said, thinking of all the markers he could call in to expedite things.

"Did you see who's representing him?" Kooch asked.

"I didn't even notice," Rawlins replied.

"Madison McCall," he said.

"Well," Rawlins said, his mind spinning, "that may not be all bad, Kooch. That may not be all bad. . . . "

Cody didn't know how to act, so he acted the way he always did. There had been times in his life when he wished he'd been a little more gregarious, but this was one time he was truly comfortable keeping his mouth shut. Part of him wanted to tell everyone that he didn't do it. Another part of him was angry and wanted to scream at everyone to stop looking at him the way they did. Instead he said nothing to his teammates, his coaches, the medical staff, or anyone. In a way, this made him feel guilty, but he was too upset and too tired to care. He needed to concentrate on playing football.

If Cody didn't end up punching out some cameraman's lights, he would be very surprised. He figured an assault charge on top of murder was like dust in a pig pen. The people were shameless. One TV station showed up outside his hotel room at eleven o'clock on Saturday night, knocking and saying that they had a special message for him. The others followed him everywhere. He had no doubt that they would have followed him right into the locker room had there been no security. Madison told him not to say anything to anyone. They would hound him for a while, but she assured him that they were like ticks; and if they didn't get any blood from the host, they would soon move on.

After the game against the Patriots the next day, he left the locker room before the press was allowed in. Because of his medical condition and his need to ice down his drugged and drained knee immediately after the game, Cody simply dressed in the training room and used Jerry's private shower. It would have been a good game to talk to the press. The team had won, and Cody delivered another exceptional performance; eleven tackles and an interception. It convinced him that the worse things got in his life, the better he played. At the rate he was going, he figured he might be able to last another season no matter what happened to his knee.

Marty promised to pick him up outside a gate different from the one used by the players. Cody snuck out the training room back door and wound his way through the maze of passages under the stands until he finally emerged into the bright Sunday afternoon sun. Marty's car was waiting for him. Cody was thankful to his agent for sticking by him when he really needed him, and he said so.

"We're friends," Marty replied.

"Yeah, but even some friends wouldn't be doing what you've already done."

"Well, then they're not real friends," Marty said with an easy smile.

Cody was relieved that Marty seemed to want to talk of nothing but the game. It made him feel almost as if the entire thing had never happened, and he was just on his way home like he was every Sunday during the season. The only difference was Jenny not being there.

"Want me to come in?" Marty asked when they'd pulled into Cody's driveway.

"No," Cody said, seeing that Jenny's car was in the garage, "but thanks."

"Call me if you need anything," Marty said. "The grand jury indictment will most likely come in tomorrow, so we'll probably have to show up again on Tuesday for another arraignment. It's just a formality."

Marty ran out of information and wondered if he'd said too much. He didn't want to ruin the guy's day any more than he needed to. He wasn't too good at all this, and he thanked God that tax law had been his calling.

"Thanks again," Cody told him as he patted Marty on the shoulder and climbed out of the car.

"Any time," Marty said. He watched Cody walk toward the house and through the open garage door. As he drove away, he couldn't help wondering what would go on inside the Grey house.

The first thing Cody did when he got inside was listen. He could hear water running but didn't know where it was coming from. He thought it was from the downstairs guest-room bathroom, and that was a bad sign. It meant that Jenny had set up quarters downstairs. He set his bag down on the kitchen table and went to the refrigerator for a cold beer. He hadn't seen or spoken to

Jenny since he was arrested on Saturday morning. He wandered through the house until he found himself sitting on the guest-room bed with his bad knee propped up on a pillow, patiently waiting for the water to stop running. It did; and ten minutes later, Jenny emerged in a towel. She saw him but acted like she didn't.

"Well," Cody said, "aren't you going to say something?"

"There's not much to say," Jenny replied.

"Do you think I did it?" he said.

Jenny stopped and looked at him. "I don't think anything," she said.

"So," he said, changing tactics, "where were you last night?"

Jenny huffed. "I don't think we're at the point right now where you need to be asking me where I am and what I do," she said.

Cody clenched his teeth. She was standing at the mirror now, brushing her hair.

"Were you with someone?" he said. He'd asked that question before, but never when he'd felt so certain that the answer was going to be affirmative. The only thing he wanted was for her to deny it one more time. That was all. That was the routine. He questioned her. She denied it. They had done it before. It worked. He was in trouble all the way around right now. He wanted her with him. He needed someone. Even if it was just pretend. He would gladly take her the way she had been for the past few months—distant, but more available than she'd ever been. He'd take her even at her worst right now, if she would only go along with the charade.

"I didn't hear an answer," he said finally.

"That's because I didn't give one," she retorted.

"I want a fucking answer!" he bellowed, rising from the bed and stepping up behind her in the mirror.

"Tough shit, Cody," she snarled, turning to face him. "Now I'll tell you what you really want to know . . . Would you like that?" she taunted.

"It's just as you've suspected for nine fucking years. It's what's haunted your dreams, your worst nightmare."

Cody's stomach turned and contracted. He wanted to smash her face in. She stood there, almost naked, her chin held high. She was daring him, tempting him.

Cody felt his hand instinctively tighten. It was like on the football field. It just happened. He bellowed with rage. There was no thought. He turned and swung his fist with all his might, he even bent his knees and coiled his hips like a natural puncher, giving the impact the full force of his entire body. As he spun, he sensed and saw the fear in her eyes. He had her attention. She knew what he was capable of. She thought he would never hit her, never have the balls to hurt her, but she had pushed him too far. In that instant before contact, he smiled inwardly at the idea of her fear. She had never been afraid of anything or anyone. It was time for a wake-up call.

The sound was like a baseball bat hitting an unripe melon, more of a crack than a thud. Cody was lucky he missed the studding. His hand burst through the plasterboard and out the other side of the wall. The terror remained in Jenny's eyes.

"I can kill you, too, you know," he heard himself saying. He wanted it to last.

"You're sick," she mumbled, stepping away.

Cody pulled his fist from the wall, sending chunks of Sheetrock and dust everywhere.

"I know," he said, before he turned and walked out of the room. "I'm sick of you."

CHAPTER TWENTY-ONE

ON MONDAY AFTERNOON MADISON AND MARTY sat down across a conference table from Van Rawlins. He had two men with him. One was Ben Cherrit, the office's main homicide prosecutor. Cherrit would sit second with Rawlins, who was trying this case himself. The other man sitting was Dale Kooch, who seemed to go everywhere Van Rawlins did these days. Also in the room was Detective Zimmer, who stood off to the side, holding a cup of coffee.

Zimmer watched the rest of them like a patient bird of prey waiting to swoop. He wasn't completely happy with the way things were going. He wanted a murder weapon, but the search of Cody Grey's house had turned up nothing more than the .357. He needed time to find it. He sensed that Rawlins was rushing things. A murder investigation wasn't something you just slapped together in two days. Things needed time to unfold. When they did unfold, an investigator needed the latitude to follow up on new leads and information without feeling the pressure of time from an impending trial.

Something else was bothering Zimmer. He had been to Board's office that morning and discovered that the file on Cody Grey was missing. It was obvious that Cody Grey would want the file destroyed, but how could he have eliminated all traces of Board's investigation? Board's boss had assured Zimmer that even if the computer version of the file was missing, a hard-copy backup should have been there in the agent's office. Yes, she'd told him, it was possible that Board would take the file home but only in one form. He would either take the hard copy and leave his laptop computer, or take the computer and leave the hard copy. He didn't need both, and there would be no reason to take them both home. Zimmer asked if it was possible that someone could have gotten into the office and taken the file. Board's boss had shrugged and told him that she supposed someone in the office could have taken it, but she knew of no reason why; and as for someone stealing it, the building was secured at night, and no one came or went during the day unannounced.

Zimmer found the computer in question at Board's home. There were very few prints they could lift from it, and they were all Board's own. A computer hack at the station had done a complete search of the hard drive. Nothing was on it. Nothing at all. The missing file and the empty computer, Zimmer knew, meant something. He just didn't know what. It didn't make sense that Cody Grey would think he could avoid an investigation simply by destroying a file. The search of his tax history could and would begin anew. For Zimmer, this fact left a gaping question. He had hoped that something in this meeting might help him find the answer.

Because of the missing weapon, Madison was prepared for Rawlins to dig in and try to use delay tactics that would push the trial off long enough for the police to find it. Just as likely, Madison knew, the gun was at the bottom of the Colorado River. Still, she expected the D.A. would try to delay things as much as possible. But it was Rawlins who had called this pretrial meeting only two days after the murder, and she wasn't exactly sure what he had in mind.

"I want to know everything you've got," Madison said to Rawlins. She didn't have to remind him not to leave anything out. He had tried to screw around with the disclosure of some evidence during a case about five years ago. It had been the last time. If Rawlins had evidence he was withholding, they both knew she would make sure Cody walked, no matter how bad things looked.

Rawlins recounted for her essentially everything she'd already learned on Saturday from Zimmer. He added the fact that everything documenting the IRS investigation of Cody Grey was either destroyed or taken. Rawlins tried to claim that that only bolstered the theory of Cody's motive to kill Board and destroy the investigation. The missing files bothered Madison as well, and it made her think again about the .22. Certainly if Cody Grey did kill Board, he would know that files or no files, the IRS would continue its investigation of his unclaimed playing-card income. A jury, on the other hand, might not look at this bit of evidence the same way.

The shoes had yet to turn up as well. Lab tests showed that the print was from the kind of turf shoe used by the Outlaws. Madison bet that the gun and the shoes were never going to turn up. The only other news that she hadn't heard yet was that the bartender at Chester's remembered Cody leaving the bar at about twelve-thirty. He had more than an hour to find Board and kill him. He had the motive. He had the means.

When Rawlins had laid out his case, he said, "So what's your position?"

He expected Madison to begin to try and strike a deal with him. He had the goods on her client. He told her he was going to ask the grand jury later that day for an indictment for murder in the first degree. He expected she'd try to bargain a murder two or even a voluntary manslaughter. He was looking forward to telling her that he intended to take this to trial with nothing less than a guilty plea to murder in the first.

"My client has an alibi," Madison said after considering the situation. "You only have circumstantial evidence. You have no weapon. Turf shoes are found everywhere. Players discard them when they start to wear. On top of that, my client may have been impaired by alcohol when he made the threat. He left the bar, yes, at twelve-thirty. He returned to his home immediately afterward."

"We both know the wife heard him coming in at 2:30," Rawlins scoffed. "And I wouldn't call an eyewitness circumstantial."

"You won't get the wife to testify," Madison pointed out. "And you can't subpoena her, you know that. So you've got nothing with which to contradict my client's alibi."

This was true, and Rawlins saw it as a possible weakness in his case, except for the fact that the jury might be smart enough to wonder why the defense didn't call the wife to the stand to substantiate the alibi. But he knew better than anyone that if you didn't serve it up for a jury on a silver platter, chances were they weren't going to get it.

"By the way," Madison said, "your witness is seventy-eight years old. He wears glasses and it was late at night. Old people have very poor night vision."

"He was under a damn spotlight," Rawlins said, amused with her tactics.

Still, he saw where she was going. Without a weapon, the real battle in this case would be the suppression hearing for his witness. If she could knock the old man out, he didn't even have a valid arrest. Rawlins was confident in the old man, though. He'd already met with him that morning and felt certain that the question of the old man's competence would at least have to go to a jury. Madison was simply posturing.

"Let's cut the bullshit, Madison," Rawlins said. "I want to set a trial date, and I want it by the last week of October. Is there anything you need that will keep that from happening?"

Madison was blown away. Rawlins was rarely so forthright. The D.A.'s case was good if the witness held up, but prudence should tell him to wait and hope for the gun or the shoes to turn up. Going to trial as things were was a great temptation to her. She knew she could out-prepare Rawlins. He was a crafty trial lawyer, good on his feet, but she was smarter than he was; and when it came to preparation, where brains were everything, she had him. She doubted even Rawlins would dispute that. A fast trial would give her the advantage. That was why she hesitated. Why was he doing this? There had to be a reason.

The answer came to her as soon as she asked the question. Rawlins didn't care so much about a conviction as he did a trial. The publicity would be just what he needed to win the election in November. He wanted this thing to go down the week before the election. The name Van Rawlins would be on everyone's mind and almost assure his victory. Madison didn't need more than a minute to realize she had to take the early trial. She might help get Rawlins reelected, but her sworn duty was to Cody Grey, and a rushed trial might just be the best chance he was going to have of being acquitted. With Cody's past and the evidence at hand, despite its being circumstantial, she was going to need every advantage she could get. She already knew Cody would be more than pleased, and she really didn't blame him. Strategy aside, she would hate to have a trial hanging over her head, especially if he was innocent.

"I want a suppression hearing on the eyewitness before I commit to anything," she said. "If he doesn't make it, this thing isn't going to trial."

"I'll give you a hearing in forty-eight hours," Rawlins said.

Madison raised her eyebrows. She liked that too; it would give the D.A. next to no time to prepare the old man.

"I'll take it," she said. Rawlins remained stone-faced, but Dale Kooch, she saw, couldn't help but smile.

As Van Rawlins's luck would have it, the judge who drew the case of People vs. Cody Grey was Walter Connack. Walter had never seen a prosecutor try to move something through the system with such speed. At first Connack balked. An immediate suppression hearing was one thing, but a full-blown murder trial in less than two months' time, when the docket was already full, was quite another. The judiciary was not a tool to be wielded in the political campaign of some ambitious lawyer. Those were his exact words to Van Rawlins.

Rawlins, however, reminded the judge that he, too, was an elected official and that the constituents of Travis County would not look kindly on a judge who had abused his power to dig up the rotting body of an Hispanic murder victim, against the vehement wishes of the deceased's family. Rawlins had found out about the exhumation from the mayor's office, where a barrage of irate calls were received from leaders throughout the Hispanic community.

"I'm prepared to do one of two things," Rawlins told the judge as they spoke in his chambers on Tuesday morning, before court went into session for the suppression hearing. "One, you don't give me the early trial and win, lose, or draw in the election, I'll see that a full-scale judicial investigation is launched against you. I'll make sure the woman who did the digging is suspended without pay and investigated. And I'll file a complaint against Madison McCall with the Texas Bar Association. The second option is that you give me my trial before the election, and I tell the mayor to go smoke a pipe because what you all did was completely within the confines of the law the way I interpret it. And you know damn well the mayor doesn't know the law from his leg, and he'll do whatever the hell I say on this. So the decision is yours."

Walter swallowed his pride and went with the program. He told himself that it was worth it if it saved the life of an innocent boy. Besides, an early trial did not compromise him, or the law, or anyone, in any way. It was merely a pain in the ass.

By the middle of October, things for Cody Grey seemed almost normal, except for his marriage. After the first days of constant media attention, the talk started to die down. He knew, however, that the reprieve from controversy and attention would evaporate as soon as the trial began. Walter Connack, the judge for the case, had set the trial date for the last Monday of October. This suited everyone, including Cody.

Madison told him that the case was going to be fairly straightforward and, barring any surprises, the trial could be over in four or five days. They could complete it during the week, and Cody would either be exonerated and play in the next game without an interruption in the football season, or he'd be in jail, probably for the rest of his life. Cody never had any doubts that he would be set free. He was innocent, and when he took the stand, the jury would see that. They had to. It was just not possible for him to think that twelve people could convict an innocent man. He knew the horror stories, but they involved the people who didn't have the means for a good lawyer. He had the best.

His marriage with Jenny was now over. She stayed on at the house, living exclusively in the guest room. The only reason she stayed at all was because Striker insisted. If the agency began to think Jenny was anything more than his sometime mistress, they might start to follow her as well.

On the rare occasions Cody and Jenny did run into each other, neither spoke. Cody stopped putting his paychecks into their joint account. He knew he was going to need all he could save. Marty had sheepishly explained to him that Madison's fee for the trial would be fifty thousand dollars. It was one time when Cody didn't want to try to cut corners and save. He knew a good lawyer was like a good doctor. She could save your life.

If Jenny was upset about his cutting her off from the income, she didn't show it. Cody supposed that once the trial and the season were over that he would look into getting a divorce. That was if Jenny didn't do something about it first. He had the suspicion that she would. He would welcome it. It would be much easier to simply stand back and watch her tear the whole thing down.

He realized that his relationship with Jenny had been infested like a house with termites from the very start. They had both let things deteriorate. When Cody was finally forced to pull the wall boards away to inspect the damage, he found that everything had essentially been destroyed. The whole thing would have to be torn down and abandoned. He would have to start his life over, building something new from scratch. It was a wearying prospect that saddened him. No matter how bad things with Jenny had become, Cody had grown used to living with her. It was the same kind of comfort that came from living in a house for years and years. Termites or not, it was still the only home he knew.

Madison worked diligently on Cody's case. She developed her trial plan and orchestrated the depositions of witnesses while she closely monitored the continuing investigation of the case. She had little time to take care of her other legal business, and she had to work overtime to try and clear her calendar for the upcoming trial. One thing she didn't neglect was to make the necessary motions to delay the trial of Yusef Williams. She didn't mind that. The delay was necessary anyway. She had enlisted the help of one of her firm's private investigators to try and find the man in black. Yusef would stand a much better chance if they could identify the mystery man, find the .22 pistol, and link them both to the boys who were killed. Because the investigator was working for free and doing the work on his own time, he warned Madison that he would probably need several months to come up with anything at all.

Occasionally, when she was thinking about Yusef's case, it occurred to her that Cody fit the description of the man Yusef said had killed his friends that night. Madison pushed this idea from her mind. She knew Cody Grey wasn't the man who had killed Yusef's friends, but there was the issue of the .22. She was obliged to show Yusef a picture of Cody and ask him if he was the man in black. No, was the answer.

She almost asked Alice to compare the ballistics from the Williams and Board murders, but she decided not to. Alice, she knew, was busy enough, and Madison didn't really want to pursue the idea anyway. It would be an unnecessary complication. To link the cases now would do more damage to Cody than anything. She certainly couldn't expect one jury to be swayed by the fact that a murder suspect in another case swore that Cody wasn't his mystery man. Even if the bullets matched, Yusef's murder case took place months ago, and anything could have happened to the gun in the meantime. It could easily have been pawned, then sold and reused by Cody months later. Rawlins would be sure to point that out. She had too many other things to think about and do without running down blind alleys. She needed something more.

Along with all her lawyering, Madison was forced to continue to deal with Joe and his attorney. She was slowly and subtly trying to poison her son's mind against the father she now believed would ultimately disappoint and maybe even hurt him. She felt ruthless and manipulative using psychological tactics that she usually reserved for the courtroom on her own eight-year-old son, but she was convinced that she had only Jo-Jo's best interest at heart. Iris DuBose gave Big Joe nothing more than a hand-slap for his unauthorized ice-cream visits with Jo-Jo. Madison had been infuriated, but with Glen Westman's help she was quickly coming to accept that there was nothing to be done about Iris until the whole thing was over. It wouldn't be until the appeal that Madison would get a chance to drag the female judge over some hot legal coals. So far, Madison had to put up with only two of Joe's temporary authorized Saturday visits. Her ex-husband had picked Jo-Jo up in the morning and returned him both times in the evening without incident.

Madison had Glen Westman digging in his heels, within the law, every step of the way to try and inflate the cost of the litigation as much as possible. She still hoped to force Joe into a settlement. She had Westman candidly tell Joe's attorney, Paul Gleason, to expect that Joe would run out on a big legal bill that didn't put any cash in his pocket up front. That knowledge, if Gleason believed it, would make the attorney work all the harder to push Joe to settle.

Madison lost the suppression hearing for Boris Hauffler's eyewitness account of Cody leaving the house after Jeff Board had been killed. It hadn't been all bad, though. She was able to learn some things about Hauffler that she knew would help her at trial. Although Hauffler's testimony would get to the jury, she suspected that she could damage him severely on the stand. Getting a judge to believe beyond a doubt that a witness was completely incompetent or that the police had coerced him into a positive ID was tough. However, discrediting a witness in front of a jury was a completely different matter. Hauffler, she learned during the hearing, didn't like young aggressive women. Madison would use this fact to get under the man's skin at trial and make him look like a near-sighted old crank who had limited night vision and a chip on his shoulder.

The real push for Madison would come two weeks before the trial actually began. She would begin to prepare Cody and all her witnesses for the stand. She would finalize her strategy and focus on getting an acquittal for her client. During the four weeks since Cody's arraignment, Madison hadn't even seen him, and her determination to keep from thinking of him as anything but a client on trial for murder seemed to be paying off.

CHAPTER TWENTY-TWO

ON THE TUESDAY THAT THEY WERE TO BEGIN preparing for trial, Cody appeared at Madison's law offices at nine o'clock in the morning. He was dressed in a plain white T-shirt and jeans. He looked remarkably out of place in the lavish and formal setting of the old firm. It was his one day off, so he was going to be comfortable. He walked into the conference room, where Madison sat waiting with Marty. The moment she saw his handsome face and his tormented smile, every emotion she'd suppressed for the past month came rushing back. She choked back a sense of self-disgust, and tried to get her emotions under control, standing and shaking his hand briskly.

They all sat down, and Madison cleared her throat before telling Cody that for the next ten days, until she started jury selection, she wanted him essentially by her side every step of the way. He might remember new things or make connections that would help in preparing his defense. They would be going over the prosecution's list of witnesses again and again, reviewing the depositions and looking for motivations, weaknesses, and contradictions that she could exploit on cross-examination. They would go over his story every day, practicing his direct testimony, and then she would cross-examine him in the same manner she knew Rawlins would cross-examine him at the trial.

Madison handed Cody a schedule that laid out the times and basic content of their next two weeks.

Cody looked carefully at it and then looked up with a somewhat embarrassed smile. "This is great," he said. "I like how thorough you're being. It's great.

"The only thing is," Cody said, looking to his agent, "I asked Marty to tell you that I can't be doing this kind of stuff during the day. I have to be at practice."

Madison looked from Cody to Marty. "Well," Marty started with a slight blush, pushing his glasses up his nose, "I didn't think it was something that should really come from me. I thought it was something that we all needed to sit down and talk about together."

"I thought you couldn't practice because of your knee." Madison said.

"I can't practice," Cody replied, "but I have to be at the meetings and watch what's going on so I know what I'm supposed to be doing in the games. I have treatment on my knee, too."

"There's really nothing to talk about," Madison fumed, rapping her fingers against the paper. "This is the schedule."

"Uhh, no," Cody insisted, looking for Marty to support him. "I don't think so. I have to be at the Outlaws facility during the day. We're going to have to do this some other way."

"I don't think you understand me," Madison said, stiffening her back. "This isn't some college biology exam that we can shift around because of your football schedule. This is a murder trial, Cody. You're the defendant. I'm the attorney. I determine what happens here. And for the next two weeks, I need your time to prepare you for this trial. In case you haven't noticed," she added with almost a wicked undertone, "this thing doesn't look so good for you."

"I'm innocent," Cody said flatly.

"I'm not talking about your guilt or innocence," Madison replied, exasperated. "I'm talking about proving it to a jury."

"Look," Cody said, "I'm not stupid. I'm not talking about not doing everything you're saying. I'm just saying that we can do it in the evenings, after practice is over."

Madison threw her hands up in the air and said, "I happen to have a life! I happen to be a single parent with some problems of my own right now. I'm sorry. Do you really think that you're the only one involved here? Are you really such a cookie cut-out of all the egocentric animals that play that goddamned game?"

A slow smoldering anger started to burn in Cody's eyes.

"No," he said, "I'm not. Are you really the tight-assed, nose-in-the-air lawyer-bitch that Joe Thurwood always made you out to be?"

"I don't have to sit here and listen to this!" Madison stormed, rising from her seat and heading for the door.

Marty grabbed her by the arm, and she shook him loose.

"Wait a minute, Madison," Marty said, obviously upset.

"No, you wait a minute, Marty!" she said. "You get your damn football player under control!"

"I'm going to get both of you under control!" Marty yelled.

The room fell silent. Marty recovered from surprising even himself with his uncharacteristic outburst and said firmly, "Sit down, Madison!"

Madison closed her mouth tightly and sat.

"All right," he said with passion, "now listen. Cody has a legitimate concern here. You want him to know about this trial backwards and forwards, and he will. But he's trying to hold his life together, too. Now I know that it's very important to you to be home for dinner with Jo-Jo and put him to bed at night, and I respect that; Cody does too. But I don't think it's asking the world for you to work on this after Jo-Jo is in bed, say from nine until midnight. You've got an office in your home, and you've been working those hours the past four weeks anyway. I think you can do it, and I think you should. This is a trial here, Madison, and I can't believe you're acting like you can walk out like it's a damn high school dance!" Marty threw himself down in his chair and stared at her.

Madison stared down at the papers in front of her and tried to regain her composure. Marty was so right that it hurt. There were so many emotions churning around inside of her. There was this trial, her ex-husband, her son, Marty, Yusef Williams, and now Cody Grey, each one demanding her exclusive attention.

"All right," she said. "All right."

Striker sat alone, reading in his chair. His leg jiggled nervously up and down. He was anxious. He usually didn't get that way. He usually managed to remain completely calm, almost disinterested; but this was his biggest operation. And it was personal. It was for the rest of their lives. He laughed inwardly. He had thought of their lives, not just his own.

Striker was getting old. He was almost fifty. His life was changing and so was he. He wondered if that was why, for the first time in his life, he was even thinking of settling down with one woman and one way of life. When this operation was complete, it would be a life of luxury and leisure. They would change identities and travel the world, staying in the finest hotels, eating the finest food, drinking the finest wines. There would be no more danger, no more looking over his shoulder. It was time, and, if he was going to do it with someone else, she was obviously the one.

Striker closed his book and wished that she were there with him at that moment. He realized that the more he saw her, the more he missed her when she wasn't there. Before Jenny, the opposite had always been true. He was even glad that she and her husband were no longer speaking. He had secretly begun to grow jealous of the time she spent with Cody. Striker chided himself for thinking like a love-smitten teenager. He felt this way more and more lately, and he didn't particularly like it. It was a dangerous way to think. It clouded his judgment. He knew that. In one way, it almost made him want to eradicate the whole thing, eradicate her. That would be the professional thing to do, and he knew it.

The people who were following him had attached themselves like parasites. At times he almost forgot they were there. But each day their very presence, and the limitations it put on him, sucked some of the life out of his existence. He had worked hard to lull them into thinking that his life was nothing but ordinary. Maybe part of his anxiety was dealing with that every day, knowing that they were there and that right now there was nothing he could do about it. His only relief was an occasional foray out into the night, and even that he only did out of necessity.

Tonight, however, was one of those nights. He had packages to pick up and packages to deliver. Striker changed into some dark clothes and black shoes. He stuffed the Beretta he carried everywhere into its shoulder holster and quietly left his apartment, taking the stairs down to the basement. He unlocked a steel door and entered the tunnel that led to the steam substation that would take him well beyond the view of the men who were watching him.

Striker had an old Pontiac that he kept on a busy side street near the university, where its constant presence drew no unwanted attention. He got into the car and headed north to the outskirts of town near the airport. About a mile from the airport was a self-storage garage that Striker used as a clandestine warehouse. The large concrete room was filled to the ceiling with boxes of surplus ammunition and weapons that he had acquired in his dealings over the years. He had enough materials to launch a small-scale invasion.

After rolling down the door behind him, Striker used his flashlight to locate a box that contained a twenty-pound slab of C-4 plastic explosives. It looked like a harmless block of modeling clay. Striker opened a suitcase that he'd taken from the trunk of his Pontiac and set it on a workbench that was in the middle aisle of the storage room, between the boxes. The suitcase had been fitted with a false bottom about an inch deep. Striker took a length of piano wire from his pocket and began slicing one-inch-thick pieces of C-4 off the main slab. He lined the slices up next to each other in the bottom of the case and then mashed them all together so they would stay firmly in place. The bomb he was constructing would be powerful enough so that it would be quite some time, if ever, before the authorities would be able to identify the person who was carrying it when it went off.

After the C-4 was in place, Striker walked to the front of the room and fished around some more with his flashlight until he found a box that contained remote detonation devices. The remotes were disguised to look like everyday hand-held cell phones. He extracted one of these with the matching detonator and brought them back to the workbench where he pressed the detonator into the mass of C-4. It stuck, looking like some kind of modern relief sculpture. He carefully resealed the suitcase and closed it up, then stuffed the remote into his jacket pocket before flicking off the flashlight and hoisting open the garage door. Striker glanced furtively to his left and right. He crossed the parking lot and got into his car. Within an hour, he was back in his reading chair. It was three A.M.

The next day Cody was out on the practice field, paying close attention. The defense was running through the coverages they would be playing against the Lions' three-wide-receiver formation that weekend. He was less than thrilled that Biggs was actually out there on the field and doing some light running. If the younger player's leg kept holding up, it wouldn't be long before he would be able to replace Cody. The word was that Biggs would run for about three weeks and then start light practicing. Two weeks from that point, he would be ready to go. It could be more; it could be less.

Besides the money Biggs was being paid, it would be easy for the coaches to justify replacing Cody for the simple fact that he could barely walk during the week, and therefore could not practice. The only thing he was good for was playing his ass off after his weekly miracle of modern medicine. That was good, but in an ideal world, the team would have a free safety who could both practice and play. It was better for everyone. But practice for Cody was out of the question. Hell, at four-thirty in the afternoon on a Wednesday, he was having a hard time just standing there watching. No doubt a healthy Biggs would mean Cody's return to the bench. He felt everything closing in on him at the same time.

A few minutes later, a loud chopping sound from above caused Cody, like most of his teammates, to look up. It was a news helicopter. It landed on one end of the field and a camera crew hopped out. Within five minutes another flew in and landed as well. Then a van from another station wheeled up and began to immediately assemble a remote satellite uplink. Cody had the sinking feeling that the sudden appearance of the press had something to do with him.

When practice broke, Cody hobbled toward the locker room with everyone else. Before he got off the field, a third helicopter came down out of the sky. A CNN crew hopped out, bent over to avoid the spinning copter blades, and ran toward him like they were all playing parts in some kind of war movie. The press surrounded him, and a CNN reporter stopped him in his tracks, not so much by blocking his path as with the question he asked.

"So how do you feel now that the police have found your shoes and matched them to the ones that left bloody prints at Jeff Board's home?" the reporter brazenly asked.

"What?" Cody said, shocked.

"Are you still contending that you're innocent?" a bleached blonde from channel seven barked at him.

"I . . . I . . ." Cody stammered. "Let me by."

He started to push through the small crowd of cameras.

The CNN reporter jammed the microphone in front of his face. "The shoes have Jeff Board's blood all over them! They're your shoes! They're Outlaws turf shoes! They have number forty printed on them! Are you going to admit to the murder?"

"What?" Cody was in a daze now. How was it possible? The first horrible thought that came into his mind was that maybe he really did do it. It was the first time he actually wondered. There was a witness. He couldn't remember the night himself. Now his shoe.

The questions were coming at him so fast now he didn't even hear them.

"I don't know," he mumbled, then stumbled by them all into the safety of the locker room, where his teammates stared at him in disbelief. He glanced around and knew that the word had spread like an electrical charge. He knew, too, that he wasn't the only one wondering if in fact he was really a murderer.

CHAPTER TWENTY-THREE

MADISON AND MARTY SAT IN HER OFFICE. Both of them were silent. They had been for almost five minutes. A little after four, they'd gotten the news from Rawlins's office that the bloody turf shoe had turned up in some weeds down by the river under the South First Street Bridge. An anonymous caller who claimed to be a jogger and said he didn't want to get involved had tipped off the police. Van Rawlins had already hit the airwaves guaranteeing a conviction. It was brazen political grandstanding, but under the circumstances it wasn't surprising.

Madison was sitting behind her desk, thinking, and Marty was watching her. He could tell she was greatly disturbed. He could tell it went beyond the news that was a brutal blow to their case. They had already talked about a motion for adjournment to delay the trial, but they knew that would be futile. Once a trial was set, it had to be something more than additional evidence to keep it from taking place at the appointed time. Considering the gravity of the evidence, they both wondered privately if a delay would make a difference anyway.

"What is it you're thinking?" Marty finally said.

Madison looked up at him in a way that let him know she'd forgotten he was there.

"I'm thinking that he did it, Marty," she said quietly. "I know I'm not supposed to think about it one way or another, but you always do, you know. I always think about it. It's not often I think I'm representing someone who actually did it, but I can't come up with any other explanation. Can you?" Her question was more of a plea for help.

Marty looked at her and pushed his glasses up before he said, "Anything's possible, Madison, you know that. Someone could have gotten a pair of his shoes. We're talking about murder. People will go to great lengths when they kill someone. Maybe Cody was framed."

"Who?" she asked. She hoped he had an answer.

"I don't know," Marty shrugged. "This guy Board was a real jerk. Maybe he messed with someone else, and they were just waiting for the chance to get him, the chance when they could make it look like it was someone else."

"And that same person not only has access to a pair of Cody's shoes, but also kills the man on the very same night Cody threatens to kill him? How?" Madison was exasperated. "And he also coincidentally looks exactly like Cody when he runs from Board's house? And, oh, yeah, he's so thorough that he actually thinks to stop and not only steal the investigatory file on Cody Grey but erase Board's entire computer hard drive?"

"We've got an alibi," Marty suggested weakly.

"Oh, yeah," Madison scoffed. "I forgot! He's going to get up there and say he left the bar at twelve-thirty and went right home. Yeah, we can insinuate that his wife heard him come in then. They can't call the wife to contradict it. I can probably even sneak it by the jury in a way so they believe it. But I'm talking about you and me, Marty. We know damned well that he didn't come home until two-thirty! We know in reality he doesn't even have an alibi!"

Marty shook his head and said, "Anything's possible. I mean, who the hell was this anonymous caller, the jogger?"

"Oh, come on, Marty!" she said. "Think about what you're saying. Only you could even say that with a straight face. Whomever the caller was, they're Cody's shoes, with Board's blood on them!"

Madison paused and said, "I think we should try to plead it out with Rawlins. I think we should push the alcoholic blackout and go for involuntary manslaughter, settle for voluntary, or if Rawlins won't take it, I think we should focus on that at trial. Concede the fact that he killed him and try to legitimize it as much as we can. Show the jury what a bastard Board was, how he was threatening to ruin Cody's life, all that stuff. We might be able to get him a sentence of fifteen to twenty. Hell, if we could do that, he could be out in eight!"

"You can ask him," Marty said, shaking his head. "I won't. I know what he'll say. He won't go for it, but you can ask him."

Madison had dinner with Jo-Jo, and afterward they played on his computer and read a chapter from *Treasure Island*. At eight-thirty he went to bed. At nine there was a knock at her door. Madison let Cody in and led him to her study without much more than a simple hello. She waited until the doors were shut and they were both sitting down before she asked him how he was feeling.

"Not great," he said, hoping she might have some words of encouragement for him. She didn't.

"It's not good news," she said.

"You think I did it, don't you?" Cody said, his stare piercing into her eyes, challenging her.

"I told you," she responded without returning his stare, "it's not my job to think you did it. It's my job to defend you the best way I know how."

"I didn't do it," Cody said emphatically. "No matter what it looks like, I didn't."

Madison wanted to scream at him to stop. She wanted to tell him that that was what they all said. She wanted to tell him to level with her and they'd see what they could do about limiting the jail sentence.

Instead, she cleared her throat and said, "I thought maybe we could talk about some backup strategies."

"Meaning what?" Cody asked.

"Meaning a deal we might cut with the D.A. in light of today's evidence."

"Like, I tell them I did it, and they give me a lesser sentence?" he said incredulously. "No fucking way. I won't do it."

Madison considered that for a moment before she said, "Did you ever think that maybe, and I'm not saying this is the case, but just maybe, you may have done this and not even remember doing it? It's not the same type of crime if you didn't even know what you were doing . . . "

Cody looked like he'd taken a knife in the gut. He shook his head. He kept shaking it. Then he stopped and looked up at her. "Yes," he choked, in nothing more than a whisper. "I thought about it. But I didn't do it. I wouldn't do that. I couldn't."

Madison stared. Her heart was filled with pity for the tortured soul who sat across from her. She felt a strange desire to hold him and brush her fingers through his hair. She pushed that from her mind. She could see that he really believed what he was saying, whether it was true or not. And she could also see that Marty was right: this trial was going to be all or nothing.

"Well," Madison said, gently patting the files that sat in a stack in front of her, "we'd better get to work."

Suddenly there was noise like a rampaging bull outside in the hall. The doors to Madison's study blasted open, showering splinters of wood into the room. Cody and Madison both jumped back as Joe Thurwood came to a stop, his fat belly heaving, trying to catch his breath as though he was having a heart attack. His long hair was unkempt and matted down. He looked and smelled as if he hadn't changed his clothes in three days. His eyes were bloodshot, and he glared at the two of them like a crazed, wounded animal.

"What the fuck is going on here!" he demanded, his body hunched over and his fists clenched as if he was ready to attack.

"What are you doing here?" Madison shrieked. "This is my house!"

"This is my house!" he screamed back, the veins bulging purple in his neck. "You don't start fucking my teammates in my house, you slut!"

As he spoke, Joe moved threateningly toward her.

"He's crazy," Madison said gingerly, more frightened now than ever.

Cody stepped deftly in front of her, blocking Joe's path. Madison felt like a brick wall had just been raised to protect her. Cody's hands were open and in the air in an offering of peace, but his body was taut and ready to spring.

"Joe," Cody pleaded, trying to cut through the psychotic rage of the large man in front of him. "Joe. It's me, Cody."

Joe's face twisted as if he were in pain. "I know, you little prick! You came to fuck my wife!"

"Joe!" Cody protested. "Calm down! She's my lawyer. She's representing me, Joe. That's why I'm here."

"At night? You expect me to believe that?" Joe said. "Put that fucking phone down!"

Madison jumped and dropped the phone. While Cody was distracting him, she had picked it up to call the police.

"Just calm down," Cody said patiently.

Joe glared at Madison with unadulterated hatred. She reached out and touched Cody's back as if to make sure he was still there. She could feel the muscles through his cotton shirt; they were tight like thick steel cables.

Joe's focus shifted to Cody. "Get out," he said menacingly.

"No," Cody said.

"He's on drugs," Madison said in nearly a whisper.

"Of course I'm fucking on drugs!" Thurwood screamed. "You ruined my life!"

"Joe," Cody said calmly, "just go. Just leave. You don't want this, man. You know I wouldn't be with your wife. She's my lawyer, Joe. She's helping me."

Joe broke out into a demented laugh, "Yeah, you need help all right, Grey. You really need help!"

"I know," Cody said. "Now please go. You don't want the cops to come here. You don't want your boy to watch them take you away in cuffs. Don't do it, Joe, just walk out and end it. There's nothing going on."

Joe considered his ex-teammate with one eye partially closed. He straightened up slightly. Cody relaxed.

"Fuck you both," Joe said flatly, then turned and walked out.

Cody followed behind Thurwood to the front hall and the open doorway to make sure he was gone. Madison came up beside him. As they watched from her front door, Joe walked off down the dark street without so much as a glance back. When he was gone, Cody turned to see Madison picking up the phone in the hallway. "What are you doing?" he asked.

"I'm calling the police," she said. "Enough is enough."

"Wait," Cody said, gently taking the phone from her hand. "Just think. I'm not telling you not to call them. Just think about it first. Can't you use it to hang over his head in your dispute? I'm a witness to what he did, if you need me. Just make sure before you call, Madison. If they come, it will be a mess. The talk will be bad, the media. For everyone . . ."

"He broke into my house," she protested.

Cody turned and looked at the front door.

"I don't even think so. He came through here, it was open when he left," Cody said, examining the hinges and locks on the front door. There was no sign whatsoever that Joe had forced his way into the house.

"He doesn't have a key," Madison said. "I changed the locks."

"Who has a key?" Cody asked.

"There are only four," she said. "I have one, Marty, Lucia, and . . . Jo-Jo. . . ."

Cody said nothing. Madison closed her eyes and moaned, "Jo-Jo."

"Mommy?" the sleepy eight-year-old was standing there in the hallway.

Madison turned and rushed to him.

"What happened?" Jo-Jo said. "It that Cody Grey?"

Cody stepped forward and held out his hand. "Hi, Jo-Jo. Your mom is helping me with my court case. We got a little loud because we were practicing for the trial."

"Oh," Jo-Jo said. He looked at Cody's hand and reached around his mom to take it. "I thought I heard my dad."

"Sorry," Cody said gently, squatting down so he was eye level with the boy. "I'll try to keep my voice down."

"That's okay," Jo-Jo said. "You're a pretty awesome player. I've got your card."

"Would you like me to sign it?" Cody said, glad to be able to distract him. Madison was still clearly upset.

"Uh-huh," Jo-Jo said, nodding his head emphatically. "It'll be worth a lot, with the trial and all."

"Jo-Jo," Madison said disapprovingly.

"Oh, I don't care," Jo-Jo said, looking at Cody. "I know you didn't do it. My mom already told me."

Cody blushed at the thought of Madison talking about him to her boy.

"Well, she's right," he said.

"Come on, Jo-Jo," Madison said, standing up and leading him away by the hand. "I'll bring your card out for Mr. Grey, and you'll have it in the morning. You have to get back to bed. You've got school tomorrow."

Cody stayed on his haunches as they walked away. When Jo-Jo turned to look back at him, Cody winked, and the boy grinned before he disappeared around the corner. Cody stood and wandered back through the house to Madison's study. He picked up the splinters of wood and assessed the damage Big Joe had done to the doors. It was minimal. A new latch and a little trim was all that would be needed. Cody walked through the room, examining the diplomas and the plaques that lined the wall. Madison already had an impressive career. He wondered how she managed it, all the while being married to Joe Thurwood. He wondered how she could have ever gotten mixed up with a guy like that. Cody knew Joe was bad news within a week of joining the team.

"Thank you," Madison said, and Cody turned to see her standing there behind him. When he looked at her, he suddenly couldn't help himself from thinking how attractive she was.

"I didn't really do anything," he said.

"You did a lot," she replied. "Especially with Jo-Jo, distracting him like that. It's hard . . . I'm trying to slowly wean him from his father. Joe resurfaced a few months ago, and Jo-Jo treated it like the second coming of Christ. He was too young to really know why Joe left in the first place. I feel like I'm walking a tightrope. On one hand I want Jo-Jo to despise his father because he's a despicable man. On the other hand, I want it to be a gradual thing to reduce the damage. He's only eight."

Cody nodded and said, "I know what it's like not to have a father. Mine died when I was a kid."

"I'm sorry," Madison said.

"That's okay," Cody replied. "I had a pretty good uncle to fill in."

"That's a big part of my problem, I think," Madison said. "There's no one like that for Jo-Jo."

Cody shrugged. He didn't know what to say.

"Do you want me to leave?" he asked her.

Her eyes looked heavy.

"I mean, we can catch up tomorrow night," he said. "You look wiped out."

"No," Madison said, rounding her desk and sitting back down in her chair resolutely. "We don't have a lot of time and we've got a trial to win."

"Okay," Cody said, sitting himself in the chair that faced her desk, "that's what I like to hear."

Chapter Twenty-Four

ACCOMPANIED BY A U.S. MARSHAL, Cody left with the team for Detroit on Saturday morning. The team was flying out and would spend the night in a Michigan hotel, then return to Austin the following evening. Striker thought it was fine that Jenny saw him regularly on Saturday nights. He knew the CIA agents watching him would be amused that he was consistently banging someone's wife whenever the guy left town. It fit Striker's profile as they knew it, perfectly. When the Outlaws played an away game, Striker and Jenny would go on different outings. One day they went waterskiing on Town Lake. Another time they took a drive up to Lake Travis to do some fishing. Each time, Striker used the excursion as a kind of training mission for Jenny, helping her to recognize when she was being followed and how.

At first she couldn't see the men following them, even after Striker had pointed them out. But gradually she learned, and by the Detroit weekend, she could spot their tail ten lengths back in heavy traffic and a hundred yards on the highway, just by the way it moved. That was saying something, considering the agents took the precaution of changing their rental cars on a weekly basis. On foot, Jenny could now pick out any one of the four agents who were taking twelve-hour shifts shadowing Striker.

She even had nicknames for them all. Two of them were older and looked like worn-out, middle-aged businessmen. She called them Thing One and Thing Two. The other pair were young and built well. One was particularly handsome, so Jenny dubbed him The Hunk. The other had the same blond coloring as The Hunk, but he was an ugly version. Jenny called him The Goon.

"Very good," Striker said, when she called out the make, model, and color of this week's car, not three miles after they'd left the center of Austin. Striker had Jenny driving, which made it that much harder to spot the tail because she also had to concentrate on the road. They were heading south to San Antonio. Jenny had never seen the Alamo, and Striker said she must.

"While we're driving," Striker said, looking over at her from the passenger seat, "I want to fill you in on what will be happening here in the next couple of weeks."

Jenny nodded. Her hair was pulled back and her black, round sunglasses were on. She was wearing a tight gray tank top and a loose-fitting pair of cutoff jeans. She was listening intently.

"When the general calls," he said, "I want you to be ready to move right away. I'm going to send you to meet him in a little town called Goldthwaite. There's a Texas Rest Inn there that I'll send him to. It's about two hours north of here, close enough so you can easily get there ahead of him. It's not that tough, your job. You'll leave as soon as I get the call. This way you'll have a day's head start on the general to watch anything coming into or going out of the town that doesn't look right. You'll be able to watch him when he arrives and see that he isn't planning any surprises."

Striker waited until she nodded, to see if she was following him, then said, "When you're sure everything is okay, you'll knock on the door to his room and make the switch. Don't be in a hurry. Wait until you're sure everything is normal. Use your instincts, you've got good ones. Then it's simple, you just bring the suitcase of money to his room, check to see that what he's giving you is the pit, make the switch, and then leave."

"What about killing him?" she asked.

"Ah, very good," Striker replied. "You remembered."

"How could I forget that?" she said.

"It's been on your mind?" Striker asked.

"Let's just say it's not something I've done before. I—"

"Don't know if you can?" he suggested.

"I can," she said.

"I know. All you have to do is think of nine million dollars and the life of a baroness, and I'm the baron. Besides, I'm going to make it easy. I told you I would."

"So," she said, "how?"

"The lining of the suitcase with the money will be filled with C-4 plastic explosives," Striker explained. "There is a remote detonator shaped like a cell phone that has a two-mile range. The general will leave first. You will watch from the window to see the direction he leaves in. There is only one of four ways he can go from Goldthwaite, and from the Inn you'll be able to see which one he chooses. Probably he'll go north on 16 or 183. Those are the most direct routes back to Amarillo. Either way, the roads are pretty empty outside the town. Take your time. You don't want him to know what you're doing. If he sees you tearing out after him, he'll get nervous. You just wait until he's out of sight, then head down the same road in your car. When you get within sight of him, you just pull off the road, dial 666-123, and hit Send. Bang, no more general.

"You'll come back," Striker continued, "and bring the pit right to my apartment. I'll contact Jamir. It will probably take about three weeks to work out the details of my meeting with him through my office because I have to go through some pretty convoluted routes and codes to communicate with him. But once I get the exchange set up, we'll disappear. I have the passports and our new identities ready to go."

Jenny almost told Striker about the coin she had been given by Jamir and how she could contact him at a moment's notice. If she used the coin, they could leave immediately. She decided against it, though. He might not like what it implied, especially since she had held onto it for so long without telling him in the first place. And she seriously doubted Jamir would be thrilled if she used the coin and brought Striker along.

"What about the money?" Jenny said. "You don't really want me to blow that up too?"

Striker chortled. "You are my kind of woman. Don't give that money a second thought. It's one of the costs of doing business, my dear."

"Couldn't you just put, like, a million and a half in there?" she asked. "Or stuff some of the packets with twenties instead of hundreds?"

"Jenny," he said patiently. "We're talking about a total of nine million dollars. If the general has figured out about how much space two million takes up, or if he leafs through some bills and sees that they're not hundreds but twenties or singles, he may do something drastic, and I don't want that. We'll have enough. Let the general take his two million to the grave."

"Can I ask a question?" Jenny said.

"Of course," Striker replied.

"But it's not a relevant question," she explained. "It's a question I just want to know the answer to, and I know you don't like those kinds of questions."

Several weeks ago, after the IRS agent had been killed and Cody was arrested, Jenny had asked Striker if it had been him or Cody who'd done the killing. Striker had looked at her with disgust and said, "Is that a relevant question?"

"Yes," she had replied. "I want to know."

Striker had grown visibly angry.

"Relevant is when a question has some possible effect on something directly related to you. Do you think it matters who killed him, Jenny? He's dead. You're safe. Your husband will take the fall whether he did it or not. How, then, is what actually happened relevant?" he had demanded. Confused and a little frightened by his outburst, she'd remained silent.

Her reference to it now was the first indication to Striker that she had been carefully listening to him, and that she respected what he'd been telling her then: don't waste his time with idle curiosity. There was no place for it in the kind of world she was living in now.

Striker smiled and said, "Jenny, it's a beautiful day, we're driving down the highway being chased by the CIA, and I'm in a wonderful mood. I'll indulge you. . . . Ask me your question."

"Where are you getting the two million in cash?" she said. "I mean, I left the last payment on the island. How do you get that kind of cash?"

"That's easy," Striker said. "Certain people have cash in this country that they want to get rid of. I have money overseas in bank accounts. I don't even have to pay two million for the two million. There are drug dealers who'll take fifty cents on the dollar to launder money they get from the street. I wind up paying far less for the two million. Understand?"

"Yes," she said. "I should have thought of that."

"Jenny," he told her, "I hope the day never comes when you do think of everything. If it does, you might not feel like you need me anymore."

Jenny looked over at him. He wore only the slightest of smiles, and she had no idea what it meant, if anything.

Cody returned from Detroit Sunday night. The team had won, and his own performance was good, if not as spectacular as the first few games of the season. He knew from the light under the door and the low murmur of her voice that Jenny was in the guest room talking on the phone. Cody took a beer from the refrigerator and sat down at the kitchen table alone in the dark. He kicked his leg awkwardly up onto the chair beside him. On the outside of his jeans, the trainers had wrapped two big bags of ice that were just now starting to melt and leak. Every once and a while he would hear a shriek of laughter coming from the guest room, and it made him lonely. How was it that she could be right there in the next room and be so cold and indifferent. Their life together had turned to shit. Maybe, he thought, it was because her life was a jackpot. She wasn't facing a trial. She was young and beautiful and smart. As much as it hurt him to admit it, he felt certain Jenny was going places.

Cody lumbered up and got another beer, but this time took it upstairs. He ran a hot bath and turned on the Jacuzzi. Unwinding the tight wrap from his knee relieved the pressure and let the pain rush in like a flash flood. He'd done extensive damage to it on the turf in Detroit. Cody dug through his black bag looking for some Percoset and washed down two with a swig from his bottle. He stripped the rest of his clothes off and climbed into the tub, letting his bad leg hang out over the edge. The last thing he wanted to do to his knee was heat it up in the tub; it would swell to the size of a basketball if he did that. The bad knee would see nothing but ice for the next seventy-two hours.

As the tub rumbled, filling with bubbles and a soothing, steady rush of water and noise, Cody began to slip into the familiar comfort of the Percoset. He wondered if he would have to go through a drug treatment program by the end of the season because of all the narcotics he took for his pain. A voice echoed off the bathroom tiles, and he realized that he had laughed out loud.

Jenny isn't the only one who can laugh, he told himself. That made him lonely again. Cody didn't really have any close friends. He had never been like that. It had always been tough for Cody to get close to anyone. He didn't know why. It wasn't intentional. It just seemed that between football and Jenny, he never had the time or the opportunity to develop the kind of friendships most NFL players did. He went out with the guys on his team from time to time, but the ones he liked the most were married with kids, and Cody just didn't have that much in common with them. Kids. Cody had wanted them for more than five years. He wondered if he'd ever have them. It almost seemed impossible now.

Suddenly he had a strong urge to call Madison. He missed her. For two nights now he hadn't seen or spoken to her. But all last week he'd spent every evening with her, talking with her well into the night. After he'd gotten over the initial sparks from her steely exterior, he found her appealing. Unlike Jenny, she was tough but had a gentleness about her. One night when their legal session was over, they got caught up talking for fifteen or twenty minutes at the door as he was leaving. The next night they talked a little longer; they sat in her study and talked until two A.M. At one point her phone rang. Some crank caller simply breathed a little and hung up. Cody calmed her down.

In those hours following their legal sessions, talk somehow turned to personal stories. They talked about mistakes they'd made and their dreams for the future. To Cody it felt strange but wonderful to talk like this after they'd finished such emotionally difficult work. It felt like a dream because everything was so intense: he was going on trial for a murder but was innocent; both his professional life and his marriage were coming to an awful end; a beautiful and sensitive lawyer comes into his life, and every night after they review crucial issues for the trial, they end up talking about their personal lives. He could very well never see her again if convicted; even if they appealed, another attorney in her firm would handle the case. Everything in his life was in a vortex, swirling and gushing about him like the whirlpool of water he was sitting in.

Cody picked up the phone that sat on a small shelf above the Jacuzzi. There was a dial tone. Jenny was off.

"Must have caught her between calls," he mumbled.

He dialed and then hung up before it could ring, suddenly feeling that he was calling too late. He looked at his watch. It was ten-thirty; that was okay. He hit the redial. On the third ring she picked up.

"Hello?"

"I know I have no business calling you at—"

"That's all right," Madison cut in. Her voice sounded sleepy.

"I woke you up?" he asked apologetically.

"No," she said, sounding soft and intimate. "No, I was just sitting here reading. How do you feel?"

"Good since I took a couple of pills. Hang on."

He leaned over and shut the air jets off. "There, that's better. I had the Jacuzzi running."

"You must feel sore," she said. "I don't know how you do it."

"It's a living," he said.

"We watched the game, Jo-Jo and I. You looked great. It's not often I get to see a client on TV."

"Unless they make the news for a jailbreak, huh?" he joked.

"My clients don't go to jail. That's why I get paid so much."

"I'll say."

That was the wrong road to have traveled down, and Cody was sorry he'd brought it up. There was an awkward silence.

"Well," he said finally, "I just wanted to tell you that I missed not talking with you over the weekend and I—I'll see you tomorrow night, okay?"

"Okay," she said.

And then in a tone that made him feel lousy because it was so businesslike, she said, "We've got a lot to cover this week because jury selection starts on Wednesday, so be ready to work."

"You got it," he said. "Good night, Madison."

"Good night," she said.

After he hung up the phone, Cody got out of the tub and dried off. By the time he got to the bed, the room had started to rock gently back and forth, lulling him to sleep. It was a wonderful feeling, free from pain and worry. Cody dropped off. His last thoughts were of Madison. He was certain that there had been a quality in her voice that was different, softer than normal, that meant she thought of him as more than just a client.

Chapter Twenty-Five

By the end of the following week, Cody knew every detail of his case and exactly how Madison was going to try to defend him. Madison had battled with Rawlins over the jury. She felt it was about as good a mix of people as she could hope for. She had done her best to get as many women seated as possible. There were six. She knew that a man as handsome as Cody Grey could influence a woman's mind just on his appearance alone. It was a sad but true fact that the defendant's appearance could give him a distinct advantage or disadvantage when it came to the jury.

Before the shoes had appeared, Madison had planned to focus her attack on Hauffler, the eyewitness, and the lack of evidence linking Cody to the crime. When the shoes appeared, Madison knew that if she was going to convince the jury that Cody hadn't killed Board, she would have to provide at least the hint of an answer as to who did and why. With Cody's shoes linking him to the killing, she now had to convince the jury that there was a conspiracy afoot, that someone else had killed Board and manipulated the evidence to make it look as though Cody was the murderer. Together they spent many hours trying to think of who and why. They came up with nothing.

Then on Thursday, they finally caught a much-needed break. Madison had subpoenaed Board's work files at the IRS in the hope that they could uncover some blemish in his past that might have somehow lead to foul play at hand. Marty was examining those files and found a man who had been investigated by Board and who looked like he might have some ties to the underworld. His name was Ricardo Lopez. He lived in El Paso and owned numerous strip clubs outside the city and in small towns around south Texas. Board had investigated Lopez and forced him to pay one hundred thousand dollars in back taxes and penalties. The thing was, after crawling through the numbers like a half-starved ferret, Marty found that Lopez had actually short-changed the government for over three million dollars.

"Something that big," Marty assured them, "usually results in a jail sentence. And a guy with as much money as Lopez would certainly be assessed at least three million dollars in additional penalties alone. Either Board was just a stupid lazy bastard and didn't see it, or he cut some kind of deal with Lopez.

"I looked into Lopez," Marty continued. "He's got a rap sheet from his younger days, auto theft, a couple of aggravated assaults. I called the D.A. in El Paso and he told me Lopez is one bad hombre, stays out of trouble now only because he's got so many people to do his dirty work for him. Supposedly his strip clubs are linked to a biker club called the Scorpions. Murder, drugs, prostitution, you name it, they do it."

"Well," Madison had said after mulling it over, "as far as we're concerned, Lopez cut some kind of a deal with Board, maybe they were in business, or maybe Board was threatening him for more of . . . whatever. Anyway, Lopez had him knocked off in a way that made it look like Cody did it. We're certainly not concerned with preserving the reputation of a dead man nobody liked when he was alive, so let's assume that Board was a real backroom dealer. It fits perfectly, Marty. If Lopez wanted Board dead, he had to wait until the perfect opportunity arose. When it would look like someone else killed him. That opportunity was Cody. This is exactly what we needed."

Marty beamed. He was delighted with Madison's praise and thrilled to be contributing to Cody's case, and this had him grinning for the rest of the week.

Madison would call Board's boss to the stand and confront her with the Lopez file. This would bolster the underworld connection theory she would make in her opening statement. She would accentuate Cody's alibi and tear into every witness Rawlins called, most especially Hauffler. For him she would reserve her most brutal cross-examination techniques. After she got done with him, she was willing to bet the man would wonder if he'd seen anyone at all leaving Board's house after the shooting. With the news about Lopez, Madison began to see a light at the end of the tunnel.

On Saturday, when Cody left for Philadelphia to play the Eagles, he felt more confident than ever about his trial, which was now only two days away.

Cody knew something was wrong when the two doctors who were draining his knee looked at each other the way they did. Instead of the usual surplus of clear yellow fluid, Cody's knee would only yield a syringe half-filled with dark, viscous blood. No matter how many angles from which Burlitz attacked the joint, none of the yellow fluid was to be found. Even though they said nothing to him that indicated anything was wrong, the grim looks on the doctors' faces were enough. And the swelling hadn't gone down nearly as much as it had on prior Sundays after the drainings.

But if the doctors were willing to give it a go, he was too. Biggs, he knew, was almost ready to play. His running during the week had gone better than anyone had expected. It was inevitable that Cody would be replaced, but he would fight it with every ounce of life he had. For some reason, it had become critical to him to keep his starting role at least until the trial began. He knew the entire state would be watching the trial, and he wanted people to know that he was still a starter, not some loser on his way out of the league. If he could put together another great game, as he had done almost every week since the beginning of the season, he might fend off the reemergence of the younger player. If Cody was doing well, there would be more incentive for the coaches to play it extra safe with Biggs. If Cody faltered, he knew he would be sent to the bench.

He slipped on his remaining leather glove and flexed his fingers to get them jammed all the way into the tips. Cody looked around at his teammates. Each one was caught up in his own individual preparation, but within minutes they would come together and throw their bodies around the football field in the synchronized patterns of the plays drawn up in the play book and practiced throughout the week. Each player had to be where he was supposed to be, otherwise the entire team suffered. That was what football was about, winning your own individual battle against your counterpart on the other team; assuring that you accomplish your part in a successful play. Cody really didn't know if he was going to be able to come through for his teammates as one of the eleven effectively functioning parts.

Instead of waiting for the rest of the players to surge through the tunnel together as he normally did, Cody decided he'd better take himself out on the field early and try to work out his knee. He knew from past weeks that the more the game went on, the more flexible his knee seemed to get. Now it was so stiff that he couldn't get the full range of motion on either his extension or his flexion. He tried to disguise the slight limp; he didn't want them pulling the plug on him before the game even began. So he began to jog. When he emerged from the tunnel, the stadium erupted with boos. Because the Outlaws and the Eagles were in the same division, they played each other twice a year, once at home and once away, so the Eagles fans knew #40 well enough to hate him the way only NFL fans can hate a player from a rival team.

Cody jogged from one end of the field to the other. Philadelphia had to be the worst place to play in the NFL. It was an Astroturf baseball field, nothing more than a thin layer of plastic rug thrown over a slab of concrete. To make matters worse, there were seams throughout the field where the baseball diamond normally was. It was the wrong place to have to play on a bad joint. And there was no question now the joint was bad. That was all there was to it. It was stiff, and even though the whole thing didn't hurt because of the Xylocaine, Cody could sense that by forcing his leg through the range of motion it took to run, he was essentially turning the gear in an engine that had no lubricating oil. Still, he was going to play.

Back in the locker room, Cody could see that Biggs was dressing. He looked around in panic and saw Dryer coming toward him. The coach pulled Cody over to a corner of the locker room where they could talk alone.

"How's the knee?" Dryer asked, staring intently at Cody's face.

Cody returned the stare and said, "Fine."

"Fine?" the coach said.

"Yeah," Cody said, "I just went out and ran on it. I can go."

"You can go?" Dryer said.

Cody nodded, "No question."

"Look," Dryer said, throwing his arm casually over the top of Cody's shoulder pad, "I know how tough you are. There isn't a damn guy on this team who doesn't. But you've got to know when enough is enough. Now, the doctors told me that you might not make it today, so I'm activating Biggs. I'd rather play you, and I'm willing to give you a crack at it, but you've gotta know that if you're hurting us, I'm gonna pull you. Okay?"

"Okay," Cody said. He wanted to thank the coach, but for some reason he couldn't.

The Eagles came out running the ball, and the strategy couldn't have better suited Cody. All he had to do was charge the line of scrimmage and clean up on the running back after the defensive linemen and linebackers had slowed him down. He could do that with even minimal mobility.

It was late in the first quarter when the Eagles threw their first really deep pass. Cody had over-the-top coverage with the cornerback playing underneath on the fade, and when the ball went up, Cody was five steps behind where he should have been. His head burned with the frustration of not being able to perform a physical feat that was normally as simple as crossing the street. The receiver caught the ball, and the cornerback got him by the jersey to slow him down. Cody caught up, and out of sheer frustration, he launched his body, throwing a forearm. He intended to hit the receiver squarely in the chest and knock the stuffing out of him. Twisted and turning, the receiver ducked, and Cody's arm smashed into the side of his helmet instead, sending the receiver into a senseless heap.

The crowd roared with rage. Cody looked down over the incapacitated player. The cornerback got up and slapped Cody's shoulder pads, pounding on his helmet in jubilation. Three yellow flags came sailing at them through the air from three different directions. One hit Cody in the chest before falling limply to the plastic grass. Cody shrugged and held his open palms skyward. These flags, he wouldn't argue about. He apologized to the player who was slowly trying to sit up, shaking the cobwebs from his brain. Cody hadn't meant to hit him in the head, and he told him so. The crowd didn't know, they didn't care, and they certainly didn't let up their storm of booing. People started throwing cups of beer from the stands. The whole thing made Cody really feel like the criminal he knew they all thought he was.

The referees marked the penalty off half the distance to the goal line giving the Eagles the ball on the Outlaws' four-yard line. The defense huddled. Cody's teammates were nothing but thrilled at his vicious hit, despite the penalty and the long pass. His ass hurt from congratulatory slaps. The network took a time-out while the Eagles' medical staff helped their receiver off the field. When both teams were lined back up to play, Cody found himself five yards deep in the end zone. The crowd still roared.

He tried to block out the sounds, but they were so close he could clearly hear their screams.

"Grey, you fucking criminal!"

"Murderer!"

"You murdering bastard! I hope they fry your ass!"

"Killer!"

Someone threw a disposable camera at him, and it shattered against the back of his helmet, making him jump. The crowd laughed uproariously. Cody spun and searched fruitlessly for the perpetrator. That he would dare turn and face them only fueled the crowd's fire even more. Beer cups rained down on him, and the officials had to halt the game. To keep the junk out of the end zone, they were forced to raise the net used to keep the ball from going into the stands after an extra-point kick.

Three times the Eagles ran the ball but were unable to get it into the end zone. On the fourth down, they tried once more from an I-formation with the fullback leading straight up the middle and the tailback right behind him. With perfect timing, the Outlaws' middle linebacker threw himself at the blocking back, and the inertia of both canceled each other out. The tailback with the ball jumped just to the left of his blocker, projecting his body up and forward to gain the eighteen inches he needed to score. Cody hit him dead on with a crack that cut through the noise of the crowd like a gunshot. The officials came charging in to spot the ball, signaling first down for the Outlaws going the other way.

The mob came to life once more with renewed hatred. Cody was washed to the sideline in a sea of his teammates. On the bench, Cody got a drink and some oxygen. Jerry came by to quickly pack his bad knee with a bag of ice. Every little bit helped. When the thrill of the defensive stand had subsided, and Cody's teammates on the sideline began to shift their attention to the offense, he found himself alone. The reality of what had happened settled on his spirits like the snow from a sudden squall. He had helped to stop the Eagles from scoring, yes, but it was his own inability to be where he was supposed to be that had allowed them to complete the long pass and get down there in the first place. He looked frantically up and down the sideline for Biggs. The younger player stood among other Outlaws close to the field, watching the action. He had his helmet off, and there was no sign that he was warming up. Maybe, Cody thought, he was going to get a second chance. He almost didn't deserve it and was certain that only his spectacular goal-line hit had saved him from the bench.

The Eagles offensive coordinator up in the box must have seen Cody's inability to cover the long pass over the top. As soon as they had the ball again, Philadelphia started throwing two out of every three passes deep to the side of the field where his coverage responsibilities were. Cody pulled out every trick he had learned in his nine years as a pro to disguise from the quarterback where he was in the coverage, in an attempt to counteract their plan of attack. It was no use. When the ball was snapped, Cody had to roll to one side of the field or the other, and the quarterback would simply choose whichever receiver was to his side, no matter who was the primary target on that particular play. After the Eagles drove down and scored, three times completing passes of more than twenty yards right at him, Cody knew it was over.

After the extra point, Cody jogged off with his teammates. He picked

Dryer out of the crowd on the sideline by looking for his cowboy hat and headed straight for him. The coach saw Cody coming and he had the decency to listen to what he had to say before speaking himself. Cody appreciated that. A lot of coaches he had known would simply have screamed at him to get his ass on the bench. Dryer let Cody do it himself. It was like letting a guy shoot his own dying dog.

"I'm done," Cody said, relaxing his muscles and allowing the leg to settle the way it wanted to with a frozen joint.

Dryer nodded and slapped Cody on the shoulder.

"You did a hell of a job while you could, Cody. You got nothing to be ashamed of," he said with a grim smile, then turned his attention back to the field.

Cody heard someone bark to get Biggs ready, and he swung his head around to watch the younger player scramble back to the bench for his helmet and begin stretching his legs for the next defensive series. Cody sat down on the bench the long way, with his bad leg resting on the seat. The emotion of the moment made it hard for him to breath. In one way he felt like he'd made it. The trial was to begin tomorrow, and until next Sunday, he would be considered a starter in the NFL. There were only six hundred and sixty of them in the entire world. Now that it was finally over, Cody felt like some wounded animal that had dragged his broken carcass back home to his den so he could lay himself down and die. It was sad, but in a way it was also a relief.

Jerry hurried up and cut away his pants at the knee. It had swollen so much that he wasn't going to be able to get them off any other way. When Jerry had pulled away the cloth and the padding and the wraps, Cody could see his knee. It was a pale, puffy orb, blotched with purple and yellow hues where the blood underneath the skin had congealed. The skin was pocked with bright red on the surface where the scabs from the repeated needle punctures had torn away. With the help of an assistant, Jerry managed to get the whole joint carefully packaged in ice.

Cody was in a bit of a daze, and when he looked up, he saw Jerry standing there above him. Jerry was not known to be a man full of emotions, but his eyes were filled with heartfelt pity. Cody saw it beyond his sharp nose, in the wrinkled corners of his deep-set eyes.

"I don't know how the hell you did it, son," Jerry said in a raspy voice, "but I can say in my thirty-six years that I've never seen anything like it."

It was the ultimate compliment.

Cody looked down at the enormous wrapping and then back up. Jerry was gone. Cody was glad for that. He didn't want anyone to see the tears that welled up in his eyes and spilled down over his cheeks. He dug the palms of his hands quickly into his face and choked back his feelings. He couldn't remember the last time he had cried.

CHAPTER TWENTY-SIX

∨

VAN RAWLINS WATCHED HIS GAP in the upcoming election close and then widen again after the initial publicity of Jeff Board's murder died down. When jury selection began to heat up and the media started to lead the local news with stories of the upcoming trial, he watched with delight as the gap began to shrink once again. By Monday morning, he was only five points behind. The trial was scheduled to begin at nine. They would go until noon and then break for an hour of lunch before resuming court until four. At seven A.M., Rawlins was sitting with Kooch at the Elbow Diner, four blocks from the courthouse. Rawlins was nervous, not so much about the trial but about the media. Kooch promised him that he had worked the local media into a fervor over the weekend to make sure they highlighted his work as the prosecutor of the case.

"I don't want to be just some local yokel," Rawlins growled at him. "I want the big boys here. I want CNN and *Dateline*. Can't you get any of the big boys down here? Hell, look at what they did with the O. J. trial."

"This isn't O. J.," Kooch reminded him. "As big as Cody Grey's name is in Austin and in the state of Texas, the national media wants something juicier to sink their teeth into if they're going to bring entire crews down here. Connack's not exactly helping us. He's treating this just like any other murder trail. I just don't think it will happen. We'll be all right. The local media will help us a lot."

"Kooch," Rawlins said with a darkened brow, "I don't want to get just the local media. Think beyond this election, goddammit. Think about Congress. Think about the Senate. Look what this kind of thing did for Marsha Clark. She's a damn celebrity, Kooch! This is the chance to put me on the map! How many times do you think a prosecutor gets a chance like this? We got to take advantage of it."

"I'd worry more about living up to your guarantee of a conviction," Kooch told him. "I told you not to do that. People in Texas don't like a guy who guarantees them something and then doesn't deliver."

"This case is a winner," Van said. "He did it."

"I know you don't want to hear it," Kooch said, going out on a limb, "but Madison McCall is as slippery as they come."

"I'll worry about the trial, Kooch," Van said with an angry scowl. "You just get some big-time media here."

"The problem as I see it is women," Kooch told him, digging into a platter of eggs that the waitress laid down in front of him.

Rawlins stopped a piece of toast halfway to his mouth and said, "Women? What the hell are you saying?"

"I'm saying that this is a trial about men," Kooch said, a little yolk dribbling out of the corner of his mouth. "'Scuse me." Kooch wiped the yolk away. "It's about a guy who killed a guy. And practically all the witnesses are guys, except for that one lady you got from the Green Mesquite. We got no female interest in this case. That's what I mean. The national TV markets are driven by women. They control what channel everyone gets to watch. That's just the way it is."

"Well, why in hell didn't you tell me about that?" Rawlins complained.

"I don't see how it could make much difference. You can't change who killed who," Kooch said, draining half a glass of orange juice with one gulp.

"Damn," Van said, knowing his man was right but wishing there was something he could do to change it.

There were more than enough cameras for Cody and Madison as they hopped out of Marty's car and started up the courthouse steps. Van Rawlins had been holding an impromptu news conference on the top step, but when the cry went forth that Cody was there, the prosecutor was quickly abandoned. Cody and Madison were mobbed by cameras and microphones and rude shouting reporters. They had agreed to say nothing to the press, so they both simply looked straight in front of them and pushed ahead. Cody led the way, and even the pushiest of the media yielded to him, giving him the space he needed to pass.

Madison and Cody went through a metal detector before passing into the courtroom. Except for the special section for the media, the courtroom was already full with the morning's witnesses and the nosy onlookers who could afford to take a day off of work to enjoy the spectacle.

A murmur went up through the crowd when Cody entered. Van Rawlins and two assistants were just sitting down at their table on the right side of the courtroom, closest to the jury. In the middle of the floor was a podium. The defense's table was on the other side, opposite the jury box. In the front and center of the courtroom loomed Judge Walter Connack's bench. It was an imposing sight that befit the man and his reputation. To the immediate right of the judge's bench was the witness box.

Cody was dazed by the speed at which everything took place. No sooner had Marty entered and sat down with them did the bailiff bark at everyone to rise. The enormous judge came in amid a litany of respect and tradition about how honorable he was, then he slammed his gavel down one time on the bench. Everyone sat. Opening statements were first, and Van Rawlins wasted no time in laying out for the jury exactly what had happened on the night in question and why. He rattled on down the list of witnesses he would be calling and why. He told them about the evidence they would see with their own eyes and assured them that when he was through, they would have no doubt that Cody Grey, the man known and celebrated for his violent nature, had finally committed the ultimate act of aggression, a coldly calculated murder. When he finished, there was absolute silence.

Madison's heart dropped. She could almost sense the jury's horror. Van Rawlins had outdone himself. She had heard him open before with equal compassion and authority, but never had she heard him be so concise in his delivery of the evidence and how it would be presented. It made her wonder if what was happening might not be beyond her lawyering skills, like it was something that had already been written down long ago. She pushed those thoughts aside and rose to face the jury.

"Ladies and gentlemen," she began with a winning smile. "I want to thank you for taking the time out of your lives to be here for this trial. I think when it is over, you will feel that you were able to help an innocent man whose life would have been torn apart were it not for your intuition, your wisdom, and your good common sense. Those are the three things it will take to see that Cody Grey had absolutely nothing to do with the unfortunate death of the victim, and I already know from talking with you last week that each of you has those qualities."

Madison paused to let that sink in. One thing she could do better than anyone was to immediately ingratiate herself to the jury without crossing the line and pandering.

"Wisdom and common sense will come into play when I show you that despite what some of the prosecution's witnesses will say, people make mistakes. People say things they don't mean. People swear they saw something that in fact they never saw at all. It happens all the time. It may have happened to you, and probably has. It's as simple as swearing you left your car keys on the kitchen table."

Madison came out from behind the podium now and moved toward the jury, standing so Cody could look toward her and in the direction of the jury. Madison had dressed him in a dark blue gabardine suit and a quietly stylish tie. He looked as if he'd walked off the pages of GQ magazine. Madison wanted the jury to have the opportunity to see his face, but it was important that he didn't stare at them. If he was looking right at them, they would glance away. If he was looking at her, the jury, especially the women, would steal frequent glances his way.

"But you know," Madison said in almost a whisper, as though she were admitting something personal to a friend, "the keys aren't on the table, and they never were. They're in the ignition where you left them. It just happens, my friends, that is exactly what happened to the eyewitness who believes, really believes, that he saw Cody Grey coming out of the victim's home on the night of the murder. But he didn't. He saw someone, I'll bet that. But it was dark. He wears glasses. It was late. When the police showed up with a black-and-white photo of Cody Grey, he cried, 'That's him!' No. That wasn't him. That was the picture of a man he thought he saw."

Madison paused and looked at Cody, drawing the jury's attention to him before assertively saying, "Cody Grey, my friends, was home and asleep.

"Common sense will show you how it happened that so much evidence has been misguidedly compiled against Cody Grey, and wisdom will help you see that despite outward appearances, he is a completely innocent man caught in a web of underworld corruption that he never even knew existed. A web with a spider that was simply waiting to pounce, waiting for a victim to come along and take the blame for its heinous crime, killing Jeff Board. The people or person who committed this crime did so with the precision and timing of a professional criminal, making it look as though the murder was committed by another man. Cody Grey was that man, and just as much a victim as Jeff Board himself.

"Now," Madison said, as though she were a sage talking to her pupils, "here's where your intuition comes in. Use it! I will show you that Jeff Board had dealings with a notorious underworld figure. I will show you that he mishandled the investigation of that figure resulting in a savings for that criminal of as much as six million dollars! And, ultimately, because of this conspiracy, Jeff Board held the thin thread that kept that underworld figure from going to jail. But Jeff Board let this man go with a slap on the wrist. Why? What sort of arrangement had they made? Did Board double-cross this man? Or was it the other way around? We'll never know, ladies and gentlemen. You and I will never know. But your intuition will tell you that there is more to the relationship between these two men than meets the eye. Your intuition will tell you that something rotten was afoot. Your intuition will tell you that if a man like the one I'm talking about was going to kill Jeff Board, he would have to make it look like it was someone else. If not, the police would have scrutinized Board's past, as I have, and found just the man I did, someone linked to Board through questionable circumstances, a killer who had stolen millions of dollars from the U.S. government. And your intuition, ladies and gentlemen, will tell you that Cody Grey, despite some hotheaded remarks after Board crudely insulted his wife, was simply at the wrong place at the wrong time. Your intuition will tell you what I already know . . . that that man, Cody Grey, is as innocent of this crime as you or I."

Madison looked at them almost defiantly, challenging them to see the truth, no matter how hidden it was. She liked what she saw, but for the next few days she was going to have to constantly battle against some very hard facts that had been stacked against them.

Rawlins called his first witness, Agnes Tuttle. Agnes was a fiery schoolteacher in her late fifties. She'd never been married, and this was the most exciting thing that had happened in her life. She recounted in great detail for the jury what had transpired between Cody and Board at the Green Mesquite. Agnes had been sitting by herself in the next booth with little else to do than listen to the conversations of those around her. She hadn't had to listen very hard at all to hear Cody's words, which he'd bellowed, in Agnes's words, "like a castrated longhorn." That brought laughter from all quarters, and Madison knew that Rawlins had called one of his most animated witnesses first to get the momentum of the prosecution off the ground. The woman was energized. She was giddy. But it was the flippancy with which she answered the questions and went into great and humorous detail that annoyed Madison most. The woman was so wrapped up in her enjoyment of the attention she was receiving that she hadn't stopped to think that she was dealing with life and death, not an open mike in a comedy club. Madison was about to bring all the fun to a screaming halt.

When Rawlins finished with Agnes, she started to get up from her seat in the witness box. Madison purposely let her get herself started down the steps before she said politely, "Excuse me, your honor, would you tell the witness that I *do* have a few questions?"

Walter boomed down from his bench, "Ms. Tuttle, you have not been excused. Ms. McCall has a few questions for you."

Madison could see that this agitated the woman, so she stared in complete silence until Agnes had returned to her seat and was completely still.

"Ms. Tuttle," Madison said with caustic abruptness, "you've threatened to kill someone before haven't you?"

Agnes looked shocked.

"I most certainly have not—"

"Objection!" Rawlins yelled, too late to stop the agitated witness from answering. "This is completely irrelevant, your honor. Counsel is badgering the witness."

Judge Connack looked to Madison and said, "I think I know where she's going, overruled."

"No?" Madison continued, looking incredulously at the teacher. "You've never said to your fellow teacher, a Mr. Lyons, in reference to a student who had told her mother that you hit her knuckles with a ruler, quote, 'I'll kill the little bitch if she takes this to the board'? You never said that?"

"I . . . that's not what I meant—said," Agnes protested. "You're taking something completely out of context."

"That's not what I'm asking you, Ms. Tuttle," Madison said firmly. "I'm asking you if you ever threatened to kill someone, namely a twelve-year-old student. Now please answer yes or no."

"No," Agnes said firmly.

"No? I have a statement right here from Mr. Lyons that he made to an investigator on October second. Do I have to call Mr. Lyons into this court to testify as to the validity of this statement? Are you saying that he is a liar?" Madison said, tapping the paper and returning the school teacher's glare.

"No," Agnes said a little softer.

"So you did say that? You did threaten to kill someone?"

"I was only—"

"Objection!" Van Rawlins roared. "Counsel is—"

"Overruled," boomed the judge.

"Your honor," Madison said with disgust, "would you please direct the witness to answer my questions and remind her that she is under oath."

"Ms. Tuttle," Judge Connack said as firmly as he could without being unkind, "please answer Ms. McCalls's questions. Yes or no will be fine."

Agnes looked like she'd been hit in the head with a brick. Madison patiently watched her struggle.

"Yes," Agnes said finally.

"I'm sorry, your honor," Madison said. "I would like a clarification, please."

The judge nodded.

"So," Madison said, with deliberate drama, "you, Ms. Tuttle, yourself have threatened to kill someone?"

"Yes," Agnes said, clenching her teeth with hatred.

"Did you mean it?"

"I most certainly did not!"

"You mean sometimes people say things like that and they don't mean them at all, don't you?"

"Yes!" the teacher said triumphantly.

"I have no further questions, your honor," Madison said, turning her back on the witness and taking her seat.

Judge Connack slammed his gavel down to signal a recess for lunch at ten minutes after noon. Van Rawlins scrambled out of the courthouse and onto the front steps to do a live shot for the noon news on seven. Other cameras hovered around, afraid they might miss a lively bite from the D.A. Agnes Tuttle did not want anyone asking any questions of her, so she stayed off to the side until the cameras had been turned off and the reporters had dispersed to get some lunch of their own. Van Rawlins was just about to step into a waiting car at the curb when she caught up to him.

"Mr. Rawlins," she said.

Van stopped and looked back. Normally he would have kept going, pretending he didn't hear, but a vote was a vote. He saw that the voice belonged to one of his witnesses, and he pasted a broad smile on his face.

"Ms. Tuttle," he said, "I'm glad you stopped me. I wanted to thank you for your time and what you did up there today."

"Well, I—"

"I know," Van said, holding up his hand to silence her, "it was uncomfortable for you. But that's how some of our less reputable members of the bar behave."

He was referring to Madison's brutal cross-examination.

"Some people feel like they have something to prove," Rawlins said sympathetically.

"I just hope I helped you put that man behind bars," Agnes said. "I knew by the way he spoke that night at the Green Mesquite that he was going to do it."

"Yes, well, I hope you'll help me next week at election time. I know you've already helped me today, thank you again," Van said, turning to get into the car.

"Mr. Rawlins," she said, stopping him once more, "there's something I have to tell you that I'd forgotten."

Rawlins turned.

"That woman," Agnes spit the words, "kept saying that the gentleman who was murdered . . ."

"Jeff Board."

"Yes, she kept saying that Mr. Board was insulting the wife, but that's just a lie." She could see that this didn't interest Van Rawlins so she cut to the chase.

"Well, after Cody Grey threw him on the floor like an animal, poor Mr. Board said he'd make him pay, and then he said, 'I found your wife's money.' And then he swore at him. I'd forgotten all about that; it didn't seem like anything. But that's not an insult, is it? That's a lie. Wasn't that lawyer lying to the jury, Mr. Rawlins?" Agnes said emphatically.

Van Rawlins was frozen in his place. He wasn't looking at Agnes Tuttle, he was staring somewhere up into the clear blue sky, thinking. When he realized that Agnes Tuttle had only paused to catch her breath before continuing to go on about Madison McCalls's lie, he looked down at her and gave her his most serious face. "I'm going to look into this, Ms. Tuttle," he said, "and I'm going to pursue it to the full extent of the law."

Agnes Tuttle gave him a curt nod of satisfaction. Van thanked her once more and escaped in the waiting car.

"Kooch," he said to his man in the front seat, "was Cody Grey's wife in the courtroom?"

Kooch thought a moment, then said, "No, I don't think she was."

"Why wasn't she there?"

"Truth is," Kooch said, "rumor has it that Grey and his wife are on the serious outs. She still lives in the house, but people who know say they don't even talk."

This news seemed to make Rawlins happy.

"Stop the car, Mike," Van said to his office's chief investigator, Mike Horan, who was driving the car.

"I've got a job for you," Van said to Kooch. "It's big. Find Grey's wife. Find her today. Tell her I want to see her in my office at five o'clock this afternoon, after the trial. Tell her not to get smart with any attorneys or anything like that. If she does, you tell her I'll be making a call to the IRS about the money Jeff Board found, the money that belongs to her. You got all that?"

Kooch spun around in his seat.

"I got it," he said.

"Go ahead," Van said, stepping out of the car.

"Now?" Kooch asked. "Where are you going?"

"I'm going to get some damn lunch at that sub shop on the corner there," Van said. "You make sure you get it done, Kooch. Take Mike with you; he'll know how to find her. We may just get CNN here and wrap up our guarantee in the same day. I'm going to blow Cody Grey's alibi into a million fucking pieces and make Madison McCall look like a backwoods lawyer to boot. Come on, Ben."

Ben Cherrit stepped out of the backseat with his mouth hanging open. Van shut the door and the car sped off.

"What was that about?" Cherrit said to his boss.

"I'll tell you at lunch," Van said.

Cody, Madison, and Marty ate in a small, windowless conference room inside the courthouse. The walls were covered with a drab, greenish-blue paint, a color that can only be found inside a government building. An associate from the firm had been sent out for sandwiches, and they sat there amid a mountain of wax paper and Styrofoam cups, eating and discussing the way things had gone in the morning. Rawlins had paraded out three other witnesses besides Agnes Tuttle who had also been at the restaurant. Madison disposed with each of them in much the same way, only with less drama and relish than she had with Agnes. The other witnesses knew what was coming and had the opportunity to learn from Agnes's mistakes, so they were much more subdued about Cody's threat. All in all, Madison made the whole incident at the Green Mesquite seem rather innocuous.

Rawlins fought back by calling to the stand three men whom Cody had assaulted over the past several years, attempting to establish that Cody Grey was not like any of the earlier witnesses who had admitted to Madison that they'd made threats they didn't mean to carry out. Van's point was that unlike the witnesses Madison had cross-examined, Cody had carried out his threats of violence before. Madison objected to these witnesses, contending that they were entirely prejudicial and had no relevance to the case at hand. Rawlins explained that he was establishing a pattern of violence that showed Cody Grey consistently made verbal threats and then carried them out.

Walter gave it to Rawlins, and Madison knew he was right. The three men had no trouble portraying Cody as a man with a short temper who had no compunction in carrying out a threat of physical violence. In each case Cody made some kind of verbal threat and then attacked. Madison did her best to tear these witnesses down, questioning their motives and their manhood. She made them out to be womanizers bent on seducing Cody's wife. Most of all, however, Madison played to the old-fashioned Texas notion that if someone else went after your woman, you had every right to punch them in the nose.

"He's going to start putting the hard stuff down this afternoon," Madison said through half a mouthful of tuna on whole-wheat. "We won't see the eyewitness until tomorrow."

"Hard stuff?" Cody said.

"Crime-scene stuff," she said. "The footprints, the shoes, the computer, the bullet that killed him . . ."

"What's the plan?" Cody asked, although he'd heard it two dozen times.

"He keeps setting it up, I'll keep trying to knock it down."

"Can I have your pickle?" Marty said, reaching over and fishing it out of Madison's wrapper.

"What do you think, Marty?" Cody asked. "How's it going?"

"I think good," Marty said cheerily.

"Let's not talk about how we're doing," Madison said. "I'm superstitious. You never know with a jury. You never know. . . ."

Cody sucked on his Coke until the straw started buckling. He jiggled the ice and tilted the cup, trying for a little more.

"Want some?" Madison said, handing her drink to him.

"Thanks," he said and took a few swallows.

Madison took it back and began drinking it again right away, flipping absently through her notes on the afternoon witnesses she expected to see.

"I'm gonna use the bathroom before we head back in," Cody said, "I'll be right back."

"It's around the corner, second door on your left," Madison said, waving her finger but not looking up.

When the door was shut, Marty said, "A little intimate there with the client, aren't you, Madison?"

"What the hell are you talking about, Marty?" she said looking abruptly up from her notes.

"Sharing a drink with the guy like that. I don't know . . . " Marty trailed off, shaking his head sarcastically.

"Hey, Marty, cut the crap, okay? I'm in the middle of a trial here!"

"I was only kidding," Marty said calmly.

"Well, I don't feel like kidding," Madison snapped.

Marty simply sat there, staring, letting his eyes lock with hers as was her habit when bickering. Then Madison dropped her gaze and looked away. He thought he saw her cheeks flush a light pink.

"Why did you do that?" Marty said.

"Do what?" she said nonchalantly, pretending to look down again at her notes.

"I was only kidding about Cody," he said. "For God's sake, Madison, I was going for a little comic relief to cut into the tension here, but you couldn't look at me. Why not?"

"I can look at you," Madison said, raising her stone-cold face, her eyes meeting his.

"But you didn't," he replied, sounding mystified.

They sat for some time in silence, looking at each other intensely.

"I was kidding," Marty said, as if finally figuring the answer to an intricate puzzle, "but you weren't. Were you?"

"Marty," she said, still holding his gaze, "I don't have time for this right now. Now, I'm going to look down. You can interpret it any way you like, but I'm going to get ready to cross those witnesses this afternoon."

CHAPTER TWENTY-SEVEN

VAN RAWLINS PRESENTED THE EVIDENCE of the footprint, the shoe, and the bullet that had been used to kill Board. Madison let the direct go on without protest or complaint, and she declined to cross. She had been willing to stipulate that the shoe that made the prints in Board's house was Cody's. She had also been willing to stipulate that the bullet found in the mess that had been Jeff Board's brain was certainly the cause of death. Rawlins, however, didn't let up. He wanted to parade the evidence in front of the jury in a dramatic display of cunning detective work. Madison let it all slide by because the sooner it was over the better.

The first time Madison rose to conduct a cross-examination in the afternoon wasn't until almost three o'clock, after Van Rawlins finished his direct examination of Robert Nusser. Nusser was the Austin Police Department's computer expert who discovered that the IRS files that should have been on Board's computer had been destroyed. It was clear after his testimony that Board's files had been intentionally destroyed. Nusser explained that even when files are deleted or erased on a computer's hard drive, even if the computer itself is mechanically destroyed, that the information stored in the magnetic fields of the disk usually survive and can be retrieved with some sophisticated software.

Deleted files, Nusser explained, are merely marked as open space for new information. So, until a vast quantity of new information is added, even a deleted file can be retrieved. Board's computer hard drive was empty except for a framework of paths that had once been used to write and retrieve the files that had existed. Nusser, with the use of an intricate retrieval program, also discovered that the computer's internal clock, disengaged when all the substantial information on the hard drive was destroyed, read 1:26 A.M., only minutes before Board was shot and killed.

"Mr. Nusser," Madison said with a pleasant smile that suggested she had no beef with him, "from what you've told us, it seems that to completely destroy the files on the victim's computer would be quite a sophisticated process, isn't that right?"

Nusser was twenty-eight, but he looked closer to sixteen. To compensate, he projected his voice with as much force as his tiny ribcage could muster.

"It's not that big a deal," Nusser said.

"To you, you mean?"

"No, or to anyone who could use a computer," he replied.

Madison nodded and said, "Could you just run through for me, from the point you turn the computer on, what exactly you would have to do to destroy an entire hard drive of computer files in the manner in which they were destroyed on the victim's computer?"

Nusser took the opportunity to show the judge, the jury, and the media how brilliant he really was. He rapidly described the steps, one by one. The commands and their sequence were overwhelmingly complex.

"That's quite impressive," Madison said. "I see you are a computer engineer with a masters in quantum mathematics, Mr. Nusser, is that right?"

"Yes," Nusser said, his chest puffed out.

"Then something that is simple to you might not be so simple for the rest of us?" Madison suggested, pointing to herself and the jury.

"Maybe not," Nusser admitted.

"And it would be next to impossible for a man who knew nothing about computers, who didn't even own one, to do something as complex as that, wouldn't it?" Madison said.

"I guess it might be pretty hard, yes," he said.

Madison nodded, indicating that he had guessed correct.

"So it is very unlikely that Cody Grey, a man who did not take one computer course in college, a man who doesn't own, hasn't owned, and hasn't even lived with another person who has owned a computer, would be able to perform this task at all, isn't it?"

Nusser looked to Rawlins before saying apologetically, "I guess so."

"Is that a yes or a no, Mr. Nusser," Madison said. "I mean as far as it being highly unlikely?"

"Yes."

"I have no further questions, your honor," Madison said, turning in time to see the looks of satisfaction on the faces of the jury. Madison thought she was home free. Rawlins was silent. Nusser started down from the jury box.

"Your honor," Rawlins said suddenly, "may it please the court, I would like to redirect the witness."

"Mr. Nusser, would you remain in the witness stand?" the judge said.

Nusser sat down, and Van went to the podium.

"Mr. Nusser," he said. "If I knew nothing of computers, nothing at all, and I came to you, or someone like you, could you write down for me everything you just said, so that I could destroy the files on someone's computer?"

Nusser smiled with relief and said, "Yes, I could."

"Thank you."

Rawlins's last witness for the day was detective Zimmer. Zimmer was the lead homicide detective on the case. He had been a good solid cop for fifteen years. Murder trials were part of his job, and Madison knew from experience that he was a tough nut to crack. Rawlins used Zimmer to tie together all the forensic and ballistic evidence, as well as the empty computer, to give the jury a clear-cut summary of why all these things meant that Cody Grey was the murderer. Together, in what Madison knew was a well-rehearsed drama, the two of them unfolded just how they pieced together the mystery of who killed Jeff Board. The climax was the shoes that were found under the bridge by the river. Rawlins sat down with a grim face. He only smiled when his head was turned away from the jury. He didn't want to come across as being smug.

"Detective Zimmer," Madison said, addressing the cop from where she stood at her own table, "How many murder investigations have you been involved with that have gone to trial?"

"A lot," Zimmer said unenthusiastically.

"About how many," Madison said pleasantly. "A thousand? Two dozen?"

"A hundred or so," he said.

Madison raised her eyebrows even though she knew full well that he'd been involved in the investigation of one hundred and seventeen murder cases that had gone to trial.

"That's quite impressive," she said. "And in those hundred cases, how many times have you found a piece of evidence like these turf shoes *four weeks* after the crime was committed?"

"Objection, your honor," Rawlins said tiredly. "Irrelevant."

"Your honor, I am simply trying to establish through this witness, whom the prosecution has touted and the court has accepted as an expert in police work, the likelihood of the events in a real murder being played out in this manner.

Please remember, your honor, that it is our contention that this entire murder was a conspiracy to make Cody Grey look like the guilty party."

"Overruled," Judge Connack said, "you may answer the question."

Zimmer thought about the question briefly before saying, "It's not uncommon at all to find incriminating evidence. Probably half."

"And when you don't find the evidence, is it simply because you didn't look hard enough?" Madison said, baiting him.

"I think probably," the detective said, "we don't find evidence only because some of the people who commit these murders are smart enough to get rid of the evidence."

"And where would they get rid of it?"

"I don't know," Zimmer answered with a smirk. "If I did, it wouldn't be missing evidence."

Some low chuckles erupted in the courtroom, causing the judge to raise his gavel and look threateningly around before setting it quietly down.

"Detective, you've been a cop for fifteen years," Madison said sternly. "Are you going to sit there and tell me that in that time, you never heard from a convict or an ex-convict or a snitch where incriminating evidence was hidden or allegedly hidden?"

Zimmer thought of Agnes Tuttle from the morning and tried to think if Madison could come up with something solid to throw in his face. He watched her pick a piece of paper up off of her desk and study it. That made him waver, and he decided to answer her honestly.

"Most times, if someone wants to lose the weapon or a garment, they'll toss it in some lake or river, or burn it."

"But this shoe didn't get burned or make it to the river, did it?"

"No."

"Why do you think that was?" Madison asked.

"You tell me," Zimmer responded hotly.

Madison looked at Walter, who was listening as if he wanted to know as well.

"That was because whoever left that shoe under the bridge wanted it to be found," she said, gazing over at the jury to make sure they followed her.

"Objection your honor!" Rawlins crowed. "Who is testifying here? Counsel or the witness?"

"Sustained," the judge said. "Counsel, please limit your cross-examination to questioning the witness. You will have the opportunity to digress in your closing statement."

"How far was that shoe from the river's edge when you found it?" Madison asked urgently.

"About . . . ten feet."

"Couldn't whoever put it there simply have tossed it into the river?" she said.

"I don't know," Zimmer responded.

"You could have thrown it into the river, couldn't you?"

"Yes."

"And I certainly could have, couldn't I?"

"Probably."

"And it's a fact, isn't it, that a man of Cody Grey's strength and athletic ability could have thrown that shoe into about the middle of that river, where it would never be found? Isn't that true?"

"I guess he could have, I really don't know."

"But he didn't?"

"No."

"Do you really expect this jury to believe," Madison said incredulously, "that Cody Grey was clever enough to commit this crime, take the incriminating evidence to the river to dispose of it, and then when he is ten feet from the water's edge, he decides to simply leave it there, right next to a jogging trail?"

"Objection!" Rawlins bellowed. "Counsel is badgering the witness!"

"Sustained," Judge Connack growled. "That will be enough of that, Ms. McCall. The witness has answered your question."

"I have only one further question, your honor," she said innocently. "Detective, in how many of your fifteen years of experience, and over a hundred murder investigations, have you had an anonymous caller phone in to the police station from a pay phone and disclose the location of a blood-soaked garment that was the key piece of evidence in a murder trial?"

Zimmer looked to the judge and Rawlins for help, then shrugged and said, "I don't really remember."

"Would it surprise you if I said you don't remember because such an event is very rare?"

"No, it wouldn't surprise me," Zimmer said, "but unusual things happen in cases from time to time."

"Would it surprise you," Madison said harshly, "if I said that never, and I mean never, has something so outrageously and obviously fabricated happened not only in one of your murder cases, but in any murder investigation in this city over the past fifteen years?"

"No," Zimmer said. He just wanted to get down.

When the trial adjourned for the day, Ben Cherrit crossed the space between the defense and prosecution tables and handed Madison several pieces of paper clipped together. He said nothing. He simply stuck them in her hands and walked away hurriedly.

"What the hell is that all about?" Marty said, looking over her shoulder as she was reading.

"Sons-of-bitches," she murmured under her breath. Then she looked up and said to Marty, "Cherrit just served me with a notice that Yusef Williams has yet to formally waive his right to a speedy trial, and that if he doesn't do so by tomorrow, Cherrit will move to begin the trial by the end of the week."

"What's it mean?" Marty said.

"It means that they're trying to do everything they can to pester me to get my mind off my cross of Hauffler tomorrow," she told him. "I have to somehow get Yusef here in this court tomorrow, or Cherrit is within his rights to force the trial, and I need more time."

"Why didn't you do it already?" Marty asked.

"Normally it's not a big deal," she told him. "But normally the D.A. isn't trying every trick in the book to win a murder case that he guaranteed to the voters one week before an election."

"What are you going to do?" Marty said.

"I'll have to deal with it," she told him with a disgusted face.

Then she turned to her client and said, "Cody, I'll see you tomorrow morning. Get some rest. I want you to take the next two nights off so you look fresh for the jury. Nothing looks more guilty than a defendant with bags under his eyes. We'll go over your testimony on Wednesday night. If things keep moving this quickly, you'll be on the stand some time Thursday. I'm saving you for last. I think together we can leave the jury with a good feeling about you, which I can slam home during the closing argument."

"Do you think we're doing good?" Cody said.

"Yes," she told him patiently, "as good as we can do. Don't worry. Go with Marty and get some rest. I'm going to talk with Walter about this other case and get it off my mind. I'll see you tomorrow."

The judge was out of his robe when she arrived in his chambers. He wore a pair of pale-yellow paisley suspenders that she imagined were big enough to hold up a building.

"Fine job, today, my dear," Walter said, his voice taking on a mellow quality that hadn't been audible all day long.

"Thank you," she said, handing him the notice given to her by Cherrit.

"What's this?" he said, putting on his reading glasses to see. "I'll be damned. I wondered what this was about. Ben put this across my desk three weeks ago, but I haven't even thought about it since. So Cherrit sprung it on you?"

"I'd say more like Van Rawlins sprung it on me," she said disgustedly. "This isn't a Cherrit maneuver."

"All right," Walter said. "Let's not get hot about it. Let's just diffuse it. The boy has to be present for this, so I'll call the jail and have him brought here first thing in the morning. You can waive the right to a speedy trial with him at eight-forty-five and still have time to start the Grey trial at nine, on time. Fifteen minutes for us both, and a ride across the county for him. No big deal, eh?"

Madison smiled warmly at the judge.

"Thank you, Walter."

Van Rawlins went directly from the courtroom to his offices. Even though it was only four-thirty, Jenny Grey was already there waiting for him. Kooch explained to his boss in the hallway outside the office that he thought it was prudent to bring her himself, to prevent her from having an opportunity to change her mind and bring a lawyer in on the whole thing.

"I found her at her country club. She really wanted to make a call," Kooch whispered, "but I said I thought it would be best if no phone calls were made until the two of you spoke. She's acting pretty cool, but on the other hand, she got what I meant and came right down here without any fuss at all."

"She's a real piece, huh?" Van said with a lurid smile.

"Damn straight," Kooch said. "I can see why Cody Grey is punching guys out all over the place. She's a number that'd be hard to walk by without taking a shot."

"All right," Van said, "come on. I want you to hear this."

Jenny remained sitting as Van Rawlins entered his office and sat down behind his desk. Jenny looked over her shoulder with a glance at Kooch before turning to meet the D.A.'s eyes.

"So, here I am," she said coolly.

"Yes," Van said, unable to keep from admiring how seductively beautiful she was in her short linen skirt and flimsy silk blouse. "Thank you for coming."

"I wasn't really given a choice, was I, Mr. Rawlins?" she said, gracefully crossing her long legs and giving him even more to look at.

"No, I guess you weren't," he said, trying not to stare.

"So, you already know from my very presence that I do not want you to pursue whatever it is you know about my problem with the IRS. What is it you want from me?" she asked, arching an eyebrow.

"I want you to testify tomorrow."

She thought for a moment before asking, "Why?"

"Because we all already know that if you testify to what you already told the police, your husband's alibi will be shot to hell. I think he's going down anyway, but there are some questions being raised about the possibility of another party being involved in framing your husband. I think if the jury knew what you know, that he has no alibi, it would pretty much kill that conspiracy theory. His attorney already told the jury in her opening statement that your husband returned home immediately after leaving the bar on the night of the murder. But we both know that's not what happened."

"And you need me to willingly testify against my husband?" she said.

Van nodded and said, "Quite frankly, Mrs. Grey, and I have reason to believe you don't care much anyway, but whether you testify or not, in all likelihood that jury is going to send your husband away for the rest of his life, however long that might be. So, as far as your marriage, if there is one left, it won't be much good to you if he's in jail or on death row. You're going to need all the resources you can get your hands on without your husband in the picture, and I can't imagine you'd want me bringing up whatever it is about this bank account to the IRS when apparently the only other person who knows what it's really all about is already dead."

"You're not suggesting that I had anything to do with all this, are you, Mr. Rawlins?" Jenny said to him calmly.

"No, that's not what I'm suggesting," Rawlins said evenly. "But I am suggesting that your financial troubles may reemerge if I have to continue to dig for evidence in this case. With your testimony, I can't imagine why I'd look any further."

Jenny sat for several minutes coolly looking over the D.A.

"When?" she said finally.

"Tomorrow," he told her. "First thing in the morning, nine o'clock."

Jenny nodded her head and stood to leave.

"Then I'll see you in the morning."

"There are some things you should know," Van said to her before she reached the door.

"What are those?" she asked impatiently.

"When you go on that stand, Madison McCall is going to try to tear you apart. I know things aren't going that well with you and your husband. I don't care. But if you've been seeing other men, or if you've spoken with your husband about a divorce, she'll ask you about all that."

Jenny seemed unconcerned, but she said imperiously, "And I have to answer those questions?"

Van nodded.

Jenny tilted her head down, then looked up and said, "So what are you telling me to do?"

"I think," Van said, "that if you simply tell the truth about your past behavior, no matter how embarrassing it might be, that the whole thing will be over a lot quicker. I'll also do a redirect to rehabilitate you if she tears you down too bad, and you'll get the last laugh."

Van knew he'd just put a whole new spin on things, but he also knew that he had her. He had Jenny Grey where he wanted her, and she would do as she was told.

"All right," she said, then turned and walked out the door. When she was gone, Van and Kooch celebrated with an enthusiastic handshake.

"Call CNN, Kooch," Rawlins said, "we're going national. . . ."

"Damn," Striker said. He was sitting with Jenny in his living room. They were sharing a bottle of red wine and waiting for the food Striker had ordered in from a nearby Italian restaurant.

"You'll have to do it," he said. She had just recounted for him her conversation with Van Rawlins.

"I know," she replied.

Then, after a slight hesitation she said, "I want you to come with me."

Striker looked at her as if she was crazy. Then he laughed with a series of low guttural grunts.

"I think you've had too much wine; I'm not going with you."

"Why not?" Jenny asked, her eyes blazing.

"Why?" Striker said, amused. "I told you, our meetings must be on a random casual basis, nothing more than serves the recreational copulation of two adulterers."

"I want you there, Striker," she said firmly, as if it were no longer a request.

There was a knock at the door. It was their food. Striker paid the boy and tipped him generously before taking the boxes into the kitchen where he put the food onto china plates. Jenny went into the dining room, bringing the bottle of wine with her. Vivaldi filled the room at a low volume. The high window at the end of the room was covered with long, elegant white and gold drapes. The table was long enough for ten people. Jenny sat down, listening to the beautiful music in silence and waiting for Striker to bring their dinner. He came in backward through the swinging door that led to the kitchen with the plates on his arms. He put them on the table and then sat down, snapping his napkin deftly before placing it in his lap. He began to eat without a word.

"This is excellent, would you like to try some?" he said after several minutes. "Oh? You're not eating."

"I want you there," Jenny said, taking a sip from her wineglass and looking directly at him. She had pulled her hair back and was wearing a low-cut, dark blue cotton dress. Her large blue eyes looked even larger than usual. "I don't think it would be inappropriate at all. We have been lovers for months now. I am in a crisis situation. I need your emotional support. I think it looks very normal. Your CIA people might even think you're partly human. . . ." Striker looked at her incredulously.

"Emotional support?" he said, setting down his fork. "You sound like a therapist."

Jenny continued to look right at him. As she did, her eyes began to brim with tears. She blinked and one rolled down her cheek. "I love you," she said, reaching her hand out across the table.

Striker took her hand in his and said quietly, "I love you too."

"I need you there. It's hard to explain, but what I'm going to do to him is . . . I know I'm leaving him, but we've been through a lot, not all good, but some good. It's been a long time. I can walk away, but to do this . . . I just want you there. Please . . ."

Striker considered her appeal. He had never seen her so emotional. He needed her to be sharp for her meeting with the general. Striker knew he would be calling any day now. He needed her resolve to be firm. He wanted to make sure she pushed that button, the one that would leave the general and the money in a trillion unidentifiable pieces all over Route 16.

"I'll compromise," Striker said, after thinking. "I won't go in with you, Jenny. It would be foolish—" He held up his hand when she opened her mouth to protest. "Let me finish. I'll take you to the courthouse. I'll drop you off in the back. You can go in there. I'm certainly not walking up those steps with you with all those cameras on us. I've made too many exceptions already with you, Jenny. I'll be there for you when you come out. But I'm not going in."

Jenny gave up with a sigh. She knew she was lucky just to get Striker to take her.

CHAPTER TWENTY-EIGHT

∨

MADISON DROVE HERSELF TO THE COURTHOUSE. She got there by eight because she wanted some time to talk to Yusef Williams. Even though she wasn't getting paid to defend him, she wanted him to know that she was on top of his case and that she hadn't forgotten him. She could only imagine the horror of being sixteen years old and in jail with the prospect of the death penalty looming. She knew Yusef wasn't a model citizen, but she didn't think anybody who'd had his kind of life could be. She was allowed to see him in a private conference room adjacent to the holding cells in the courtroom. The room had no windows, and the table and two chairs were simple pieces of scratched and battered oak. Still, it was the most dignified setting she'd seen him in to date. Except for his bright orange jumper with a number stenciled across the chest, the meeting could have been nothing more than a high-school student with his guidance counselor plotting his future.

"Have you thought about what I said about getting back into high school after the trial?" Madison asked him.

Yusef nodded. He still had a hard time looking at her, or anyone.

"I been going to the classes they give in jail," he said quietly, stealing a glance to see how she took that information.

Madison smiled broadly at him.

"That's wonderful, Yusef," she said. Then sternly she reminded him, "Because, you know, if we can get you out of here, it's only the beginning. I want you to remember that. If you don't get through high school and some kind of training or college, you'll end up right back here, I promise you.

"And I don't do two free trials in the same lifetime," she added lightly.

This brought a smile to the boy's face, and he looked at her sheepishly and mumbled something incoherent.

"I'm sorry, Yusef," she said, "what did you say?"

"Said, thanks," he grunted.

Madison knew from the torment on his face that it took a lot for him to say that. He probably had never thanked anyone for anything in his life. He'd probably never had cause to.

"You're welcome, Yusef," she said. "You really are.

"All right," Madison said, back to business, "here's where we are. You know already that I've got the bullet, and it matches the wound in Ramon's ear, we've been through all that. You know I've got a detective working on trying to find out more about the man in black. He's got nothing so far, but he'll keep working. If the man in black is out there, maybe he'll appear in the neighborhood again somewhere. If a tall, thin white man with dark hair walks into the neighborhood, he's going to stand out, so let's keep our fingers crossed. Also, the detective has taken the list you gave me of the friends and family of your . . . your . . . the two other boys who were with you. He's going to go to each one of them and try to see if they know of someone matching that description. We're really doing everything we can think of.

"The reason you're here today, Yusef," she continued, "is because you have the constitutional right to a speedy trial. In other words, you can force the issue. The state can only keep you incarcerated so long before they have to either give you a trial or let you go. Sometimes, in fact oftentimes, like in your case, the defense, us, wants to delay the trial to have time to accumulate more evidence to . . . to get you off. But only you can waive those rights yourself, in front of the judge. I can't do it for you.

"So, if that's okay with you, I'm advising you to waive those rights so my friend the detective can find out some more information that's going to help us get you out of here. I know it's not a pleasant prospect to stay in jail while you wait, but I don't want to go to trial until I think we can put forth our best case. Okay?"

Yusef nodded and mumbled something.

"I'm sorry," she said. "I didn't hear you, Yusef."

He looked up at her and said, "It's not so bad, bein' in jail."

That was what she thought he'd said. That was what she was afraid of.

"Well," she said, "that's good that it's not so bad. You just keep working on those classes, and when we get you out, we'll see what we can do about getting you a place to live that's even better, so you can get your life going in the right direction."

Yusef nodded. It didn't really seem possible to him, but he was willing to give it a shot.

"I'm going to go out to the courtroom now," she told him. "They'll bring you out later and we'll go through the procedure. It's nothing to get worried about. It's no big deal. There may be some people there, but don't worry, they're not there to see you. They'll be coming in for another trial I'm doing that starts at nine."

"Cody Grey trial, huh?" the young boy said, looking up with stars in his eyes.

"Yes," she said, "it's his trial."

"Yeah," Yusef said, nodding with satisfaction, "I told them boys I had the same lawyer as him when we saw you on TV. No one believed me. . . . You think you could get his autograph for me?" he said, looking directly at her for an instant before turning his gaze back to his hands.

Madison smiled and wondered what it would feel like to bring so much happiness to a young boy, even as desperate as this one, with something as simple as signing an autograph.

"I think I can do that," she said. "You keep going to those classes, and I'll have it for you the next time we meet."

Yusef, Madison could tell, was nervous despite what she'd said. When he came out into the courtroom through a side door with the bailiff, his eyes got wide and he glanced around uneasily. The courtroom was now filling rapidly with people and press. They went through the pleading, and Judge Connack was as gentle as he could be without losing the authority that made him stand out as one of the most respected judges from Dallas to San Antonio. Madison took care to glare at Van Rawlins when he came in and sat down beside Ben Cherrit. She wanted him to know that she knew he was simply trying to waste her time by forcing this pleading now, before the trial. Van returned her look only briefly. His smile was smug, as if to say that she'd seen nothing yet. And she hadn't.

When the pleading was over, Madison shook Yusef's hand, and he was led away. She turned to look for Cody and Marty, and it was then she saw Jenny Grey walking into the courtroom from a side door, escorted by Ben Cherrit. Jenny was dressed in a conservative, dark gray suit with a bright red blouse. She looked stunning, much different from the last time Madison had seen her, the morning after the murder. Without thinking, Madison ran her fingers through her own hair. Jenny Grey had that effect on other women.

She looked like she was just passing through on her way to Beverly Hills.

Cherrit sat her down without any commotion near the back of the courtroom and then joined Van in the front. Madison had a sinking feeling in her stomach. She couldn't think of any good reason why Jenny Grey would be in the courtroom. She glanced over at Van Rawlins, who had also seen Jenny and was looking on with a smile. Madison knew what it meant, and she was furious.

Marty and Cody walked in and passed right by Jenny without looking at her. They left a wake of press behind them at the door. Madison could see that Cody was upset, and she figured correctly that the press must have somehow gotten wind that Jenny was here and had been badgering him to get a comment on his feelings about his wife's unexpected testimony. Madison realized Ben Cherrit was at her shoulder, and she turned to him. He was holding a sheet of paper out for her.

She took it and said disgustedly, "Let me guess, Ben, an amended witness list."

He looked at her apologetically and said, "We faxed a copy to your office first thing this morning when we knew for sure."

"And, of course," she said, "I was here, so I didn't get it. . . . Good one, Ben. I'll remember this."

"Sorry."

"I'll bet," Madison mumbled. Cody and Marty were beside her now, and she knew that they knew.

"What can we do?" Marty asked. "Do you think she's going to sink us?"

"I can't think of anything else," Madison said. "We didn't ask her to testify, and she's not here to watch."

Madison saw that Cody had spotted his wife in the back. She imagined that his face was calm the night he'd slammed Jeff Board around at the Green Mesquite compared to what it was right now.

"First off," she said, looking sternly at Cody, whose face was red with rage, "Cody, you've got to cool down. I can see you're upset; anyone would be. This is . . . I can't believe she's doing it. But if she is, she is. I'll try to do what I can, but I've got a bad feeling. . . . But you've got to calm yourself. If the jury sees you looking at her like that, they'll convict you for sure."

"Ms. McCall?"

Madison turned around. George Freeman, the court bailiff, was leaning over the bar and tugging at her sleeve. She couldn't imagine what he wanted.

"I'm sorry, Ms. McCall," he said, "I know you're getting ready for the trial, but we're having a time of it in the back with the boy. We tried to get him out of here. They want to take him back to the jail, but he's got himself wrapped around the steering wheel of the county bus and won't let go for nothing. I'm afraid he'll get himself hurt by those boys from the county. They're either gonna mace him or use their sticks. He's gone half-crazy, and he's screaming that he has to see you. Could you come?"

Madison looked behind her. The jury was being led in and she knew the judge would soon follow.

"All right," she said, starting for the side door.

"Marty," she said, turning back to her open-mouthed friend as she walked away, "Ask to approach the bench and tell Walter what's up. I'll be there. Just stall. . . ."

There was a ruckus out in back of the courthouse. Yusef had his arms and legs wrapped around the steering column. Outside the bus stood the driver and various workers from the courthouse. Inside, two county guards and a policeman were trying desperately to pry him loose. Each of them was screaming directions to the other, and Yusef was howling in pain and determined rage. His eyes were shut tight, and tears were streaming down his face. Madison ran to the doorway of the bus.

"Stop it!" Madison cried. "Stop it!"

Her shrieking voice cut through the din, and Yusef's tormentors backed warily away from him and down the steps of the small gray bus.

"He's gone crazy, ma'am," the cop said to her in a heavy southern drawl, "you better stay back."

"I'm his damn lawyer," she said, shoving the men out of her way. When it was quiet she held her fingertips to her temples and said to Yusef, "Are you all right?"

"Yes," he said, shaking with fear and exhaustion, unwrapping himself from the steering column. "I'm sorry. I had to talk to you."

He was facing her now, looking at her beseechingly.

"It's him!" he said. "He's out there!"

Yusef was pointing toward the front window of the bus.

"The man! The man in black! I saw him! I saw him drive up in a car!"

"Wait," Madison said, "calm down. What are you saying? You saw him?"

"He was right there!" Yusef was furiously stabbing the air with his finger, pointing outside the bus. "When I came out, he pulled up in a big gray car! A woman got out, and he drove away!"

295

Yusef could tell she was doubting him. "I told you the truth about Ramon's ear, didn't I?" he pleaded. "I'm tellin' you the truth now!"

Suddenly Madison said, "Was she tall, with dark hair?"

"Uh-huh," Yusef nodded. "She was—"

"Was she wearing a dark gray suit?"

"I think so," Yusef said, frowning, "and red, a red shirt. . . ."

As the trial was beginning, on the other end of Texas, in the panhandle, the general drove to a shopping center on the outskirts of Amarillo on his way in to the office. He drove his Jeep around the lot for five minutes, looking for the closest spot to the stores. He was tempted to park in a handicapped space, he'd done it before. But today he didn't want to draw any attention to himself at all, not even a parking ticket. The general walked briskly to a pay phone on the brick wall outside the grocery store that anchored the small center.

He picked up the phone and noticed that his hands were shaking. He couldn't help it. He hated having the pit with him. He hadn't been able to decide where to leave it, so he took it wherever he went. It was now sitting in the back of his Jeep in its case. The general felt almost giddy with the idea that within a few short hours he would have the rest of the money, and the last pit would be out of his hands. It was as if he were carrying around a life sentence, which he was. If caught with the pit, he certainly had no conceivable defense to explain it. He would tell them everything if he was caught, but he knew they would tear him apart anyway. He knew exactly what would be done. They would take him to a remote warehouse somewhere where these kinds of things were done. He would be put into a sensory deprivation chamber and given hallucinogenic drugs until sanity was stripped from his mind. Then they would grill him.

It would take about ten days, and during that entire time, he would be under a suicide watch because he, like anyone who had ever been interrogated thoroughly by military intelligence or the CIA, would prefer death to what they would do to him. When it was over, he would be all right—a little shell shocked, but he would recover. Then they would put on a court-martial for the media and convict him of treason. He would be put away somewhere in a military prison, where books weren't written and prisoners didn't enjoy the vast array of rights that common serial killers, child molesters, and rapists did in the civilian penal system. He would simply cease to exist. He would disappear. The general wanted to disappear, but not in that way.

He dialed the number. On the third ring a woman's voice said, "Gem Star Technologies."

"This is Ken Frost," the general said. "Is Mr. Moss available?"

"I'm sorry Mr. Frost, he's busy at the moment, can I take a number?"

"Yes, please have him call me at seven, nine, five, eight, eight, two, two, six, one, nine."

The woman repeated the number. The general confirmed it and hung up. He looked at his watch to note the time. In thirty-six hours he would have the money. In two months he would be in Grand Cayman. From there, who could say?

The general looked around him carefully before leaving the phone. He saw nothing and no one unusual. He wiped the dried spit from the corners of his mouth and a smile crept across his face.

Madison entered the courtroom and went immediately to the bench where Marty and Van Rawlins were arguing with the judge.

"Thank you, Marty," she said.

"They had a small problem with Yusef Williams," she explained. "I'm sorry, your honor." Judge Connack's stern look faded instantly.

"Well?" he said. "Are you ready to proceed with this case now?"

"No, your honor," she said. "I want an adjournment for at least a week. The District Attorney has found it necessary to spring a surprise witness on me this morning, as I'm sure you already know, and I'm not prepared for this witness, your honor."

The judge scowled. Madison knew the last thing he wanted was a delay in this trial. He didn't want to have to deal with the media circus any more than he had to. He had already fouled his schedule for three months to come because of this trial.

"Mr. Rawlins," he said. "There's no paperwork here that suggests you have ever deposed or even interviewed this witness. Just what exactly is going on here?"

"Your honor," Van said, "I'm sorry that the court and counsel were not informed of Mrs. Grey's appearance as a witness, but it wasn't until yesterday evening that I knew myself she was going to testify. She is here for the single purpose of telling the jury exactly when Cody Grey arrived at home on the night of the murder. I have no written statement from her. I don't even have any trial notes from my brief discussion with her, your honor. It's as much a surprise to me as it is to counsel. We tried to question Mrs. Grey weeks ago and were told that she was invoking her right to spousal immunity. Apparently, she has changed her mind in the interests of justice."

Madison scoffed at that.

"Ms. McCall," Judge Connack said, "that really doesn't seem unreasonable to me. If Mr. Rawlins is limiting his direct examination to that one question, I don't see why we can't proceed, can you?"

"Your honor," she said, "I need time to prepare a cross-examination of this witness. I need time to investigate her past and find if there is anything that would impeach her credibility as a witness against my client."

The judge thought about that for a moment, then said, "All right, Ms. McCall, I'm granting your motion for an adjournment. I will reconvene this court in one hour."

"Walter, an hour?" she blurted out, forgetting herself completely.

He didn't like her calling him by his first name, especially in front of Rawlins.

"Yes, Ms. McCall," the judge said, "you have the witness's husband at your complete disposal. If he doesn't know how to impeach her, no one will."

With that, Judge Connack turned to the jury and said, "Ladies and gentleman, I apologize for the delay, but I must call a brief adjournment. Court will reconvene in one hour."

The judge let the gavel drop once, and then he was gone.

CHAPTER TWENTY-NINE

∨

MADISON WORKED FURIOUSLY WITH CODY for the full hour. She focused every bit of her energy on finding out everything she could about Jenny Grey, every bit of dirt, every weakness, every strength she had. It was a good exercise for Cody, anyway. She could tell it was cathartic for him to revisit every evil aspect of his wife that he could think of. It helped lessen the pain of seeing her sitting there, looking like a million dollars. Madison took the final fifteen minutes to sketch together a cross-examination plan. She didn't have much, but she'd do her best to cast at least a little doubt about Jenny's veracity. She couldn't figure out why she felt so eager to tear into Cody's wife.

On their way back into the courtroom, as the three of them walked down the aisle, Madison leaned Marty's way and said hurriedly in a low voice, "When Jenny Grey leaves this courtroom after she testifies, you follow her, Marty. I can't explain it all now, but when she's done, she'll probably go out the side door to the back. If she does, I think she'll get picked up by a man in a big gray car. Get the license number, Marty. I can't explain it all now, but I have to have it. Cody's life may depend on it."

No sooner had they sat down than George began to rattle off his litany, and Walter Connack's imposing figure appeared from his chambers. He climbed the stair to his bench like a giant mounting the turret of his castle. He slammed his gavel down and called the court to order. Van called Jenny Grey to the stand, and the crowd began to murmur.

Jenny took the stand and the oath with her head held high. Van Rawlins poised himself strategically at the corner railing of the jury box so Jenny would have to look toward the jury to answer him, and they could see her face clearly. The imperious look she had worn when she first walked in was gone. In it's place was the look of confident humility and sincerity.

"Mrs. Grey," Van Rawlins said gently. "I know it is very hard for you to be here today, and I will not belabor your personal pain, but I must say that I am moved by your willingness to testify and your commitment above all else to the truth."

Van let that sink into the jury while Madison fought to keep the disgust off of her face.

"I am only going to ask you a few simple questions, Mrs. Grey," Van said benevolently, "and then I'll let you go. . . ."

Madison knew exactly what he was doing. He was setting her up to be the insensitive bitch-lawyer who would torment the helpless and distraught wife of a killer in cross-examination.

"I know that on the night of Jeff Board's brutal murder," Van began, "you left your husband after he viciously beat Mr. Board at the Green Mesquite."

"Objection, your honor," Madison said calmly, "is counsel giving us his closing argument, or is he questioning the witness?"

"Sustained. Get to the point, Mr. Rawlins."

"What did you do after you left the restaurant?" Van said without missing a beat.

"I went home and went to bed," Jenny said. She was speaking in the timid voice of a little girl.

"And did you wake up during the night?" Van said.

"Yes."

"What woke you up?" Van asked.

"I heard Cody coming in," she said. "I was staying in the guest bedroom next to the garage. He hit a trash can or something when he pulled in, and the crash woke me up. I listened to him come into the house and go upstairs."

"What time was that, Mrs. Grey?" Van said, as if he dreaded the question himself.

"Two-thirty in the morning," Jenny said.

"How do you know?"

"There's a digital clock right next to the bed. I looked at it," she said, and a tear actually spilled out of the corner of her eye. Jenny let it roll all the way down her cheek and fall onto the front of her jacket before she bothered to wipe her face.

"I have no further questions, your honor," Van said quietly, and then sat down to watch.

Madison rose from her seat and walked over to a corner of the jury box, the exact spot Van Rawlins had spoken from only moments ago. But her reasons were different. She wanted to stand by the jury so Jenny would look in their direction, but by positioning herself as if she were a juror, she also wanted her voice to seem like one of theirs—so the jury would feel as if Madison's perspective and line of reasoning were their own. She took a deep breath and let it fly.

"Mrs. Grey," she said softly, "how long have you known your husband?"

Jenny hesitated, wary of some trap, then said, "About fifteen years."

"Since high school, isn't that right?"

"Yes."

"And in that time, your husband has been in some trouble, hasn't he?"

"Yes, he has."

"And you have unfortunately had to witness these outbursts, haven't you, Mrs. Grey?"

"Yes, I have."

"But isn't it true that in each one of these outbursts, Mrs. Grey," Madison said in a normal tone, "that you were the direct cause of the problem?

"Objection, your honor! Counsel is badgering the witness, there is no relevance to this whatsoever!" Van bawled.

"Sustained."

"It is true," Jenny said anyway, and there was absolute silence. "He's fought over me since I knew him."

"And you liked that, didn't you, Mrs. Grey?" Madison said wickedly. She wanted the jury to know that this beautiful woman was nothing but trouble from the start.

"Your honor, objection!" Van said desperately.

"Sustained. Ms. McCall, I see no relevance whatsoever, here. Please move on."

"Isn't it true that you lie on a regular basis, Mrs. Grey?" Madison said.

"Of course not," Jenny replied, her lip curling up in contempt.

"No? Well, do you think that deceiving your husband on a daily basis and breaching your marital vows is being honest?"

"I don't know what you're implying, but I don't lie."

"Isn't it true that you have had before and are at this time having an extramarital affair, Mrs. Grey?" Madison said with as much nastiness as she could muster. She knew that if a woman like Jenny Grey had a lover now that it wasn't her first.

Jenny paused. She glanced briefly at Cody, then said, "Yes."

The court erupted, and Judge Connack slammed his gavel twice with a warning. "There will be no more of that in this courtroom, or I'll bar you ladies and gentlemen from the press. This is not a circus. This is a court of law, and for those of you from out of town, just ask the people who know me. I mean it."

Van looked over his shoulder for the CNN people, hoping they hadn't been too offended.

Madison let the notion of Jenny as a coldhearted slut sit for a while. She stood there until she was certain everyone in the entire courtroom was uncomfortable, even Jenny.

"Isn't cheating on your husband a lie, Mrs. Grey?" she said abruptly.

"No," Jenny responded.

"No? What would you call adultery, Mrs. Grey? Is it cheating or is it lying?"

"My husband never asked. I never told. If he'd bothered to ask," Jenny seethed, "I would have told him the truth."

"So you would have us believe that you are really nothing more than a cheater, and not a liar?"

"I don't think of myself as either."

"Mrs. Grey, your husband has made a substantial amount of money over the past nine years as an NFL player, hasn't he?"

"Yes."

"And you've lived well, haven't you?"

"Yes, fairly well."

"You drive a Porsche, don't you?" Madison asked.

"Yes."

"Objection, your honor," Van said.

"Your honor, may I approach the bench to explain my line of questioning?" Madison asked politely.

"I wish you would," Judge Connack responded.

"Your honor," Madison said in a whisper as Van Rawlins hung over her shoulder to hear her every word, "this woman has spent every penny my client has made. Because of his age and his injuries, his earning potential is about to drop off to relatively nothing. I believe that she is planning to divorce my client because of this. If he was sentenced to jail, then Mrs. Grey would have grounds for an easy and cost-free divorce. I believe that this may show some bias of the witness toward my client in this case. That is the line of questioning I am pursuing."

"Preposterous, your honor," Van commented.

Walter thought a moment, then said, "I'll allow it."

Madison returned to her spot.

"Besides the Porsche," Madison said, "you live in a three-quarter of a million dollar home with a pool, isn't that right?"

"Yes," Jenny huffed with boredom.

"But you don't have any money in savings, do you, Mrs. Grey?"

"Not much. Not really."

"Isn't it a fact that if your husband were to lose his job today that you would have to sell your home?"

"Probably."

"And you wouldn't like to have to live in any other way than the one you've become accustomed to, would you, Mrs. Grey?"

"I suppose not. Who would?"

"And your husband, Cody Grey, is at the end of his career, isn't that right?"

"Yes."

"And he won't be making that money much longer, will he?"

"I doubt it."

"And you're planning on leaving your husband, aren't you?"

"Not because of that."

"But you are planning on leaving him, aren't you?"

"Yes."

"So you'll want a divorce, correct?"

"I guess I will, yes."

"So you can marry someone who does have money, isn't that right?"

"Objection!"

"Ms. McCall," the judge said, "now I really am starting to lose patience with you."

Without pausing to absorb the rebuke, Madison said, "And you're aware that if your husband is convicted in this case that it will be unspeakably easy for you to divorce him, aren't you?"

"No, I didn't know that."

"You don't really care what happens to your husband, do you, Mrs. Grey?"

"I care," she said.

Madison looked toward her with disbelief, in clear sight of the jury. She counted off her fingers as she spoke: "You cheat on your husband, you're planning to divorce him, you came here today under absolutely no legal obligation to testify against him, and you say you care what happens to him? Are you lying to us now, Mrs. Grey, or simply cheating again?"

"Objection! Your honor! This has gone too far!" Van was steaming and Judge Connack wasn't too far from boiling.

Madison didn't care. She didn't give a damn if Walter threw her in jail overnight. She had probably gone too far, and she was going to go even further. It was a question she knew she shouldn't ask because she had no good faith belief that it was true, but she had to do it. She had to link this woman's testimony against Cody to something more than a divorce. The jury would want a stronger motive to kick around when they were deliberating.

"Has one of your illicit affairs been with a man named Ricardo Lopez?" Madison barked. "And didn't he drive you here to this courtroom today?"

It wasn't in Jenny's response; she said nothing. It was the momentary shock on her face that let Madison know she had struck a nerve with mention of the man who dropped Jenny off. She had no idea if the man was Lopez or if he had something to do with Lopez, but one thing was certain. That man had something to do with this case. He might even be the real killer.

Van was yelling, the judge was yelling, and the entire courtroom was in an uproar. But the jury heard, and Madison knew she'd battered Jenny's image around enough so that they'd remember. They'd make the connection between the cheating wife and the mobster who had a plausible reason to want Board dead. They might even buy her whole theory now.

"I would like to redirect, your honor," Van said after he'd calmed himself down enough to speak and Judge Connack had finished his bellowing. Van walked calmly back to his place beside the jury.

"Mrs. Grey," he said, "why do you want to leave your husband?"

Jenny looked pointedly at Madison before she turned to Van and the jury.

"Because he is a violent man and I can't stand it anymore. I think he may be addicted to painkillers. He's been using them for over three months now, nonstop."

The people were quiet except for the rustling of clothes as every head in the courtroom craned to get a view of Cody Grey.

"Did anyone ask you not to testify here today, Mrs. Grey?" Van said.

"Yes," Jenny replied, pointing her finger at Madison, "my husband's attorney told me to say nothing to anyone about what time he came home."

The courtroom erupted with a quiet murmur. The judge looked shocked. Van smiled. He had never had any intention of questioning the ethical behavior of another member of the bar in open court, not even Madison McCall's, but she had gone too far. She asked for it.

Van nodded and said, "Finally, Mrs. Grey, why did you tell us that your husband came home at two-thirty?"

"Because that's what happened."

"Thank you, Mrs. Grey."

Jenny got down off the stand and walked with her chin still held high, looking straight ahead, right out of the side door of the courtroom that she had come in through. Madison nudged Marty and he quickly got up and followed.

Madison wasn't upset about what Rawlins had just done to her. It was smart on his part. Under the circumstances, she would have done the same thing. Her father used to tell her, and it was true, that if you're going to bite and kick, you're going to get bitten and kicked back. She looked at Cody sitting next to her. He was stone-faced, not an ounce of emotion detectable on his face. She put her hand on his arm and gave it a friendly squeeze. He looked at her and smiled weakly. He looked like a condemned man already. Madison had a moment to consider what Jenny's testimony did to their case and realized it all but killed them.

Van Rawlins got back to business. He called Alice's boss to the stand, the Travis County Coroner, to go through the gory details of what exactly had killed Jeff Board, the struggle that took place, how he had defecated and cried right before death. Van was trying to get the jury to see Board in their minds, begging for mercy.

Madison made it as hard for Van as she could, protesting at every step of the way about the prejudice such morbid talk was casting on her client. Walter, however, wasn't disposed to let her have her way any longer, and Madison was relieved when court was finally adjourned for lunch.

CHAPTER THIRTY

MARTY WALKED INTO THE COURT even before Madison had finished packing up her things to go to lunch. She looked at him expectantly.

"Marty," she said quietly, so Cody couldn't hear, "did you get it?"

He nodded and quietly said, "Yes."

He figured correctly that Madison didn't want to wound Cody any deeper than he already was by openly discussing the man with whom his wife was obviously involved.

"Good," Madison said. "Listen, I want you to track it down. Find out who this guy is and what he does, okay? Can you do that tonight?"

"You got it," Marty said. "I'm like a real private eye here. First I'm a tax attorney, then I'm an agent, then a trial lawyer, and now I'm a private eye. Be friends with Madison McCall and see the world."

"Thanks, Marty," she said. "You go with Cody to our room. I'll meet you."

Madison went to a bank of pay phones outside the courtroom and dialed Alice Vreland's office.

"I'm sorry," the young man who answered the phone told her, "Alice is in the field. She won't be back until later this afternoon. Can I help you?"

Madison chewed her lower lip and said, "No, thanks. Just tell her that Madison called, and I have to speak to her today. I'll try back around four-thirty. If she's not going to be around, please have her leave me a message where I can reach her. It's very important."

Madison hung up the phone and went to the same room they'd eaten lunch in the day before. She found Cody and Marty eating the same sandwiches they'd had the day before, as well. Things weren't as upbeat as they were a day ago, though. Jenny's testimony put a damper on everyone's spirits, and Madison didn't want to share her possible new lead until she had something more concrete. She couldn't, however, keep her mind from jumping to all the possibilities that could exist if she were able to link both bullets to a real person. She had to push those thoughts from her mind, though. She was in the middle of a trial, and what happened with the prosecution's eyewitness over the next few hours could prove to be more important than a matching bullet and a man in black.

The afternoon was a slow, meticulous battle. Van carefully built up Boris Hauffler as a credible and completely unbiased eyewitness. Hauffler seemed to become more nervous and forgetful as the time wore on. Seeing that fatigue was setting in, Van tried hard to get right to the point as well as sneak in some leading questions that were not allowed on direct examination. Madison was certain that everyone in the courtroom was growing tired of the words, "Objection, leading the witness," but that was her job, and she did it well. By the time Van was through with his direct, Hauffler was tired and frazzled. Still, without hesitation, Hauffler had pointed directly to Cody Grey as the man he saw running from Jeff Board's house the night he was killed.

Madison had a complete history on Hauffler, and she attempted to impeach his credibility for every indiscretion he ever committed, grilling him thoroughly on things as mundane as some unpaid parking tickets and as embarrassing as the time he beat a neighbor's dog with a shoe after it allegedly bit his dog. Madison also knew that Hauffler's wife had left him twenty years ago and run off with a fitness center owner who had once been a semi-pro baseball player. Her theory, challenged unsuccessfully by an irate Van Rawlins, was that Hauffler maintained a grudge against any and all professional athletes as a result and was thus a biased witness against Cody Grey.

By the time she got to the important things, both Madison and the jury knew from the tone of his voice that Hauffler hated her vehemently. Madison went into great detail on the exact way in which the police had presented the picture of Cody Grey to Hauffler. She suggested that from the instant he was told that it was Cody Grey, the famous athlete, Hauffler was convinced that Cody was the killer, but that the man Hauffler saw running from the house was not the man in the picture.

Hauffler stuck firmly to his story, as Madison knew he would have been coached to do. Suddenly Madison paused dramatically. It seemed she had come to a dead end. Then she lifted a stack of papers four inches thick from her table and said, "Mr. Hauffler, are you aware of how many cases there are in this state alone where innocent people have been convicted of murder by eyewitnesses who were later proven to be wrong?"

"Objection, your honor," Rawlins said, rising tiredly from his chair. "Is counsel trying to admit those papers to evidence? If so, I'd question their relevance; if not, I question this method of unfounded suggestion."

"Ms. McCall, are you presenting those papers as evidence?"

"I think I'd like to, your honor," Madison said, as if it were the first time she was even considering it. "I realize it is unusual, but I think these cases are critically important for Mr. Hauffler and the jury to consider. These are real cases, your honor. Cases like this one, with witnesses, like Mr. Hauffler, who claimed to be just as certain that they had made a correct identification. They were wrong, your honor, as the respective courts later determined. Unfortunately, your honor, in two of these cases, the defendants were executed before the truth was discovered. . . ."

There was a low murmur throughout the courtroom.

"All right, Ms. McCall," the judge said with a heavy sigh, "that will be enough. Please submit copies of this to the court as well as to the state."

"I object to this, your honor," Van said. "I see no relevance to this case whatsoever."

"I just don't want this jury," Madison said compassionately, "or Mr. Hauffler, to have to live with that kind of guilt, your honor."

"I understand," Walter said impatiently. He certainly wasn't buying Madison's phony concern, but he did think it was a legitimate body of evidence to consider. "Please submit the evidence, Ms. McCall."

When she'd finished her cross, Madison felt certain that she had done everything she possibly could. Once again, however, despite all her work, Van Rawlins was able to use his redirect to build his witness back up. His final question was simple and to the point: "Are you absolutely certain that you saw that man, Cody Grey, coming out of Jeff Board's house right after he was murdered?"

Hauffler answered yes with the certainty of a king.

Madison was beginning to think more and more that if they were going to stand a chance at all, it would come down to Cody's testimony and how well he stood up under Van Rawlins's cross-examination.

After the trial was adjourned for the day, Madison left Cody in the care of Marty and excused herself. She went immediately to her office to call Alice Vreland. Her friend was there.

"You want me to what?" Alice exclaimed.

"Don't you know anyone in the D.A.'s office that can get you in the vault?"

Madison said. She wanted Alice to go to the D.A.'s office and sign out the bullet that was in the evidence locker being used for Cody's case. Whenever evidence was needed for a trial, the D.A.'s office secured it from the police. They would keep the evidence for each case in their own vaults until the trial was over. The only way Alice could check to see if the .22 slugs found in the wall of the garage and in Jeff Board's brain were the same was to put them under the comparison microscope together. To do that, Alice would have to get the slug from the D.A.

"Yeah," Alice said, "I know a gal in the felony bureau who could probably do it, but why? You don't think there's a connection between Cody Grey and our smelly corpse, Ramon, do you? I mean, Cody's your client."

"No," Madison explained. "It's not Cody. It's the man who Yusef claims made him pull the trigger. He, Yusef, saw him this morning, dropping Cody's wife off in the back of the courthouse."

"What?" Alice said, mystified.

"Yusef was in court for a pleading this morning," Madison explained. "When they were taking him out to the bus to take him back to jail, he saw him. I guess he pulled up in a car and Jenny Grey hopped out."

"Wow," Alice said, "the plot thickens, but you've lost me."

"I admit I'm a little lost in all this myself," Madison told her, "but I can't do anything until I find out whether these bullets came from the same gun. I'd ask Rawlins if I didn't think the press would hear about it before anyone has a chance to find out who this mystery man is. I don't want him disappearing or having a chance to ditch the weapon if he hasn't already. Matching slugs without having this other guy only makes things look worse for Cody."

"Well, I'll find out for you today," Alice said. "I can't say how soon, but I can do it. Getting the stuff won't be a big problem. They're pretty loose with evidence at the D.A.'s office when it comes to us. You know, we're supposed to be on the same side. But if I do get a match, I don't want you to go telling everyone until tomorrow. If I'm gonna do this on the QT, you've got to give me a chance to get the evidence back in the vault."

"No problem. Thanks, Alice," Madison said sincerely. "I owe you."

"Again," Alice reminded her. "You owe me *again*, honey."

Before Marty could begin his investigation for Madison, he had to take Cody home. Marty didn't want to just drop Cody off after the day's events, so they went to a restaurant where they could get a secluded table and a couple of steaks. Afterward, Cody asked Marty to go to the video rental store and get *The Bishop's Wife* for him. It was an old black-and-white Cary Grant film. Cody had seen it before, and he knew it was good—the kind of movie that might take his mind off things for a brief time. Marty doubted if anything could make him feel good in those empty moments when he was by himself, but the movie would be a good reprieve. After picking up the video, Marty dropped Cody off at home and promised to be back by seven-thirty the next morning. Before he got out of the car, Cody sat for a moment, looking straight ahead.

"Marty, I really want to thank you."

"Hey, I'm your agent. I told you I'd stick by you, through thick and thin."

"I know," Cody replied, still looking out the windshield, "but you've gone beyond the agent point. You've been a great friend, probably the only one I have. . . ."

Marty didn't know what to say. He could tell Cody meant it. He had never had a client talk like this. Most of them expected him to do the things he did for them. No one had ever really thanked him with anything more than a perfunctory mumble.

"I appreciate it, Cody," he said honestly.

Cody nodded. They had talked of nothing the entire evening but the trial, what Madison said and did and how things looked. Cody would go from elation with the certainty that he would be acquitted to total depression at the idea of going to jail, all in the span of ten minutes. Up and down he had gone, the entire evening. Not once though, did he mention Jenny's name or what she'd done to him. Marty said nothing about her either; instead, he had patiently stayed with Cody every step along the way of his emotional roller coaster ride, assuring him that things were going extremely well.

Marty thought Cody was going to get out of the car, but he stopped after opening the door and said suddenly, "I can't believe she did it, Marty."

Marty looked at him and pushed his glasses up while he cleared his throat.

"I'm sorry," he said. "I know that must have hurt. It was awful."

"I mean, I know I've never been the greatest husband," Cody said. "I'm not saying it's all her. There were things I could have done that I didn't. But she's bad, Marty. I always knew it, I guess. I knew it, but I could never admit it to myself. I never let myself see it. She's bad."

"Yes," Marty said solemnly, "she is."

"How did I marry a girl like that Marty?" he said. "I'm not that bad a person, do you think?"

"No," Marty said, "I know you're not. You're not a bad person at all. You've got a hot head, but I don't think there's anything bad about you, really. I think you just fell in love with beauty, and that's all that was important then. It happens to a lot of people."

"Yeah. Well," Cody said, getting out of the car, "I'll see you tomorrow, Marty. Thanks again."

The house was dark. Despite himself, Cody couldn't help wondering where Jenny was. The answering machine was blinking. He didn't bother to play the messages. It would be the media trying to get him to do their interviews or some other people who didn't really care. He was alone and he knew it. There was beer in the fridge, and Cody took a six-pack out, bringing it with him to the TV room where he settled down on the couch to watch his movie. He took a Percoset from his pocket and washed it down with a swig from his beer. He was as content as he could be under the circumstances. A good movie and some good beer were all he usually needed. Each would do their part, along with the Percoset, in taking him away from the place he was.

About an hour into the movie, the phone rang. Cody ignored it, but when he heard Marty's voice on the machine in the kitchen, he reached over and picked up the phone that was next to him.

"Cody?"

"Yeah."

"Oh, I thought you were there—"

"I am," Cody said.

"Uhhhh," Marty hesitated. "I'm not too good at this. "

"Marty, what the hell's wrong?" Cody demanded in an even voice.

"Okay, the team called. They're worried about the roster and, you know, they need to pick someone up—"

"What are you telling me?" Cody said, "They put me on the injured reserve list?"

"No, they cut you. I didn't know if I should—"

"They can't *cut* me, Marty. I'm hurt," he insisted, certain Marty had made some kind of mistake. "You can't cut an injured guy. You put him on IR."

"I know," Marty said. "We're going to have to sue them. They cut you. No settlement. No payout. Just cut. They said they needed the room on the roster, and they didn't have any extra money under the cap to bring this guy in from Green Bay on an undisclosed trade. They said they didn't want to do it, but they had to. They need another safety."

"That's bullshit!" Cody yelled into the phone. "They have room on the roster with me on IR! They can't cut me!"

They were silent for a moment.

"They did," Marty said. "It had something to do with the salary cap. They *had* to pick up the contract of the guy they signed. I'm sorry."

"You tell those motherfuckers . . ." Cody roared. He was hyperventilating now. "You tell them . . ."

Cody's voice broke, and he fought to regain control. He bit the inside of his mouth.

"I gotta go, Marty," he said.

"Are you okay?"

"Yeah, I gotta go—"

"We'll sue their asses off."

"Sure," Cody said, then hung up.

Striker and Jenny had dinner at the Four Seasons. It was his send-off to her. After Jenny delivered the pit to his apartment, they were going to take a few days off. The media would be hounding Jenny, and after the last few days, Striker thought it best to give it a rest.

"When you leave here," Striker told her, "make sure no one is following you. I'm not worried about the agency, but you never know if one of those reporters hasn't gotten enough from you today."

Jenny nodded. That made sense to her.

"Here are the keys to my Pontiac. It's on Twenty-second Street, just off Guadeloupe. It's a big old gold thing with no hubcaps. You'll see it. Get the suitcase out of the trunk and head for Goldthwaite tonight. I don't have to tell you to make sure that you take that case with you wherever you go. Keep things simple. Don't talk to anyone, and get yourself holed up in that Texas Inn there tonight. Tomorrow morning I'll call the general back and tell him where to meet you. If anything funny is going to happen, it'll happen some time after about nine. Are you okay?"

"Yes," she said.

He knew she was still shaken by the trial, but had gone to lunch afterward, where they drank a bottle of wine. Then they went back to his apartment to work up a sweat in bed. She seemed better now, but he was still concerned.

"You say that, but you're not completely okay, are you? Maybe you should talk about it."

TIM GREEN

"I just feel . . ."

"Guilty?"

"No," she said calmly, "no, I feel sad. I didn't think I would, but I do. I knew it would be hard. I just thought that once it was done, I could walk away and forget it. But I'll be fine. I think I just need a good night's sleep."

"Well," Striker said, "I hope that's all. It's bad timing, the general calling today, but nothing can be done about that. I know he wants to wrap this up, and we can't risk letting him sit around with the pit. He's liable to fuck it up. You just keep your mind on what we're doing. You'll be fine."

"I will be fine," she said. "I'm glad I told you, though. I think I needed to say it. You don't mind, do you?"

"No," he said, leaning across the table to kiss her lips, "I don't mind at all."

Cody drove for some time. He went up to Lake Travis and pulled off the highway at a remote Catholic church high up on a ridge overlooking the lake. He got out of his truck and limped across the grass and through a covered walkway that stretched between the church and its offices. It was a cool fall night, and Cody wished he'd brought a jacket. There was no one in sight. Once through the walkway, the Texas sky unfolded like a new universe. The moon was full and rising. Its heavy beams danced on the lake that lay hundreds of feet below him, sprawled out between the dark jagged hills. It was a magnificent sight, and it made Cody momentarily forget the problems that had rocked his life like a catastrophic earthquake. Everything he had worked so hard for over the years to build and maintain had been smashed to the ground. A breeze blew in his face, and in a few minutes he was shivering.

He hobbled slowly back to his truck, reluctant to leave the beautiful sight. He scoffed at the idea that he might not see that sight again, but it was true. By the end of the week he could be in jail. If he wasn't, he would really have no reason to stay on in Austin. His career was over. The Outlaws had slashed him open and salted the wound. There was no going back now. What they had done only confirmed that the doctors believed his knee was well beyond any hope of recovery. They wouldn't have done to him what they did if there was any chance of his return. It twisted his insides to even think about the media, but he couldn't help it. They would make a big deal out of his being cut. Everyone would know that he was done, a true has-been. It was exactly why he had suffered so much these past few weeks: the fear of being humiliated and perceived as a total loser.

Cody had no intention of going to Madison's home, but to get home from where he had been, he had to pass her neighborhood on the way. He wondered if that wasn't what he was doing up at Lake Travis all along, just giving himself a route home that took him so close to her that he couldn't do anything but stop. He made the decision at the last second, right before the turn. He had to cut it sharp. His tires squealed. He wound his way through the hills and down her long, wide street where you couldn't get a house for under a half a million. He pulled up into her driveway as he had most nights for the past two weeks. It didn't seem intrusive to him at all.

He rang the bell. Madison's voice was harsh and threatening.

"Who is it?" she demanded.

Cody looked at his watch. It was only nine-thirty. "It's me," he said quietly.

"Cody?" she said, her voice softening.

"Yes," he said. He felt like he was picking her up for the prom. He was that nervous.

Madison opened the door and stood there. She was wearing an old T-shirt and a pair of faded green cotton sweatpants. Nothing, not even those clothes, could hide the fact that she had a wonderful body.

"Can I come in?" he said.

She jumped as if she had been daydreaming.

"Of course," she said. "Is everything all right?"

"Yes," he said, stepping inside. "Let me take off my boots. I got them muddy."

"That's all right," she said, "can I get you a drink or anything?"

"No," he said.

They stood there looking at each other uncomfortably.

"You look so sad," she said gently, reaching up to put a hand on his shoulder.

Cody's face contorted in pain, and he bit his lower lip.

"They cut me," he said.

"Oh, Cody," she said compassionately, pulling him into a kindhearted hug.

He let his hands fall around her waist. He pulled her tight, and a small sob escaped.

"What happened to my life?" he heard himself say through his tears. "Why am I here?"

Madison looked up at him. She put her hands on his cheeks.

"Shhh," she said. "I'm glad you're here. I'm glad."

Cody looked down at her. She was so kind, and the most beautiful sight he had ever seen. He knew then that so much of his life had been a mistake. Everything for years had been so sick and so wrong. Here was the answer he had always hoped and longed for, a woman who would love him and stand by him; a woman who was strong, yet beautiful and delicate; a woman he could trust to be there whether times were good or bad. He was at the lowest point he had ever been right now, but he knew, from her eyes, that that didn't matter in the least.

Then Cody kissed her. She stiffened only briefly, and then it was as if he had torn down a floodgate of emotion and desire. Madison pulled the shirt out of his pants and ran her hands up and down his torso, groping desperately over every muscle and striation. He pulled his shirt off and put his fingers into her hair. It was thick and soft, and it felt just as he imagined it would.

Madison began backing away from him, slowly moving up the stairs. Each of them was careful not to break the kiss that connected them and electrified them, afraid that if they did, the spell of passion would break and end any hope they had right then and there. They made their way slowly to the top of the stairs and into her bedroom. When they were at the edge of her bed, Cody let his jeans fall to the floor, and he wriggled out of them until he stood there before her wearing nothing at all. Her hands continued to grope his body as if she couldn't feel enough of him at one time. He undid her pants and she twisted out of them, then tore off her T-shirt and threw it to the floor. Cody pressed himself up against her and felt the softness of her burning skin.

Cody hooked his hands around the backs of her thighs and gently lifted her off the floor. It was the first time Madison had had a man in over two years. She turned into a frantic animal, twisting and gyrating wildly with him; every part of her was wrapped tightly around his body, squeezing him like a hungry serpent. Then Cody laid her down on the bed. He arched his back and rose above her on his hands so he could watch as she turned and twisted in ecstasy. He began a slow, steady rhythm that intensified until Madison was moaning wildly, and they both collapsed in the throes of pleasure.

Cody rose up above her, admiring her beauty in the light of the full moon that was shining in across the bed. She was beautiful in a different way than Jenny ever was. Jenny was picture-perfect, alluring, and seductive, like a sexy lingerie ad. Madison was attractive in a wholesome way. Her features weren't sculpted like Jenny's, but she was just as beautiful, if not more. A warmth emanated from her. It was like the difference between a diamond ring and a new puppy. Cody put his hand softly against her cheek, and she smiled without opening her eyes. Madison reached up and pulled him to her, kissing him tenderly on the lips.

"I never felt so good about acting so completely unethical in all my life," she whispered into his ear.

"How is this unethical?" he asked quietly.

"Because sexual relations with a client can get you disbarred. Although I don't think there's ever been a case where the client was a man and the attorney a woman. . . ."

"You amaze me more and more each day," he said.

They lay there quietly together for some time.

"Wait," Madison said, "don't move."

She tore herself away for a moment to get up and set her security system, then she set the alarm clock next to the bed.

"You'll have to leave early," she said apologetically, "before Jo-Jo gets up."

"No problem," he told her. "I'm glad you're letting me stay at all. The last thing I want is to be alone tonight."

Cody found his pants and took a Percoset out of the pocket, swallowing it dry. Madison pulled back the covers and beckoned him to her. He climbed underneath. He lay on his back and Madison snuggled tightly against him, resting her head on his bare chest. They were perfectly still. Each in their own thoughts but sharing the same happiness.

"It seems like everything is all right," he said in a tired voice. "I mean, like you and I have been like this forever, and the world is perfect . . ."

"Right now, it is," she said sleepily.

Cody smiled as the Percoset took effect and the incoming tide of sleep washed slowly over him.

When he drove by and saw that all the lights were off and Cody Grey's truck was still in the driveway, Joe Thurwood screeched to a halt and jumped out of his car with the engine running, right there in the middle of the street. He was halfway up the driveway when he realized he was being stupid. But he was so enraged to see Grey's truck there at three-fifteen in the morning that he was seeing nothing but red. He would smash Grey's bones. He knew that. Not only had Cody lied to him, the son-of-a-bitch was fucking his wife, and doing it with his kid in the house!

Joe walked warily down the driveway and got into his truck. He drove out to the main road and left the truck on the shoulder. He took the bat from the floor of his backseat, then made his way on foot back to the house that had once been his. He crept up the front and into the bushes where he stopped to take a baggy out of his pants and have a snort of powder. He sat down in the dirt to let that settle in. There was something comforting about sitting there in what were once his own bushes. His senses were heightened from the coke. He became increasingly aware of the sights and sounds around him, the smell of the wooden baseball bat resting against his cheek, the crickets screaming in his ears. He started to move, then a car drove down the street. It was unusual for someone to be driving at this time of night. Joe froze in his spot for almost twenty minutes, the paranoia of the drugs holding him there like quick-drying cement.

When he thought it was safe, Joe crept out of the foliage and up to the front door. He took a key from his pocket and slipped it into the lock. He was going in. He turned the key, but it didn't budge.

"Damn!" he cursed, waving the bat in the air. "That bitch! Changed the fucking locks!"

He stood back, preparing to throw his full weight into the door and smash it down. He'd be upstairs and pummeling Cody Grey before he knew what was happening.

"Stupid," Joe said to himself suddenly, stopping before he broke the door.

He began to think. That's what he needed to do, think, not just act. Madison had taught him that over these past two years. She'd taught him that in the outside world, outside of football, you could fuck people up if you only stopped to think carefully about how to do it. If he went in now, he would probably activate the alarm and the cops would come. If he went in now, the noise would wake his son and he'd be scared shitless. If he went in now, he'd fuck up everything he'd worked for over these last few months. His lawyer warned him of that, that he'd only get one second chance.

A thinking man wouldn't make a lot of noise. A thinking man would walk away quietly and come back when it was cool. Cody Grey was here almost every night as far as Joe could tell. He came about nine. He stayed late, but then went home. They worked in Maddy's study. Tomorrow, Joe would be waiting for him. Cody would arrive, and it would be dark. Joe would sneak up behind him, quietly. Joe would leave him in a bloody heap on Maddy's own doorstep. Maddy would worry about him. She'd come to the door and take a look. She'd see him, her boyfriend, smashed to smithereens and oozing blood all over.

Then she would call the police, and they would file a report. Maddy would cry. She would think it was him but wouldn't have a shred of proof. The cops wouldn't care, not as long as he didn't kill him. Grey was going to the can anyway. Then, after he'd gotten his money and was ready to split town, he'd call Maddy and tell her that it was him. Then he'd tell her that he'd be coming for her some day soon. Not too soon, but soon. That would give her something to think about. He knew how she liked to think about things like that. Shit, she couldn't even handle a crank phone call. Joe smiled wickedly and started to back away quietly, looking around nervously through coked-up, bulging eyes. He made a promise to himself. He would be back.

CHAPTER THIRTY-ONE

WHEN THE ALARM WENT OFF AT SIX-THIRTY, Cody had no idea where he was. Then he saw Madison lying there next to him, reaching sleepily to turn off the alarm clock. Cody felt sick. He was sure that she was going to regret what had happened between them last night, but when she turned to face him, she gave him the warm, sunny smile a bride gives to her husband on the morning after their wedding night. "Good morning," she said with a little yawn.

"Hi," Cody said, leaning over to kiss her lightly on the lips.

"I'm glad that wasn't a dream," Madison said.

"Me too," Cody said in a husky voice, running his fingers through her soft hair. "But it would have been a hell of a dream if it was."

"I like those kind of dreams," she said.

It was so strange for Cody to see her like this, with her guard down. She wasn't a lawyer, she was a beautiful woman waking up on a cool fall morning, happy with herself and the man she's slept with. It was so simple, but their lives were so complex.

"You have to go," she said sadly. "I don't want Jo-Jo to see you. He's not ready for that, yet."

"Yet?" Cody said hopefully.

"Yeah," she said, the corners of her mouth turning up just a bit, "I think one day it will be fine. It may take some time, if you want that. . . ."

Cody looked deeply into her eyes. "I want that more than anything."

"Except being acquitted," she said seriously.

"If I can't get acquitted, I can't be with you," he reminded her. "So I guess I'm wishing for both at the same time. It gives you some extra incentive."

"Is that why you came?" she said lightly.

He looked at her lovingly, without speaking for a moment.

"I don't know why I came," he said, as though he was searching for an answer. "But I know that it was the best thing I've ever done. I know I needed you. I needed you more than I ever needed anyone, and you were there. It was like . . . It was like it was meant to be."

"Maybe it was," she said dreamily. "Maybe both of us have suffered long enough. Maybe good people end up together in the end."

"You think I'm a good person?" he said.

She looked intently at him and said, "I know you are, Cody. If you weren't, I wouldn't be here with you like this."

"Well," he said happily, getting out of bed and pulling on his jeans, "I'm off."

"Cody?" she said, sitting up straight in bed.

"Huh?" he said, looking down at her.

"There's something that I want to tell you about."

"Okay."

"I don't want to get your hopes up," she began hesitantly, "but I may have found a man linked to the gun used to kill Board—"

"What?"

"Don't get too excited," she told him. "Nothing is for sure. It's just a possibility."

She told him about Yusef Williams and his claim that he saw the man responsible for the killings in his own case.

"He was with Jenny?" Cody said, his face showing bewilderment.

"I think so," Madison told him. "If Yusef is telling me the truth, and he's right, then Jenny may somehow be involved with this guy. The same caliber bullet that killed Board was found in the wall of the garage where Yusef's friends were murdered. And a twenty-two is not a gang's weapon of choice. I'm having Alice Vreland, from the coroner's office, do a comparison of the slugs today. It may be nothing. Yusef may be mistaken, or it may just be a coincidence. I've got Marty trying to find out who this guy is. He got the license plates yesterday."

Cody sat down on the edge of Madison's bed, still bare to his waist, and stared off into space.

"The thing I can't figure," Madison said, "if I'm right about this whole thing, is what Jenny's connection to Board's death could possibly be."

"The money," Cody said suddenly.

"What money?"

Cody looked at her and said, "That night at the Green Mesquite, Board said something to me about finding my wife's money."

"What did he mean?"

322

"I don't know," Cody said thoughtfully. "I'd forgotten about it. I guess because it didn't make any sense to me at the time. But if Jenny had something to hide . . . I just can't believe she would be involved with someone who would have Board killed. I just can't believe it."

"I hate to say this," Madison said, "but after yesterday, I'd believe anything about Jenny. And if she had something to hide, that may explain her link to the killer. It would certainly explain how he got a hold of your turf shoes."

Cody winced and shook his head, "Yeah, you're right. I guess it's just hard for me to believe someone I've known for so long could be that bad, someone I was, or am, married to. But after yesterday . . . She wants me to go to jail. I just don't know why."

Madison put her hands on his shoulders and massaged them gently. Cody lifted his hand and rested it on hers.

"Maybe it's not that she wants you to go to jail but that she'd rather it be you than her. We don't really know anything yet," Madison said. "I just wanted you to know what's going on."

"If the bullets match," Cody said, "What will you do?"

"Try to find the gun," Madison said.

"Will you tell the police?" Cody asked.

"I don't know," Madison replied. "It would be hard to get the police to get a warrant to search this guy's place based on this convoluted theory and a chance citing by Yusef Williams. It depends on who this guy is. If I could get one of my investigators to snoop around and make sure this guy has the gun, then I'd could get the police to act for sure. Besides, if the bullets match and we don't have the gun, I'm afraid it won't help you any. If we push the issue, Rawlins will just use it to link you to the Yusef Williams case."

"But that wouldn't make sense," Cody said. "Why the hell would I be involved in something like that?"

Madison shrugged and said, "I know that, I'm just telling you what Van will do. Remember, he's promised his voters a conviction. But listen, that's enough of this. We've got a trial to think about. Let's not get too immersed in this until we find out who this guy is and if there's a match. You'd better get going now."

Cody stood up and shook his head, "This whole thing is unbelievable."

"It is what it is. . . . By the way, let's make sure we keep a professional distance in court. The last thing we need is the press, or Rawlins, speculating about a romance."

"No problem," Cody said, pulling on his shirt. "When I walk out of that door, you're Madison McMean, ruthless lawyer and jock-hater. But seriously, I hope your Alice and Marty can find something, Madison. I know you're the best, but this whole trial is killing me. That Hauffler swearing he saw me, and Jenny killing my alibi . . ."

Madison sighed and said, "I know. But it will work out."

Madison saw Cody to the door. They kissed each other before Cody went out to his truck. The phone was ringing. Madison stopped waving and shut the door. She picked it up in the foyer.

"Sorry to call so early," Marty said.

Madison felt a wave of guilt about Cody.

"That's okay, Marty," she said as normally as possible. "I was just about to wake Jo-Jo."

"I didn't want to call you late," Marty explained, "but a friend of mine at the sheriff's office called last night. He ran that license plate. It's not registered to a person. It's in the name of a corporation called Gem Star Technology. The address is a downtown office building on Eighth Street. It's where the offices of Ridley & Shaw are. This morning I called a buddy of mine who works over there, and he couldn't tell me a thing about it. He never heard of Gem Star. So, what do you want me to do? What is this all about, anyway?"

"Marty, can you hang on?" she said. "I want to tell you, but I've got to let Abby out and make sure Jo-Jo is up and going. Hang on."

A few minutes later Madison was back on the phone in the study, with the door shut. She told Marty what Alice had said about comparing the bullets.

"So you think this guy has something to do with both murders?" Marty asked.

"I want to find out who this guy is," Madison replied. "I can't say for sure he's involved with both until Alice checks the ballistics. If it is the same gun, then it's almost certain this guy is somehow involved in both killings if he wasn't the killer himself."

"So what should I do?" Marty asked.

"Find out who this guy is, but that's all," she told him. "If this guy really is the killer, then he's dangerous, Marty, so you steer clear of him. I've got Alice working on getting those bullets and doing a comparison of them today. If they match, and we find the gun, then it might clear both Cody and Yusef. Hell, Marty, if we can find the .22 *and* this guy, this trial will be over."

"I just can't see Jenny having a guy killed to frame Cody so she could divorce him," Marty said. "Where's the connection? It just doesn't fit."

"What about this," she said. "What about her having Board killed for something to do with her. He was investigating them both, wasn't he? I assume they filed together. And those files were destroyed by someone. Why would Jenny's boyfriend bother to destroy those files if it wasn't to protect her?"

"No," Marty said. "It doesn't fit. Board didn't care about Jenny, and she knew it. Cody was taking the fall himself, one hundred percent. He was the one Board wanted, not Jenny."

Madison didn't want to say anything about Jenny's money. She had no way to explain how she'd gotten that knowledge. Instead she was silent for a time before saying, "Maybe we were right all along, Marty. Maybe this guy is from Lopez's organization. Maybe they sent him to get close to Jenny so he could get Cody's shoes and set him up to take the attention away from Lopez. Maybe Yusef's friends were just part of another deal that involved Lopez."

"I don't know," Marty said. "But it sounds like the most plausible scenario yet. Otherwise, there's just no reason for this guy to kill Jeff Board, none that I can imagine."

"Well," Jenny said. "We'll know a lot more after we find out who this guy is."

"So, that's what I'll do," Marty said. "I'll work on it today and see what I can find. Hey, can you pick Cody up for me? I told him I'd drive him."

"Sure," Madison said.

"Are you going to tell him about what's going on?" Marty asked.

"Yes," Madison said. "I'll tell him today, Marty, and thanks, for everything."

"Hey, I'm enjoying this," he said. "I may end up being the hero in this whole thing."

She laughed and said, "I hope so, Marty. But don't do anything risky. If you find where this guy lives, call me, I'll get one of the investigators on it."

"Don't worry about me, I'll call you tonight," Marty said enthusiastically, and then he hung up. One thing was certain. If there was a little danger, he wasn't going to shy away from it. He could see it now; finding this guy out and then running to the firm to get someone else to finish the job, a typical tax lawyer, afraid of his own shadow. Madison's plea only made him more determined to see this thing through to the end.

That morning Van Rawlins called his final witnesses to the stand. They were a couple of psychologists who testified that violent crime among professional athletes has increased, particularly athletes at the tail end of their careers or after their careers were over. The tendency toward violence among these men was undeniable. While this went on, Marty was asking everyone he could find in the office building on Eighth Street just where the offices of Gem Star Technology were. The security guard in the lobby said there was no such business listed there. Marty asked people coming in and going out, but no one had heard of it. He had really given up hope and decided that the whole thing was a ruse; that Gem Star didn't exist but had only been used for the vehicle registration. Outside, he saw a U.S. Postal truck that had just pulled up. Marty dug into his briefcase and found some stationery from his firm. He quickly folded a piece of paper and put it inside an envelope, then scribbled the Gem Star address on it. The postman was pulling mail out of the back of his truck and stashing it in his bag. Marty walked up to him as if he was in a hurry and handed him the letter.

"Could you just drop this for me?" Marty said. "I'm in a hell of a hurry, and it's real important."

The mailman looked at him out of the corner of his eye.

"Get yourself a damn stamp and put it in the box," he snarled.

"Oh, I see," Marty bumbled, "I forgot the stamp, but don't you think you could just take this up with all your other—"

The mailman stopped what he was doing and turned to face Marty. He looked up at him and squinted in the late morning sunlight.

"Look," the mailman said, "what do I look like?"

"You're from New York, right?" Marty said in a friendly way.

"Yeah, I am!" the mailman said. "And what's it to you? This ain't no charity outfit. This is the damn post office. If you want it to get there so bad, why don't you take it up yourself? You got two good legs."

"Well, if you put it that way, I will," Marty huffed.

"Good!" the mailman said, turning back to his mail.

"Uh, just tell me where this office is, will you?" Marty said.

The mailman turned his head, grabbed the letter from Marty, and squinted to read it.

"Gem Star, that's the third floor, last door on the left," he said, and thrust the letter back at Marty.

"Thanks," Marty said and disappeared.

He found a door where the mailman said Gem Star would be. But there was no indication on the door and nothing in the hallway to suggest that it was the correct door. Marty took a deep breath and walked in. He could tell by the look on her face that the thirty-something black woman behind the desk wasn't used to many visitors. Marty simply handed her one of his cards and sat himself down on the small leather sofa against the wall. There was only one other door in the room besides the one he'd come in through, so he knew that Jenny's boyfriend was probably just on the other side.

"I'm Marty Cahn. I have an appointment," he said, looking expectantly at the secretary as though he'd set up this appointment three weeks ago.

"You have an appointment with Mr. Moss?" she said.

"Yes, Mr. David Moss," Marty said, holding out the leather dayplanner he'd produced from his briefcase as proof.

"You mean, Mr. William Moss?" Clara said, mystified.

"Isn't this Ridley & Shaw?" Marty said, as if he'd made some terrible mistake.

Clara shook her head. "No, this is the office of Gem Star Technology. I didn't know Mr. Moss had an appointment. Let me buzz him."

"Oh, no, no," Marty said, holding up his hands for her to put down the phone. "I don't have an appointment with William Moss, I have an appointment with David Moss. He's an attorney with Ridley & Shaw."

"You can't get into Ridley & Shaw from the third floor. You have to go in through the second or the fourth," she explained to him.

"I am so sorry to have troubled you," Marty said, standing hastily to go. "Thank you for your help."

When he was gone, Striker buzzed Clara.

"Who was that in there?" he asked.

"Oh," she said, "just some man who thought he was in Ridley & Shaw. I sent him back down."

"Oh," Striker said, then clicked off.

Rawlins rested his case before the noon adjournment. Madison had her first day's witnesses there at one o'clock. She began to meticulously construct Cody's tenuous defense. She began by calling Patti Short, Jeff Board's boss, to clarify the bizarre nature of the Ricardo Lopez investigation, suggesting that Board may have been involved with that dubious figure. Next, Madison had a detective from the El Paso police department lay out exactly who Ricardo Lopez was and establish that he was certainly capable of orchestrating a conspiracy of the type Madison was suggesting had taken place. It was important that Madison fill in all the details of exactly how and why someone would go to such trouble to frame Cody Grey. Her plan was to establish her theory, then focus on Cody's own story.

Probably tomorrow she would call the bartender who served Cody to suggest that he was too drunk to plan out and commit the kind of crime that had been committed. After that she would build Cody's character up with testimony from members of the communities in which he had volunteered his services. She had a parade of witnesses ready, and by the time she was through, the jury would have a completely different view of Cody Grey than she was certain they had right now. The contrast would be to Cody's advantage. Finally, Madison would call Cody to the stand. It might come as early as Friday. But during the entire proceedings, Madison couldn't help being haunted by the thought that the probable verdict did not look good.

While Madison was questioning Patti Short, Marty was in the county sheriff's office with his friend, Dalton Pollgraft, a sheriff and small-businessman who owned three convenience stores for which Marty did the tax returns every year. Pollgraft was a true Texan with a ten-gallon hat, a cheek full of leaf chew, and a drooping walrus mustache. Marty did the obvious. He called information to learn what he expected, that William Moss had an unlisted number. Pollgraft, Marty knew, had ways of getting around things like that.

"Got yourself a mystery-man, Yankee," Pollgraft drawled as he punched away at his keyboard, using the nickname he'd given Marty upon their first meeting. "But even a mystery-man can't hide in the modern-day world of computers. Gotcha!"

Marty leaned over the terminal and looked on.

"Mr. William Moss," Pollgraft read, "1100 Colorado Street, fancy, apartment 18-G, real fancy, must be a penthouse way up that high. This guy's got some greenbacks."

"Yes," Marty said. "See what else you can find out about him with that computer of yours. How extensive is this network?"

"Hell, Yank, this here is state-of-the-art law enforcement here in Travis County. I can link into every law enforcement agency in the U.S. of A., from the local yokels to the Feds."

"How about the IRS?" Marty asked.

"I need a social security number for that," Pollgraft explained. "Here, this will take a minute. Want a cup of coffee?"

"No thanks," Marty said, sitting back down to wait. They talked about Pollgraft's stores for a few minutes before the heavyset sheriff said, "Here it comes."

"And . . . nothing," Pollgraft said. "William Moss, at that address, doesn't show a damn thing. Sorry, Yankee."

"Well," Marty said, standing up and shaking Pollgraft's thick callused hand, "thanks, Dalton. I appreciate the help."

"Wasn't much help," he said.

"I got the address," Marty said. "That's more than I had."

"What're you gonna do with an address?" Pollgraft asked casually.

"I don't know. Poke around, I guess."

"Well, you be careful pokin'," Pollgraft said. "You ain't a poker by nature. You need some help?"

"Yes," Marty said thoughtfully, "I could use some help, but I don't think it's anything you want to get involved with."

"Then you need my help even more," Pollgraft said.

"I need to get into this guy's apartment," Marty told him.

Pollgraft raised his eyebrows and brought a battered paper coffee cup to his lips to disgorge a wad of spit.

"That's some serious pokin'," he said. "Lot more serious than I thought—"

"I need to get this guy's social security number. I need to see if he's got a certain kind of gun. I . . ." Marty looked at the sheriff sheepishly, "I can't really explain."

"Don't want you to," Pollgraft said. "So you need to git in there, and you need to do it now, no cops, no search warrant or anything messy like that; and you aren't too concerned about a breaking-and-entering charge, huh?"

"I kind of figured you could help me out if there was a problem with that," Marty said hopefully.

"Mmm-hmm." Pollgraft was thinking.

"This is a big favor," Marty said. "Really big. I can't really imagine how I could bill you for this year's return if you helped me with this. No, it just wouldn't seem right to me."

Pollgraft's eyebrows disappeared up under the edges of his sandy brown bangs.

"Well, of course, I can't really tell you how to do something like that, " he said. "But if you did need to get into your own place, or somethin' like that, and no one had any keys . . . well, there's a guy I know, a locksmith, and he's got this little ditty called a coredriller that I'm sure can get you into anywhere."

"Let me see," Pollgraft said, wheeling his chair over to his desk and leafing through his Rolodex. He found the number and picked up the phone.

"Johnny, how the hell are you, son? I've got a favor to ask you. I got a friend o' mine, a damn Yankee," the sheriff drawled, "locked hisself outta his house. He's a cheap sumbitch, Johnny, too stingy to break a damn window, and he won't pay you to go out to his place. But I owe him a favor, an' you owe me, so I want you to lend the sumbitch that core-driller ditty you got there at the shop, an' tell him how to use it, okay? Bet your ass I'll be there Saturday night, you horned-toad bastard. Right. Thanks. Bye."

Pollgraft hung up the phone and wrote Johnny's address down on a piece of paper, handing it Marty with a wink and a smile. "Need a new outboard for my bass boat, Yankee, just about the same price as what it costs me to have you do those damn taxes. So, it's a hell of deal. Just remember this," the Texan warned him, "if you get your ass in a sling an' git caught, don't say a damn thing to the city cops. You just tell them to call me, that's it. I'll see what I can do if the need arises. Don't go gittin' yourself into no hot water trying to play big-shot lawyer, okay?"

"Okay," Marty said, taking the address. "Thanks."

"I don't know a damn thing," the sheriff said, holding his open hands up in the air. "Far as I know, you got yourself locked out, an' you're too cheap to break a window or pay the smithy."

Jenny sat with her ostrich-skin cowboy boots propped up on the air-conditioning unit that sat below the window in her room. She was wearing a faded pair of jeans and a snug-fitting, navy cashmere sweater. Her hair was pulled back tight. The suitcase with two million dollars was right beside her on the floor with her 7mm automatic resting on top of it. The gun was locked and loaded. Her Porsche was parked out back behind a dumpster where it couldn't be seen. She had chosen a room on the second floor facing west. She knew the reflection of the afternoon sun would allow her to see out without letting anyone else see in. She could see the entire parking lot of the Texas Inn, so she'd know for certain when the general arrived, or when anyone else did for that matter. At two, a Mexican couple had pulled in, driving an old Chevy station wagon. The couple appeared to be in their thirties, and they looked fairly innocuous, but Jenny kept a sharp eye on their room anyway. She remembered Striker's words: expect the unexpected. She knew that it was the smallest details that could give away agents posing as tourists or common folk, things like someone peering out of a window repeatedly or a piece of luggage that didn't quite fit.

At four-seventeen, the general's Jeep wheeled up to the office in a cloud of dust. She watched him get out and survey the area furtively from behind a pair of mirrored Ray-Bans. He went into the office and after a few minutes came back out and drove to the parking spot in front of his room. It was on the first floor, and Jenny could see the door and window clearly. She watched with a racing heart as the general took a duffel bag and the case that she knew held the plutonium pit from the back of his Jeep. In another minute he had disappeared inside his room.

Jenny had her feet down now. She leaned toward the window with a pair of field scopes and carefully examined the general's room from the outside. When his face appeared suddenly in the window, she jumped. He scanned the area carefully for several minutes before drawing the shades once more. Jenny used the scopes to scan the rest of the area. There was a gas station across the road and some trees beyond that. She would watch everything around her until dark. Then, like Striker said, if she had a good feeling, she would go down to the general's room and make the switch.

CHAPTER THIRTY-TWO

MARTY SAT IN HIS SILVER FLEETWOOD for half an hour, looking at the luxury apartment building across the street and trying to build up his nerve to go in. The contents of his briefcase lay stacked on the seat beside him. In their place was the core-driller that Johnny had given him. He finally decided that the only way he could get in would be through the parking garage beneath the building. There was a doorman in the front lobby, and Marty preferred not to have to contend with him. If he could get in the garage, he could probably get up the elevator and to the eighteenth floor without any questions from anyone.

Marty exhaled and picked up his car phone. He dialed Madison's home office and got her answering machine. He left a message telling her what he was going to do. This way he figured if he got into any trouble, at least someone would know what happened. Leaving the message gave Marty a new burst of courage and resolve. He got out of his car and crossed the street. He sauntered up and down the sidewalk as purposefully as he could until he saw a woman with a beige Jaguar signaling to turn into the garage. Marty eased up behind her and watched as she ran her card through the sensor. The garage door rose, and the car slowly advanced into the garage. Marty waited until her car had disappeared well inside the garage before he dashed for the door that was beginning to close. He just made it inside and he glanced around frantically, afraid the woman might have seen him. She was just getting out of her car in the back of the garage. Marty ducked behind a fat concrete pillar and waited until the click of her heels faded away.

He made his way toward the middle of the garage and saw that there was a surveillance camera mounted above the two elevator doors. He ducked into a row of cars and crouched down to wait. He only had to wait about ten minutes more before a younger woman in a business suit drove in behind the wheel of a Mercedes sedan. Marty stood at his hiding place and timed it so he arrived at the elevators after the woman had used her elevator key and the doors were just opening. Marty smiled at her and got in. He looked like a tax attorney, the kind of person who belonged in a building like this. The woman got off at twelve, and Marty continued on up to eighteen. His hands were sweating now, and his heart was pumping as if he'd just downed an entire pot of coffee. It was quiet in the hallway; he wondered how much noise the drill would make. He was betting that most of the people who lived on the eighteenth floor would be out at that time, working.

When he stepped off the elevator, his heart sank. There was a short hallway to his left, at the end of which was apartment G; there was a maid's cart in the hallway and the door was open, but Marty had come too far to turn and run now. He calmed himself and listened. A vacuum was running somewhere inside the apartment. Marty looked around the hall, then crept closer to the door. He peered inside. There was no one in sight, and before he could even think about it, he found himself standing upright in a coat closet, his knees shaking as he listened to the maid vacuuming.

After about ten more minutes the vacuum was shut off, and Marty heard the maid clattering around in the kitchen—from the sounds of it, emptying the dishwasher. That didn't take her too long and he heard nothing for some time. Then he heard the rustling of a skirt and the sound of the vacuum being rolled past the closet and out the front door. He heard her load the vacuum and some other things onto the cart, shut the door, and turn the locks from the outside. Marty stood there frozen for almost twenty more minutes before he came out. He looked at his watch. It was quarter to five, and he knew he shouldn't be there too much longer, so he took a quick look around and found the bedroom.

There was a desk that he searched through, being careful not to disturb anything in a way that would let William Moss know he was there. Marty found nothing of any consequence in the desk. He went through the bureau drawers, still nothing. It was three minutes to five. Marty figured the Gem Star offices were ten minutes away on foot and five by car with the heavy traffic. Assuming Moss would leave his offices at five, Marty thought he had about ten minutes more to be safe. He looked briefly through the bathroom, then went into the open clothes closet. There were more drawers there, and he looked but still found nothing. It was strange. There were no papers of any kind anywhere, he could see. Most people had something. Here, there wasn't even any old mail to be checked over. He thought about where he kept his own mail, in the kitchen. He started out of the bedroom then stopped when he was halfway out the door. Behind a sitting chair by the foot of the bed was the outline of a closet, set flush into the wall. Marty moved the chair and a lamp and found a small gold ring in the door. He pulled at the ring and then turned it. It was locked. Marty was certain that whatever he needed to find was behind that door. Just below the ring was a keyhole. Marty could feel the outline of a deadbolt tumbler through the wallpaper. He hurried to the hallway and returned with his briefcase. He took out the coredriller, placed its bit against the tumbler, and pulled the trigger. He hit the jackpot.

Marty pushed his glasses up nervously and tried to swallow. His throat had gone dry as a desert. There, right on the back of the door, was a mini-arsenal, the likes of which Marty never knew even existed. There were exotic machine pistols, a chrome-plated gun with a laser scope, and many small arms. In the middle of the whole conglomeration was a long black pistol. Its grip was coated with a sticky substance that Marty suspected would leave no fingerprints. He picked it up and looked at the barrel. It was a smaller caliber than the rest, he guessed it was the .22 Madison had told him to look for. Marty tried to think of what to do. He looked at his watch. It was three minutes after five. He had to go. He hesitated for another couple of seconds, trying to decide if he should just take the gun or leave it and come back with the police. Then he heard the front door open.

Striker walked into his apartment and knew immediately from the smell that the maid had been there. That was good. He liked cleanliness. He hung his coat in the closet and took off his jacket, tossing it on the back of the couch in his living room before going over to the wet bar to pour himself a drink. He poured three fingers of good scotch and put on a CD of Strauss waltzes. He sat down in his favorite leather chair and drank his scotch slowly while he listened to the entire disk.

When it was over he refilled his glass, and then, drink in hand, he picked up his jacket and headed down the hall to his bedroom. He froze in the doorway and his eyes shot around the room with the trained awareness of a guard dog. The carpet had been vacuumed, but crisscrossing through the room were the footprints of a pair of men's dress shoes. They led to his closet and didn't come out. The chair had been hurriedly put back; he could see the marks in the carpet where it had been moved, and it wasn't quite in its original spot.

Striker set his jacket and drink down quietly on the floor and took off his shoes and socks so he wouldn't slip on the carpet if he needed his footing. Carefully, without making any noise, he pulled the chair away from the door so he could pull it wide open. He could see where the lock had been bored out. With his Beretta in one hand, Striker crouched down beside the door, setting on the floor a pillow he'd taken from the chair beside him. Then he reached up and jerked open the door. The door slammed against the wall with a crash, and Striker quickly snatched up the pillow and whipped it straight into the closet at what he figured was eye level with a full-grown man. Then he darted into the doorway, still in his crouch, aiming the gun up at a man's chest.

"Don't move!" Striker commanded.

The pillow had caught whoever was there off guard, and by the time he had recovered, Striker's weapon was aimed at his heart. The intruder had Lucy in his left hand, and Striker could tell by the way he was holding her that he didn't have a clue.

"Drop the gun," Striker said calmly. A professional would have either dropped it by now or tried to shoot him. Striker knew that one of the most dangerous things you could deal with was a novice; he would be unpredictable, and that could get even the best agent killed. So Striker didn't want to shake him up.

The man looked at him and, trembling, dropped Lucy to the carpet. Striker kept his gun aimed at the man's chest. He was tall and lanky, about six foot four with thick glasses and a balding head. He looked like an accountant, not an agent or a cop. When he was within striking distance, Striker threw a blade kick to the man's groin, doubling him over, then boxed his ears to disorient him. Striker stuck the Beretta in the back waistband pants, and then carefully, so as not to kill him, he took the man's head in both hands and popped him underneath the chin with his knee, driving the man's jawbone back into his skull. The shock left him in an unconscious heap on the floor. Striker kept one eye on the inert figure while he felt around on the shelf right above him for a fat roll of gray duct tape. He found it, then knelt down with his knee in the man's back and started taping.

When Marty failed to show up at the courthouse after the trial had adjourned for the day, Madison was more excited than she was worried. She figured he was hard at work. She tried to get ahold of Alice from her car phone but couldn't. Then Madison called Lucia to tell her to go ahead with dinner and have Jo-Jo get ready for bed. Then she asked to speak to her son.

"I've got some extra work I have to get done tonight," she told her son as she looked over at Cody and smiled. She wasn't really lying. Cody was still her client and the top priority in her legal career at the moment. If Marty wasn't going to be there, she wasn't going to let him eat dinner alone. She wasn't going to bring him home to her house yet, either. The best thing to do was simply to have something with Cody, then go home and put Jo-Jo to bed. Cody could go to his house and change his clothes, then meet her later. They could go over his testimony one final time and then afterward, well, that would take care of itself. There would be an afterward, though. She knew that, and just the thought excited her.

"Get all your homework done," she said, "and get everything ready for bed, Jo-Jo, so when I get home I can help you with any problems you need help with, and then we can spend the rest of the time before bed playing on your computer, or reading, whatever you want."

"When will you be home, mom?" he asked.

"I'll make sure I'm back by seven-thirty." Then, as an afterthought, she said, "I'll let you stay up an extra half hour tonight too. How's that sound?"

"Wow! Great, mom! Thanks!" Jo-Jo said.

Madison wished the entire world was as easy to please as an eight-year-old boy.

"I've only got until seven," Madison told Cody when she hung up the phone.

"I feel bad . . . taking you away from Jo-Jo like this," Cody said. "You really don't have to. If you just want to drop me off home, I can fend for myself."

"That's all right," Madison said. "I wouldn't want you to eat alone."

"I don't mind eating alone," he said.

"Well, I can't stand it," she told him. "Besides, we're almost there. We'll eat, I'll drop you off, and then I'll go home. I want to have dinner with you."

Madison took him to Chiang Juang's for Chinese food. There was a booth in the back where they could sit undisturbed. She knew the people who worked there wouldn't know a football player if he fell on them; and even if they had seen Cody on the news, they would be too shy to make any kind of scene.

"So," he said after they'd ordered, "what do you think about Marty?"

Madison shrugged and said, "He must be on to something. Marty's like that. When he gets into a project, he'll just keep digging until he finds the answer, like with the Lopez stuff."

"What about the trial," Cody said, "how do you think that's going?"

"I knew you were going to ask that," she said.

"Why? Because I haven't asked it in five minutes?"

She looked at him seriously and reached across the table for his hand.

"I want to tell you that it's in the bag," she said quietly. "I want to tell you that more than anything in the world. I'd give everything I have except my son to have that jury acquit you. If they don't, I don't know what I'll do. I don't . . .

"But the truth is," Madison continued, "that a jury is the most unpredictable thing in the world. People settle cases for millions of dollars in order not to face a jury and take a chance. There are no rules. There's no rhyme or reason."

"We've got to have good odds," Cody said with a hopeful smile. "I mean, with you and everything . . ."

"Don't say it like that, Cody," she said, wincing at his words. "I'm not the answer. I'm a good lawyer; yes, I am. But the case against us is bad. It's very bad, I'll be honest."

"But you've been killing their witnesses. You make them look so bad. Look what you did to Jenny. I thought she was going to come over that railing and try to tear your eyes out. Look what you did to Hauffler, all those other cases you threw in his face. The jury's got to believe us!" he said, squeezing her hand.

"We can win," she said, "don't get me wrong. I just don't want you to stand there in shock if they give us a guilty verdict and the bailiff steps up to lead you away. I want you to be ready. It could happen but I don't want it to. . . . I don't know. I just want you to be ready.

"Believe me," she told him, "it would be so much easier for me to just talk about how good everything is and how we should win this, and then if we lose, they take you away and I feel bad, but my life goes on. But that's not how it can be . . . I love you, Cody. I do. I know that might sound strange. In a way we don't even know each other. But in another way I feel like I've known you all my life."

Cody looked at her without saying a word. He just held her hand and wished with all his heart he had met her, somehow, years ago.

"The day I saw you at the jail, I felt it then, something," she said. "I fought it. Oh, I fought it hard. I wanted to hate you. You were everything I thought I hated. You were like another Joe Thurwood to me. Then, over the past two months, I couldn't help but see that on the inside you were the furthest thing from Joe Thurwood a man could be. And that makes me love you even more, the fact that you can be so hard and so tough and so handsome, but at the same time, good and gentle and kind."

They sat quietly looking at each other for a few moments before Cody said, "Thank you, Madison. Thank you. I feel the same way about you. I'm so confused and lost right now that I almost can't believe you're real. It's like while my whole world is being destroyed around me, I finally found the one thing I always wanted, but the one thing I never had. It makes me think that maybe that's why I've been so angry for so long, at least angry some of the time, when I play football, when I fight. So I just can't believe anything except that the jury will see the truth and let me go. I don't see how they couldn't. I'm too close to having you. I finally know what it is that I want and what it is that I need, and I've found out that you want me too?"

Madison was crying silently now. The food arrived. The girl noticed Madison's tears, so she set everything down quickly and left. Steam rose up from the blue-and-white porcelain bowls filled with soup and the egg rolls that sat on smaller, matching plates.

Madison was crying because she'd seen it before. She'd seen people believe before. She'd seen their hopes be placed in her skill, seen them believe that God would never send them away for a life of agony in a prison full of animals. But it happened—not often, but it did. If the evidence was against you, the jury just might send you away. Madison had never had a case where she was so totally convinced that her client was innocent and the hard evidence was so heavily weighted against him.

"I just don't want to lose you," she whispered.

Cody leaned across the table and kissed her softly on the lips.

"You won't," he said quietly. "Something will happen. Marty will find this guy. Maybe the bullets will even match. Hey, if not, I'll get on that stand tomorrow or Friday and I'll show them. They'll believe me, Madison. They will."

Striker knew that you couldn't hurry an interrogation. He'd seen North Vietnamese officers tear the fingernails out of every finger and toe, sending the victim into shock that sometimes took hours to bring them out of. The inexperienced interrogator would inevitably get frustrated and mad and end up killing his prisoner without learning a thing. Striker had also watched master interrogators within the agency extract information from the most hardened and ruthless people imaginable in a matter of hours. The anticipation of physical suffering, not necessarily physical suffering itself, was what caused most people to break. The body had mechanisms for dealing with pain, shutting it off, but the mind did not.

When Marty came to, he found himself naked and facedown on top of Striker's bed. He was hog-tied and soaking wet. Striker knew from his wallet that his visitor's name was Marty Cahn and that he was a lawyer. It was easy to make the connection with Madison McCall, then check the yellow pages and find that she was a member of his law firm.

Marty began to struggle and moan as soon as he realized where he was. His hands and feet were bound tightly behind his back with tape, and his legs were pulled up and secured to his wrists with more tape. A rubber ball filled his entire mouth, making it impossible for him to scream, bite, or swallow his tongue. The ball was secured with a band of tape that circled his head but still allowed him to see and breathe through his nose.

Striker had a large twelve-volt flashlight battery on the floor with two long wires coming out of it. One he had attached to a metal bolt that he'd inserted into Marty's rectum while he was unconscious. He held the end of the other wire with a pair of needle-nosed pliers whose handles were insulated with rubber. He jammed the pliers into Marty's ear until his body started to tremble and smoke. That settled him down a bit, and Striker was ready to go to work. He had a lot of questions to ask, but he wouldn't even ask his first question for another hour. First he would do what was necessary to get Marty in the right frame of mind.

Joe waited until the sun went down before he left his Blazer and walked to the house. He didn't want to sit around forever in the bushes, but he didn't want to miss Cody Grey, either. He had plenty of snort to keep going, so he wasn't worried about not being able to hold up even though he hadn't had more than three hours sleep today. While he sat, Joe began thinking about Madison. In order to help keep himself under control, he'd made a promise to himself that before he left for New Orleans, he'd have her one last time. He would drug her and take her where he could really work on her. He'd leave the bitch with a fucking she'd never forget. That's what he promised.

He started thinking about New Orleans and the good life he'd have there, no more bullshitting around. That city was the big-time for him. Not for the first time, he thought about simply taking off. Fuck his lawyer; he didn't give a shit about that rat turd. The money he would like, but it was pissing him off that it was taking so long. He figured the bitch would have tossed an easy six figures out on the table by now, but they weren't even close. Maybe he'd just give her her fucking and bolt, go to New Orleans and get on with it. He could pop his long-haired boss for a couple of grand just by keeping the stash he'd collected today. That would be enough to get him there and buy him a new suit. Yes, maybe that was the way to go. The car and the apartment he wanted could come later. Well, he'd have to see what happened tonight. If he pounded the hell out of Cody Grey without a hitch, maybe he'd stay. If the shit went bad, though, he'd rape his ex-wife and then blow town. That was a good way to do it. Let fate determine where he would be tomorrow.

Inside the house, Madison finally got Jo-Jo off to bed. She thanked Lucia and sent her off to bed as well, then picked up the paper and made her way down the hall into her office. The light on her answering machine was blinking, and she sat down at her desk to listen to her messages. There were two. She hoped one was Alice, and it was.

"Honey," came the voice from the machine, "I'd say we got ourselves a mystery here. I checked these two bullets, and there's no doubt they came from the same gun. I got the slug back to the D.A.'s vault already, so no one except my friend knows . . . I hope this helps. Let me know if you need any more help, honey. Bye."

Madison clicked off the machine and jumped to her feet, she was so giddy with excitement. She dialed Marty's house and let the phone ring a dozen times before she tried him at the office. She finally gave up and called Cody.

"The bullets match," she told him the instant he picked up the phone.

"Madison," he said, "that's great!"

"I know," she said. "Now when we find out who this guy is, we can go from there. But I've got a feeling, Cody. I think this whole thing is going to blow wide open."

"God, Madison!" Cody said. "My God. Thank you so much."

"I didn't do it yet," she said, "but maybe. I've really got a feeling."

"Should I come over?"

"Yes," she said, "come. We need to work on your testimony anyway. I'd try to get an adjournment, but I know Rawlins and Walter Connack wouldn't go for it."

"I'll be there in a little," Cody told her.

When she'd hung up, Madison tried Marty again, wringing her hands the whole time. She gave up and sat back down, trying to calm herself. She should get her papers ready for Cody, and she still wanted to take a shower. Then she realized that the light was still blinking on her machine. Someone had left another message.

"Madison, hi. It's Marty. I found the guy. His name is William Moss. He lives at 1100 Colorado Street, downtown, in apartment 18-G. I'm outside the building now, and I'm going to go in and check it out. I know you told me not to, but someone has to, and I can do it just as well as anyone. Don't worry, I had someone give me some help on getting in. I'll see what I can find, and hopefully I'll see you later tonight. Bye."

"Oh, my God," Madison said. She yanked the phone from its receiver and dialed Cody.

"Listen," Cody told her, "just calm down. I'm sure everything's fine, Madison. I'm sure Marty is fine."

"But I haven't heard from him!" she was near hysterical. "This man is a killer, Cody, and Marty was going in there!"

"Hey," Cody said, "this guy may not even be around. He's probably somewhere around town with my wife. Listen. Relax. I'm out the door now. I'll go downtown and check it out. You wait there and don't do a thing."

"Should I call the police?" she said.

"And tell them what?" Cody replied. "Let's just see what's going on. I'll check it out and call you from there. Marty will probably call you before I do. Okay, let me run."

"Go," Madison said. "I love you."

"I love you too," he said, and then he was gone.

342

CHAPTER THIRTY-THREE

EVEN THOUGH HE WAS NEARLY INAUDIBLE, Marty was crying uncontrollably. His body was limp. Every ounce of energy was gone, drained from the shock waves of pain that had racked his body for what seemed like forever. His mind drifted into a moment of clarity, and he realized he'd never known what pain was before. He never knew unending pain existed. He only hoped Moss would kill him. He didn't want this. Death would be a welcome reprieve. It seemed so simple, so peaceful. Marty felt the pliers touch the skin in his armpit and his body was wracked again with the burning shock that tortured his entire body. He welcomed the smell of his own flesh burning because he knew it meant that soon the shock would stop, and it did.

His mouth worked slowly. He was thirsty beyond description. Moss had taken the ball out of his mouth a while ago. By then he was beyond the point of screaming, and Moss seemed to know it.

"So there is no one else who knows?" Moss was saying for what seemed like the tenth time. His voice seemed to come out of nowhere. It was a soothing voice, a voice Marty had come to love. When he heard the voice, he knew there was no pain. It was only when the voice stopped that he knew it was coming. That was the pattern. It hadn't taken him long to learn it. Nothing left an impression quite like wave after wave of excruciating pain.

"No," Marty whispered. Then he was struck again with another moment of lucidity and remembered telling Moss about Pollgraft and Madison. How could he have told about Madison! In his mind he could still hear the flipping of pages as Moss went through the phone book looking for what Marty knew, even in his state of shock, was Madison's home address.

Tears from some unknown source in his completely dehydrated body began to stream down his face once more.

"I believe you now," he heard Moss whisper suddenly. He smiled. He wanted Moss to believe him.

When Marty felt the barrel of the gun poking gently at his lips, he knew what it meant. He was sad, but he didn't even bother to struggle; he was afraid that if he did, the talking would stop again, and then . . .

He never heard the sickening, muffled spit of the .22.

Striker was about as angry as he had let himself be in a long time. He knew from Marty that the whole thing had been caused by the fucked-up thing he'd done months ago, totally unrelated to the operation. Well, damn it, he told himself, he certainly deserved it. He deserved it if the cops came blowing through his door and shot him dead where he stood right here and now. It was so stupid to get involved in someone's personal life, and it was totally uncharacteristic. He didn't care about anyone. Who the hell had he thought he was, getting involved with Clara and her son? He knew better. He'd known better than that for a long time. Now he was going to have to kill two people in one night, and not quickly either. He had to find just how far the word had spread about him. If the cop had told his wife, she'd have to go too. If the lawyer told the judge . . .

"Damn!" Striker said, jabbing Marty's corpse angrily with the butt of his pistol. If too many people knew about the killings, he'd be forced to take the pit and run. That could possibly cost him the nine million he would get from Jamir. He was not an easy man to make contact with. No one knew exactly who he was or with whom he did his business. Taking and delivering coded messages from his office was an essential link in the intricate network necessary to communicate with him. If Striker tried to reestablish communications any other way, Jamir might think it was a trap. The procedure had been prearranged; there had never been any reason for Striker to believe that there would be any difficulty whatsoever in staying right here where he was until the deal was complete.

And he had this mess to clean up as well. Well, the maid had been in already today, so he didn't have to worry about anyone coming. He'd just have to leave this and see if he could get the other things straightened out before daylight. He looked at his watch; it was 9:15.

Cody raced through the streets of Austin and pulled up into the circular drive at 1100 Colorado Street. His heart began to race. He'd seen Marty's silver Fleetwood on the opposite side of the street as he pulled in. He hopped out of his truck and went in. The doorman looked up pleasantly at him from his desk.

"Hi," Cody said with a nervous wave, as if he had every right in the world to walk into the building and proceed upstairs. He had no intention of stopping to talk or to answer any questions. Marty's car meant Marty was here either going through the killer's apartment or snared by the killer himself.

"Excuse me," the doorman said, leaning across the side of the desk to address Cody as he stepped onto the elevator. "Can I help you? I need to announce you, sir."

Cody stepped onto the elevator and punched number eighteen before he turned to face the doorman.

"It's okay," Cody said with a calm, knowing smile and a wink, "I'm Cody Grey."

Cody could see instant recognition as well as befuddlement on the young doorman's face as the doors closed. Just before he was blocked from sight, Cody was sure he saw the man give him a half-smile and a nod. Everything was fine. He was a celebrity, and that meant he was always welcome. Besides, Cody acted like he'd done this before.

In truth, Cody thought to himself as he shot upward, he didn't care if the guy followed him or even called the police. Something wasn't right. Cody knew that for certain. The more he thought about it, the more nervous it made him. Cody's adrenaline carried him down the hall to 18-G. He paused briefly in front of the door, wondering what in hell he should do now. He knocked. There was no answer. Cody felt the rush of adrenaline that made him feel like it was ten minutes before kickoff in a big game. He knocked again and listened. Nothing. He looked around. There was no sign of another person on the entire floor. Cody rocked back and with his good leg kicked the door as hard as he could. The noise seemed incredible, but the door didn't budge. This only gave him an added boost of adrenaline. He reared back again, this time aiming carefully for the part of the door closest to the knob. The door burst inward with a splintering crash, and Cody raced inside.

"Marty?" he yelled, truly scared now. "Marty! It's me! Cody! Are you in here!"

Cody wanted to find his friend and get out. He didn't want to be here when the owner returned or if the police showed up. He dashed through the unfamiliar apartment. When he burst through the bedroom door, he froze.

"Oh, no," he said out loud. "Oh, God, no! Marty."

Slowly Cody approached the bed, as if he were sneaking up on a wounded wild animal.

"Marty," he whispered, touching his agent on his bare shoulder. It was cold. Cody realized Marty was lying in a pool of his own blood. He could see where it had leaked from his mouth and out onto the bed, soaking the white sheet. Marty's eyes were open, but he was clearly dead. There was a chair beside him as if there had been a priest present, administering last rites. Beside Marty and the white sheet, the bed was bare. A battery lying at the foot of the chair had orange wires connected to Marty in a bizarre way.

Cody's eyes drifted instinctively to the phone book that lay open on the night table next to the bed. Amidst this carnage, the book meant something. That was as clear to Cody as if he'd heard a voice telling him so. Cody looked down at the book.

He jumped for the phone almost before the realization became a conscious thought. The book was open to the page where Madison's address and number could be found. Cody dialed frantically. He got a busy signal. He tried again and cursed out loud at another busy signal. She had two lines. He called her office phone. It was busy too. That was impossible. He called the operator. He told her it was an emergency. He needed to break through on the line.

"I'm sorry, sir," the operator said pleasantly, "there seems to be a problem with both of those lines. Would you like me to call customer service?"

Cody dropped the phone and ran.

Striker drove past the house that was listed as belonging to Madison McCall. Striker knew how Marty felt about the female attorney. Striker could always tell the sentiments a man had for the people he was tortured to talk about. People a man loved required a level of pain and psychological manipulation that was ten times that of someone for whom they had no real feelings. Pollgraft, for instance, hadn't been difficult at all compared to the pain he had to deliver to get Marty to talk about Madison. Striker kept going down the street in his Pontiac until he found a dead end off the main road with a vacant lot between two large houses. He backed the old car up off the road and barreled slowly into the brush, making as little noise as possible. When he got out he was careful to close the door without more than a subtle clicking sound.

Striker looked carefully around to make sure no one had been watching him, then set out down the street wearing a dark green sweat suit as if he was one of the neighbors going out for an evening stroll. He knew better than to skulk around the bushes. When he got to Madison's house, he simply turned up the driveway like he was paying her a visit. When he got to where there was some foliage, he turned slowly to scan the area before he darted into the shadows. He quickly found the phone box, and with a tool from his pocket he jimmied it open and cut the lines. That done, he walked back toward the driveway. He stopped on the edge of the shadows to carefully study his surroundings. He was looking for neighbors walking their dogs or taking a jog. He was concerned with the house diagonally across the street that had a view of Madison's doorstep, but after a careful assessment, he presumed they weren't home. Everything else looked quiet, so he crossed the driveway and started up the walk. As he was climbing the steps, Striker sensed some movement behind him, and he spun instinctively, ducking at the same time.

Joe's bat hit Striker level with his waistline, shattering the tip of his hip bone. This knocked Striker sideways to the ground. He rolled with it and came up in a crouch despite the pain in his hip. Joe was too quick for him to avoid the next blow either. He had redirected with Striker and was smart enough to swing the bat in an arc that was parallel to the ground and stood a much better chance of connecting than a swing that came straight down. The bat caught Striker in his left shoulder, knocking it painfully out of its socket and sending him sprawling again.

Striker didn't bother trying to rise, he dug his fingers into the mulch bed where he lay and advanced toward his attacker on his belly, like a lizard. He got to Joe's feet when the third blow hit his buttocks, doing little damage. Striker pushed and then yanked Joe's left ankle, sending the bigger man into the air. He flipped his hands over like a car in a high-speed crash, keeping his hold on Joe's foot and snapping the bones and ligaments in his ankle with the crack of a woodsplitter. By the time Joe's body hit the ground, Striker was within reach of his groin, and he grabbed his testicles with an iron grip and yanked down hard. Joe saw stars and lost his breath.

Striker used his grip on Joe's groin to pull himself forward. He got his other hand high enough to hook a finger behind Joe's eyeball and yank it out of its socket with a bizarre sucking sound. Joe let out a primal roar when he felt the eye being ripped from his skull. During the fall Joe lost the bat, but it fell fortuitously beside him. He grabbed it by the fat end and slammed it like a pool cue into the side of Striker's head, knocking him senseless.

Joe pushed the limp body of the man he still thought was Cody Grey off from on top of him. He stood uncertainly, his legs still weak from the damage done to his groin. He dropped the bat, grabbing for his face and whining in a high-pitched voice that sounded nothing like his own.

"My eye, my eye, oh, my fucking, my fucking eye!"

He felt it, a slippery oblong superball, hanging by what was left of his optic nerve, dangling against his cheek. He heard the high-pitched spitting sound of the twenty-two as the bullet ripped through his chin and tore through his nasal cavity, lodging in his septum. It made Joe dizzy immediately, and he staggered backward, choking on the blood that gushed down his throat. The next bullet hit him square in the chest, piercing the left ventricle of his heart and sitting him down hard on the concrete walk. The final shot he never felt. It struck him between the eyes, killing him instantly.

Joe's body fell backward and the front door opened at the same time. In the split second it took the woman to realize what had happened, and before she could scream, Striker pulled the trigger again, hitting her between the eyes as well. Abby raced through the doorway over the fallen body with her teeth bared and snarling. Striker shot the dog. He kept his gun raised at the ready. He was laying on his belly, half on and half off the walkway. Along with his hip and shoulder, blood was now flowing steadily from his ear. He struggled to his feet. The world spun for a moment, and Striker was afraid he might lose consciousness again. As quickly as he could, he moved carefully toward the open door.

The Mexican couple's lights had gone out a half hour ago, and they hadn't shown any sign of life since. Jenny felt she'd waited long enough. Striker told her to act on her feelings and not worry. "If he was going to cross me," he had explained, "it would probably have happened already. Probably with the first pit. Relax. Be ice. He's like a mean dog; he won't fuck with you if you look him square in the eyes."

Jenny pulled on her jeans jacket, then stuck the pistol into her pants and hefted the suitcase. She opened the door and looked around carefully one last time. When she got to the general's door, she took a deep breath before knocking twice. The door opened wide, and there he stood with a leering grin. He peered past her as if he expected that Striker might have come after all.

"Come right in, little Lucy," he said, closing the door behind her with one last glance out the door. "Oh, I know that's not your name. That's just what Striker likes to call his women, after the real Lucy of course."

Jenny looked at him coldly, showing no emotion, but the remark had hit its target. She couldn't help herself from wondering how this man knew about the first Lucy and how many other Lucys there'd been.

The general was chuckling to himself now; his eyes roving up and down her body with a freedom he hadn't enjoyed the last time they'd met, when Striker was there. Jenny hoisted the suitcase onto the bed.

"Let's get this over with," she said with contempt.

"Oh, why?" the general said with mock disappointment. "Don't you want to give me any of that poon you've been dishing out to our friend Striker? Hasn't he shared you with any of his associates yet?"

"You're a pig, old man," Jenny said with a snarl. "Where's the pit?"

"Oh, where's the pit?" the general said, mocking her. "Let's see the money, cheesecake, then you'll see the pit."

Jenny stared coolly at him for a moment, just to show him that she wasn't jumpy. Although his comments about Striker were having some effect on her, she wasn't about to let it show. She reached down and popped open the suitcase, revealing wad after wad of hundred-dollar bills packed tightly in the case. The general stepped over to the bed and picked up a few random stacks, leafing through them as Striker had predicted he might.

"It's all here, huh?" the general said with an evil look.

"Why don't you count it," Jenny said sarcastically. She was inwardly delighted that she had lifted two ten-thousand-dollar packets and stuffed them underneath the driver's seat of her Porsche, despite Striker's warning. She knew there was really no way the general would be able to tell, and it wasn't enough to bother with even if he could, but it was something. Even if it was only in a small way, she was fucking him, and that's what counted.

The general didn't say anything. He went around to the opposite side of the bed and lifted the metallic case from the space between the bed and the wall. He set the case on the bed between them and opened it. He reached inside but instead of the pit, the general extracted a snub-nosed .38. He pointed the gun at her chest. Jenny smiled in disbelief, like it was a bad joke. The general wasn't joking.

"Get that fucking smile off your face, you cunt!" he bellowed, coming from behind the bed and pistol-whipping her face to let her know he meant business.

Jenny didn't think about the gun in her own pants until the general yanked her head up by the hair and jammed the barrel of the .38 up under her chin.

"Oh, I'm gonna teach you a few things, you little cunt," he whispered into her ear. She could smell the stench of onions and liver on his breath. The smell and her fear made her think she would vomit. "You don't play in the boy's sandbox unless you're ready to get fucked!

"Now," he snarled, "I'm real nervous, you hear me? I don't want you to make a fucking noise. I don't want you to make a cockeyed move. I don't want you to do anything but what the fuck I say, and then you make sure you know what I said. We're walking out of here, you and I. You're going to shut both these cases and pick them up, then you're going to walk out of here with me right behind you. You'll get into the front seat of my Jeep on the driver's side and slide across. The fucking gun will be aimed at your guts the whole time. You got that, bitch?"

Jenny nodded her head and bit the inside of her lip to keep from blubbering. She fought to control herself. If she could control herself, she might get a chance. That's what Striker would do, wait for a chance. If she got it, she would kill him. She would look into his eyes and watch him die. She had no way of knowing then that she wasn't going to get that chance.

Madison was in the shower. She had to get clean, and she had to do what she could to calm down. The hot water helped. She never heard Joe's wail of agony as he groped for his dangling eye. Cody was probably right, she thought. He'd find Marty, and everything would be fine. She had to just relax. She had briefly gone over her plan for Cody's testimony, but was unable to concentrate. Lucia was cleaning the kitchen, and Madison asked her to stay there and answer any phone calls until she got out of the shower because, she admitted to herself, ever since the recent incidents with Joe, she didn't feel safe in the shower anymore unless it was daytime or someone was standing guard. When she got out she dried off, then took two towels off of the towel-warmer and wrapped one around her head and the other around her body.

She pushed her feet into her slippers and pumped some moisturizing cream onto her hand. She assessed herself in the mirror as she rubbed the cream into her face. There was the faintest hint of lines at the corners of her eyes, and she wondered if Cody knew she was at least three years older than he was and if it would matter. She couldn't stop herself from thinking that way. She truly believed now that with Alice's match of the ballistics that Cody would be exonerated. They could come out of this and maybe have a life together. A sigh escaped her and she spun around.

She thought she'd heard something in her bedroom.

"Lucia?" she said, stepping warily to the door and putting her ear against it. There was nothing.

Slowly she opened the door and peered out into her bedroom.

"Come out."

Madison shrieked and jumped backward, slamming the door shut and fitfully pushing the lock. It was quiet.

"Come out," the voice said. "I've got your boy."

"Jo-Jo?" Madison cried. "Jo-Jo?"

"He can't speak at the moment," the voice said, "but I'm sure he'll be happier when he sees your face."

Madison stepped back into the bathroom, reaching quietly with a trembling hand into the water closet where there was a phone on the wall. She picked it up. It was dead.

"I'm getting impatient. I'd hate to have to hurt him."

Madison opened the door and stepped out into her bedroom. Jo-Jo lay face down on her bed, knotted up tightly with the sleeves of two of his own sweatshirts. A pair of socks were stuffed into his mouth, fastened down with a third sweatshirt. He was straining his head up to see her, and his eyes bulged so far out that she thought he was being strangled.

"Jo-Jo!" she cried, "Oh, oh, oh, God, no . . ."

The man was sitting next to her son on the bed. Half of his face was covered in blood that continued to spill from his ear. He looked like he'd walked out of a horror show. The white comforter that covered her bed was stained crimson, and there was a trail across the carpet to the bed.

"Sit down," he said tiredly, "right where you are. On the floor where I can see you. We have to talk."

Madison realized it was Jenny's boyfriend. The gun he held, she imagined, was the same one he had used to shoot Ramon Gustava and Jeff Board. She knew that he was going to kill her. She couldn't let herself think that he would kill Jo-Jo too, but the thought pounded wildly against the closed door in her mind. She fought to keep from being completely hysterical. She could see that her crying was scaring her son even more than he already was.

"What do you want?" she begged, looking up at him through her tears, wiping them dry in an attempt to get herself under control.

"Who else knows?" he said. His eyes closed briefly and then opened.

Madison thought he might pass out. If she could stall him, she had a chance.

351

"What do you mean?" she said.

Striker shook his head and said, "Oh, no, don't you do that to me."

He raised the gun and shot Jo-Jo.

Madison let out a wailing scream and jumped up off the floor to go to her son.

"Stop!" he commanded. "The next one goes in his head!"

Jo-Jo was thrashing on the bed. The bullet had gone through his forearm. When he saw the blood he fainted. Madison froze halfway across the bedroom. The gun was pointed at Jo-Jo's head.

"No one," she said. "I only told Marty. The boy, the boy you made shoot the others. He saw you . . . No one knows. My son doesn't know anything. You've got to let—"

"Shut up!" he screamed. He was trying to think. His head was pounding and the room was starting to spin. He closed his eyes for an instant. When he did, Cody Grey sprang from the hallway.

Jenny was bent over the hood of the general's Jeep. She had nothing on but her boots. The general had her put the boots back on as an afterthought. The general had been worried more than anything that he was going to be killed by Striker as he walked away from the motel. He used Jenny as a shield, then took her to an abandoned meadow down a dirt road off of Route 16 that he'd found on his way into Goldthwaite that afternoon.

"You're gonna get the pit," he had told her at gun point, calmer now because he was certain they hadn't been followed.

"I'm gonna give it to you," he had told her. "But first I'm gonna fuck you good, like you want to be fucked. So start taking those clothes off before I get antsy and just gut shoot you for the fuck of it."

"You see," he explained, his eyes greedily upon her as she undressed in the moonlight beside the Jeep, "I know there's only one thing Striker would come back to me for, that's the pit. I have no doubt that he would find me and kill me if I screwed him on that. So I won't. But I can screw you. He won't like it, but he won't risk his ass trying to kill me over you. It'll be my little good-bye present to him. He won't give half a shit. He's probably got your gravestone picked out already anyway, or haven't you noticed? People seem to die a lot around your friend Striker."

When she was naked, he made her stand there for a few minutes so he could look at her. She began to shiver. He wished he hadn't had to hit her twice already, once when she smirked at him in the motel room and the second time when she tried to pull the gun out of her pants in the Jeep. She wasn't nearly as pretty with a big bleeding knot above her forehead and a gashed and swollen upper lip. Still, he knew she looked better than anything he'd ever put the pipe to. She was outrageously gorgeous. He told her to put the boots back on and bend over the front of the Jeep. She heard the buckle jangle as he undid his pants and dropped them to his knees.

She felt the rough razor stubble of his beard rubbing up against her bare bottom as he started to lick her. The general pressed the barrel of the thirty-eight into the soft flesh above her hip while he worked. Jenny's skin crawled at the touch of his slobbering tongue. She cringed when he finally stood and jammed himself inside her. The general started to pound his hips against her, reaching around the front of her and groping at her breasts with his free hand while he pressed the gun into her ribs with the other. He worked angrily for about ten minutes before he hit her in the back of the head with the pistol once more. She let out a shriek. The general was breathing heavily now, frustrated and sweating despite the cool night air and the gentle breeze.

When he had finally satisfied himself, the general began beating her about the head with his pistol once again, this time flailing wildly until he had her knocked off the hood of the Jeep and into a cowering heap in the tall grass beside the dusty road. Keeping an eye on her all the while, the general tossed the metallic case out of his car into the grass beside her.

"I imagine a nice-looking girl like you won't have any problem getting a ride back into town," he said. "Hell, you can walk it in an hour."

He threw her pistol as far as he could off into the weeds, then fished through her clothes one piece at a time, checking to make sure she didn't have any weapons. There was a coin in her pants pocket. He didn't look close enough to see that it was gold and let it simply drop to the ground. He found a small cell phone in the inside pocket of her jeans jacket, and he threw it on the road where it smashed against a rock, the pieces scattering in several directions. The last thing he came to was her underwear. They were a pretty, black, see-through lace. The general put them up to his nose and sniffed deeply.

"I think I'll keep these," he said, laughing to himself and stuffing the panties into his pants pocket.

The general climbed into the Jeep, did a quick three-point turn, then raced away in a choking haze of dust and burnt fuel. Jenny scrambled from the grass and searched frantically for the pieces of the cell phone on the road. Blood was flowing into her throat from both her mouth and nose. It was hard for her to breathe. She heard the Jeep bounce along the dirt road and then reach the highway where its gears began to whine as the general punched the accelerator, increasing his speed steadily and driving farther away. She was sobbing with rage as she picked up two small pieces of the phone. She found the main body, but the flat battery that attached to the back of the phone was nowhere to be found. She began to tear through the grass. It was hopeless. She had no idea what she would do or what she would say to Striker. Then she found it, the battery.

She snapped it onto the back of what was left of the cell phone and pushed the power button. Nothing happened. She pushed it again and again. Still, nothing. It was broken. The general was probably almost out of range by now, but the urge for murderous revenge would not allow her to give up. She took the battery off and blew furiously on the contacts before clipping it on again. She pushed the power button again. Nothing. She tried again and, the phone emitted a loud, sour tone. The numbers now glowed. Jenny's fingers trembled as she dialed 666-1234. She frantically pushed the send button. Instantly there was a flash of light from down the highway. The flash seemed to momentarily light the entire northern sky. Jenny felt the warm gust of air from the explosion and heard the roar of the blast. She grinned. If anyone had been there to see her, they would have seen that three of her front teeth were nothing more than jagged stumps of dentine. Jenny didn't even care. She only wished she could have seen his face.

When Cody drove up to the house he knew instantly something was wrong. The front door was open. He jumped from his truck and raced up the walk where he saw Joe's dead body, then Abby's, and finally Lucia's lying across the threshold, faceup, with a tiny bit of blood trickling into one eye from a small hole just above the bridge of her nose. He didn't waste a second. Cautiously he darted into the house. The adrenaline rushing through his body made him forget about his knee, which began to throb as soon as he started to move. He instinctively made his way to Jo-Jo's bedroom. He didn't know why that was his first thought, maybe it was because that would have been Madison's first concern. He hadn't gotten to the kitchen when he heard Madison's shriek from upstairs. Cody wheeled around and headed for the stairs.

Quickly, but still quietly, he climbed. Then he heard their talking. He listened, trying to figure what was happening and how best to act. He heard the threat to shoot Jo-Jo in the head. When he heard whoever it was shout at Madison, he assumed she would be killed. He peeked around the corner just as the man he knew must be his wife's boyfriend shook his head and closed his eyes in obvious pain. Cody didn't hesitate. He sprung from his place, took one step, and launched himself through the air.

He hit Striker in the side of the head with a viciously thrown forearm just as he opened his eyes. The pain was dizzying for the already wounded man, and the two of them tumbled together onto the floor. Cody had Striker's head cradled in one arm while he pounded his face brutally with his free fist. Cody heard the gun spit twice before he knew what the zinging bees that had shot past his ear actually were. He instinctively rolled away from Striker just as the gun went off again.

Despite his hasty retreat, Cody would have taken the next bullet in the head if it wasn't for Madison. After pulling Jo-Jo off to the other side of the bed, she tore the clock radio off of the night stand and threw it with all her might at the raised hand in which Striker held his gun. The corner of the heavy clock caught his hand perfectly, knocking his shot wide and spilling the gun from his grasp.

Cody reversed his directing, diving for the free gun and finding it on the floor with Striker already on his back. He felt Striker's hand plastered to the front of his face, the fingers slowly creeping up toward his eyes. Striker got his index finger high enough on Cody's face to punch it into Cody's socket. Cody reached over his shoulder as if he was scrubbing his back in the tub and pulled the trigger of the gun repeatedly. Two of the seven shots that were left in the gun imbedded themselves deeply in Striker's brain.

CHAPTER THIRTY-FOUR

V

CODY SAT ON THE SAME HARD CHAIR in the same white room he'd been put in almost two months ago on the morning after Jeff Board's murder. He'd been there since around midnight, and it was now 3 A.M. Zimmer had given Cody several cups of coffee to help him stay awake while he recounted a dozen times what had happened at Madison's house. When Madison came through the door with Zimmer, Cody rose and she rushed to his arms, hugging him tightly.

"Is he all right?" Cody said, the concern in his eyes real.

"Yes," she said. "They operated to remove the bullet, and when he came out I spoke to him for a while before he went to sleep. The doctors gave him a sedative, so he'll sleep until sometime tomorrow afternoon. I can't . . . this whole thing is . . ."

"Why don't you sit down?" Zimmer said, pulling out a chair for her.

"Thank you," she said.

Cody and Zimmer sat down as well. Madison refused to be questioned alone. She told Zimmer that she would recount the incident from her perspective after she'd spoken with Cody. Zimmer knew better than to try to bully her, so he had acquiesced in order to get to the bottom of everything much quicker. Madison sat next to Cody. She unabashedly held tightly onto his hand, which rested on her leg. Madison looked tired, but the relief at having her son safe was as evident as was her gratitude to Cody Grey, who she was sure had saved both their lives.

"Please tell me from the start everything that happened," Zimmer said.

Madison recounted her story, beginning with Yusef Williams's story, then how he saw the man in black with Jenny Grey at the trial, through to Cody's arrival and struggle with that same man only a few hours ago.

"So this person you call 'The Man in Black,'" Zimmer said, chewing the inside of his cheek thoughtfully, "you're telling me he was the one who killed Jeff Board?"

"His name is William Moss," Madison explained. "He had access to Cody's shoes through Jenny Grey. And he could have known from her about Cody's altercation with Board and that it was the perfect opportunity to eliminate Board and have everyone think it was Cody. He was probably the one who arranged for Board to run into Cody at the Green Mesquite."

"How do you figure?" Zimmer said.

"Simple," Madison replied, "he could have just called Jeff Board and told him he was Cody and that he wanted to meet him. Board hadn't heard Cody's voice enough to recognize it. He could have said he wanted to talk about a deal.

"Moss even fits Cody's description," Madison continued. "He could easily have been the person Hauffler saw coming out of Board's house. I'm still not convinced Hauffler had a clear view of him. Come on, Zimmer, you know as well as I do that that the shoes turning up looks as much like a frame as any murder you've ever seen."

Zimmer looked at her candidly and said, "Off the record, you're right, but what else could I think? Why would William Moss do it? What reason would he have to kill Board?"

"I don't know," Madison said. "I don't know why he killed Yusef Williams's friends either, but I know he did it. Maybe there really is some link between Moss and Ricardo Lopez, I don't know. But I would be more willing to bet that the reason he killed Board had something to do with Jenny."

Cody looked at Zimmer and explained, "I told Madison that the night Board was killed, he said something at the Green Mesquite about how he found Jenny's money. I didn't know about any money she had. It never made sense, until now. I'm not sure if it does even now."

"Well," Zimmer admitted, "if this guy Moss is the kind of person who's not afraid to sneak around at night killing people with a twenty-two, it would figure that he could also be capable of getting into the Federal building and getting the files on Board's investigation of you and your wife. That always bothered me, that both sets of files were gone. I honestly could never figure your motivation to take them."

"He also probably had the capability to erase the hard drive of Board's computer at his home," Madison added. "Either way, I'm willing to bet we'll know a lot more when you're able to find Jenny."

"Well," Zimmer said thoughtfully, "one good thing is, that dumb bastard Rawlins will get his ass kicked in Tuesday's election when the press gets wind of this fuckup. I can't say it was his fault really, but I can say that it couldn't have happened to a nicer asshole.

"But what about Joe Thurwood?" Zimmer said. "Where does he fit into all this?"

Madison shook her head. "I don't know. The only thing I can think of is that he was outside the house and got into a fight with Moss. I don't know why he would have, maybe he was just in the wrong place at the wrong time."

Madison briefly described for Zimmer the problems she'd been having with Joe over the past few months, adding that it didn't really surprise her that he was lurking around outside her house.

"Sounds like for you he was at the right place at the right time," Zimmer said. "So, what about Marty Cahn?"

Madison looked from Zimmer to Cody.

"Oh, my God," she said, her mouth dropping open, "Marty . . ."

Madison chewed absently on the back of her knuckle, choking back her tears as they raced through the streets of Austin toward 1100 Colorado Avenue. She and Cody were riding in the back of an unmarked car with Zimmer driving and his partner, Bortz, in the front seat beside him.

Mark Britain couldn't be more bored than he had been with the assignment over the past three months. He knew, though, that it was a part of his job that had to be done and done well. He and his partner, Conrad Maddox, hadn't been the ones who'd lost Striker on the road during the summer. So far, he and Maddox had a perfect record following him, but it wasn't really saying much. It had been easy, almost too easy. Now the two of them sat there in the predawn gloom, fretting, trying to decide what to do. They'd seen Cody Grey go racing into the building and figured some kind of jealous quarrel would ensue. They waited patiently outside, hoping for some real fireworks. The only thing they needed was popcorn.

Then they had heard Cody's desperate attempts to call someone over their wire tap. It didn't make any sense at all. Striker hadn't come out of the building, and yet Cody Grey had come and gone, even tried to make a phone call from Striker's apartment. The panicked tone of Cody Grey's voice also told them something was very wrong. Still, it wasn't a decision either of them wanted to make. Instead they waited for a call back from either Teitlebaum or Garbosky to see if they should go in. They certainly didn't want to tip Striker off to the fact he was being followed if there was no cause to do so.

"Call," Maddox said, "ask for someone else, wrong number. See if he's in there."

Britain nodded and picked up his phone, dialing Striker's number. He let it ring twenty times. There was no answer.

"You think we lost him?" Maddox said, staring toward the main door. They could see the entrance for the building from where they sat, as well as the garage all the cars had to come out of and the loading dock on the side of the building where deliveries and garbage pickups were made.

Britain shook his head and said, "I don't know. He could have gone out a window, I guess. That's the only other way out."

Suddenly their phone rang. It was Teitelbaum. Maddox explained the situation.

"Go in," the boss said. "Something's wrong. Don't make any noise about it. Just check it out, then call me. I'll stay by the phone."

Together the agents got out of their burgundy New Yorker and pulled their suit coats on over their firearms before walking briskly across the street. The two of them were tall and muscularly built, with blonde, closely cropped hair. Despite the similarities, their faces looked nothing alike. While Britain had the looks of a Nordic god, Maddox was just plain homely. They showed their badges to the doorman, who raised his eyebrows with concern and let them pass. They took the elevator up to the eighteenth floor and gently pushed open Striker's broken door, entering the apartment with their guns drawn.

"Jesus and Mary, mother of God," Britain said, crossing himself when they saw Marty's pale dead body lying on the empty bed.

"Awww," Maddox said in horror and disgust, picking up the loose wire that still hung from the battery. "Look at this. This guy was tortured. You ever seen anything like this?"

Britain nodded his head, "Yeah, in Beirut one time. The Syrians got a Lebanese guy like this. They say it's the worst fucking way to get it. Beyond fucking medieval."

"Striker?"

Britain and Maddox spun around with their guns leveled at the woman who had just entered the apartment and was standing at the opposite end of the wide hall that opened from the entryway into the living room.

"Don't move!" Britain commanded. It took a full minute before he recognized Striker's slam-piece. He knew she was a married woman, and he had no respect for her. Britain had a wife of his own at home, and watching

Jenny Grey carry on over the past few months had filled him with loathing. She looked like she had gotten a little medicine, though. There was a large purple goose egg over her left eye, which had swollen almost completely closed. Her face was bruised, and her lips were swollen and freshly scabbed over. When she spoke, he could see her broken teeth. She wore no makeup, and she looked like hell warmed over.

"Who are you?" she said. She was carrying a metallic case, the kind Britain knew you put camera equipment in.

"Just set that case down and raise your hands nice and slowly," he said.

"Looks like Striker got her too," Maddox said. "Why don't you tell us what's going on here, Mrs. Grey. Do you know this man in here?"

Jenny walked slowly toward the bedroom with her arms raised, leaving the case behind her.

"No," she lied, glancing only briefly at Marty's twisted angular body.

Maddox turned to his partner and whispered, "Lets take her back to the office and find out what the hell she knows. Striker's gone, and he's not coming back. I think it would be easier to squeeze her there than in the middle of all this mess."

Britain shrugged and nodded his head. The agency had rented them some offices to use as a base of operations while they were in Austin. It would be better for the agency if they did their own interrogation before the locals got to her with a lawyer. If Striker was on the run, Jenny would be their best bet of finding him.

Maddox gave Jenny a cursory frisk, even though there was no reason to believe she would be carrying a weapon. They knew she was a civilian, and it wasn't part of her profile.

"Mrs. Grey, we're with the Central Intelligence Agency," Maddox said to her, showing his badge. "I think you better come with us. We have a few questions we want to ask you."

"All right," Jenny said quietly, obviously in shock from what had already happened to her and what she had seen.

"What's in the case?" Maddox said as he hefted it off the floor.

"Just some video equipment," she said. If they looked she already knew she'd plead ignorance, but they didn't. They simply led her down the elevator and into the back of the New Yorker. Maddox put the case into the trunk and slammed it shut before getting into the passenger seat beside his partner. Neither of them spoke to her. They would let her sweat a little and save their questions for the office. Britain started the car and pulled away from the curb.

A patrol car suddenly appeared, racing around the corner with its wheels squealing and its lights flashing. Two more came from the other direction, followed by an unmarked car. They all screeched to a halt helter-skelter in front of the apartment building. The police hustled inside.

Maddox and Britain looked at each other simultaneously.

"Shit," Britain said.

"What are we going to do?" Maddox said as his partner slowed down the car and pulled over to the curb.

"I'll go talk to them," Britain said. "You stay here with her."

"Are you going to tell them about her?" Maddox asked.

"I'll see what they know," Britain replied. "If we can get her alone for a while, I'd prefer that, but if they ask me about her . . . Well, I don't want to stir up too much shit."

Britain shut the car door behind him and Maddox watched him go. He turned around and looked at Jenny Grey. Unlike Britain, he had been fascinated with her over the past few months. He was single, and he envied Striker's conquest of a woman he would have bedded down in a moment's notice, married or not. Some things were too good to pass up. Maddox smiled at her despite the agency's unwritten code of stone-faced indifference. Jenny smiled weakly at him and looked sadly out the window at the apartment building and all the commotion. Maddox felt a little bad for her. She sure was beaten up pretty badly.

Madison was wailing uncontrollably, and Cody, with the help of Bortz, had to pull her off of Marty's body. Cody had a sickening knot in the pit of his stomach. Madison began to wretch, and he led her out into the living room, giving her a wastebasket to throw up in.

"No! No! No!" she moaned between sobs.

Cody held her closely and gently stroked her hair.

"Shhhh," he whispered in her ear. "Shhh . . ."

"He . . . took . . . care . . . of . . . me. . . . ," Madison sobbed. "He . . . came . . . here . . . for, for me!"

"Shhhh," Cody whispered quietly, "I'll take care of you, Madison. I'll take care of you."

She hugged him even tighter and continued to cry. She was horrified. She was crushed. But despite her sorrow, with Cody holding her she felt somehow safer than she ever had in her life. Zimmer had warned Cody that it would be best if Madison didn't come, but she had insisted.

From out of nowhere, Cody heard his wife's name. He turned his head to see Zimmer standing near the door talking with a handsome young man who was built like a linebacker

"I've got her in the car outside," the young man said, answering Zimmer's pointed question almost reluctantly. "We wanted a chance to talk to her. I realize your jurisdiction here, detective, but we may be talking about the difference between catching and not catching a ruthless criminal, an agent of our own who can elude the locals in ways you never imagined."

Zimmer took exception to the young agent's condescension, so it was with pleasure he said, "Well, even us locals can't lose him now. Your big agent is on a slab down at the county morgue."

Britain removed his glasses and stared incredulously with his sky-blue eyes at the detective, saying, "Are you sure?"

"I am," Zimmer said flatly. "So if you don't mind, I'll take custody of Mrs. Grey. We have reason to believe that she is deeply involved in all this, although I'm not exactly sure what all this is. . . ."

Zimmer briefly filled the agent in on what had happened.

Britain replaced his glasses and said, "Come on, but we'll still want to question her with you."

"That's fine, Agent Britain," Zimmer said dryly, "I'm sure you can teach us how to interrogate a suspect. . . ."

Britain didn't even notice the jab.

"Madison, I'll be right back," Cody said to Madison, passing her to a uniformed officer.

"I'm coming with you," Madison said, pulling away from the officer.

Together they followed Zimmer and Britain into the elevator. No one said a word as they descended to the ground floor. The cop and the agent weren't giving out any information to each other until they had a chance to sort everything through and get to know one another a little better.

Britain led them out the lobby and started briskly toward the street. When he got to the curb, he pulled his gun abruptly and started to run toward the New Yorker, which sat in the beam of a streetlight with its trunk popped open.

Zimmer followed, and Cody did his best to keep up. Cody and Madison got to the car and cleared the trunk in time to see Britain yank open the front passenger side door. A man in a suit was slumped forward in the seat, his head twisted at an awkward angle and resting against the dash. His forehead was missing, and the windshield was cracked and splattered with blood and flecks of bone and brains. The back of the man's white dress collar was crimson from the blood that ran out of a hole in the back of his head, where the 7mm slug had entered before it exited along with the front portion of his skull.

Zimmer was looking around frantically, and Cody looked away from the gruesome sight to follow his gaze. He saw the same thing as Zimmer: a dark, balmy October night in Austin, Texas, and the trees that lined the street, shrouded in darkness and blowing gently in the breeze. An occasional piece of paper flipped along pell-mell in the gloom. Nowhere at all was there any sign of Jenny, the woman who had not long ago been his wife.

"I'll catch her," Cody and Madison heard Britain say. "She won't get far."

The young agent's jaw was set and his face was grim. His partner's blood was still wet on his hands. "Even if she gets out of the country, wherever she goes, I'll find her."

EPILOGUE

∨

ON EMERALD ISLAND IN THE FIJI ISLANDS there are two hotels. One is for people who like to see the sun rise, the other is for those who like to watch it set. The east side is the more sedate setting, it tends more toward older people and families. The west side is a haven for jet-setting young people, mostly from Australia and South America. The island is nothing more than the very tip of a small volcanic mountain. Its tremendous conical height, however, is entirely verdant, and thus the name Emerald Island. There is only one treacherous road that could get a person from one side of the island to the other, and there are very few cars with which to make the journey. Emerald Island is a vacation spot for only the very rich. And they usually know which side they prefer, and they stay there.

On one particular afternoon, a blonde American tortured the gearbox of an open jeep in order to make the unusual trek from one side to the other. He had done it before. He was looking for someone. He rounded a bend in the perilous descent, and he could see it, the Grand Beach Hotel. It was nestled into a nook of white sand and lush vegetation formed by the protective barrier of an ancient finger of lava that extended out toward the ocean before it hooked lovingly back toward the land. The hotel rose like a gem out of the jungle. It was a large, white stucco structure with towering gables topped by steep-pitched ceramic tile roofs. The design was European. It was intricate and exquisite.

The man pulled the jeep into a small turnaround that was almost completely shaded from the afternoon sun by the wild, overgrown palm trees. The door he went into took him to the back side of the hotel lobby. Most of the guests arrived from the ocean side, where a seaplane would land and take off several times a day from the lagoon. When the man at the desk looked up and saw him, he smiled nervously. The blonde American stood out in his lightweight gray flannel business suit. The man at the desk wasn't certain if interrupting the guest this man was looking for would be welcome or not. He had people to answer to, and it never went over well if a hotel guest was disturbed in any way. The American, he knew, was here to see one of Grand Beach's more frequent guests. She was a South African heiress who tipped extravagantly and would come and go at a moment's notice, sometimes staying for a month, other times for just a day.

Rumor had it she traveled the globe collecting men like trophies. There were usually men with her, one, or sometimes even two. If she arrived alone, the staff would get edgy. She was a huntress, and if she didn't bring her prey with her, she found it somewhere on the island. Occasionally she would even venture to the other side. A year ago, one of the waiters, a handsome man from Taiwan with a broad back and long black hair that he tied in a ponytail, had taken up with her. When she left, he tried to follow. No one had seen or heard from him since. She, however, had returned alone a month later.

On this particular trip she had also come alone.

"Where is she?" the tall American asked. He was wearing sunglasses that he seemed to prefer not to take off.

The man at the desk quietly said, "The south beach."

The American nodded solemnly and handed him a twenty-dollar bill before walking out through an intricate maze of winding paths that led to various tropical pools and, ultimately, the beach. There was a large cabana built just inside a line of palm trees where the sand began in earnest. It was here that liveried waiters hustled to and from guests who sat on the sand and around pools, bringing them everything from cold bottles of beer to champagne and chilled lobster tails, sometimes setting formal tables complete with linen and silver under some secluded cluster of palms that a romantic couple had decided to call home for an afternoon. The south beach was the most secluded area on this side of the island where you could still receive service from the hotel. To get there you had to walk about half a mile and cross a footbridge that traversed a stream feeding the lagoon. It was more of a place to go if you wanted to be alone, so the guests from the Grand Beach Hotel were rarely found there.

The American followed the winding path that went south. He took off his jacket and swung it casually over his shoulder. When he reached the south beach, he could see that a waiter was just scurrying away from her, leaving a silver ice bucket and a bottle of champagne. There was a small bamboo table beside her lounge chair. She sat facing the crashing surf. In the distance were a cluster of uninhabited volcanic islands. The beach was empty. It was a glorious sight, and sitting there with her back to him in her white bathing suit, stretched out on the chair, she looked the picture of paradise. Her hair fell to her shoulders and was the color of late summer wheat. Her body was long and tan.

He took his shoes and socks off and left them neatly at the end of the path. He wondered if she would try to run. The waiter, a short fellow with a page-boy haircut, scrambled past him with a smile, hit the path, and disappeared into the jungle. Now they were really alone.

When he was halfway across the beach he realized that on the small table the waiter had left two champagne glasses instead of one. He wondered if she somehow knew he was coming and was going to simply surrender herself to him, or if there was someone else. He looked around warily. It wasn't something he had expected, another person, but it certainly was possible. When he reached her, he stepped dramatically in front of her and looked down at her, a beautiful figure lying in his shadow. She tried to screen the glare of the sun to see him better.

"What do you want?" she said.

"I want you," he told her, taking off his sunglasses so she could see his face more clearly.

She sat straight up now and got into his shadow so she could see his face. It was very familiar. It was an unforgettable face, strong and determined, with piercing blue eyes that some would say were almost as beautiful as her own.

"I know," she said. "But I'm staying. . . . Would you like a glass of champagne?"

"No," he said, taking an official document from the inside breast pocket of his jacket. "You'd better look at this before you say anything more."

He held the document out to her. She casually took a sip of champagne before taking it from him and opening it.

"How did you get this?" she asked with a worried look on her face.

"Don't worry," he told her. "I didn't have to give up everything. I flew here right from Reno. That's why the suit. Everything was completed, well, it was this morning when I left. I did what you said. I gave her the houses in Malibu and Aspen, but the chalet in Zermatt is mine . . . and half the money. Now, come with me. I want to leave this place."

Grand Beach held some unpleasant memories for Paul DuMont. More than once he'd snuck away from his wife on the other side of the island, only to find Jenny bedded down with someone else. Some ugly scenes had ensued.

"I'm glad," she said, letting him drop to his knees in the sand and kiss her on the mouth. His constant reappearance in her dreams made her think she just might love him. Besides being distractingly handsome, he was a subtle cross between Striker and Cody. She would marry him now, now that he had done as she had told him, divorced his wife without losing everything he had in the process. Besides his looks, he was smart and cultured, like Striker. He had some of Cody's naiveté and the same jealous hot temper. And his wife, or ex-wife, was so rich that her family would probably disown her for losing half her fortune to a man who had run off with another woman. But that was okay, because she was that other woman. Jenny had toyed with Paul DuMont now for over two years, seeing him sometimes when he was staying on the other side of the island with his family, other times in Zermatt, Switzerland, where he and his wife would go skiing in the winter or the spring. Never in the United States, though. Jenny had never gone back to the States. She never would.

She got out of Texas slightly ahead of the large-scale manhunt they'd formed to catch her. Fortunately, she already had a new passport and identity from Striker. It was a simple matter of cutting her hair and dying it to match the doctored Dutch passport of one Greta Hammerstam. She'd rented a car outside Austin with a card Striker had given her. Then she drove to Laredo, where she had hooked up with a trucker who agreed to let her ride in his sleeper cabin across the border into Mexico for a thousand dollars. It was the first time the trucker ever heard of someone trying to sneak *into* Mexico. Jenny wasn't taking any chances. From there she went to Monterey, where she got a flight to Paris. Shipping the plutonium had been as simple as a curbside check-in. In Paris she used her coin to contact Jamir.

From Paris, she wasn't quite sure where it was she'd been flown to, but she thought it was an island somewhere in the Aegean. Jamir was hospitable and greatly pleased to see her, for sexual as well as business reasons. She delivered the pit to him, completing the transaction that Striker began, keeping the nine million dollars in cash for herself. Despite the pleasure of her company, Jamir, like she, had many things in life to do. Jamir had advised her on how to elude the long-reaching arm of the CIA. He'd seen to it that she was given new documents, this time from South Africa, and introduced her to a discreet speech therapist as well as to equally discreet and competent doctors who had changed her appearance, while still leaving her beautiful. Within six months, the old Jenny Grey was gone forever. That was four and a half years ago.

In the interim she had searched for a man with whom to share her life. She didn't know if the one before her was the one she would stay with forever. That seemed too long a time to even think about, but she would certainly marry him now. A marriage with Paul would only increase her wealth, and that was something that did interest her lately. Her money was generating almost a million dollars a year in interest, but she had no problem spending that. Recently she had grown to want more, and Paul DuMont was the man who could give her more, as well as satisfy so many of her other needs.

Jenny had become so busy in her pursuit of men and money that there were times she would go for days without thinking of Cody Grey. She'd run into the son of an American real estate developer in the French Riviera about six months ago who claimed to be friends with Jason Storm, the Outlaws quarterback. Jenny was able to learn from the developer's son only that Cody had remarried and that he was supposedly teaching school somewhere and coaching high-school football. The young man thought Cody also had a couple of children, but he wasn't certain about any of it.

If she thought about Cody at all, it was usually late at night, right before she slept, when her mental guard was down. She'd think about his quiet way of looking at her and smiling, the way he did in the good times. In fact, those were the only times she could recollect with him, the good ones. Occasionally she would fantasize about going back to him to take him with her. She thought now, with all the money she had, they could definitely be happy together. Looking back at all the men she'd had, even Striker, she realized that not one of them had been as much of a man as Cody Grey.

Even with all she had, she found herself thinking of Cody. She wondered what had made her unhappy with him in the first place. She supposed it was the direction he had been heading—kids, teaching, little leagues, PTA. Those were things she just didn't want and couldn't understand. There wother thing that bothered her even more than the fact that she no longer had Cody. In fact, it haunted her. It always would. She had everything now that she'd always dreamed of then. But now she dreamed of him.

THANKS TO:

Jerry Petievich, former agent for Military Intelligence and the
U.S. Secret Service, for his patient tutoring on the inner workings
of the United States intelligence community.

Mike Berryhill, chemist, and David Krueger, nuclear engineer, for their
instruction on the properties and handling of weapons-grade plutonium.
Super cop and fellow attorney, Mike Kerwin, for answering my
late-night questions about the inside world of police work.

My brother Kenny, for helping me work out my final plot twists
on our twenty-four hour drive to Florida.

And Bertha Wolkoff, for keeping me well fed during the home stretch.

NOTE:

For the sake of this fictional story, I have taken the liberty to use
existing legal principles and procedures that may or may not
conform exactly to the laws of the State of Texas.